The Metal Woman

Project Orpheus, Book 3

Frank J. Cavill

COMMUNITY:

All my books: relinks.me/FrankJCavill
Web: frankjcavill.com
X: @FrankJCavill
Facebook: facebook.com/frankjcavill
Threads: @frankjcavill
Instagram: @frankjcavill
Tiktok: @frankjcavill
Bluesky: @frankjcavill

Mail: frankjcavill@gmail.com

Cover by:
Pilar García (pilargarcia.net)

Translation by:
Christy Cox

Edited by:
Peter Gauld

Prologue
The nomad people

Shyiich finished swallowing the last piece of dried meat left over from his frugal breakfast. Meanwhile his son, barely seven Keplerian years old, watched him closely from the other side of the table. He made faces at the boy until he made him smile. He could have spent his whole life watching that pure smile, and yet he had to get going; there was work to do.

Yiiÿa was swaying in the dark wood rocking-chair which Shyiich had crafted with his own hands shortly before she had given birth to her firstborn. After clearing away the remains of breakfast and kissing his son's head he went over to her, kissed her on the lips and stroked her prominent belly. Once again their lives were to be blessed. They were looking forward to the birth of a fourth member for his humble family.

He fetched his satchel from where it was hanging on the back of the door inside the cabin, together with a waterskin of fresh water, and turned to his wife.

"I'll be back at noon, in time for lunch. Try not to make any effort."

"Don't worry. Be careful, and if you feel hot, stop."

"I don't think it'll be necessary, it's not going to be hot today." He opened the door of the cabin. "I love you."

"And I love you too."

This looked like a good day for gathering wood in the forest. Yiiÿa always told him to take advantage of the cooler days to do the work that needed more physical effort, so that he would not get too tired. Today, for a change, he heeded her words. Sometimes he had the feeling that he was the one who was expecting a baby. Yiiÿa was always attentive to what he did, trying to prevent him getting hurt or helping him with the house repairs.

He knew he was lucky to have married her. Despite living in a small nomad village Yiïÿa was very beautiful and had not lacked suitors in every single one of the Keplerian villages. But she had always been in love with him, ever since they had been little and had been taught together by the village teacher.

They had spent some time in a very quiet spot, far from the buzz and frantic life of the three large Keplerian villages. Here life followed a different rhythm, homes were built around the trees, as in the large villages, but after a few years they moved somewhere new, to gather wood and cultivate the earth. It was a different life, more peaceful and quiet, more satisfying, or at least so Shyiich thought. More and more Keplerians were deciding to live away from the large cities. Apart from being able to live a quieter life, they would have a better chance of passing unnoticed when the Khol came back.

He fetched his sharp axe and the small wooden cart which was parked at the door of their cabin and prepared to cross the little village of nomads toward the south. There was something he had to do that day.

"Morning, Shyiich," his neighbor called as he passed.

"Good morning, Fosh. How's the garden going?"

"Well, it's coming along," was the reply. "Though I was expecting more rain by now."

"Yes, this year it looks as though the rain's taking longer than usual."

"I think it'll rain this afternoon, though," the old man said. "I can feel it in my joints."

"Could be. There's certainly plenty of humidity in the air. And to judge by the light, I'd say it's cloudy."

Fosh noticed the tools his neighbor was carrying in his cart. "Gathering wood today?"

"Yes, I'll see if I can strip a tree nearby." He pointed to the south. "I think Laankhol wants to build another stable four rows further on."

"Well, well, well!" Fosh said. "At last that stubborn old man's seen reason and decided to build it away from the rest of the cabins. Better late than never."

Shyiich smiled. "Yeah, it looks as though he listened to your complaints at last."

"I doubt it. He's so stubborn he's sure to have some other crazy plan to make our lives even more difficult, if that's possible."

"True, but after slaughter-time he always gives us all some meat."

"If it weren't for that I'd have left long ago," Fosh admitted. "My brother-in-law Khipshii says that three days or so north of here, around the snowy mountain, there are lands that are far more fertile, where you can sow grain and in a few days it sprouts, even without sunlight."

Shyiich looked surprised at this. "And how on earth does your brother-in-law know that if he barely so much as comes out of his cabin to do what he has to do?"

"That's exactly what I asked him. But his kid is apprentice to an old cattle-farmer, and it seems he has to move around a lot, beyond the Thako iron mines. He says he's thinking of visiting the place."

"But that's a long way away," Shyiich objected. "If he does that it'll be harder for him to take his goods to the big markets. How does he intend to take the grain to the big cities?"

"I asked him the same thing," the old man replied.

"Well, what did he say?"

"That I think too much about everything."

Shyiich burst out laughing. "Ha, ha, ha! The things we have to hear! Well, anyway, I'm off to see if I can make the most of the morning. I told Yiïya I'd be back at noon."

"All right. Stop by on your way back and you can take some vegetables. How's she doing, by the way?"

"Fine. She still has a few days left before she gives birth, but everything seems to be going as it should."

"I'm glad about that," said Fosh, "Although I'd advise you to get ready for it. With one it's easy to share out what has to be done, but with two you're going to have to work hard to tame the beasts."

Shyiich smiled broadly. "Yes, I realize that."

The old man knew very well what it meant to have a number of children. He himself had had six of them. In a way he treated Shyiich like his own son. He was a good Keplerian and cared about his neighbors, whom he helped with what little he produced from his garden. Shyiich always brought him the wood he needed, which for him did not represent much of an effort, but for Fosh it meant a relief for his battered joints, especially during the wettest time of the year.

Shyiich went on his way between the dozen cabins which made up the little nomad village. He greeted another of the neighbors, who was feeding her domestic animals in her little corral, then finally left the village.

His work was simple enough: he climbed the trunks of the trees with strong fabric cinches and stripped them clean of branches up to four or five meters. That way he would get wood for the coldest time of the year, as well as preparing the ground ready for putting up new buildings. Apart from a woodsman Shyiich was an expert carpenter who could build beautiful, functional cabins out of whatever nature herself provided them.

He had spent some time up the tree the village farmer had asked him to strip when he began to feel thirsty. He came down carefully and went to the cart, where he had left the waterskin. He grasped this by the base and tilted it all the way to quench his thirst.

He wiped his face with his hand, ignoring the temptation to take a bite from the chunk of grayish bread his wife had baked a couple of days before. It was too early for a snack, and hunger might make itself felt again before he was expecting it. He concentrated on finishing the work that still remained to be done. He was not going to have enough time to finish before noon, that was pretty clear. That tree was one of those that were a thousand years old, so he would have to come back in the afternoon.

All of a sudden the air was filled with the echo of furious metallic roars which rent the calm silence of the forest. It was like the distant rumble of thunder, a symphony of unnatural jolting that seemed to defy all known logic. He was sure the sounds were coming from the village.

A shrill scream froze the blood in his veins. Unmistakably, it had been a yell of anguish.

"Yiïÿa!!" he shouted in terror.

He ran to the village, and even though he had not gone far away, that scream made the journey back seem to last for ever.

The repetitive metallic sounds went on coming from the cabins, sounding closer all the time. When he reached his neighbor's house he found her lying in the doorway, with her apron soaked in the blood that was flowing from two small circular marks on chest and stomach. A wide red pool was beginning to spread under her body, but there was no trace of the weapon or of the arrows which had caused it. The sounds were still coming from the other end of the village.

He went on running. Old Fosh lay on his face among the flowers he had looked after lovingly. His blood was beginning to soak the earth his kind neighbor had put in so much effort working on. There was no trace of the attackers, and Shyiich was beginning to fear the worst.

He ran faster, driving his body to the verge of exhaustion, desperate to reach his cabin. Something or someone was attacking the little nomad village which he and his family had decided to join shortly after their marriage.

Suddenly the strange noises stopped.

Shyiich raced across the little garden in front of his home, full of those flowers with intense green petals that Yiïÿa liked so much. The door was ajar and he hurled himself against it, shoving it so forcefully that it slammed against the wall of the cabin. Beside the rocking-chair was the motionless body of Yiïÿa, his wife, his only love, the reason his life made sense.

With tears in his eyes he turned in every direction in search of his son, little Ziip, then muffled a scream, his hands to his head. His son was lying on the floor, in the corner where they would both play with the little wooden toys he himself carved. His eyes could not hold back the tide of tears, which like a torrent of emotions were beginning to run down his cheeks and onto the cold floor of the cabin.

His only two loves, the lights that guided his life, stripped away by someone utterly unscrupulous, someone who could murder an innocent child and his pregnant mother in cold blood. He knelt on the cabin floor with a sense of impotence, broken by pain and grief. And yet despite this, it was not long before he noticed a strange presence in the place. Something, or someone, was blocking the light from outside.

Shyiich turned around very gradually. What he saw in the doorway froze his blood. It was a being enfolded in a kind of gray metal armor, with an orange stripe down the left-hand side and an inscription in an alphabet he did not know. Through a small slit in its helmet he was able to see a pale being whose small eyes were watching him closely. In its right hand it held a long object he could not identify, but which he knew without a doubt was what had caused the thunderous metallic sounds he had heard a few moments before.

"Who… are… you?" he muttered through his tears.

The being directed the tip of its artifact toward Shyiich and spoke in a language he could not understand.

"My dear friend, this is your lucky day" said the being in a cruel voice. "You're going to be the only witness to this operation,"

Shyiich heard one last metallic burst and felt a stinging pain in his left leg. He looked down and saw that a deep hole had opened which was bleeding profusely. By the time he had taken this in, the being had turned and was leaving the cabin. Even so, he could hear it raise its voice in the distance.

"Sergeant Reynolds! That's it! I found the last one! Move!"

Then there was only silence, only weeping and loneliness. Shyiich had been left alone in the cabin. He had been left alone in the world.

1
The chosen

November 6, Year 0

Gaal-El Village, Kepler-442b

They had managed to arrive safe and sound at the Gaal-El temple after crossing the mountains and the snow-covered Dipyaa pass. Had it not been for the experience of Haagar, the intrepid old Keplerian hermit, they would never have made it. But they were so driven by necessity after losing one of the mules in that pass that Emily, Rakesh, Robert and Ferrara had no choice but to get back to the base as soon as possible. Otherwise they might have ended up having problems if they were to run out of oxygen or electrical supply in one or other of their exosuits.

They still could not understand what had happened that morning. Finding dozens of cultists prostrated in front of Emily, thinking she must be a kind of goddess from another world who was destined to save them from slavery, was not something that happened every day.

"Are you all right?" Robert asked her. He was concerned by the silence in the back of the cart they were travelling in.

"Yeah, don't worry." She was leaning against the wooden floor to stop herself swaying too much, what with the potholes and the slope.

"You seem a long way away."

"I'm… surprised by what happened."

"Care to talk about it?"

She shrugged. "I don't know. What can we do about it?"

"Maybe if you could tell us what you talked about inside the temple," Rakesh put in, "we might be able to come to some conclusion about all this rigmarole."

"Nothing out of the ordinary happened, that's the strangest thing of all. Liikmi and I went into the temple in search of the high priest. The place is an ancient cave, a pretty big one. I'd even guess there's a lot more

space behind the temple itself."

"Yeah, that makes sense," Rakesh said, "seeing the space it's enclosed in,"

"Apparently it was a cave where their ancestors hid from the Khol in ancient times. At some moment in history it was converted back into a temple for the Gaal-El cult."

"Accidents of nature have always provided shelter in difficult times," Rakesh pointed out.

"The priest was at the far end," Emily went on, "beside a kind of altar. But before we got to him, Liikmi filled a clay amphora with water from a small basin at the entrance."

"What did he want the water for?" Ferrara asked.

"It turned out that the cult leader was stretched out on the floor beside the remains of what must have been a binge, so he emptied the jar on top of him as soon as he got to where he'd fallen asleep."

"It sounds as though Haagar was right when he said he was partial to a drink," Ferrara pointed out.

"Yeah, looks like it," said Emily. "But though it might sound odd, he seemed to me to be quite intelligent and honest."

"What did he go on to tell you?" Robert asked.

"That's what's really strange. He showed me around the place and talked about the problems the cult had, how it had fallen into oblivion, how he himself had lost hope. But while we were inside he never gave me any sign that what happened outside the temple later was on the cards."

"We saw Liikmi running out as if the devil were after him," said Robert.

"Yeah, Waafdiv reproached him for not warning the others. He said this was no way to welcome his guests."

"That's why he appeared with all the others later," Rakesh pointed out.

Emily nodded. "Right."

"Did he say anything else?" Ferrara asked.

"Just that we weren't what they were expecting."

"Not what they were expecting?" Ferrara protested. "What sort of a welcome is that? And what the hell were they expecting?"

Emily smiled at this indignant comment. "We need to bear in mind that they've been waiting for someone to free them from the Khol."

"The advent of a Keplerian deity," Rakesh said with a nod. "It's logical that he should be disappointed at first. I can understand that their imagination must have run riot when Khikhya came to see him and told him about us."

"What I don't understand," Emily went on, "is what made him change his mind when we came outside again."

"The only thing I can think of is that he's deliberately playing a role," Robert said.

"What? Like in a play?" Ferrara asked.

"Yes. If we understand that there's a strong political component in everything the Keplerian tribal leaders do, then he might want to play the messiah in front of his fellow cult-members. After all, the fewer Keplerians who know the truth, the easier it'll be to keep up the subterfuge."

"Could be," Rakesh reasoned. Then he turned to the young Keplerian with them in the cart. "Yisht, you haven't said a word during the whole trip. What do you think?"

The young woman swallowed when she saw that all eyes had turned to her.

"Me?" she said shyly. "Actually… I don't know what to think. I mean, the Gaal-El cult stopped being as important as it used to be centuries ago. There are hardly any sites of worship left in the villages, and fewer and fewer followers. In my family, to give just one example, we were never believers. And I think that's widespread. Even so, we all study the cult of the Gaal-El at school, though more from a historical and political point of view than a religious one."

"And what's your take on what happened this morning?" Rakesh asked.

"I don't know what to say. But whatever the reasons the cultists were driven to do what they did, even without being a believer, I had a sense of euphoria and hope that I find hard to describe." She looked closely at Emily and added: "I don't know whether you really are the one sent to deliver us, the one the sacred scriptures speak of, but if the other Keplerians have this same feeling with half that intensity, I can tell you in advance that my people will have hope all over again, they'll believe they can be free at last."

Emily was unable to bear the young Keplerian's hopeful gaze for very long. It was too much responsibility, too much pressure added to all the problems humanity already had. As if it were not enough to have found a new home and to have found out what had happened to the Galileo, on top of this they were going to have to deal with the unfounded expectations of the Gaal-El cult. She could not hold back a deep sigh of frustration as she put her head on her knees.

Robert, who was sitting beside her, put his hand on her shoulder. Although she was in her exosuit she was able to feel that at least she was not alone in this insane adventure. They were all silent, meditating the words of hope Yisht had just shared with them. They would have to weigh up the implications of what had just happened very carefully, whether or not it was a deliberate move on Waafdiv's part.

Ferrara broke the long, uncomfortable silence in the wooden

carriage. "How far have we got left to Wiikhaadiiz ofiz?"

"We'll get there in the early morning," Rakesh said.

"I'm beginning to get pretty sick of this uncomfortable contraption," Ferrara complained.

Emily had agreed with Waafdiv that because of the accident with the mule and their particular situation, they would need transport which would allow them to reach some point near the base and pass through the military checkpoints the Khaavahki had set up along the roads which separated the Keplerian villages.

The leader of the Gaal-El had provided them willingly enough with the cloth-covered cart they were currently rising in and had ordered a couple of cult members to take them to the village of the Wiikhaadiiz ofiz. The journey would be a long and rather winding one because of the terrain, but it would allow them to reach the base before their exosuits had run out of oxygen.

"What is this ceremony Waafdiv talked about?" Ferrara asked.

"Apparently they have ancient forms of government that allow any citizen to become the sole leader of the Keplerian villages," Emily explained.

"It's the sole command," Yisht explained. "But it's centuries since anyone claimed it."

"But why do you have to pass that test?" Ferrara asked.

"It's a trial by ordeal," Emily explained. "It seems that to claim sole command, I have to first pass a test that'll officially make me a Keplerian citizen."

"To become an adult all of us Keplerians have to pass a test," Yisht told them. "The nature of this test will depend on the village it's held in."

"In the case of the Gaal-El," Emily went on, "it's a kind of quest."

Yisht nodded. "That's right. The Gaal-El send teenagers in search of a stone that symbolizes wisdom and the commitment to serving society. And I understand that it's customary among them to give that stone to their mentors, as a sign of respect for the knowledge they've gained."

"What did you have to do yourself to be accepted among the Wiikhaadiiz ofiz?" Ferrara wanted to know.

"My people have the responsibility for looking after the injured, among many other things, so that in my case I had to help at one of the village hospitals for some time."

Ferrara nodded. "I see. And what about you, Emily, are they just sending you to get a stone?"

"Oh! But it's something very dangerous," Yisht exclaimed. "Not all the novices survive the quest."

Robert frowned. "Dangerous?"

"Yes, the stones we're talking about are special, they can only be found at the bottom of a freezing lake, inside a mountain… And besides, no-one's allowed to help the candidates in any way."

"Did you know all this, Emily?" he asked in alarm.

"No, I didn't. I guess Waafdiv forgot to mention those minor details."

Rakesh looked at her with interest. "And when d'you have to pass this test?"

"Waafdiv said as soon as possible, so I'll get ready as soon as we get to the base."

Suddenly a Keplerian claw gently drew aside the cloth that separated the inside of the cart from the cult-members who were driving it.

"We're coming to a checkpoint," he whispered loudly enough for everyone inside to hear. "You'd better stay silent. Leave us to deal with it."

Robert and Ferrara put one knee on the floor of the cart and aimed their rifles at the rear opening, which was still blocked by the canvas cover. The cart stopped.

"Hi there!" they heard someone call in Keplerian a few meters away, "How's it going, then, lads?"

"Morning, sergeant," called one of the cult members.

"Where are you going? It's not Tuesday today, there's no delivery."

"It's an extraordinary order from Khikhya, the leader of the Wiikhaadiiz ofiz. You know, from when she was here a couple of days ago. She asked our leader for a special delivery of sweets."

"A special delivery?" another voice asked in disbelief.

"Yes, Lieutenant. Apparently the leader of the Wiikhaadiiz ofiz has suggested a small change in the recipe for the sweets."

The hidden passengers were sharing the interior with a few dozen boxes of the special sweets the Gaal-El themselves baked in the monastery stoves. They must have been quite famous among the Keplerians, and they represented one of the ways the Gaal-El still had at their disposal to finance their conservation work at the temple. For this they used a syrup extracted from the same tree they used to prepare the alcoholic drink their high priest was so fond of. In fact it was also normal for the noble families of the various villages to ask for a few amphorae of the Gaal-El drink.

"This is rather irregular, Zofi," said the one who sounded most senior. "No-one said anything to us about any new shipment."

"Well, I'm sorry about that, Lieutenant. But we have everything in order, let me show you."

The cult member put his arm through the back of the carriage without opening the curtain and took out four boxes with a small paper file

on top.

"Here's the permit. And I think I can say once again that we've lost a few boxes on the way. The road's pretty irregular along some stretches, and now and then a few boxes go to waste."

There followed a silence which seemed endless in the back of the carriage. It was obvious that none of these Keplerian soldiers would be superior to the semiautomatic guns Robert and Ferrara carried, but at all costs they wanted to avoid any kind of confrontation that could reveal the Gaal-El's clandestine activities.

"Hey, try a bit of this, Lieutenant!" the first voice exclaimed. "They're a lot better than the usual ones!"

After another long pause, the Keplerian lieutenant confirmed his sergeant's opinion.

"That's right, they're very good. Is it a touch of ginger I can taste?"

"I don't know what ingredients they put in it," the cult-member admitted. He turned to his partner. "What about you, Ghurvik?"

"No idea. The closest I've been to an oven is to warm my balls in winter."

The four Keplerians burst out laughing at this coarse reply.

"All right, you can go on," the lieutenant said.

"Thank you, gentlemen," Zofi said as he shook the reins of the fhores to urge them on again.

The curtain at the rear of the carriage did not part again until they had covered a good distance. Ghurvik took a peek back into the enclosed section.

"The danger's over now," he said.

"Are bribes normal among the Khaavahki soldiers, then?"

"Yes, they are. In fact we always carry more than usual to allow for this sort of thing and avoid any problems."

There were no more interruptions, nor did they come across any other military presence during the rest of the journey. They reached the clearing without any problems, where they said goodbye to Yisht and agreed to keep in touch. She would inform Khikhya about everything that had happened.

The embrace Robert and Emily gave one another once they were at the base after days of being unable to do anything of the sort would have been longer if after four days in their exosuits their bodily hygiene had not left a lot to be desired.

"We need a shower," Emily said with a smile, surprised by her own smell.

Ferrara wrinkled her nose. "I think we could all do with some severe hygienic treatment."

"And have something solid to eat for a change," Rakesh added.

"I think I'm going to stuff myself as soon as I've had a shower," the private added.

"And you and I will talk about it later," Emily whispered to Robert with a mischievous smile.

She could not remember ever having been so keen to take a shower and have some solid food. Not even being able to brush her teeth was making her feel dirty and uncomfortable, but she was certain that she would remember those days for a very long time. She found it extraordinary that her body had not felt the need to evacuate; the chemicals which had been added to the oat mash had worked to perfection.

She brushed her teeth as she waited for the water to heat for her shower. She could not help an intense moan of pleasure as the precious liquid began to slide over her skin.

I never thought anything as simple as a shower could be such a pleasure, she thought.

A good while later, after finishing all the usual morning routines, even though it was still the small hours of the morning, they gathered in the mess-hall to have something to eat which was not in the form of pap. Exhaustion began to make its presence felt.

Emily was the last to arrive. She longed desperately to hug and kiss Robert, but she merely gave him a kiss on the cheek as she passed him to avoid making anyone uncomfortable.

She went straight to the food printer and looked through the list of possibilities. She dismissed the idea of anything sweet, as they were soon going to bed and she did not want a lot of carbohydrates or sugars in her system. She settled for some fish burgers, which were not remotely her favorite, but tonight she fancied something with a taste of the sea.

"You didn't have to wait for me," she said when she saw that her three comrades had not yet started. "If you're half as hungry as I am, you must be famished."

Robert dismissed this. "Oh, it's no trouble. It's nice to have a proper meal at last."

"You can say that again!" Rakesh said. "If I had to see Haagar and Yisht eat all that again, I'd have been quite capable of taking my suit off and gulping down their food."

"I nearly did that at breakfast, before we went up to the monastery," Private Ferrara admitted.

They did not talk much after this, as everyone was concentrating on the dishes in front of them: steak for Robert and Ferrara, chicken filets for Rakesh.

Afterwards they went into the common bedroom, trying to make as little noise as possible, since everyone else on the base was still asleep.

Emily slid silently into Robert's bed, noticing the way the heat of his body contrasted with the cold she was feeling in her limbs. They huddled together in the narrow bed.

"This is wonderful," he whispered.

But her body had given up the moment she had felt his warmth, and her breathing, which was already deep and rhythmical, showed that she had already fallen asleep.

She woke up alone in the room to find that all her comrades were busy at their own tasks by now, including Robert, who had got up without her realizing. Nor was this surprising, given how tired she had been and the deep sleep she normally fell into.

She stretched, then took a shower in water which was cooler than usual to try to get her stiff body to recover from its accumulated exhaustion. When she came out of the shower she met Evelyn, who was organizing the infirmary.

The nurse gave her a hug. "Emily! It's so good to see all four of you safe and sound! You all looked dead tired. It's obvious it must have been a long, hard journey."

"It certainly was, and the suits are very useful, but they don't offer much comfort."

"I know. But come on, get your breakfast quickly, because you have visitors."

"Visitors?" Emily asked in surprise.

"That's right, the deputy director and Commander Bauer are here."

"What? And here I am lingering in bed like a teenager!"

She took a hasty leave of Evelyn and ran to the base meeting-rooms. Here, just as Evelyn had told her, the deputy director and Commander Bauer were waiting for her, deep in talk with Robert, Rakesh and Private Ferrara.

"Sorry," she said hastily as she sat down. "I'd no idea you were here and I think I overslept."

"Good morning," the deputy director said. "Don't worry, that's entirely understandable. It's been a long journey, full of excitement. I'm glad you're all well. Your comrades are updating me with one or two details about the journey."

"Yeah, I can imagine."

"However, now you're here we'll have a recap of what happened up there."

She nodded. "Of course."

"Maybe the most important thing is to determine what our next steps should be," he went on.

"Sure," Emily agreed. "Waafdiv, the cult leader, told us that in view of what's happened he's going to organize a conclave with the other Keplerian leaders."

"A conclave? What kind of conclave?"

"We're not sure about that, but we know it's a kind of meeting between the different factions which hasn't been celebrated for centuries, if not millennia. It seems to be an ancestral custom that could be requested by any of the leaders of the four main villages."

"And what'll this conclave be about?"

"Well…" she said nervously, "in theory… they're going to discuss my… new condition."

"I get that. The Gaal-El want to present you to the society as their chosen one, is that right?"

"Yeah, it'll be something like that."

The deputy director thought about this for a moment, looking concerned. It was obvious that the situation they were in was an extraordinary one, but despite the esoteric, even fantastic, component of the prophecy which foretold the advent of the Keplerian Gods, this might represent an advantage for the project. Having the Keplerians as allies was something to bear in mind, given the threats which were gathering over the planet.

"I'm going to go straight to the point," he began in earnest. "What do you all think about all this blatant mumbo-jumbo?"

A slightly uncomfortable silence fell on the hall.

"It's obvious that we're dealing with an ancient religious legend," Rakesh said at last. "It's almost certain that at some point in Keplerian history the Khol began to enslave the much less advanced Keplerians. The creation of myths and superior deities which would help the oppressed to defeat their oppressors obeys a perfectly logical need. Human religions have done the same, to a greater or lesser extent, during the course of our own history. Imagine what would have happened if humans had come across a superior alien civilization during the Bronze Age. I'm convinced that the myths and legends we know would have been directed towards their liberation."

Green nodded. "What you say makes all the sense in the world, Dr. Kumar."

"And yet," the theologian went on, "we can't dismiss the fact that even if it's a false myth the power it might have over Keplerian civilization is enormous. And that, I regret to tell you, Emily, is a double-edged sword. If it can be managed well, we might unite the Keplerians as a single people against the Khol. But if it goes wrong, it could lead to the extinction of both in the face of an enemy which seen from every angle is far superior."

Emily lowered her head, aware of the importance of the new and uncomfortable role she was now being called on to play.

"Unfortunately, Dr. Kumar is right," the commander said. "We need to be very careful with the next steps we take. One false one could prove fatal for all of us."

"There's something I'm not clear about yet," the deputy director went on. "What led them to believe you're the chosen one who's come to save them?"

"Quite honestly, I don't know," Emily admitted. "I know the Gaal-El have some kind of very ancient library or historical register, but we don't know anything about what their sacred scriptures say about these supposed deities. All I know is that they were expecting Keplerians with some kind of superior technology."

"And yet they referred to you as 'The Woman of Metal'," the deputy director pointed out. "What in the name of sanity does that mean?"

"I don't know," she repeated. "Maybe somehow the fact that we were wearing exosuits led them to believe we show some of the characteristics of their supposed saviors."

"And also," Ferrara added, "you said yourself that the leader himself acted differently when it was just the two of you inside the temple,"

"Yes, that's true."

"What does that mean?" the deputy director asked.

"When he first showed me the temple he seemed to open up to me," Emily explained. "He told me it wasn't what they'd been expecting, but even so, it might help them to unite all the clans. The point is that he seemed sincere and quite hopeful."

"And what happened afterward to make them end up worshipping you as their messiah?"

She shrugged. "We don't know. He saw something in us, I don't know what, but then his expression suddenly changed, and that was when he addressed us as Gods of Copper."

"As suddenly as that?" Commander Bauer asked.

"Yes, and I have to say that his reaction seemed quite honest to me. Either he's the best Keplerian actor of all time, or else he really did change his mind and it turns out we really were what they were expecting."

"Where does all this business about the Gods of Copper come from?" the deputy director asked. "The exosuits are made of a latest-generation alloy, and they're not even copper-colored."

"We don't know where it comes from. We presume it must have something to do with their beliefs."

"My theory is that their oldest scriptures go back to a distant time when the Keplerians worked in bronze," Rakesh said. "Although without

17

being able to get access to their writings it would be very complicated to work out a more elaborate theory."

"Even so," the deputy director said, "it seems obvious that there's some relation between our exosuits and their deities. Could it be that they were waiting for a third alien civilization that had already visited the planet in ancient times?"

"That's one of the possibilities," Rakesh admitted. "This planet might have been visited by other advanced civilizations."

"I get that." The deputy director smiled briefly. "What's clear to me is that nothing's clear. So what agreement did you come to?"

"The Gaal-El are going to summon the sacred conclave," Emily said in summary. "We'll receive a message with instructions so that we can attend it."

"Who'll be able to do that?"

"Unfortunately, only the leaders of each faction and myself. But to do that I'm going to have to pass a test."

"A test?" David repeated. "What kind of test?"

"It seems to be like the initiation test the Keplerians themselves have to go through to reach adulthood. In this case, I'm going to have to get hold of a kind of special stone which can only be found inside the mountain."

"That presupposes a considerable risk."

"Yeah, I know. But I'm ready to run it if it means we're able to help the Keplerians, and the main goal of the project, of course."

"When do you have to go through this initiation test?"

"Tomorrow. And I have to do it alone."

"That's not something I'm very keen on, but I trust your good judgment," the deputy director said reluctantly. "We'll have to work out a strategy, we can't act lightly. We'll wait for news of the Gaal-El while we go on with the colonization plans for the planet. I want you to know that I've given the appropriate orders for us to start extending this base with new facilities and personnel. And more than that, we're going to start the necessary moves for the installation of another base some way away from here."

"How far away?" Ferrara asked.

"We're talking about the second site, in the other continent, the one near the sea."

Emily gave him a worried look. "That's where we had the accident with the storm."

"Yes, but we were able to establish that storms, as a general rule, are more electrical than on earth, so what we have to do is be prepared for these kinds of meteorological events, whether storms, dense fogs or any other kind of phenomena we don't yet know anything about."

"Who's going to lead that expedition?" Robert asked.

"We haven't decided on the names as yet," the commander admitted.

"But don't worry," the deputy director reassured them. "They'll be trustworthy people."

2
Investigations

November 6, year 0

Magellan Base, Kepler-442b

The deputy director and the commander returned to the space station once their small meeting ended. Emily was then able to enjoy a relaxed meal with the rest of the team.

"So, what's the village of the Gaal-El like?" Paula asked.

"The truth is it's worth seeing," Ferrara said. "The way there reminds one quite a lot of the roads and paths to those Buddhist monasteries lost in the middle of the mountains."

"Yes, and the temple itself is very similar to the settlement of Petra in Jordan," Rakesh added.

"It's certainly a special place, that's for sure," Emily admitted, "although I believe time has taken its toll in the carvings and stone of the place. It's a shame, but a couple hundreds of years ago it must have been an even more impressive place."

"What can there be of truth in their beliefs?" Chad asked curiously, "Do they really believe you're the chosen?"

Emily felt a small shiver hearing how Chad used the word.

"I don't know," she replied. "It's difficult to assess how fervent the cultists are, but I think they have great expectations set on us, and it scares me that they believe we can do something for them which we really have no capacity to do."

"Defeat the Khol?" the biologist asked.

"Yeah, especially that."

"If it's true that this planet belongs to them, I'm afraid we'll have no choice but to face them," said Taro.

"So, what's the plan, now?" Kostas asked.

"Tomorrow I'm leaving to do some kind of initiation ritual that will make me a full-fledged Keplerian citizen."

"A ritual?" Chad asked. "Like those in which they sacrifice goats?"

"No," Emily smiled. "I don't have many details, apart from the fact that it seems to be dangerous and that all Keplerians do something similar when they reach adulthood."

"She also has to go alone," Rakesh added.

"Oh dear," Chad's face changed, "That doesn't sound like fun."

"Why are they making you comply with this ritual?" Paula asked.

"Afterwards I will be summoned to the conclave with the rest of the Keplerian leaders," Emily explained. "An in order to be able to attend I need to be a Keplerian citizen, I guess that from the conclave we'll gather more information and the next steps will be decided."

"We'll have to wait for the events to unfold, I guess," Gorka said, "Whichever way we're with you to the death, Emily."

"That's right," Paula added. "We're in this all together. We'll be with you and do everything you tell us to."

"Hear, hear!" Taro said.

"Thank you all, it means a lot to me."

After finishing her steak, Emily decided to spend some time with Chad and Taro so they could bring her up to date. They had been working for a long time and she did not know their latest advances in their investigations. So, the three headed to the lab.

"How are you doing with the *fhores,* Chad?" Emily asked. She had brought two draft animals to the base when she was rescued, together with Shildii, from her capture.

"Ha!" Taro cried. "How he's doing? He spends more time with them than at the lab. They're his new pets."

"Despite the obvious exaggeration of my esteemed colleague," said Chad with forced solemnity, "the truth is that indeed I have grown quite fond of them and I believe they like me too. They're very noble creatures. Who knows how their former owners treated them, making them work hard all day."

"I'd say that he's really spoiling them, he feeds them all the time. They've put on quite a bit of weight since they've been here."

"What can I do if Pegasus and Rocinante weren't well fed?" Chad protested with his arms on his hips.

"Pegasus? Rocinante?" Emily said.

"Yes, he's given them the names of famous horses," Taro said mockingly.

"Of course!" Chad cried ignoring the jokes. "Pegasus, for the mythical animal of the Greek Mythology, and Rocinante to honor Don Quixote de la Mancha's horse. And in spite of your constant jokes, they're

21

delighted with their names and they come when I call them."

"They come because you feed them," Taro corrected him.

"I'm glad you're enjoying the animals so much, although let me remind you that they might belong to someone so don't grow too attached to them, just in case."

"I think it's already too late for that," Taro said laughing.

"But tell me," Emily said, "what have you found out during these days?"

"We haven't made any great progress," Taro admitted, "but we've noted again that the molecules had an interesting effect, although never lethal, on all the bacteria and organisms we've exposed them to."

"That's not anything you normally see in nature, is it?" she asked.

"No, it isn't," Chad agreed. "We do believe they will affect them, but in a positive way, something similar to what's happened to the fungi and bacteria we've exposed to the molecules."

"Or similar to what Kostas is doing with the fields outside," Taro added.

"Are you sure that nothing bad will happen to them?" Emily insisted.

"We don't think so," Chad ventured, "and it would be one of the first steps to see what the effect of the molecules is on humans."

"We were already exposed to them a few weeks back," Emily noted.

"Yes, but in a very limited way, and the truth is we haven't noticed any kind of problem, at least not in the short term. Unfortunately, it seems the planet is filled with those obelisks that spread the molecules and, even if we managed to destroy them all, many of those molecules are already scattered throughout the planet. It would be very complicated to eliminate them completely to avoid exposure."

"The obelisks!" Emily remembered suddenly. "I had forgotten. Do you know we saw one during our trip?"

"Yes, we all saw it," Taro reminded her, "That means they can be almost anywhere,"

"In fact," Emily went on, "I asked Ada to try and find more all over the planet."

"That's right," said the AI, "And I already have the results, there are thousands of them," she continued ´no half measure, "And they're distributed with almost pinpoint accuracy throughout the three continents of the planet."

Ada showed them the images with the location of the obelisks, which clearly traced a pattern of lines and squares on firm land.

"Wow, it's true there are thousands," taro cried.

"Eighty-four thousand, two hundred and seventy-eight, to be

exact." Ada said.

"What's the distance between each one of them?" Chad asked.

"It depends on the latitude" the AI explained. "In latitudes closer to the poles, the distance is less, but it goes from the sixty kilometers of the latitudes you're in, to the shortly fewer than forty as we get closer to the poles. They form an almost perfect network of obelisks."

"Wow, that's impressive," Emily admitted. "Whoever their creators were, they were very precise."

"Yes, and although the network isn't distributed or aligned perfectly," Ada added, "I'd say that it's necessary to have tools of great precision in order to achieve this. The fact hasn't escaped me that the more diverted obelisks regarding others are near the tectonic plates of the planet, which means that although nowadays their placement isn't altogether exact, it was indeed thousands of years ago."

"Could you date their antiquity?" Emily asked.

"Impossible, I'd need to study the planetary geological activity and the tectonic movements carefully. But I doubt they're less than a hundred thousand Keplerian years old."

"D'you think it was the Khol who built them?" Taro asked.

"I don't know," Emily admitted, "and I doubt the Keplerians themselves know who raised them, really. All I know is that they are sacred to the Gaal-El."

"Wow!" Chad cried. "Then I don't think we'll get the other request we were thinking of asking you."

"What are you talking about?"

"We want to dismantle an obelisk," said Chad.

"Dismantle it?" she replied. "You mean like knocking it down to study how it works?"

"That's it," Taro said. "We believe that the obelisks are only the tip of the iceberg. If they've been working for thousands of years, they must have alien technology inside, or underground, perhaps."

"I'm not sure we'd be able to understand how they work," Chad added, "but it might help us understand how the molecules are created. It would be fascinating to check the creative process of something so advanced. The applications of a technology like that would be unlimited, they would undoubtedly lead us to a technological revolution. It might even help us build something that would allow us to terraform the planet."

"Yes, I understand, but I'm afraid it won't be that easy," said Emily, "At least considering that the obelisks are sacred to the Keplerians. Although we don't really know what it is they worship of them."

"Well, we had to try," Chad shrugged.

"The idea is interesting," Emily agreed, "but I'm afraid that right now it's not as easy as going up to one of those structures and knocking it down."

"By the way, Ada, where's the nearest obelisk to this base?" Taro asked.

"That's an interesting question," Ada replied. "The obelisk found during the trip is the closest in a straight line, followed by another located three kilometers from the cave of the Yokai."

"What's interesting about that?" Emily asked blankly.

"Well, there really should be an obelisk right on the other side of the river," Ada said, "For some strange reason, there's an obelisk missing."

"What do you mean there's one missing?" Chad asked.

Ada zoomed in on the images and marked the place on the planet where there ought to be an obelisk with a red X.

"If you look closely, there's a void in the middle of this perfect distribution."

"I believe I know the answer, but, where's the spot you've marked?" Emily asked.

"I'm afraid your suspicion is correct," said Ada. "It's half-way between the villages of the Wiikhaadiiz ofiz and where we think the Khapabir are located."

"The Khapabir?" Chad was interested, "I'm not much up to date on Keplerian geography. Who are those?"

"It's the largest of the Keplerian villages," Emily explained. "Yisht, Khikhya's assistant, was born and raised there. It's a people ruled by technologists. I think we'll eventually have to pay them a visit. Yisht says that they already master some kind of energy to move carriages."

"I see, but why would they destroy it themselves if they're sacred?" Chad asked.

"That's a very good question," Emily said.

"Maybe it fell by itself," Taro suggested.

"I doubt it. If that had happened I guess Ada would've found more voids in the network, and she's only found one, right Ada?"

"Correct, I only found that void."

"It can't be coincidence," Emily reasoned, "Someone, Keplerian, Khol or of any other species, has destroyed the obelisk that ought to be there."

"This planet never stops throwing enigmas at us," said Chad.

"Exactly," Emily agreed. "But we'll solve all those mysteries, one by one, for our own good. Is there anything else you want to tell me?"

"Not for now," said Chad, "but we'd like to have some animal or embryo to study the effects of the molecules on living beings. That would be the most important right now."

"Good, I'll see what I can do," said Emily. "We have our own Noah's ark in the silo at the station. I guess we can count on some of the specimens."

"That would be great," said Chad.

"I'll let you know," Emily said as she was leaving.

Talking about the obelisks, apart from giving her something to look into when they visited the other Keplerian villages, had reminded her of something she had to check and that she had found curious during the trip. Perhaps it was nothing, but she would rather make sure. She headed to the storage that was right in front of the door to the labs. Emily took a terminal from a nearby table and a stool and sat down beside the surviving mule from the disaster of the Copernicus. She switched it on and it gave off the characteristic electric hum that indicated it was operative and awaiting orders.

Emily manipulated the terminal she had just grabbed and put the mule in a maintenance mode. She wanted to check in case that mule had had a different behavior than the one that ended up falling off the snow-covered mountain pass through which they had arrived at the village of the Gaal-El. She did not have the mule that had had the accident to contrast the state of both, but she might find some explanations with the one that was left.

First she checked the manufacturing facts: date, place of assembly and name of the company purchaser of the Defense Department contract.

"American Dynamics" she read.

"Ada, the company American Dynamics has been in charge of manufacturing all the autonomous devices of the expedition?" she asked.

"It has," she replied, "The specifications of the Department of Defense of the New United States encompassed all the autonomous machinery for the two official expeditions. This mule you're manipulating was manufactured in the second batch."

"And what about the mules of the Asimov?" she asked. "Where did they come from?"

"There was no type of public contract to provide material to the Asimov."

"If the ship was already planned and in construction before the attempt, I guess the contests would include extra material to provide the third of the arks," Emily thought out loud.

"Most likely," Ada confirmed. "The Galileo carried less material than was supposed to have been manufactured."

"I guess that only two thirds of that planned, which together with the extra third of what the Copernicus was going to carry, would provide the material for the ark that was hidden from public knowledge."

"Indeed, your estimates coincide, roughly speaking."

"I guess it makes sense. And the department of defense being in charge of managing everything and considering how secretive the two projects were, the fact that more material than was necessary for two arks was manufactured went unnoticed."

Emily went on reading the characteristics of the mule: model, serial number, and software version. Emily stopped there.

Version 4.0.0.

"Ada, what is the last available version to be installed in the mules?" she asked.

"The 3.14.2," she said.

"What? … No, it can't be…"

"Yes, the version 3.14.2 is the last one," Ada confirmed. "Besides, it was modified already here, on Kepler-442b."

"Who made those modifications?"

"Erik Johansen, one of Director Patel's robotic engineers."

"I know who he is, I gave him access to some of your functionalities a long time ago. Can you put me through to him?"

"Sure."

Emily needed to know why this mule had a software version which did not even exist in the code records of the space station. It was extremely odd. Sometimes there were mistakes in the updates, but that would imply having an obsolete version of the software, never a superior one. That was impossible.

"Hello?" she heard a young voice. "Oh, Hi Emily! How's everything down there?"

"Hello Erik," she said. Very well, finally back at the base, it's been non-stop for the last few days. How about you?"

"Fine," he replied, short. "We don't get bored up here either, you know there's always something to fix or improve."

"Yes, I understand. I'll try not to take up too much of your time, but I have with me, here, one of the surviving mules of the Copernicus."

"We brought several that hadn't been taken to the Copernicus yet when everything happened."

"I know, but you see, the thing is I've seen this mule doing different things from another labeled for the Asimov."

"Well, tell me which one it is and I can check it over, it might have an older version of the firmware. Sometimes the updating process fails."

"I know, and that's the first thing I checked, but that's not the problem," Emily went on. "In fact, I'd say that its behavior has been way superior to that of the other units."

"Way superior?" he asked. "What do you mean?"

"I know it sounds odd, but the software of this mule is much better that the others'. And I haven't told you the weirdest yet. Its version is the 4.0.0."

"Let me check it for you," the young technician said. "It can't be," he said shortly after. The last available version is the 3.14.2, I'm looking at it right now on my terminal. In fact, the last two software checkups are mine, a few months ago. I fixed a couple of problems that made the servomotors not respond correctly in certain circumstances. But there is no 4.0.0 version."

"Well, I can swear that this unit has that version installed," she insisted. "Check my screen."

"It can't be," he said taken aback. "Unless someone installed a version that hasn't passed through the space records, but for that we'd need the manufacturer's credentials. No-one in the station should have them."

"What can we look at apart from that?"

"Well, I'm afraid we can't know at what date this version was compiled, but in the terminal you can see when the unit was last updated. Go to the firmware tab, select 'Record' and at the bottom there will appear a list with all the updates and when they were made."

"It can't be…" Emily whispered upset, once she had followed the indications.

"What? What date did you find?"

"It says here that this mule was last updated on June 14 of 2292."

"And what's impossible about that?" Erik asked. "I mean, apart from the version number. That only means that the mule hasn't been updated since before we left Earth."

"You still don't realize, do you?"

"Realize what?"

"That's the date of the attempt against the Copernicus," she told him. "This mule was updated with a non-existing version on the same day in which part of its batch was blown up."

"Wow, I don't know what to say."

"I need you to check it," Emily told him. "I'll speak to the director so he knows, but I want you to analyze it in depth, to decompile the software it has installed if necessary, in order to know what this version of the firmware does."

"All right," he said. "I'll ask Director Patel to send someone to bring it back."

"No, I'll bring it myself, personally, in two days time," Emily said. "I need it to come with me tomorrow on an important mission."

3
The ordeal

November 7, year 0

Near the Magellan base, Kepler-442b

Together with her mule, Emily approached the clearing on the far side of the river. According to Waafdiv, to undergo the ordeal which would grant her citizenship she needed to do the test on her own, but he had said nothing about using tools or technology, so she had loaded the mule with all kinds of things that might be helpful.

She waited for some time until she saw a small Keplerian procession approaching the clearing from the north. From out of a cart came two figures. The first was Liikmi, the high priest's faithful assistant, the second one Waafdiv himself. They came up to Emily and greeted her with bows which must have been the result of her new status.

"Greetings, Metal Woman," Waafdiv said ceremoniously.

She blushed. "Please get up. None of this is necessary."

Two more figures came down from the carriage.

"These are our brothers Hoyth and Khasbelt," the high priest said. "They are to act as witnesses and make a written record of the result of the ordeal."

"Hello," she said as they too bowed to her. "But really, none of this is necessary," she insisted uncomfortably.

"Since all parties are present," Waafdiv began, "we can begin the ritual."

"Wait a moment, Waafdiv, I don't really know what I have to do yet."

"You have to cross the waterfall on the mountain. Within it lies the great lake, and within that rest the sacred stones of the Gaal-El."

"What are these stones like?"

The high priest indicated with a gesture. "Dark and smooth, the size of a *fuj*'s egg."

"And how do I find this lake?"

"You will have to go into the cave of the waterfall. There you will have to follow your own instincts. You will only have a single rotation to achieve it."

"And if I don't succeed?"

"I know you will," he replied confidently.

"How can you be so sure?"

"Because you are the chosen one."

Emily sighed. This test left her feeling very uneasy. Alone, on an unknown planet, inside a cave which had been hollowed out by the action of water. What could possibly go wrong?

"Now let us begin the ritual," Liikmi announced. "In the presence of both parties, on the one hand the candidate Emily, of the human village, and on the other the people of Gaal-El, represented by the high priest Waafdiv. We state publicly the candidate's intention to become a member of the Gaal-El people. Entry into the cult will be granted only if she returns to this same place with one of the sacred stones within a period of time which is never to exceed a full rotation. Are both parties in agreement?"

"We are," the high priest said.

"I am," Emily repeated, although she was not very confident about her chances.

"In accordance with our laws," the assistant said, "we declare the ordeal to be under way. Begin."

She looked at them uncertainly. Waafdiv was smiling in satisfaction. Seeing that neither of them said anything more, she decided that the moment had come to depart for the waterfall. She turned toward the mountain, sighed and set off.

She had seen the waterfall a few days earlier, when they had followed Khikhya's instructions for reaching Haagar's cabin. But on that occasion they had come from the other side of the river. She weighed up whether to cross it again, but then she thought that if the candidates for admission into the Gaal-El all did the same test, there might be a path which would allow her to avoid the eighty-meter height of the waterfall.

The mule, laden with supplies and tools for almost any unforeseen event, followed obediently a few meters behind her.

"Which way do I go?" she asked.

"I'll draw you a route to the base of the waterfall," Ada said. "Once you're there we'll work out how we can go into the mountain."

Emily speeded up as much as she could. She only had a single Keplerian day, one rotation, to complete the test, so she tried to cover the distance to the waterfall as quickly as she could. She had no doubt that she would come across difficulties on the way, so there was no time to be lost.

She made her way through undergrowth until after a while she came upon a small path. It did not look as though it was much-used, but it was obvious that it led to the waterfall. Ada modified the instructions she was giving to her so that she could follow it.

After four hours of walking she began to hear the water crashing against the source of the river. She was very close now. Suddenly the path forked. To the left it seemed to lead to the foot of the waterfall; on the right it began to climb, but was soon lost to sight.

"Which way do I go?" she asked again.

"I'm not sure," Ada said. "I can't see anything from the satellite."

"In that case I think the most logical thing would be to take the left-hand path. Maybe from the riverside we'll find a way to access the mouth of the waterfall."

She took the path that veered to the left, toward the sound of the water breaking against the base of the waterfall. It took her barely five minutes to reach a rocky area which allowed her to contemplate the spectacular descent of the water, which caused a cloud of spray in the form of millions of tiny droplets which were borne on the breeze to spread through the atmosphere.

In the distance she saw the spot where they had stopped to rest on their way to Haagar's cabin. "We're further along than when we saw the waterfall from the other bank."

"Yes, seventy-five meters or so further."

"Do you see anywhere that'll let me get to the mouth of the waterfall?" She looked up at the enormous opening the water was falling through.

"There seems to be a small path which goes right under it."

"Under it?" Emily repeated in surprise.

"That's right. If you look closely, on the left of the waterfall there's a flatter area that seems to give access to the opening."

"So that we have to go up from this side of the river, but then go in by the left, is that it?"

"That seems to be right," said Ada. "And something tells me that if we follow the other path we'll come to the way across the waterfall."

"I'll take the opportunity to get my strength back."

After resting for a while and ingesting some mash and water, she retraced her steps as far as the fork and took the path on the right. She went on for a long time, and as she did so the terrain began to climb slowly, but not too steeply as yet.

"I seem to be going further away from the waterfall."

"That's right. But I presume that later on it'll turn left. It's veering away from the river so that the path doesn't get too steep."

The vegetation was still abundant in that area, which made it difficult to carry out a satellite survey to see where the path went. So far there was no indication that it was turning back toward the waterfall again.

"Any news?" Robert asked, alert to her progress.

"No, nothing. I'm following the path. We think that further along it must turn west, through the rock."

"Yeah, I'm looking at it now. Are you sure you don't want me to come with you? I can be there in the blink of an eye."

"No, I have to do this alone. It's something very important for them, and I can't risk doing anything that could ruin it all. They might take that as an insult."

"Okay, then. Anyway, I'll be on the alert all the time."

"Thanks, though it's possible we might get cut off the moment I go into the cave."

"Ada," he asked, "do you know whether that could happen?"

"I'm not sure. It'll depend on the composition of the rock the waterfall starts from and how deep Emily needs to go. But looking at precedents, the probability is that we won't be able to maintain communication."

"Thanks, Ada. Anyway, we'll be on the alert and ready to set out if there's any difficulty. Balakova's up-to-date too, and the ship's ready."

"Thanks. I hope it won't be necessary."

It did not take long for the path to swerve nearly a hundred and eighty degrees and then turn back again toward the waterfall exactly as they had expected. With every step she took, the rock of the mountain became more visible and the tall, leafy trees gave way to others that were smaller and more scattered. The slope of the path remained at a steady but comfortable level of difficulty. Ten minutes later it had turned into a narrow ledge the same size as the ones they had had to cross at the snow-covered pass on their way to the Gaal-El village.

Emily watched the mule out of the corner of her eye as it followed her only a few centimeters behind her. It seemed to be bearing up quite well. She had only loaded it with a couple of batteries, together with oxygen and food. Apart from these supplies she was also carrying a few tools and other useful extras: rope, a torchlight, material for making fire, a blanket and various small utensils she thought might come in handy. She was still puzzling over what she had found out the day before. Why did this mule have a more advanced version of the software which had been installed the day before the attempt on the Copernicus? She hoped Erik, the engineer who worked with Director Patel, might be able to shed some light on the mystery.

The narrow path went on ascending as it drew nearer the waterfall. The sun was already beginning to decline and was shining from the east, a sign that it would be dark the moment she went into the cave.

She supposed she would have to spend the night inside the mountain, though everything would depend on when she managed to find the lake.

The faint sound of the waterfall began to reach her ears from ahead, and soon she saw the spray which the wind was raising from the water. The path was completely surrounded by stone now that the vegetation had disappeared, but even so, the trees at river level were so tall that they prevented her from seeing much further. The path was getting narrower and narrower and the slope was already notable, almost vertical. The stones were wet with water from the fall, which by now was coming into view a few meters above the path.

The water was falling forcefully from the little ledge which ran seven meters or so above the path. At last they were in the area they had seen from below. The stones were slippery, and many of them were covered with a kind of red slime which obliged her to take great care as she went.

She glanced back at the mule. A single misstep on those stones would be enough to provoke a fall down the cliff. The path had narrowed so much that the mule had modified its way of walking; it had lowered its center of gravity and was leaning against the almost-vertical wall. Emily's steps became shorter and more careful. Then she came to the stretch which ran just below the level of the water. It was dark, the path was very narrow and she could almost have touched the water with her left hand as she went on.

For a moment she lost her concentration. Her right foot trod unwittingly on one of the slippery stones and she was thrown against the right-hand wall so that she struck it hard with her helmet, and although this softened the blow she was left rather stunned. By the time she realized this, her body was slipping toward the precipice. She managed to hold on with her arms on the narrow path, but her torso and legs were left hanging in the air. The dense spray did nothing to help the situation. She tried to heave herself up, but the suit was not responding as she would have expected.

"Emily!" came Robert's voice. "Are you all right?"

"No!"

"Try to lift yourself up, very carefully."

"That's what I'm trying to do!" she shouted uneasily.

"Keep calm. Breathe deeply."

She tried to calm down, but the situation would not let her. She was hanging nearly seventy-five meters up. The fall might not kill her, but she had no desire to establish either the depth of the source of the river or the capabilities of the exosuit. Suddenly a metal leg, taking small but precise steps, stopped at the level of her hands. The mule wanted to help her out of that sticky situation.

She grasped its hind leg with her right hand, and the mule reacted

32

by throwing its weight toward the rock wall. It seemed to be inviting her to hang from it so that the suit would find it easier to use its abilities. She grasped the foreleg with her left hand and at last was able to maneuver more easily. First she leaned her feet against the waterfall wall, then with the help of her improvised holds made the effort required to lift herself up from there and stand upright. That mule had done it again.

"Are you all right?" Robert asked when the danger had passed.

"Yeah, I'm okay." Her heart was still in her mouth. "I don't know what this mule has, but it just saved me from a certain fall."

"It's a survivor," Robert said, sounding calmer now. "Just like you."

"It was nearly left all by itself," she joked.

"Better not think about that. Get out from down there as soon as you can."

Emily did this, but this time she was much more careful. She kept an eye on every step she took, every stone she stepped on, until she was past the area of low visibility. A few meters on she came to a spot where the way ahead was blocked and the path turned back. From here it climbed to the mouth of the waterfall itself. With her heart beating more slowly by now, she was able to get her breath back and get ready to enter the cave, which was now visible a few meters ahead.

"The comms'll probably get cut off from this point," she said.

"I'll wait till you come out again. Be careful in there."

"I'll do my best," she promised him, but she did not feel in the least confident.

She took a few steps forward and found herself at the cave-entrance. It was much larger than it had appeared from below. The waterfall itself did not even fill even a fifth of the entire opening. It was not the snow-melt season, so she supposed that the volume of water the river was carrying at that altitude would not be at its maximum. The stones in the entrance seemed to suggest this, as they were covered with reddish algae like those which grew over the rocks they used to cross the river. They were damp, but they did not look as slippery as the ones that had caused that minor accident. Even so, she was very careful when she stepped on them.

At last she was inside.

The cave was very spacious. The good news was that there was more than enough space to walk with no risk of falling into the river, which ran through the cave with enough strength and volume to put anyone in a tight spot. Even so, she decided to switch on a light. She did not want any more surprises.

The sound of the water filled the cave. Suddenly a muffled sound reached her from inside the cave, as if dozens of rocks were falling somewhere far away, very deep inside. It seemed that to all the dangers she might have to face there she now had to add falls of rock. She went on toward the far end of the cave, which for the moment was large and offered space enough to move, even though she had to dodge boulders, stalactites and stalagmites. Despite all this, neither she nor the mule found it difficult to move on.

"We have no comms now," Ada informed her.

After going up a few meters more she reached an area where there was a wide opening to her left. She focused her helmet-torch to inspect what looked like an artificial distributing hallway. This led to the former mines, and from there four tunnels excavated into the rock continued on their way. A strange sound, above that of the water, came to her ears. She did not know what it was, so she asked Ada to filter it and amplify it. What she heard left her frozen.

A moan of pain was coming from one of those artificial corridors, as if some creature were in agony. It was not continuous, but instead stopped for a few moments at a time, then the desperate moans started again. Whatever it might have been, Emily's blood froze at the thought that it might be a Yokai. Instinctively she looked away from that particular corridor and focused on the mission which had brought her there. Once again she turned toward the interior of the cave and went on, ignoring those unsettling moans.

She had no idea how long she had been walking, but she supposed by now it would be the middle of the night outside. The place was immense, and although she passed stretches which were far narrower and more dangerous, and was even forced to cross a small stream, she always came to other areas which were wider, with enough space to move on. The path was ascending. Not too much, but because of gravity the water was filtering down the side-walls and then joining the stream. She had not heard any sound which was not caused by the underground river.

The sound of the water grew when she came to an opening in the cave. When she directed her helmet torch she saw a small inner waterfall. It was not very high, barely five meters, but the path she had been following until that moment vanished. In its place a group of smooth rocks lay piled up in one of the corners. She would be able to use them to get up above the level of the waterfall, and with a bit of luck this would be the last obstacle before she got to the lake.

The mule followed her footsteps, leaping from rock to rock as they went up. It seemed to be managing without any trouble. In the final stretch Emily supported herself on her hands to manage the last meter and a half. The mule, on the other hand, used a series of rocks in between, leaning against them to reach the necessary height. She illuminated the place with her torch. The ceiling was some six meters high and the underground hall was so large she could not see as far as the end. The water filled the whole expanse, and the surface was so calm that only the sound of that waterfall was able to disturb it. She had just found the lake.

"How deep is it?" she asked.

"There's no way I can tell," Ada informed her, "but to judge by the incline of the lake-bed at the corners, it could be over ten meters in the central area."

"And the temperature?"

"Bearing in mind that this water is filtered from the snowy summits, it might vary between one and five degrees centigrade."

"I don't know how the Keplerians manage to get in there."

She decided that the safest way to approach the lake would be to go further into the cave and tie herself to the mule with one of the ropes in case there were currents which could drag her to the waterfall. She tied a lark's head knot around one of the legs of the mule, then tied the other end around her waist. She tested the strength of the hold a couple of times to see how the mule would react, but it seemed to bear the pressure without any trouble.

"Here we go," she said to encourage herself as she began to get into the lake.

Soon the water had reached her waist. The temperature was two and a half degrees, and she began to feel an intense cold. The suit compensated for this by giving off heat. She decided that she could go under safely, so she went on walking until the water covered her completely. Her helmet light was powerful and she could see the bottom of the riverbed quite clearly. However, the stones there were more or less normal. Waafdiv had made it quite clear that as soon as she saw them she would know what kind of material they were talking about.

Have I mistaken the place? she wondered uneasily.

She went on deeper into the lake. The depth was approaching four meters by now, but the stones at the bottom were still utterly plain and normal. Suddenly she saw a dark line deep in the bed. It was twenty meters or so away, almost in the center of the lake. Here the water was eight meters deep. Without the suit she would have found it impossible to reach the spot. There were thousands of dark stones with a reddish tinge which seemed strange to her. She knew she had found what she had come in search of. The stones, slightly smaller than a hen's egg, were very familiar. She took one of them and turned around.

The mule pulled her outwards, and very soon she was out of the water again. The suit must have been hot, because thick steam was coming out of it as a result of of the contrast with the water temperature. She was clutching the stone in her fist. As soon as she had untied herself she unclenched it.

"It's an almandine garnet," Ada said. "It's formed in metamorphic conditions, which means that this place must have experienced changes in temperature and pressure in the past. From an economic point of view it has no special value, or at least it didn't on Earth."

"That's not what strikes me about this stone."

"And what is it, then?" the AI asked.

"That it's the same type of stone as the one in the pendant my aunt Helen gave me when I was little."

Emily retraced her steps in the direction of the cave entrance. It had taken her over four hours to get there, she was tired and her body was anxious for rest, but she had to keep going. A couple of hours later she reached the area where the four artificial galleries began, the relic of a previous mining era. Once again she asked Ada to mute the sound of the river. All she could now hear was silence. She waited for a few moments without knowing very well why. And once again she heard it, far weaker and more muffled than it had been hours before.

"I hope I won't regret this," she said as she crossed the rocks which led her to the distributor area.

She listened carefully at each of the galleries. Two of them went up, the other two down. They must surely have linked different sections of the mine with the river. Perhaps long ago the miners had channeled the water in some way to make it reach other places, but no-one would remember that by now. The sound was audible through the third of the galleries; she had to go up.

She went into that corridor which had been carved out of the rock itself. The gallery was spacious, though every now and then she came across areas where part of the wall or the ceiling had collapsed, although they never blocked her way. She went up two hundred meters or so in a straight line, then the gallery turned thirty degrees to the right. Whatever might have been there had heard her in the distance. She came to another natural dome from which three more galleries set off. This was a real labyrinth. The moans became cries of despair. Something was moving in the entrance to one of the galleries. A Yokai. It was trapped.

The desperate cries became stronger and stronger when she focused her light on the creature. On top of it was a pile of rubble which had fallen from the ceiling of one of the galleries, trapping both legs of the demon so that it could not escape. Emily understood that the light from of her helmet must be hurting it.

"Light out," she said. "Change to infrared."

The creature seemed to calm down a little, though it went on shaking its head and emitting a steady growl of terror. Its arms, smaller than she remembered, were trying to protect the rest of its body. It was only a pup, and it was very frightened. She hesitated about coming anywhere near, because she knew well enough what its elders' claws and jaws could do. But

36

something within her took pity on that frightened, defenseless creature.

"I can't believe what I'm about to do," she said to herself.

She approached the creature, which tried to struggle free once again from the rocks which were holding its body down.

"Easy now," she said softly. "I don't mean to hurt you."

She drew back one of the upper rocks of the pile. She wanted it to understand that she was going to help it get out of there. She drew back another. It seemed to calm down a little, though it went on giving that anguished moan. It must have been in great pain. She took away a third, much heavier than the other two, and this seemed to relieve the young Yokai considerably. Now it was able to free its left leg. It rubbed the wound, obviously painfully. She realized that it was shivering; it was only wearing a small loincloth and it must have been very cold there. She pulled back a few more rocks, until at last the creature was free to move. It used all the strength it had left to crawl to a corner, where it huddled into a ball. It was weak and frightened. That cave-in had taken it by surprise when Emily had gone into the cave, and since then it must have been trying to warn its fellows, which would have been too far away to hear it. She retreated very cautiously, not wanting to scare it, and fetched an isothermal blanket from the mule. She went over to the creature again and draped it over its shoulders. At first it gave a start, then seeing that its rescuer's intentions were good, it seemed to calm down.

There was nothing there to eat, but she knew that if she left it there with its legs crushed it would be sure to end up dying right there. She remembered the Yokai families they had seen when they had gone through the mountain on their way to the Gaal-El village. Those Yokai had not looked so threatening; most of them had been females and pups, younger even than this poor unfortunate. She sighed and went up to the creature, which covered itself again in fear. It calmed down once it realized that she simply wanted to pick it up in her arms. She pointed one by one at the three entrances to the galleries which started from that point. The creature, which kept shaking its head compulsively, stretched out its arm and pointed at the central gallery. Its family must be in that direction.

She went into the narrow corridor. Once the Yokai had relaxed she was able to feel it and take a closer look at it. Its skin was very pale, almost waxen, and though it was not very tall, its limbs were very long. Although it was a pup, its claws looked sharp enough to tear an adult man in half. But what most impressed her was its head. The absence of eye-sockets and that disproportionate mouth with a multitude of sharp fangs inside it gave it an air of horror.

She went on as fast as she could, but even so, they had to walk for some time until the little demon showed signs of excitement because of something it had heard further ahead. She slowed down out of caution, and after a few moments she began to hear a multitude of growls and cries, and these were not in the least reassuring. Her blood froze. It was not long before she saw movement ahead in the gallery. An adult Yokai with a very unwelcoming look was coming toward them at great speed.

Instinctively she put the young Yokai down on the floor of the gallery and took a few steps back. Very soon the adults reached them and assessed the situation with threatening postures. The little one tried to get to its feet and come between the first of them and Emily. Both of them exchanged growls, while the adult checked the pup's state. For a few interminable moments she thought she was done for, that these Yokai would take her and her adventure would come to an end as Private Parrish's had when they had first set foot on the planet.

However, the little one seemed to persuade the adults, who relaxed their attitude a little. Emily decided that this was the right moment to get further and further away from there, walking backwards without taking her eyes off that strange family reunion. Once she had lost sight of them she turned and ran out of the gallery, followed by the tireless mule. Soon she was back at the mouth of the cave. It was the dead of night. She had more than enough time to get back to the starting-point with the precious sacred stone.

The first rays of light were beginning to show in the sky when she reached the clearing she had set off from. Here the four Gaal-El who had seen her off the day before were waiting. They seemed to have slept in the same cart they had arrived in.

"Welcome once again, Emily," the high priest said.

"God morning, Waafdiv."

"Did you attain your goal?"

"I have it here." She took the stone out of one of the mule's saddlebags.

"Fantastic!" Waafdiv cried. "Liikmi, take note that the candidate has managed to retrieve a sacred stone from the great dark lake."

"We can consider the ordeal over," the assistant added.

"And now what?" she asked.

"The Gaal-El tradition says that you must give your stone of wisdom to the one who has been your greatest mentor or teacher. I trust you know who will have the immense honor of receiving it."

"Yes," she said firmly. "I know that very well."

4

Promotion

December 1, year 0

Asimov Space Station

"Good morning," Emily said as she kissed Robert's cheek tenderly.

"Morning," he replied sleepily. "I think I must have fallen asleep."

"Yup." She stroked his pecs with her fingertips. "And I have to tell you, Lieutenant, that you look very cute when you're asleep."

He returned the caresses as he pushed away a lock of rebellious hair from her face. "Do I?" Does that mean you've been spying on me?"

"I plead guilty," she said in a whisper. "You can arrest me if that's what you'd like, Lieutenant."

"I'll have to think about it." He kissed her on the lips.

"How did you sleep?"

"Very well. What about you?"

"Me too." She leaned her chin on his shoulder. "I think we ought to do this more often. Last night was very good. I needed it after everything that's happened over these last few days."

"Yes, it was great. But wouldn't it seem a bit odd if both of us left the base so often?"

"Well it's normal enough if we have things to do in the station. I don't think having a little privacy is a crime. And anyway, I don't care what other people might think."

"No, that's not really my point. It's just that I feel I'm not doing my duty protecting the base."

"Right now you're protecting the chosen one," she said mockingly.

"That's true."

She had noticed a slight change in his expression. Something seemed to be troubling him.

"If you like," she suggested, "we could just spend the night together when both of us have to be here."

"I don't want you to think I don't want to be with you." He looked into her eyes. "In fact I'm dying to repeat what happened last night."

"Don't worry." She stroked his hair. "I think I understand you. In a way, the responsible part of my brain is also prompting me to stay at the base and avoid these moments of folly."

"And how do you manage to ignore it?"

She shrugged. "No idea. I guess the part of me that does crazy things shouts louder."

"I think the part of me that does crazy things has lost its voice."

"Well, it's a just a question of cultivating that area of the brain a bit more. I can teach you how to do that."

"Oh yes?" He put his arms around her and stroked her back. "And how would you do it?"

"I could start by kissing you here…" She put her lips on the dimple on his chin. "And then I could kiss you here." She went on along his left cheek. "And then here…" she added, kissing his neck softly. "And perhaps here too…" She kissed his lips.

Both of them felt the warmth and moistness of the other's lips as they played with their tongues. Emily felt a sudden but growing fire beginning to stir inside her again. The memory of the night before was spurring them to resume the lustful dance they had enjoyed so much before their healing sleep.

She could not help an idiotic smile as the water ran down her body in the shower. Never before had she experienced anything like what she was feeling at that moment, could not imagine that there could be anyone better to share her life, her experiences, her fears, her hopes with. Robert was everything she was looking for in a man, and she loved him. As she wrapped a towel around her body she thought how lucky she was to have found him.

And yet when she came out of the shower again she found him sitting on the cabin bed, lost in thought. Something was genuinely troubling him, and it did not seem to be his conscience telling him he had to get back to the base to get on with his work.

"Is everything all right?"

He nodded. "Yeah, I'm fine. It's just that…"

"What is it?" She crouched and stroked his knees. "You can trust me."

"Yeah, I know. It's just that…"

She sat down beside him on the bed and put her arm behind his back. "What's bothering you?"

40

"The commander's offered me the position of captain,"

She could not see that as a problem. "Hey! That's fantastic! Congratulations!"

"Thanks."

"But I don't understand. Isn't that good news? It's an acknowledgment that you're doing your job well, right?"

"Yeah, that side of it's fine," he said barely changing his expression.

"Well then, what's the problem?"

"The problem is that if I accept the promotion I'll have to leave the base, and it's possible that I'll have to coordinate the expansion, or even investigate the activities of the rebels. That'll mean we won't be able to be together so often."

Emily said nothing. Now, at last, she understood what was troubling him. And her own inner selfishness was asking her to try and prevent that promotion. She was well aware that she could persuade him it was a bad idea: more responsibility, more subordinates, a great deal of time.

However, the responsible part of her brain suddenly recovered its voice.

"It's still a great opportunity for you. I think you should accept."

"But what happens about us, then?" he insisted, looking at her. "Just now everything was beginning to make sense."

"We'll manage. Quite honestly, I can't think of anyone better to replace Captain Garth. I'm sure you'll do it really well."

"But I don't want to be away from you," he protested.

"Nor me from you." She clasped him firmly. "But I guess it's the price we have to pay for this great adventure we're having."

"I'm not sure I want to pay that price."

"I don't want to pay it either, but right now it seems to me it's necessary. It'll be good for us, we'll see each other now and then and we'll talk every day if we have to. And besides, you'll have to spend more nights up here, so I can find some excuse or other to come and see you."

He looked at her tenderly. Her words had eased his mind,

"Did you know you have a gift?" he told her as a shy smile appeared on his face.

"Oh yeah?"

"Yes. When I'm with you, every problem seems less complicated. I feel I'm capable of doing almost anything."

She smiled. "Well, well, well. It turns out I have a superpower, and there was me not knowing."

"I suppose I'll accept the promotion," he said after a long sigh.

"I'm very happy for you, Captain Beaufort."

He smiled. "My skin prickled just hearing you say that."

"Yeah, that's another of my superpowers. I can make your skin prickle whenever I want."

Both of them laughed. But at that point several doubts arose in Emily's mind, and she sat up again.

"I have a question. If you stop being the officer responsible for the base, who'll take on the role?"

"My first act as captain will be to promote Sergeant Ortiz to lieutenant. He'd be in charge of leading the base. Although he's a medical officer, he knows how everything works very well. I know he'll do a good job."

"Yes, of course. He's very capable."

"And also I'll propose that Ferrara's promoted to sergeant. The two of them make a great team."

"I'm very happy for the three of you," Emily said, smiling. "You all deserve it."

"Well, for the moment it's just an idea. I haven't spoken about it to anyone yet, just you. First they have to accept the commander's proposal."

"And do we know who's going to lead the new base yet?"

"We're considering a few names, but whoever it is, it'll be someone we trust. The two candidates served with me on the Copernicus, but they're still in cryo."

"I'm sure the one who's chosen will be the most suitable. I trust your good judgment."

Robert was nervous. Wearing his dress uniform, he was about to take a major step in his short military career. Urgency and the needs of the project had forced things to move fast, though without in the least detracting from the importance of what was about to happen. Beside him, Sergeant Ortiz and Private Ferrara flaunted their dress uniforms proudly. Emily was watching the scene from one of the chairs in the atrium. Almost a hundred people had gathered there from both the civil and military personnel of the expedition. All her friends were there. At the highest point of the atrium Commander Bauer was preparing to address everyone there.

"My dear colleagues, I'd like to begin by thanking you all here at this ceremony. It's no secret that we're living in an uncertain time. Our responsibilities to mankind are often a heavy burden on the shoulders of each one of us, and even though the latest developments have not been entirely positive, there can be no doubt that today is a day of celebration.

"Today we celebrate the dedication and unlimited efforts of those of our colleagues who are present. But first I'd like to remember and honor those fallen in battle: Privates Parrish, Garcia, Dimitrova and Singh, as well as the ill-fated Jonathan Wiśniewski and all those who were not even able to get as far as this point." Silence fell on the atrium. "I would also like to extend my gratitude to all the members of the space station, the settlers at Magellan Base and all those who form part of what might be the last human stronghold in the universe. Thank you for your dedication and your efforts. Humanity is in debt to every single one of you."

There was generous applause in appreciation of Commander Bauer's kind words.

"Lieutenant Beaufort!" he called.

Robert left the row he was in and walked forward to stand before the commander. They both stood to attention in a choreographed maneuver.

"For your bravery and dedication to the service," the commander said, "I, Timo Bauer, Commander-in-Chief of the army of the Project Orpheus human colony, hereby appoint you Captain Robert Beaufort."

He took a small silver badge from the hands of an orderly. With a trace of clumsiness he removed the old lieutenant's badge from the epaulette of Robert's suit and replaced it, then repeated the process with the one on the other side. Once both stripes were on, he saluted the newly-promoted captain, who returned the salute proudly.

"Sergeant Ortiz!" the commander called.

As Robert had done, the sergeant came to stand in front of him.

"For your bravery and dedication to the service," the commander repeated, "I, Timo Bauer, Commander-in-Chief of the army of the Project Orpheus human colony, hereby appoint you First Lieutenant Carlos Ortiz."

He replaced Lieutenant Ortiz's stripes on his sleeves, rather less clumsily, both of them saluted again, and the lieutenant went to stand beside the captain now that his promotion had been effected.

"Private Ferrara!" came the final call, and she came to stand before him as the others had done.

"For your bravery and dedication to the service I, Timo Bauer, Commander-in-Chief of the Project Orpheus human colony, hereby appoint you Sergeant Giulia Ferrara."

He placed the patch with three arrows pointing upward which would identify her as a sergeant on the sides of both her sleeves, and after repeating the salute, Sergeant Ferrara went to join her two newly-promoted superiors. The ceremony ended after the commander had bestowed the rank of sergeant on two other soldiers whose actions had played an important part in the military operations to date.

Robert went on receiving congratulations from his colleagues as Emily did her best to get to his side. She waited for her turn to have a word with him at last.

"Congratulations, Captain Beaufort."

He came close to her and kissed her tenderly, and they joined in a warm embrace.

"Thanks, Emily. I'm really happy, even though this looks like being a great responsibility."

"I know you'll be great at it. You were born for this."

He smiled. "I'm not so sure about that."

Gorka stood to attention in front of him and gave a clumsy imitation of a military salute. "Congratulations, Captain!"

"Thanks, Gorka," Robert said, and gave him a friendly hug.

"Congratulations, Robert," Paula added, and he answered her with another hug.

After this Chad, Taro, Evelyn and Kostas congratulated him one after another. And though Emily was very happy for him, she could not help thinking that in a way this promotion was going to separate them a little. They would have to get used to carrying on their relationship at a distance. Unfortunately they would not always be able to escape their working duties so that they could be together. Soon the group was joined by Lieutenant Ortiz and Sergeant Ferrara, both showing off their newly-awarded stripes.

"Congratulations to both of you!" she said, giving each of them in turn a hug.

"At last I can be the one who gives the orders!" Sergeant Ferrara exclaimed. "It's high time these young upstarts knew who the boss is here!"

"That's the way to talk!" Chad said. "Let them know who's in charge!"

Gorka and Paula appeared suddenly with a couple of bottles of champagne and some glasses the project crew had handed out across the atrium. They handed these out, and after the bottles had been loudly uncorked, the golden liquid was poured out for everyone.

"I'd like to propose a toast," Robert began.

"Yes, sir!" Chad shouted.

"I'd like to thank all of you for your friendship and your love. And I think I speak on behalf of my two colleagues if I say that this entire experience wouldn't have been possible without every single one of you. We think of you as our family, and as such I know we'll fight for each other. So we'll drink a toast to the future!"

"The future!" they all shouted as they heard the glasses clink.

"And I'd like to make it official that as of this moment, Lieutenant Ortiz is responsible for the safety of Magellan Base." He raised his glass again. "I wish you the best of luck in your new post, Lieutenant."

"Lieutenant Ortiz!" Ferrara cried happily.

The celebration did not last for very long. After all, it was a mere formality, and everyone in the station had to get back to their work. Hence everyone, except Robert himself, made their way to the hangar to go back to the base.

Emily began to put on her exosuit again. "Are you sure you're okay?" she asked.

"Yeah. It's just that I hadn't quite realized we'd have to part till this moment."

She put her arms around him tenderly. "Don't worry. We'll talk every day, and get together now and then."

"I know you'll be fine with Ortiz, but it's hard to part from you all," he whispered. "Though the thing I'm most unhappy about is being away from you."

"I'm really going to miss you," she whispered back. "But we'll be fine."

They shared one last kiss. Although it had a bitter-sweet quality, it was a passionate one which they would both remember for a long time. And although Emily knew she was going to be all right, she could not help a tear rolling down her cheek at the sight of the person she most loved in the whole universe saying goodbye, waving from the space station hangar.

5

The enlargement

December 2, year 0

Asimov Space Station

That same morning work on the enlargement of the base began once again, and Director Patel's engineers were already there transporting the habitat modules for it. As an experienced director of engineering, he watched from a distance as the transports unloaded their cargo onto the area just in front of the current facilities, a few meters from the greenhouses Kostas had rebuilt.

"Morning, Emily!" he called.

"How's the work going?" she asked.

"On schedule. Today we're going to make various trips to unload the modules onto their sites. Tomorrow we'll assemble and seal them, then in less time than it takes a Keplerian rooster to crow, we'll have the facilities up and running."

Emily indicated the infrastructure behind them. "The new facilities'll be like these, right?"

"Not like, identical," he corrected her "If something works properly, why change it, wouldn't you agree? The only difference between the two facilities is that instead of a lab there'll be a robotics workshop, and instead of the gym area and infirmary there'll be a complete operating theater."

"That's great. I presume for the moment we have enough material to keep expanding?"

"Yes, don't worry about that, we have enough equipment at the station to build a hundred facilities like this. That little... incident with the rebels only delayed us a little. And besides, this time all the leveling and excavation were under way, so some of the work had already been done."

"I see there's a lot more security than usual." She was referring to the two dozen soldiers who had set up a couple of defensive posts in the area.

"That's right. That new captain friend of yours seems to be very clear about things. He doesn't want to leave even a single crack Captain Garth could use to take advantage of the situation."

"He's very capable," she said proudly. "In fact all the soldiers we have here are."

"Of course. We're very lucky to be able to rely on all of them."

"Do we know who's going to form part of the expedition?"

"You mean the technical personnel?"

She nodded.

"Yes, I've decided on some names. First there's Marko, who I think you know. Right now he's responsible for medical equipment and consumer electronics."

Emily nodded. "Of course. We coincided when you showed us the Copernicus for the first time. And he was here a few days ago too, for the re-inauguration of the base."

"That's right," the director said. "And one of my most talented pupils is going to settle here too: Erik."

She smiled. "That's wonderful. In fact I spoke with him a couple of days ago. It'll be great to have him here with us."

"And there's a welder, Emma, we've just finished bringing out of cryo. And Dr Schmidt has decided to send Yara, a generalist doctor who'll be in charge of medical matters for the whole base, in close collaboration with Evelyn of course. In fact the medical equipment we're going to install at the base is more modern than the equivalent at the station itself. The operating theatre, for example, is completely automated, and it was the very latest when we left Earth."

"Hey, that sounds good. Although I sincerely hope we never need to use it."

The director nodded in agreement. "Quite right, let's hope it just collects dust. Although the idea of installing one is to establish that the equipment works correctly in planetary conditions."

She sighed. "Do you know anything about which of the others will be part of the expedition?"

"I don't know anything about that," the director admitted, "but I'd imagine the deputy director will pass on the reports to you soon enough."

"All I hope is that they won't cause any trouble, and that they'll be able to integrate well into a community as diverse as ours is."

"Integration of the passengers from the station will be vital if the colonies are to work."

"And what about you, Director Patel?" she asked. "Don't you see yourself as a settler?"

He groaned. "Oh dear, I wish my schedule would let me. But I fear I have too many tasks at the station even to think about it. And besides, I'd rather leave the planet to you young ones. An old rocker like me would be sure to be in the way."

"Don't say that, Director," she said reproachfully. "We'd be delighted to have you here with us. Your experience would be very useful."

He smiled. "You're very kind. But be careful, there might come a day when I accept the invitation, and then you won't be able to get rid of me."

Both of them laughed until Ada interrupted them.

"Emily, the deputy director has just left the station on his way to the base. He asked me to let you know he'll be arriving very soon."

"Understood, Ada. Director Patel, I'm afraid we'll have to go on with this conversation some other time, the deputy director's on his way."

"I'd imagine he's coming to update you on the same subject."

She laughed. "And to keep an eye on you!"

"Well, that could be! Though I've no idea what I could turn to if he fired me all of a sudden." He laughed heartily.

"I think there's a need here for hands to do the plowing."

He smiled. "Well, I'd be delighted, Emily. Though I dare say my back wouldn't agree."

She said goodbye fondly to Director Patel when the transport which was bringing the Deputy Director appeared through the abundant cloud of the morning. The ship landed near the construction zone, so she went over to the rear ramp, which was already beginning to open. Inside she had the impression of huge quantities of equipment. In fact by now one or two technicians were looking out from inside.

The deputy director came down from the ship in his gray exosuit with a darker gray vertical stripe, a sign that this was someone from the station's administration and government.

"David!" Emily called. "I'm so glad to see you here! We weren't expecting you!"

He laughed. "I've come to see whether you've tidied up your room."

She too laughed. "Well, I think you're in for a pleasant surprise."

"How's everything going here?"

"Fine. Director Patel has started coordinating the works. He says we'll have the new facilities very soon."

"Great. That's exactly what I've come to talk to you about."

"I thought so."

"Can we talk inside?"

Both of them went into the original facilities and discarded their suits, then Emily threw her arms around him.

"Much better this way," he said. "With these wretched suits you feel as if you were wearing medieval armor."

They went into one of the meeting halls, and both of them sat down.

"I didn't see you at the ceremony yesterday," said Emily.

"I'd have liked to be there, but unfortunately I had some other urgent matters to deal with."

"Oh dear, I hope it wasn't anything bad."

"Nothing catastrophic, to be honest. But in a way it has to do with this base."

"Do I need to worry?" Emily asked.

"No, don't worry, we'll get to that later on, First of all, how are you?"

"Me?" she asked in surprise. "I'm very well, why do you ask?"

"Well, as I understand," the deputy director said very seriously, "Captain Beaufort and you have a very close relationship."

Emily blushed immediately.

"I… I mean…"

"Emily!" He burst out laughing. "I'm joking! I'm very happy for you. Well, actually, for both of you. Although it annoys me a little to have had to find out all about it from Commander Bauer,"

"Commander… Bauer?" Emily managed to say. She was nervous, and her face was still red. "Does he know too?"

He smiled broadly. "Yes. I hope it wasn't a secret. There's nothing wrong with it. And I think he's perfect for you."

"But… we've tried to be as discreet as possible…"

"Emily," the Deputy Director said, "in this life there's only one thing more powerful than love, and that's a good bit of gossip."

"Dear God!" she cried with her hands to her head. "We're the talk of the station!"

He smiled. "Don't worry, I don't think it's gone as far as that. "Now, seriously, how d'you feel?"

"I was all right until you told me half the station's talking about us behind our backs."

He was still laughing. "Sorry, but I couldn't help myself. Are you really all right? With his new position it's going to be a lot more difficult for the two of you to be together."

"Yeah, we've talked about it, and we agreed to try and deal with it as best we can. I think Robert deserved that promotion, and I know it's the best thing for the Project."

"Of course it is. He's very resolute and responsible. I've no doubt the commander made the right decision."

"I agree."

"I'm glad you're taking it so well," he said. "But if you need to talk at any other time, you know where I am. I'm no expert when it comes to relationships, but I suppose it might help to talk these things over with a familiar face."

"Thank you, David," she said gratefully. "That means a lot to me."

"It's the least I can do," he said with a touch of sadness. "I'm sorry your father isn't here to see it, he'd be very proud of the maturity you've shown ever since we reached Kepler-442-b."

"Do you miss him too?" she asked.

"Yes, very much so," he said without hesitation. "I remember him every day. We shared many experiences, you know, long before we joined the Project and also while we were organizing it all. I know I mustn't go on clinging on to vain hopes, but I still dream that we might find them and that all this is just a horrible nightmare."

She put her hand on his. "Yeah, I feel the same way."

"But… I think we need to be pragmatic and fight for the people of the Asimov."

"You're right. Whatever may have happened to the Galileo, it'll be difficult for us to do anything about it."

"That's right. Well now, you don't think I've come here just to talk about the station gossip, do you?"

"No, I'd imagine you want to tell me who our next-door neighbors are going to be."

"Correct, that's exactly what I'm here for."

"Well, that was to be expected," she said. "Although before we get on to that, I'd like to give you something."

"Oh yes?"

She took a small handkerchief with something wrapped up in it out of her sweatshirt pocket.

"You see"—she began to unwrap the handkerchief—"this stone is sacred to the Gaal-El. It represents the wisdom that's been accumulated by the individual when he or she passes from childhood to adulthood. It's traditional for new members of their society to give the stone to the person who's done most to help them to take that step forward to maturity. I'd like to give it to you in gratitude for everything you've done for me over these years, for all your advice, and for the love you showed my grandmother and me."

"Well…" he said, deeply flattered. "I don't know what to say."

"Don't say anything. It's the least I can do."

David took the stone and clasped it in his hand.

"It's really pretty. I'll keep it with all my love. Thank you."

Both of them joined in a heartfelt embrace which left the deputy director very moved.

She changed the subject. "And now tell me, who are our new neighbors going to be? Although Director Patel has told me in advance who the team of technicians for the new facilities is going to be."

"Good, so we'll focus on the others. Captain Beaufort"—he could not restrain a mischievous smile—"has already selected a handful of young soldiers who'll be under the command of Lieutenant Ortiz. I trust his judgment fully, so we'll leave the introductions for another day. Let's go directly to what concerns us: the passengers on the station who'll form part of the colony."

"All right. But before you start, can I ask you a question?"

"Sure. Fire away."

"How did all these people manage to join the project?"

"I guess it's logical that you should ask," the Deputy Director said. "We signed binding contracts with every one of them. Obviously all of them, to a greater or lesser degree, paid for their passage."

"What did the contracts specify?"

He was thoughtful. "That's a rather complicated question. Let's say it wasn't simply a matter of a few clauses. The lawyers on both sides studied each particular case and wrote specific contracts for each passenger. But in general, all the contracts include clauses that specify the moment they'd be brought out of cryo."

"Interesting," she said. "And why should that be specified in a contract?"

"Think about it. The idea of colonizing a planet might sound very romantic when you read a book or experience a story in virtual reality. But the truth, as you've experienced directly, is very far from that. The first years of any kind of colonization are always very complicated. You can expect a lack of resources, discomfort, even having to face all sorts of dangers. Not everyone is capable of coping with those circumstances when you're used to all the comforts that existed on Earth.

"Even so, some passengers were attracted by this experience, the sense of facing new challenges and new situations, of forming part of one of the most important milestones in the history of humanity. Many of them were fed up with the monotony of their life on Earth, others simply wanted to escape from an uncertain future. Which means that every contract reflects those different realities. I won't talk about numbers, because that's confidential, but based on all these details, the passengers paid a greater or lesser amount of money."

"I understand," Emily said. "I suppose that in this case the new settlers are people with a profile that's more... let's say adventurous, right?"

"Yes, you could say that, though it won't always be so. There are also people who could only pay the minimum and weren't very hopeful about the results of Project Atlas."

"I see."

"Well then, if you have no more questions, I'll introduce you to your new comrades."

"Go ahead,"

The deputy director operated his terminal and showed Emily the file of an Asian man who must have been less than forty.

"This is Park Min-jun. On Earth he was general manager of a leading robotics and applied science company in Seoul. In fact he was interested in being part of the passage because he was a supplier for the project during those last years on Earth. There's no doubt that he's a genius. He comes from a humble family, but he was able to create a billion-dollar empire from scratch. I'd imagine his knowledge and his skills will be very useful to us here."

"He sounds like one of the ones who are attracted by adventure."

The deputy director nodded. "Correct. And besides, he knows the project equipment very well. One of the clauses he negotiated was to have unlimited access to the technology which would be used here."

"Fine. It looks as though he might be an asset for the colony."

"Yes, it'll be interesting to have him here. I was able to speak to him yesterday, after he'd been awakened. I've brought him up to date on the situation, and he's dying to start."

She nodded. "I'm glad to hear that. Actually, I was a little worried about the kind of people who were going to join the base."

"Well, don't get ahead of yourself. Let's just say I wanted to begin with the ace to liven up the gathering, but I'm afraid we have a little of everything."

Emily's expression changed, to the point that the deputy director was obliged to correct his last words a little.

"Don't worry, it won't be anything you can't manage."

He operated his terminal again, and on the screen there appeared a young man with a Nordic look, straw-colored hair and light eyes. He could barely have been more than twenty, and in his profile picture there were still signs of acne.

"And here we have Martin Karlsson. He's only twenty-one, and unfortunately he has neither a job nor any known activity. His greatest achievement is being the son of a Swedish cargo transport multimillionaire. As with Mr. Park, we contacted Mr. Karlsson's father because his company was contracted to transport a lot of the materials we used to build the ark."

"And what about the father?" Emily asked. "Is he a passenger too?"

"It's curious you should ask that. But no, Karlsson senior isn't among the passengers."

"Wow, a father saving his son from certain death?"

"Or a father who can see his son has no future on Earth and wants to send him to the other end of the universe."

"How horrible!"

"Problems of a rather eccentric family, I'd imagine. With this one, and now I'm speaking in a non-official capacity, I would think you'll have to be careful if you don't want to end up with a rebellious teenager who only knows how to photosynthesize."

"I get you," she said. "I hope I can lead him the right way."

"Great!" the deputy director said as he operated his terminal again. Now came the turn of a middle-aged Central American, with carefully tended black hair, weathered skin and a neck covered in religious tattoos. "Our next passenger is Mr. Alberto Mendoza. His fortune is, shall we say... of dubious origin, but he defines himself as an entrepreneur in the service of God and the Catholic religion. You can guess from all that that he's a fervent believer, one of the few who are left. His whole family are at the station, but he asked expressly to be wakened with the first group. He paid a real fortune for the whole package, and for being able to choose the exact moment for his relatives to be wakened."

"They seem very odd clauses. How many relatives are we talking about?"

"Twelve."

Emily gave a loud whistle.

"I'm not going to hide the truth from you," he went on, "he sounds like someone very dangerous. One of the ones it's best to have on your side, but his whole family is here, and right from the start he showed a great interest in the project. He saw it as a gift from God so that humanity could start again somewhere else. I think he'll cooperate in whatever's needed."

"Let's hope so," she said.

"He will. Since we woke him he's done nothing but thank everyone for the chance he's been given to be here. He seems genuinely anxious to do something useful."

"Good. I'm glad to hear that."

"I think you'll like our next passenger."

A woman of color appeared on the screen, aged around thirty, with frizzy hair and an intellectual look.

"Melissa Hudgens, neurosurgeon, one of the best-regarded ones of our time. Although her family had a lot of money, she's a very hard-working woman. She decided to join the project out of conviction, she believed she could be of use here. And though her resumé is enviable, let's hope we won't need to use her knowledge."

"Yeah, let's hope we won't need much in the way of surgery."

"I've left the main dish for last," the deputy director announced sarcastically.

A white man in his mid-thirties appeared on the screen. Apparently fit, and with one or two tattoos peeping out from under the collar of his luxurious shirt.

"And lastly, James Coogan. Ace of finance, a star of extreme sports. Multimillionaire, eccentric. I don't think he needs any further introduction."

Emily could not help giving a deep sigh. She knew the man; in fact she doubted whether anyone on the station or on the planet Earth did not know James Coogan.

"This I really wasn't expecting at all," she admitted resignedly. "He's a bloody misogynist, arrogant and overpowering."

"You're absolutely right, but unfortunately we have a contract to fulfill with him. In fact yesterday I was unable to attend the military ceremony here because Mister Important here set off quite an uproar when he realized what he'd signed for when he'd got all the way here."

"What happened?"

"When he started to regain conscience he was very rude to the two nurses in charge of bringing him out of cryo. It seems he was expecting a five-star hotel with free drinks laid on, on a planet like Paradise."

"And how do you expect us to live here with an idiot like that?"

"I don't expect it," the Deputy Director said. "At the slightest problem he'll spend a few weeks in one of the station cells, the ones which unfortunately you're already acquainted with. You just give me a reason, and I'll take care of the rest."

"Well, we'll try to make him cooperate with us. With a bit of luck he'll only have been playing a role just to make himself known. Although if he behaved like that yesterday, I very much fear the actor's going to be just as stupid as the character he's playing."

"That may well be true," he admitted. "Anyway, as soon as they've all settled in, at the slightest complaint we'll find a solution."

"Fine. Anyone else?"

"No, that's all for now. Very soon we'll start working with the team that'll be going to the second location."

"It looks as though it's taking shape."

"Yes, except that we still have plenty of problems left to solve, I'm afraid."

"The Yokai, the Khol, the fact that the planet's uninhabitable..." she said sarcastically. "I don't know what you mean."

"Well, no-one said this was going to be easy, did they, Miss Chosen One?"

"Oh that's enough of that, don't remind me. We'll have to see how I can manage that."

"Well, if you want some advice," David said, "take the opportunity and try to use it to your own advantage. It's a chance we've been offered, and I think we can make something out of it."

"That's easy to say."

"I know, but I haven't the slightest doubt that you'll choose the right way at all times."

She smiled. "Thanks, David. Except that sometimes that overflowing optimism and confidence of yours can be rather overwhelming."

"Relax, I know what I'm saying. You just need to have a bit more confidence in yourself. You'll go far, a lot further than you think at this moment, and you'll save us all."

The meeting came to an end, and the deputy director went back to the station. But in Emily's mind his last words echoed again and again. What had he meant by them?

6
Safe conduct

December 3, year 0

Magellan base, Kepler-442b

The morning was going normally. A fine rain was watering the base surroundings, water which would certainly be very welcome to Kostas and his germinating crops, but which made the work of expansion rather more difficult. Emily was following her usual routine of organizing her next steps, oblivious to the bustling activity of Director Patel's engineers outside. She knew she needed to stay out of touch with the Keplerians, at least until she had news from the Gaal-El. For the time being she preferred to maintain the status quo with the Keplerian diplomacy.

The threats of the Khaavahki soldiers and her own unsuccessful kidnap had done nothing to lessen her determination to cultivate relations between the two species. All she could do was wait, but waiting would be a lot easier if at least she had a rough date for taking the next step. Hence she decided to do some tedious bureaucratic work and process Chad and Taro's requests for access to the space station silo. Both scientists wanted to carry out experiments which involved exposing complex organisms and small animals to the molecules of the planet. It was a significant step toward being able to analyze their effect on humans, so that it was best to start as soon as possible.

She wrote a couple of messages and with Ada's help filled out the appropriate forms. Luckily for all, bureaucracy at the station had been simplified considerably, and she soon received the deputy director's call.

"I've just received the application form. Could it be that yesterday you forgot to mention it in person?"

She smiled innocently. "Yeah, I completely forgot. So many things have been happening lately, I don't know where my head is."

"Don't worry, that's quite normal. If it weren't for Ada I wouldn't be able to remember half the things I have to do."

"I'm at the service of your inferior brains," the AI commented mockingly.

"Be careful, Miss Circuits," the deputy director joked. "Or do we need to remind you how well that superior brain of yours was working when Emily woke up in the station?"

"Touché."

"Well, I'm going to grant the request," the deputy director said. "But be careful, remember that according to Earth laws, testing on animals is forbidden by the Treaties of Manchester. Our laws were drafted bearing in mind the needs of an extraterrestrial colony and we have no ban on that, but make sure the treaties are complied with as far as possible."

"I'll do that. Thanks, Deputy Director."

"Anything else you might have forgotten to mention?"

"No… Or actually yes, but I want to wait till I have more information before I raise the alarm."

"Oh dear, I don't like the sound of that."

"I'm almost certain it'll turn out to be nothing, or that it'll have a rational explanation," Emily said. "One of Director Patel's technicians is looking into it. It's a software problem."

"Right. I can't help much with that, I'm afraid. But if you get somewhere, I'd like to know. Keep me informed."

"I will. Thank you, David."

She got up from her seat once she had finished the conversation with the deputy director, took her empty cup and went to the mess hall for a refill. Evelyn was there, with the same idea.

"I slept really badly last night," the nurse told her. "I don't know what happened to me, but I had one nightmare after another and kept waking up."

"It's happened to me sometimes, it's awful," Emily said as she poured herself coffee from a metal thermos.

"How are things out there?" Evelyn asked.

"I haven't gone out yet. It's raining, and it's a drag having to dry the suit so that the floor doesn't get wet. But I looked out of the window before, and it looks as though they're not stopping. They've got the structure in place and they've started work on the inside of the new facilities."

"This morning the mess hall looked like a shopping mall at rush hour," the nurse joked, referring to the number of soldiers who had spent the night on the base.

"I suppose that's the price we have to pay to stop the rebels trying to take our equipment again."

"I'd imagine they'll have been on watch duty outside," Evelyn said. "Right now there are quite a few of them resting in the dorms."

Suddenly Ada interrupted the conversation.

"Emily, two Keplerians are approaching."

"Oops, sorry, Evelyn. Who are they?"

"One of them I don't recognize, as he's wearing typical Gaal-El clothing. It could be the emissary you've been waiting for."

"And what about the other?"

"The other one is certainly Yisht."

"How can you be so sure?"

"Because she's wearing the green showerproof jacket you gave her."

"All right, I'll get ready to go out. And just when I was looking forward to a quiet day…"

She got into her exosuit. When she was outside she saw Yisht and her companion coming toward the facilities.

I need to suggest that they build a covered area for visitors, she thought. *As it is, I'm not going to be able to offer them any shelter, apart from a tree.*

"Hello, Emily!" Yisht greeted her.

"Yisht! How good to see you!"

The young Keplerian was very likeable. Emily had become friends with her during their journey to the Gaal-El village. It was a real shame that they were unable to keep in touch, even by radio via the communications backpack they had left in her house. But without any way of knowing how the rebels might be able to monitor the activities of the project, it might even put Yisht herself in danger.

Her companion pushed back his hood to reveal his face. It was Liikmi, the personal assistant to Waafdiv, the high priest of the Gaal-El.

He greeted her with a deep bow. "Hail, woman of metal!"

"Get up, please, there's no need for you to bow," she said, uncomfortable with these constant displays of respect. "We'd better go under that tree. I'm afraid you wouldn't be able to breathe inside our buildings, so I can't offer you shelter. Forgive me."

"Don't worry," Yisht said as they went over to the shelter offered by the large leaves of one of the great trees near the base. "I have to say this garment is wonderful at keeping the wet out." She stretched the material to show that the water was repelled completely the moment the tiny drops touched the surface.

"I'm glad you like it."

"All right then, let's not waste any more time," Liikmi said urgently once they were under the leaves.

The Gaal-El assistant took out a sheet of thick, rough paper which bore a round seal, inside which a crossed key and scroll could be made out. At the top of the seal four toothed circles formed an irregular diamond with another circle, slightly larger than the others, on its upper right-hand corner. At the bottom of the seal seven smaller circles formed an irregular trapezium, set at an apparently random angle, with three lines emerging in different directions which connected with the same number of circles. One of these toothed circles was larger than the others.

Emily opened the parchment, which as was to be expected was handwritten in Keplerian, and spread it out. Ada helped her to read it, superimposing the translation via her eye implant:

Greetings.

I, Waafdiv, high priest of the cult of the Gaal-El, hereby extend a cordial invitation to the supreme conclave which will be held in the Temple of Khormak. The conclave will be conducted according to our ancestral traditions, and will have as its sole purpose the union of our people, involving the establishment and reinforcement of relations between the different factions of our society.

The conclave will take place on the fifth of this December. I request that you confirm your attendance to bearer of this message.

The recipient of this message and her companion will be given a safe-conduct which will permit them to move with total freedom through the territory involved.

WAAFDIV, HIGH PRIEST OF THE GAAL-EL

Emily rolled the parchment up again into an almost perfect cylinder and turned to Liikmi.

"I confirm my attendance, and that of Rakesh."

"Your attendance honors us deeply," Liikmi replied, and once again bowed deeply.

Once again she began to feel uncomfortable with all this bowing, but she assumed that for better or worse it was going to be the normal procedure from now on, at least as far as the Gaal-El were concerned.

"May I take it that you'll arrive at the Gaal-El village tomorrow evening?" the cultist asked.

"Yes, we'll be there."

"Good. I'll inform the high priest."

"Anything I need to know before the conclave?"

"Nothing special," said Yisht, "Just that one like it hasn't been held for several generations, so it's going to be something of a novelty for all of us, I'm afraid."

"What do they consist of?" Emily asked.

"The leaders and their respective assistants gather around a round table and discuss the business which has inspired the conclave. Once the different points have been discussed and all sides, voices and opinions have been heard, they'll all withdraw for five days, during which time they have no contact with anyone else. During this period of reflection the leaders and their assistants will have to weigh up matters and make the appropriate decisions."

"I see," said Emily. "So I suppose on the day of the conclave itself no decisions will be taken."

"That's right. The decision will be taken communally at another conclave, then there'll be a vote and a discussion of how the various resolutions which have been proposed should be formulated."

"It sounds pretty democratic," Emily commented. "Although it looks like quite a slow process."

"Yes, it is," Yisht admitted. "In fact it can go on for several weeks, because some of the leaders might require more information, or bring it, about the matters in question, if they haven't been made clear during those earlier conclaves."

"Which means we might have to travel a number of times over the next few days."

"Yes, that could be."

"Right. And how long can a conclave last?"

"My understanding is that it'll depend on the questions to be dealt with. I don't think this one will last more than a day, but according to the history books some lasted for hundreds of days."

"Well, they certainly must have had things to sort out."

"It certainly looks like it."

Emily came to a decision. "Right, we'll meet there."

"And please," Liikmi said, "remember that the invitation itself will act as a safe-conduct which will allow you to move freely throughout the territory."

"I understand."

"Good. So if you'll excuse me, I have to finish my duties." He made another exaggerated bow.

"Yes, and I need to go back with him," Yisht said regretfully. "The usual thing is to deliver these messages by messenger bird, but we haven't any that are trained to fly here, so Khikhya asked me to go with him and show him the way."

Emily was surprised by this. "I'd no idea you had a way of communicating at a distance."

"Yes. It's quite normal for the leaders of the different villages to exchange short messages. But in order to deliver this one, Liikmi had to come in person."

"Oh dear, I'm very sorry about that, Liikmi."

He bowed again. "It doesn't matter, my lady. I do it with pleasure and devotion."

"All right. We'll meet tomorrow, before sundown."

The two visitors went back along the same path they had arrived by, and she went back to the base. She saw Director Patel, who was directing the enlargement works as usual, and asked him whether it would be possible to add a small additional module without any life-support system inside, only a meeting hall and a couple of rooms so that they would be able to welcome visitors.

"Sure, Emily," he said cheerfully. "Let me organize it. We have smaller modules at the station, so you can count on it."

"Thanks, Director Patel."

He saw that she was still looking thoughtful. "Is there anything else you need?"

"Well… I'm not sure." There was something more on her mind. "You see, I was wondering whether it would be possible to make some kind of device so that the Keplerians could survive in our atmospheric conditions."

"You mean to breathe our air, or else to have their own life-support?"

"Yeah, exactly that."

Patel was thoughtful for a few moments.

"It would be very interesting from a diplomatic point of view," she added, "and why not say it, from the sociological point of view as well, to be able to invite Keplerians to our base, or even take them to the space station. Their reactions might be worth studying."

"Yes, it certainly would be intriguing, to say the least," he admitted. "We have plenty of non-assisted suits available, like those of the ancient astronauts. If we leave aside the different proportions of our bodies, in theory it would be possible to adapt some of those suits for Keplerian use."

"And what about oxygen?"

"I suppose we could regulate the suit's oxygen supply so as to match it to the level on this planet. Not using the air supply would actually be even simpler than the system you have in your exosuit."

"Could you make a suit available so that we can carry out a test?"

"Let me look into it with one of the engineering specialists, but I very much doubt whether we'll find any snag."

"Yes, of course. Thank you, Director."

Emily went back inside the facilities, and after thoroughly drying the suit she got out of it once again. She had a trip to organize, and she hoped to have it all sorted out before the day was over.

"Hello there, Deputy Director."

"Hello, Emily. What have you forgotten to tell me this time?"

She laughed. "Nothing, don't worry. It's just that there's news about the conclave. We have the invitation now." She showed him the parchment, which she had put in a bag before going to the facilities to avoid any kind of contamination.

"Right. When's it to be?"

"The day after tomorrow,"

"At the Gaal-El village, I gather."

"That's right."

"And how do you plan on getting there?"

"Among other things, that's why I'm calling. I'd like to know whether we can use another rover to get us there. It's over forty kilometers, and even with our exosuits it would take a long time and use a lot of electricity. And apart from that, at the moment our only mule is being studied by one of Director Patel's technicians."

"Of course, Emily," the deputy director said. "Leave it to me. This same afternoon I'll have a rover sent down to you, along with a couple of extra mules."

"Thanks, they'll come in very handy."

Emily had just settled the most important thing, which was transport. Now she had to tell her traveling companion the news. She found Rakesh in the common area by the mess hall, sitting on a comfortable sofa and leafing through some documents on his terminal.

She shook the bag she was holding. "We've got the invitation now!"

"Well, well, well," he said in surprise. "How did it come?"

"Liikmi and Yisht brought it."

"When do we set off?"

"The conclave's in two days. The deputy director will provide us with a rover, so we'll set off after lunch tomorrow. We'll be there in an hour and a half, more or less."

"And how are we going to cross the river with that thing?"

"I'll tell Lieutenant Balakova to take us to the clearing on the far side of the river."

"Good." He got up from the couch. "We'll have to get the equipment and supplies ready. Do we know how long it's going to last?"

She shook her head. "Not really. So try to get some rest tonight, because tomorrow you're very unlikely to be able to with the exosuit on."

She left him in the common area. There was only one more detail left. Bearing in mind that the safe-conduct was only valid for the two of them, it did not seem proper to take a military escort. Still, she decided to speak to Robert, not just for strictly professional reasons but because she needed to hear his voice.

"Hi," she said.

"Hi there, how are you?"

"Fine. Organizing a trip."

"Has the invitation to the conclave come?"

"Yup, just a little while ago. It'll take place in two days' time, at the temple. The only ones who can go are Rakesh and me."

This seemed to worry Robert.

"Take it easy," she said, getting ahead of him, "we'll be fine. I don't suppose they'd summon us all the way to a conclave to sacrifice us to their gods."

"It's not the Gaal-El who are worrying me," he said, "it's Captain Garth and his new Khaavahki friends who are stopping me from sleeping."

"I don't think they'd risk a confrontation that'd set them against the other Keplerian leaders. We'll be fine."

"Still, I'll have a couple of transports in the air, far from any prying eyes, so that we can act quickly."

"All right," she agreed. "If that makes you feel better, I won't get in your way. But we'll be fine, really. And we're going in one of the rovers, so the journey'll be much less risky than last time."

"Do you have one there?"

"No, but the deputy director told me he'll send one this afternoon."

"I could do it myself."

"No, he said he'd do it. But let's not talk about the conclave, for a change. How are you?"

"Well. With plenty to do, but well. This new job involves more responsibilities than I thought." He smiled. "But it's bearable. The hardest thing is being away from all of you, away from you in particular."

"Yeah, I miss you too," she admitted sadly. "And I know the others do as well."

"I'd love to be there with you right now."

She nodded. "And I'd love if it you could be here. But I dare say we'll have time for that…"

"Yes. Now all we can do is wait,"

"Any news up there?" she asked.

"No, nothing noteworthy. Half the engineers are working on the enlargement and the other half on the plans for the second base."

"And what about you?"

"We've started getting the ones who'll make up the new replacement ready."

They spent a while longer chatting. Both of them missed one another, and they were finding it hard to have to spend so much time apart. And although they were pragmatic and knew that what really mattered at that moment was the project, they could not help thinking that their relationship might have been easier in different circumstances.

After this she finished her preparations for the rest of the journey. That afternoon the deputy director sent one of the exploration rovers from the station. With the help of her exosuit and a mule she loaded the batteries, the oxygen tanks and the supplies into the rear of the vehicle.

7
The journey

December 4, year 0

Magellan Base, Kepler-442b

Emily was walking through a huge cavern. The water to either side ran in small streams whose source was the dampness of the walls. Someone had attracted her attention from the bottom of the cave. It was Steven Rhodes, her father. And yet no matter how quickly she tried to get to him, he would always move away faster than she could manage. However strongly she called him and ran after him with all her might, her lungs made no sound, and he moved further and further away all the time. She had the impression that the cave was growing larger every moment. The stony path seemed to be growing wider and wider, changing its shape as she tried to call her father, with tears in her eyes.

She sped past all the Yokai families which lived inside there. She saw the pup she had helped to get out of the passage, wearing the isothermal blanket she had covered it with. As the cave grew both longer and higher, she began to see trees inside. They were larger and larger as she went on and had structures fixed to their trunks, as if there were a Keplerian village inside. She saw Shildii as she raced past, saw Yisht and even Khikhya. But she had to go on running, even though her father was further and further away all the time. Every now and then he would look back, as if he wanted to make sure that she was following him.

There came a moment during the expansion of the cave when it had grown so large that she could barely make out either ceiling or walls. Suddenly she saw her father entering the Gaal-El temple. When she reached the spot and crossed the two enormous entrance doors she realized that there was no floor inside. She fell for several interminable seconds; she moved in her dreams until she realized that she was no longer in the cave, but in space. She was floating, without the need of a suit or any kind of life-support.

She turned in every direction in this weightless state and searched for her father. There was no-one else there. But then she saw something which surprised her: the Galileo Station. Beyond it, a planet with three large continents whose reddish surface stood out amid the blue of its oceans. Beyond both of them was a black hole.

"Watch out!" she tried to shout in her dream, but no sound came out of her throat. She waved her arms desperately and tried to come closer to the station. "That black hole is going to swallow you!" Nothing.

Just when she seemed to be beginning to move from where she was held, a pod flew out of the station. At that same instant, seeming to take barely any time at all, the planet was deformed in the direction of the black hole, forming an infinite thread along which it vanished. Only a little later the space station went the same way. And finally she herself felt the hole pulling at her, stretching and swallowing her in barely the tiniest fraction of a second. She felt the enormous force of attraction of the black hole and the equally enormous weight of its core on her deformed body. Then she woke up, almost two full hours before her alarm was due to ring, soaked in perspiration.

When she went to the mess hall she was still shaking from the nightmare, remembering every detail of it. Rakesh was there, enjoying the morning tea which was now his habit.

"Couldn't you sleep?" he asked her in surprise.

"I had a terrible nightmare."

"Oh dear, I'm sorry to hear that. Is anything troubling you? Do you need to talk?"

"Thanks, I don't think so. I just need to calm down a little."

"I can make you a cup of tea if you like. But the real kind, not the slop that comes out of that wretched machine."

"That would be great."

The anthropologist heated some water and took a few leaves from a metal box he kept in one of the cupboards. He boiled them all, and when this was done he added milk. Once it was all ready, he offered Emily a cup.

"This is *Gakhir Sah,* one of the most widely-grown varieties of tea in my old country. The usual thing is to take it with milk, sugar and spices. Unfortunately I have no spices here, but the tea's still very good."

Emily sniffed the aroma, and after cooling it by blowing on it she took a small sip.

"It's very good," she admitted. "Nothing to do with what the machines make."

"Yes, I know. This is the real thing, made in the traditional way."

"Where did you get it?"

"Let's just say I have my methods for getting hold of quality items. That, and the fact that I made it a condition when your father wanted to recruit me: the possibility of bringing a good quality tea with me and having it available."

Emily smiled at the anthropologist's odd demand. She relaxed and laughed for some time during her conversation with Rakesh. She had realized the first time they had spoken, many months ago in the station mess hall: there was something in his voice that in some way managed to soothe her.

"At least you've got some color back," he said. "To judge by your complexion, it looked as if you'd seen a ghost."

She merely nodded, though deep down she thought that perhaps that was exactly what had happened.

"I feel a lot better now. Thanks, Rakesh."

"You're very welcome." He checked his watch. "It's a good moment to start thinking about the final preparations for the trip, wouldn't you say?

"Yeah, we'd better get down to it."

The two of them carefully prepared all the equipment and supplies they were going to need during the journey. They got rid of the seats at the rear of the rover and loaded it with enough to survive for ten days. They did not want to take any risks, and they had no idea how long the conclave was going to go on for. They would also be carrying a mule so that they would be able to travel through the temple or the village if they had to do without the rover.

They said goodbye to their comrades after lunch, and when the sun had passed its zenith they set off. Balakova the pilot took them to the clearing where they had met the Keplerians before. Once they were there, now in the land vehicle, they left the ship and set off for the Gaal-El village.

The rover was an autonomous vehicle and hence did not need to be driven, and though it permitted manual control neither of them was so enthusiastic about driving as to take up the offer.

"We have about an hour, more or less, to the village," Emily said, "bearing in mind that the road won't be entirely straight and level."

"Pity there aren't any aero-taxis here," the anthropologist said ruefully, "or else we'd be there in a flash."

She smiled. "Actually, this isn't really so bad. I find it relaxes me to travel on the surface. And also we lack the infrastructure for the autonomous air transports to work here, at least with any guarantee of safety."

"Yes, I know. I dare say many years will go by before we can enjoy all those comforts we used to have on Earth."

"But at least this means we can talk during the journey."

"In fact that's what people did in those cases," he said with a smile. "So, let's talk. What d'you think this conclave will be like?"

"QuiteQuit honestly, I have no idea. I've tried to imagine it, but nothing much occurs to me. I suppose the leaders'll get together and discuss the Gaal-El proposal."

"And what do you think they're going to propose?"

Emily shrugged.

"I'd imagine it'll be something to do with us and their sacred scriptures. Maybe they'll talk about a unified rule for the Keplerian peoples."

"Do you think the other tribal leaders will be willing to give up their command?"

She shook her head. "No, I don't think so. If Keplerian ambition and hunger for power are even half as strong as they are for human leaders, I doubt very much whether any of them'll be capable of even getting their heads round the idea."

"On that we agree," Rakesh said. "Above all, seeing the way Vaahur's lieutenant talked to us when he burst into Khikhya's rooms."

"What do you think it'll be like?"

"I'd imagine that as it's something traditional that hasn't taken place for so many years, Waafdiv will have dug out some ancient scripture or other from oblivion so that it can be done exactly the way it was done the last time. I imagine it as something very spiritual, even a little pompous. It's possible that some kind of sacred text will be read out, something that reminds them of their ancestors. Or they might even carry out some kind of ceremony or religious liturgy."

Emily felt a slight shiver as she imagined herself in the midst of a ceremony like that, if not as a central part of it.

"After the formalities and the pomp," Rakesh went on, "I suppose they'll move on to politics. Waafdiv will give the reasons why the conclave has been called, and the other leaders will decide whether or not they support whatever he proposes."

"That's right, though Yisht warned me that there'll be another conclave to make the decisions of each leader public. Which means I'm afraid we're going to have to make more journeys like this one during the next few days."

"You know, it's fascinating to find ourselves in the midst of all this," Rakesh said. "I still can't believe we're dealing with an intelligent alien race."

"Yeah, everything's going too fast."

Both of them noticed that the road and the terrain it crossed were rather irregular in some areas. But although they had been this way before inside the Gaal-El carriage, they could not recognize any of the places they had seen from the vehicle. In fact they would not even have known how much of the journey was still left had it not been for the screen in the rover, where Ada indicated their position at every moment. Less than fifteen minutes had passed since their departure when Emily saw movement on the road a few meters ahead. It was a cart, with a draft animal at the front and a Keplerian sitting in the rear of the wooden structure.

"Someone's coming," Rakesh said.

"That's right, it looks like an ordinary Keplerian transporting something."

As the cart drew closer they saw the Keplerian, who was holding the reins of a *fhore,* more clearly. He seemed not to be concentrating, almost asleep. But then quite suddenly, after becoming aware of the rover, he gave a start on the narrow board he was sitting on and almost fell off.

The Keplerian stopped his cart almost completely and waited expectantly for them to pass him. When Emily and Rakesh did so they could not help laughing out loud at his look of incredulity.

"What do you think he must have thought?" Emily asked. She was watching the Keplerian on one of the screens as he set off again.

"I don't think he'll have thought we were an animal," Rakesh said. "But considering that according to Yisht the Khapabir have vehicles that run on some technology like steam, he might have taken the rover for some kind of Keplerian invention."

It was not long before they reached an area which was rather more complicated for vehicles. The road wound through endless trees and up and down a succession of small hills, and by now had begun to climb toward the mountains. It was clear that they were getting closer and closer to the single narrow pass which allowed access to the domains of the Gaal-El. A few minutes after beginning the ascent the road ran between two mountains, with less vegetation to either side, so that it was a perfect spot to carry out an ambush or establish a military checkpoint, as was the case here.

Both of them could see a small wooden stand in the distance which served as a sentry-box for the Keplerian soldiers on watch duty at the pass. Nearby, under a huge tree which stood by itself in a small stony field, they caught sight of a large wooden building. This must be the base for the detachment which guarded the pass between their destination and the other Keplerian villages. Vaahur had increased the military presence on the roads since the appearance of the humans on the planet; no doubt he wanted to check the travelers' movements.

One of the Keplerians, wearing a green doublet and light metal breastplate and carrying a long, threatening halberd, raised one arm and motioned them to slow down.

"Now we'll find out how valid those safe-conducts Liikmi gave us are," Rakesh whispered.

"I hope they're good," Emily said nervously.

"Unlike that peasant, this soldier hasn't even blinked at the sight of the rover."

The military presence was heavy in the area. They had not been able to check the size of the garrison when they had passed this way a few days before, but on this occasion Emily could count up to seven soldiers, two of them riding *fhores*. In addition to this, she was convinced that there were a lot more in the barracks to one side.

Ada stopped the rover at a safe distance, neither too near nor too far; she did not want to make any movement which could be seen as a threat. The first of the soldiers approached calmly and confidently, looking closely at the vehicle without paying too much attention or seeming to be surprised by its presence. They had clearly been warned about its arrival.

Emily activated the control to lower the glass of her door.

"Good afternoon," she called.

The soldier looked at her, then noticed Rakesh, but said nothing. He went on to the rear of the rover and walked around it, then went back to the small sentry-box and spoke to someone inside.

After a while another soldier came out. He was not wearing a breastplate, only a doublet of the same green as the one before. Both of them came back to the vehicle, with the one who was obviously senior in front.

"Good afternoon," the Keplerian officer said sharply.

"Good afternoon," Emily repeated.

"I imagine you're the foreigners we were expecting."

She shrugged. "I suppose so."

"You have a very interesting transport," he said, without looking altogether surprised.

"Thank you."

"What are you carrying at the back?"

"Supplies."

"I understand there won't be any problem about checking those supplies."

"Not at all." She opened the door and got down from the vehicle.

She went with the two soldiers to the rear and opened the hatch. Inside, piled neatly on both sides, were dozens of bundles containing oxygen and the food which would be needed for the next few days. In the middle, its legs folded and in a position of repose, lay one of the mules from the Asimov expedition.

The Keplerian officer examined the bundles on either side and then noticed the mule.

"What's that?"

"It's a device for transporting heavy objects where access is difficult," she explained.

The soldiers stared closely at the mule, unable to see how that complex of latest-generation metal and polymer could possibly do what she was telling them.

"Ada," Emily said, "make the mule get off the ship."

The mule deployed its legs without warning and moved toward the rear door. The soldiers started back a couple of paces. One of them lowered his halberd and aimed it at the mule, while the officer drew his sword from the sheath at his belt.

"By the ancient gods!" he burst out, staring in disbelief. "What the hell is that thing?"

"Don't worry," Emily said, caught halfway between caution and laughter. "It's just a metal animal. It's harmless."

The officer, slightly shocked as he realized that this thing was still determined to come out, took several steps back, pointing vaguely at it and at her.

"Make it stop!" he shouted.

"Ada, stop the mule," Emily said with her hands raised.

When the mule stopped, the officer relaxed a little. None of them had found the demonstration amusing at all. She and Rakesh could not afford to take the risk, so she ordered Ada to send it back into the rover.

"I need to see your safe-conduct," the officer demanded very seriously as he put his sword away.

"Of course."

She went back to the pilot's seat, fetched the invitation to the conclave and handed it at once to the tense officer. He looked carefully at the parchment, then after a while looked up from it and gave it back to her with some disdain.

"You may continue. But make sure that thing in the back there doesn't cause any trouble."

"I will," she said, and got back into her seat again.

The officer made a sign to the other soldiers in the garrison to let the rover pass. From that moment the road became considerably steeper and more twisting, though well within the capacity of the autonomous vehicle.

Emily gave a sigh of relief. "I have to say there was a moment when I didn't think he was going to let us through,"

Rakesh nodded. "That's right. When he drew his sword I wasn't too sure of our odds either."

"It looks as though they have orders to let us pass."

"The Khaavahki leader knows he has to defeat us through politics," Rakesh commented. "So far we humans haven't done anything that could be seen as a threat. If the Gaal-El and the Wiikhaadiiz ofiz support us, he'll have to move very carefully if he doesn't want to provoke the opposite of what he wants."

Emily considered this. Rakesh was right, which made her wonder why Vaahur had made the decision to kidnap her. If by then she had had the support of the Wiikhaadiiz ofiz, why try anything? Did the Gaal-El have the power to make them change their minds and their strategy with regard to her?

Whatever the case, it did not take them long to reach the edge of the Gaal-El village. As they were not sure about the agenda of the conclave, they went to the small inn where Liikmi had put them up on their previous visit. They were hoping that as had happened before, someone would be waiting for their arrival. And they were right: waiting for them there was Waafdiv's solicitous assistant.

Ada stopped the vehicle behind the lodge, where it would not be visible from the main avenue. Emily got out of the rover, holding out her hand.

"Liikmi, I'm so glad to see you again!"

"I'm delighted to see you too," he replied with a deep bow. "The high priest sends you greetings and begs to be excused for not being here to welcome you. At the moment he's in the temple, preparing tomorrow's ceremony," he added as he invited them inside the small, but cozy, inn.

"What do we have to do when it's time for the conclave?" Rakesh asked.

"Tonight we'll sleep down here. Tomorrow, at dawn, I'll go with you to the temple. There you'll attend the ceremony which opens the conclave, and during the day you'll be taken to it."

"Won't we be at the conclave from the start?" Rakesh asked in surprise.

The assistant shook his head.

"Only the Keplerian leaders can participate. However, given the extraordinary condition of the chosen one, there will be an exception when the moment comes. That is what is stipulated by our ancestral traditions."

"I understand."

"Have the other leaders arrived yet?" Emily asked.

"Vaahur, the Khaavahki leader, and Khikhya, the Wiikhaadiiz ofiz leader, are now in the presidential chambers of the monastery. Khaÿ, the Khapabir leader, hasn't yet made his appearance. Although it's still early, and I'm afraid punctuality isn't one of the Khapabir leader's characteristics."

He was right: it was not yet even mid-afternoon, so there was time to spare before night fell.

"What can we do in the village until evening?" Rakesh asked.

"You can wait," he replied, not really understanding the question. "I've prepared the same rooms as last time."

"Oh!" Emily exclaimed suddenly. "I think we'll both sleep in the same room this time."

Liikmi stopped in surprise, not understanding this sudden change. But looking at them he seemed to realize that they must have different customs, so he let it pass without asking any further questions.

"As you wish. Am I to suppose you won't need me to prepare anything for dinner or breakfast?"

"No, thank you, Liikmi," said Emily. "We'll eat our own food."

"All right, then. If you need me, I'll be in one of the two dwellings opposite." He bowed deeply once again, then left his guests by themselves in the ancient inn.

8
The ceremony

December 5, year 0

Gaal-El village, Kepler-442b

Rakesh and Emily spent a boring evening contemplating what little activity there was to see in the avenue. Only a couple of Keplerians going back home and a Keplerian girl chasing her rebellious domestic animals, which were not very keen to go back to their pen. After this they tried to get some sleep, though it was hard to do this in their exosuits. Ada woke them as soon as the first rays of light appeared through the trees around.

"Did you manage to sleep at all?" Rakesh asked her.

"Not really," Emily admitted. She had dreamed again about the cave where she had come across her father. "It took me quite a while to nod off. It's this wretched suit that's so uncomfortable for anything apart from moving around. What about you? Did you sleep?"

"Yes, not too badly. Despite my age I can still get to sleep more or less wherever I am. Or perhaps it's just that I'm getting used to being inside this tin can."

After having breakfast in their room, they went downstairs and out of the inn. A fine rain was falling through the treetops, creating an attractive and rather curious scene.

"Look at that!" Rakesh exclaimed. "It's impressive. It looks as though it's raining under the trees."

"Yeah, it's a lovely effect."

Liikmi came over quickly, attentive to any movement on the part of his guests. Emily was not sure whether it was because of his helpful nature or if instead it was a question of safety, to stop anyone catching sight of these peculiar foreigners.

He came over with one of his now-familiar deep bows.

"Are you all ready?"

"Yes," said Emily. "Except that we have to fetch a few things from the vehicle before we begin the climb."

She and Rakesh loaded the mule with enough supplies to last a couple of days. They had decided to leave the rover there, as they did not want to take it up to the temple in case it posed a problem; they remembered some stretches with steps, and they were not sure where they would be able to leave it. In the village, hidden from inquisitive eyes, it would be fine. And in any case, if it turned out to be needed, Ada could bring it to the temple.

"We're ready," she said.

"Perfect," said Liikmi. "In that case let's go to the temple."

Together with the mule, which followed Emily's steps closely, they began the ascent of the ramps which led to the Gaal-El temple.

"Has the Khapabir expedition arrived yet?" she asked.

"Yes, they arrived when it was nearly dawn."

"That's quite late."

"Yes, they must have had some kind of problem with one of their vehicles without *fhores*, Up to a point it seems to move by magic, like yours."

She smiled. "There's no magic behind that, it's just technology."

"Forgive me, madam," he said. "I've never managed to understand any of the prodigies of the Khapabir, and yours look even more magical."

"That's natural. No-one's born knowing these things. It's civilizations and societies that have to give their individuals knowledge, so that they can help their societies to evolve with new creations and wonderful things."

The road, perhaps because they had traveled it before, or perhaps because they were looking forward to arriving, seemed longer to them. Even though the exosuits meant that tiredness was not a problem, it was tedious. Emily wanted all her doubts resolved as soon as possible.

By the time they reached the open area in front of the monastery it had already stopped drizzling. And as though announcing their arrival, some faint rays of light were beginning to break through the heavy clouds which had been discharging their load during the last few hours.

The three of them went up the wide flight of steps which led to the temple, leaving behind the busts of the previous high priests which decorated both sides. On the flat area at the top, almost at the temple entrance, hundreds of cult followers, organized in perfect rows, formed something which resembled a chessboard. Except that there were far more cult followers than pieces on that imaginary board. They were all equipped with immense wooden staves and had left a central corridor with enough space for the guests of the conclave to enter the temple.

"What are we supposed to do now?" Emily asked.

"Go into the temple," Liikmi said. "That's where the ceremony which precedes the conclave will begin shortly."

"Do we have to take part in it in any way?" Rakesh asked.

"No, only the leaders will do that. Once the ceremony's concluded, the leaders will meet in the Chamber of Concord, where the conclave will begin. You'll be summoned when the high priest deems it suitable. Meanwhile you'll need to wait inside the temple."

"All right," Emily agreed, satisfied with this explanation. "I think we ought to go in."

She and Rakesh, together with Liikmi, who stayed two meters behind them, began to follow the path which separated them from the temple entrance. As soon as they reached the first row of cult followers, the two who happened to be closest to them banged the floor hard. The wood echoed against the huge slabs of stone which decorated the open area. Immediately the two behind did the same, as did the others, one pair after another, until the final two. Emily nearly stopped dead in her tracks because the gesture had been so sudden, but they were so well-coordinated that it was worth watching.

The same action was repeated when they reached the second row, then with those after it. It was a curious way of announcing the arrival of the guests at the ceremony. Rakesh was looking to one side and then the other, impressed by this welcome. They crossed the threshold of the temple, whose elaborately-worked doors, engraved on a thin sheet of copper-colored metal, impressed Emily once again and amazed Rakesh, who had not been able to examine them from so close before. It was a few seconds before the visors of their suits adjusted to the light and they were able to see what was in the interior, which in spite of the timid sunbeams filtering in through the door was still in shadow.

The hall had been cleaned and prepared for this great event, and what Emily had perceived a few days before as somewhere antiquated and badly-cared-for now merely looked old. Even so, Rakesh gave a muffled sound of admiration when he looked up and saw the frescoes in the ceiling of the cave which sheltered the temple.

Someone had lit two small braziers at the front, but though each held a small, playful orange flame, they did not give enough light to fill the huge hall. Emily saw that five rows of benches had been installed, separated by the small aisle which led to the altar. In addition, numerous carvings of important Keplerians had been set up along the sides of the temple. Some paintings, in a deplorable state of conservation, had also been hung along the walls.

All this wasn't here the other day, she thought. *Waafdiv and his cult-followers have been very busy these last few hours.*

76

There was no-one in the benches, but at the far end, in front of the altar, in the shadows, a figure could be made out. It stayed immobile, resting on its knees, making no sound. It was impossible for it not to have heard the banging of the cult-followers outside, so that it gave the impression that this apparent passivity was premeditated.

Liikmi motioned them to take their place in the last row. Obediently they sat down in silence on the old wooden bench on the left of the aisle. A few moments went by, during which both of them, far from wanting to break the silence by exchanging impressions, took the opportunity to look around. Rakesh focused on the ceiling, while Emily never took her eyes off the inert figure. Despite the mysterious quality of the situation, she was sure it was Waafdiv.

Suddenly new sounds of wood being banged came from outside: several outbursts, closer and closer to the entrance.

A procession of four Keplerians came into the temple. Emily and Rakesh turned to see who they were. Both of them recognized Khikhya and her three counselors, though Yisht did not seem to be among them. The four Wiikhaadiiz ofiz were accompanied by another cult member, who like Liikmi, motioned them to take the seats two rows in front of Emily and Rakesh. Khikhya, who wore a beautiful jeweled blue cloak and was leaning on her inseparable staff of office, sat down on the left-hand bench beside her counselor. Her two other companions did the same on the one on the right.

Emily presumed that protocol marked every one of these movements, such as the fact that they had taken their seats two benches in front of them, or that Khikhya had not even glanced at them. The mysterious figure went on in an apparent trance, not moving an inch from its position.

Without giving any time to think, a new burst of banging once again announced the arrival of the next procession. Emily watched the behavior of the Wiikhaadiiz ofiz carefully. Although someone was crossing the threshold now, this time none of those who had just arrived turned to see who the new guests were. Once again it was four Keplerians, all of them men. The one leading them wore a khaki dress uniform. His expression was one of displeasure, so that it was hard to avoid the conclusion that he had not the slightest desire to be there. On his head several prominent protuberances displayed his high position and social status. Under his left arm he carried a hat of the same color and in his right hand an elegant wooden staff.

The three Keplerians who followed him were wearing similar clothes, except that in their case these were dark blue. They were all high-ranking officers in the Keplerian army, but were of different ages: one looked considerably older than the other two, another much younger. What they had in common was that all of them were proudly displaying the numerous decorations on their lapels. Emily could only recognize the middle-aged one: Lajlab, the colonel who had stormed into Khikhya's chambers and threatened the two from Earth, but more especially poor Yisht. As with the Wiikhaadiiz ofiz, a cult member motioned them to sit in the second row of benches.

That just leaves two rows free, she thought.

Then she became aware of something she not noticed until that moment. Two wreaths, one on either side of the row, lay on the benches of the row in front, the one which separated the Wiikhaadiiz ofiz from them.

A new burst of sound came from outside. Emily presumed this must be the Khapabir delegation, and something told her that they would take the front row. Now there could be no doubt that they were being organized in order of importance in the context of society. But what was the meaning of the floral decorations on the fourth row? Did they represent the Gaal-El themselves? Or could they have some other significance?

A new procession, this time made up of five Keplerians, made its entrance. The leader of the group was an old man escorted by three Keplerians of different ages and another, who although he was an adult was notably younger than the others.

The old man wore a curious white garment, halfway between a breastplate and a tunic. Over it he wore a wide stole in vivid orange which covered both shoulders. Its two ends met across his chest in an enormous golden brooch, leaving the ends hanging. The stole was decorated with a pattern which revealed a crest, but though the old man was walking slowly, all she could recognize was a kind of hammer, crossed with another tool. The old man was leaning wearily on an elegant metal staff. It was golden, almost coppery, the same color as his brooch.

As she had guessed, this was Khaaÿ, the leader of the Khapabir village. He and his retinue of counselors, also dressed in their best attire, took their seats along the front row of benches.

Coincidence or not, we've come in in reverse order, she thought as she observed her surroundings attentively. *Even so, there's still the bench in front, if anyone else is coming.*

During all this time the mysterious figure had not moved, oblivious to the entrance of the delegations, but went on sitting there on its knees in silence. Several endless minutes went by in which no-one either did or said anything. Only the odd cough or the sound of someone clearing their throat broke the deep silence inside the temple. None of the Keplerians seemed to be looking to either side; they were clearly utterly absorbed in the solemnity of the event.

The timid flames of the braziers went on crackling in unison, but at last the high priest seemed to react. Maintaining the same posture, he leaned forward and touched the floor with his forehead, then stretched his arms forward as far as he could as if he were making an exaggerated bow. Then, all of a sudden, he got to his feet and went to the altar at the front without even giving the attendants a glance. When he reached the wooden reredos which decorated the front part of the temple with bucolic images typical of Keplerian society, he stopped.

Emily heard a metallic sound, as if a huge lock were being opened. A rectangular hole the size of a Keplerian appeared in the reredos itself: there was a room behind the altar, or perhaps more than one, to judge by the size of the cave. For a few moments Waafdiv vanished into the darkness, to reappear carrying a book. This did not seem to be any old book; its size and state of dilapidation seemed to indicate that it was a very old and important one, far more so than any she had ever seen. And given the relevance of the ceremony, she was sure that it must be a very special one.

Waafdiv placed it with great care on the altar, and his concern to avoid damaging it in any way was almost palpable, then he opened it at a page marked by a bookmark. When it was open he raised his arms in a sudden gesture.

"Keplerian brothers and sisters," he began solemnly, "I welcome you and thank you for your presence in this sacred temple of the Gaal-El. Many centuries have gone by since the last time our villages came to the call of our creed. Too many, there can be no doubt."

He paused briefly. Emily did not know whether this was to emphasize his words or whether he was unsure how to go on.

"My predecessors, like many of us, gave their lives for our creed, for our people, for our species. I would like to keep a few moments' silence in memory of all the fallen, for everyone, for all those Keplerians who sacrificed their lives so that all of us could be here today."

Once again a sepulchral silence filled the temple. Everybody who was there bowed their heads in a gesture which honored the lives which had been lost throughout Keplerian history. It was an emotional moment which Emily and Rakesh honored with respect and politeness.

He broke the silence, raising his arms once again: "I, Waafdiv, high priest of the Gaal-El, and in view of the latest events which have taken place in our villages, invoke the ancestral and sacred conclave of the Keplerian peoples. And I hereby yield my command to the disposition of the conclave while the future of our society is determined."

With a distinctly theatrical gesture he raised his staff above his head and touched the front of the altar, where there seemed to be a small hollow ready for it. Then he fetched a wooden bowl from one side of the altar, together with what looked like a dagger from the other, and raised both objects.

"And to seal my commitment to the Keplerian people, I hereby offer my own blood in token of submission."

He put down the bowl, seized the dagger with his right hand and made a cut on the palm of his left claw. Thick drops of a dark, dense liquid fell into the bowl. Then he moved away from the altar and bowed his head very ceremoniously.

Without a word Khaaÿ, the ancient Khapabir leader, got up, not without some difficulty, from his seat in the front row. Staff in hand, he took Waafdiv's place at the altar and repeated the same words.

"I, Khaaÿ," the old man began, "leader of the Khapabir village, yield my command to the disposition of the conclave while the future of our society is determined."

In the same way as Waafdiv before him, he put his staff down on the left-hand side of the altar. Emily saw that there were five slots in it. Waafdiv had put down his staff in the third, while Khaaÿ had chosen the first.

"And to seal my commitment to the Keplerian people," he went on as he raised the dagger and bowl in his aged claws, "I offer my own blood in token of submission."

After he had stepped back and taken up his position to one side of the high priest, Vaahur, the Khaavahki military leader, got up from his bench.

"I, Vaahur," the soldier said, "leader of the Khaavahki village, yield my command to the disposition of the conclave while the future of our society is determined."

And in the same way, he laid his staff in the second hollow.

"And to seal my commitment with the Keplerian people, I offer my own blood in token of submission."

Then came Khikhya's turn.

"I, Khikhya, leader of the Khaavahki village, yield my command to the disposition of the conclave while the future of our society is determined."

She put her staff in the fourth hollow.

"And to seal my commitment to the Keplerian people," she repeated, "I offer my own blood in token of submission."

No-one claimed the fifth hollow, so Waafdiv himself, standing in the center of the tribal leaders, took a step forward and spoke again.

"We will always remember our fallen brethren," he said solemnly. "Wherever you, the *Wiijof jikhaashyush,* may be, we beg you to bless both this ceremony and your brethren here."

And making a small, ceremonious gesture with his hands above the bowl, he picked it up and went to one of the corners of the altar. There, in a stone basin, he poured the blood of the Keplerian leaders from the bowl. He took a small torch and lit it carefully from one of the braziers.

"May the light guide us in darkness!" he called. "May our fears be devoured by the sacred flames! May our enemies be consumed by the heat of the fire! May our blood reawaken from its ashes and keep the history of our people alive!"

He brought the torch close to the basin, and after a powerful burst of flame two trickles of orange fire came from the sides and ran down all four walls of the temple, lighting up the hall. What had been darkness was now light.

After this he put the torch back in its place, picked up the sacred book again and went back to the center of the reredos. One by one, in strict order, the leaders went through the door. Once all four were inside, it closed. A familiar metallic sound told them that no-one else was to be allowed in.

9

The conclave

Now, with better light, Emily and Rakesh were able to admire the beauty of the frescoes and the details of the carvings and figures along both walls and ceiling of the temple. Even the floor, which was of a rosy stone, seemed to be of exceptional quality.

"Now all we can do is wait," Rakesh said. He was paying close attention to everything around him. "Even without being very clear about the year this temple was built, I have to admit that Keplerian materials and skill are of truly exceptional quality."

"Yeah, all this is beautiful," said Emily, looking once again at the frescoes on the ceiling. These were far more visible now that Waafdiv had illuminated the hall completely.

On the other benches the counselors were talking among themselves in low voices, without paying much attention to the others. And as was to be expected, they did not mingle with the other delegations. Some had stood up and were pacing around looking at the works of art, as Emily and Rakesh were from the last bench.

Liikmi and the other three cult-members who had attended the ceremony in silence from the end of the temple, close to the exit, looked like mere statues. It was then that Emily noticed someone. Out of everyone there this was the only one, apart from the cult-members, who had not yet exchanged a word with the others but merely went on sitting there immobile. It was the youngest of the soldiers. Although the other two had got to their feet and were looking closely at a bust while they exchanged impressions, her attention was drawn by the fact that this young man had not made the slightest gesture. Who would not at least make some comment to his peers after attending a ceremony which had not taken place for centuries? Or go to look at some of the works of art of his own civilization, works of art which very few ever had the chance to see?

With every minute that went by, her doubts about the whole business grew. Several times she was tempted to get up and go up to someone to try and resolve them. Still, she decided to be cautious and avoid troubling anyone. She did not want to cause any undesired reaction among the Keplerians, especially considering how they were glancing aside at them whenever they could.

When they had been waiting for almost an hour, she and Rakesh felt the need to stretch their legs, and decided to get up from their bench. They walked aimlessly around the temple looking at some of the statues, which were of a beautiful white marble. Among them were historical personages and ancient high priests, but also more bucolic carvings, such as one of an enormous buffalo grazing in the shade of a tree. They also stopped to admire wood-carvings which portrayed small everyday scenes: shepherds with animals of every kind and size, traders, farmers milking and even fishermen.

"It's curious," Rakesh said, "that as a cult which worships deities they don't have any kind of idol, or messiah. If you look closely, all the scenes shown here in the figures and the frescoes belong to their daily life. Things you could come across in the course of a stroll through any of the villages."

"That's right," Emily said, "I'd noticed that. And it's odd that there are no references to the Khol. It's as if something were missing here."

They made a complete circuit of the temple. Emily was still intrigued by the passivity of the youngest soldier, who had still not moved from the bench. The others went on chatting, some more animatedly than others. Even the two older and more senior soldiers had taken the liberty to go outside for some fresh air. As they themselves were inside their exosuits, they were not aware that the atmosphere might be rather stale in there by now.

When they came alongside the four cult-members, Emily decided to speak to Liikmi.

"Can you talk?" she asked him.

The young Keplerian came over to them, ready to help. "Of course. What do you need?"

"Oh, nothing, we're fine, but we were wondering whether you could answer some questions."

He bowed. "Most certainly, my lady. Whatever you need."

"Why is there an empty row of benches?"

"In ancient times there were five villages which made up the Keplerian nation. Apart from the four you already know, there were the *Wiijof jikhaashyush.*"

"And what happened to them?" Rakesh asked.

Liikmi looked down sadly. "We don't know for sure. It happened thousands of years ago, after the Great Revolt. It's thought that they moved away gradually from the other villages and their blood grew thinner until they died out."

"That's really sad," said Emily.

"Yes, it certainly is. The Gaal-El try to keep the history of the Keplerians alive, but unfortunately our knowledge only goes back as far as the relatively recent past."

"Don't you have books from before the Great Revolt?" Rakesh asked.

"We have scrolls and books from long before then, but some are written in the language of the ancient Keplerians, which none of us knows how to interpret now. And also, much of our most ancient library was lost in a fire centuries ago."

"What a pity," Rakesh murmured. "I see that this kind of problem isn't exclusive to our own species."

"How big is this cave?" Emily asked. "I can see there's another hall behind there, but are there more?"

Liikmi nodded. "The cave is enormous. Even though very few can go beyond the hall of the conclave, it's a sacred place for us."

Rakesh looked interested at this. "Why is it sacred?"

"Because this is the cave where our ancestors first took shelter from the attacks of the Khol. No-one knows for sure when that happened, but it must have been at least several hundred generations ago. As I say, there are very ancient writings, but fewer and fewer of them all the time, and nor are there many Keplerians who know how to interpret them. I fear that there are fewer and fewer of us cult-members too."

"I understand," said Emily.

"Liikmi," Rakesh asked, "is there any engraving, or anything we could see here, which tells of your gods?"

He looked around in surprise. "Of our gods? No, I don't think so."

"And doesn't that seem rather strange to you?"

"I'm afraid I don't understand the question, I'm sorry. There are engravings and ancient paintings of exquisite craftsmanship here. Why would we decorate it in any other way?"

"Oh, forgive me, I didn't mean to be disrespectful. The temple is wonderful. I was simply wondering whether there was anything that could help us to a better understanding of your cult."

"There's no need to apologize," the young Keplerian said, sounding a little embarrassed. "I'm sorry if I sounded rather abrupt, it's just that your question surprised me."

84

Emily tried to explain. "You see, where we come from it was quite usual in many of our cults to carve or paint figures of the deities. Although there were others where it was forbidden, we simply wanted to know why we hadn't seen anything like that here."

"I see," he said in some puzzlement, "though in fact I don't know the reason, if there is one."

They spent another couple of hours without any news from inside the conclave. The others were beginning to get tired of waiting, with no distraction apart from their own thoughts and sporadic conversations with their colleagues. Then, without warning, five cult-members suddenly came into the temple. Except for the first of them, whose hands were empty, they were carrying small covered trays. The eldest tapped three times on the reredos door which gave access to the conclave chamber.

A few seconds later they heard the metallic grinding of a key turning in the lock. The door opened, and one by one the five cult-members went in with their trays, then came out a few minutes later empty-handed. Then the same old man went from group to group, inviting them by gestures to leave the temple.

When he came to Rakesh and Emily, he spoke to them politely and helpfully.

"We're serving food for our guests, but I understand that you're unable to eat it. Is there anything I can do for you?"

Emily shook her head. "It won't be necessary, thank you."

"Very well. In any case, our other guests have gone to the dining-hall in the monastery. If you need anything, please don't hesitate to let me or any of my brothers know."

"Thank you very much, but I don't think it'll be necessary."

The old man nodded and took his leave with a deep bow, which once again embarrassed her. She could not help grasping him by the arms to get him back to his feet.

"Really, there's no need for all this bowing," she said with the trace of a smile.

"As you wish," he said, and left the temple.

Only the two of them and Liikmi were now left inside. Emily called him over.

"I suppose you must be hungry. Why don't you go and have something to eat?"

"I'm fine," he said. "Besides, I have to stay with you at every moment."

"But you're aware that we aren't going to eat, presumably?" Rakesh asked.

"Yes, I know."

"But would you be able to eat in the dining-hall if we were there?"

Emily asked. "Even if we didn't eat anything?"

"Yes, I suppose so."

"In that case take us to the dining-hall."

The three of them went across to one of the buildings within that open area. Most of them were of stone, and although the façades were reasonably well-kept, the roofs did not seem to be in such a good state, presumably because of the effects of time and the lack of resources.

Liikmi invited them to enter through the side door of one of the largest buildings. It was well lit, thanks to the innumerable inner courtyards which admitted the sunlight. They crossed one of them, with a large tree in it which was taller by far than the building, and came to a huge wooden door. This admitted them to a hall with three rows of tables and long benches on either side of each of them. The atmosphere was rather dark, as was the wood which covered the entire hall. In that airy space six hundred or so people would be able to eat comfortably, but at the moment there were not even fifty, including both cult-members and guests. The delegations had spread themselves over several areas of the hall, but they all stopped what they were doing, turned toward the door and stared at the new arrivals. An uncomfortable silence followed until Emily and Rakesh sat down with Liikmi at one of the free corners. The moment they did so, the subdued buzz of conversation broke out again. She found herself looking once again at the strange soldier, who seemed to be ignoring everything that was happening around him. He was finishing the last spoonfuls of some kind of stew.

Another young cult-member approached Liikmi and offered him a generous plate of meat and vegetable stew.

"May… I… offer you…. anything?" he asked them, very shyly.

Emily smiled politely. "No, but thank you all the same."

Instead of eating, Liikmi seemed to be waiting for something.

"Oh," said Rakesh, "don't worry about us, we can eat whenever we want."

"That's right," Emily said. "You go ahead and eat, or else it'll get cold."

Liikmi narrowed his eyes in delight and set about eating his stew avidly. There was no saying when the high priest's poor assistant might have broken his fast that day, as he was always attentive to the needs of others. Meanwhile Emily and Rakesh too took the opportunity to eat their own food.

The sun was beginning to trace its downward curve by the time they went back to the temple, where the delegations from Wiikhaadiiz ofiz and Khapabir had already taken their places. Emily and Rakesh sat down and prepared to wait patiently for some news from the Keplerian leaders, who were still locked inside the chamber.

Another couple of hours went by before once again they heard the metallic grinding of the door as it opened. Liikmi and the three other cult-members who were accompanying the different delegations hastened toward the reredos. They went into the chamber, and Emily presumed that they would be receiving instructions. Sure enough, shortly afterward they came out and each of them went to their respective delegation.

Liikmi came over to Emily and Rakesh.

"The leaders have finished the first part of the conclave. The spokesman has explained the reasons why he decided to call the leaders. Now they'll let one of the counselors in so that they can share what they consider opportune. All with the aim of making the most objective possible decision."

"Do we need to do anything?"

"No, I'm afraid you'll have to wait until this second part is over. Afterwards you might be called in."

"All right," Rakesh said resignedly, "in that case we'll wait."

Liikmi went back to his place at the temple entrance, after making a deep bow. The two of them had no choice but to wait patiently for their moment to arrive. They decided to take another tour around the hall to try and calm their nerves.

"How strange the fire here looks," Rakesh commented as he watched the flickering of the flames as they danced in the braziers

She nodded. "It's very different from the fire on Earth. Here the lower level of oxygen in the air makes it harder to put out, and it also means that it burns very differently."

"There are still a whole lot of things I can't get used to which I understand are everyday matters for the Keplerians."

She smiled. "That's natural enough. We've only been here a few weeks."

She thought of what she had just said. She had still not fully realized what all this they were currently experiencing meant for humanity. Only fifty-four days had gone by since she herself had first set foot on the planet. Fifty-four days, during which they had met two different intelligent alien races. Fifty-four days during which they had discovered constructions and biological material belonging to a third species. In only fifty-four days, she herself had experienced at first hand events which would be recorded in the annals of mankind's history. Simply thinking about the supreme importance of what they were experiencing made her legs tremble.

She tried to calm her nerves, but she was still uneasy about what they must be debating inside the conclave at that very moment. Then she heard the metallic sound which announced that the chamber was being opened again. Once again the parade of cult-members came hurrying in.

After a few endless minutes, Liikmi came over to them.

"The leaders request your presence in the chamber," he announced with an ostentatious wave of his right arm, inviting them to cross the threshold.

Emily sighed loudly and thanked him with a nod. Both of them went across to the reredos and went in determinedly. The chamber was not very large; in fact its low ceiling was surprising in comparison with the rest of the temple. Although they had to go down a couple of steps to get to it, it was obvious that the ceiling here was much closer to the floor. The hall was rectangular and seemed not to occupy the whole width of the temple, which made her think that behind those walls there must be a generous empty space between them and the walls of the cave itself.

Everything there was of wood, including the ceiling. A dark variety of wood, very well-kept considering that it was inside a cave, though it too reflected the inexorable passage of time. Even so, and even though they were unable to pay very much attention, both of them could not help noticing the richness of the hundreds of carvings which adorned the walls. It would be worth visiting that chamber on some other occasion, without the context of an important conclave, to be able to enjoy its splendor in full.

Inside was a large pentagonal table with a large hollow in the center in the shape of another, smaller pentagon. It was the same color as the rest of the hall, and in each section were engraved the five crests of each of the Keplerian villages. Sitting around four of the five sides were the leaders themselves, with their companions standing, beside their respective leaders.

Behind them stood the Gaal-El high priest. He locked the door once again and turned to the new arrivals with a polite gesture.

"Please take the place of our ill-starred brothers."

Emily and Rakesh obediently went to the part of the table he was indicating. Rakesh offered the only chair available to Emily, who accepted, even though she did not like to leave her partner standing. She was reluctant to contradict her hosts, so she sat down between Khikhya, who barely so much as looked at her, and Khaäy, the leader of the Khapabir village.

Waafdiv cleared his throat before speaking.

"I think we can go on now. To bring our guests up to date—he waved toward Emily and Rakesh—"I'll give a brief summary of what's been discussed so far and what this conclave will be dealing with. For the last few days I've been isolated in our sacred libraries"—he waved toward the chamber door—"gathering information about our most ancient traditions. I've checked scrolls written in the language of our ancestors, I've compared the ancestral prophecies with historical writings and even the opinions of my predecessors." He paused briefly, which sharpened expectations.

"Everything I could find has led me to the same conclusion. The humans are those we have spent millennia waiting for, the ones who'll free our people from the yoke of the Khol."

A murmur spread through the chamber.

"That can't be true," said the counselor from Khaaÿ.

"That's impossible!" cried Vaahur, the Khaavahki leader vehemently. "It even goes against your own cult. Isn't it written that our foretold saviors would be Keplerians? Gods in our own image and likeness, with a range of supernatural skills and powers which would help us defeat our enemies?"

"All this is preposterous!" added Lajlab, his counselor.

"We should allow Waafdiv to explain his words," said Khikhya firmly at this disturbance.

Waafdiv stared at his detractors. "You're right, all of you. I too thought the same, but I've found ancient scrolls which date from a few hundred years before the Great Revolt. At that time the Gaal-El cult was going through a complicated period, the faith had been lost, the villages were divided. The Wiijof Jikhaashyush had long since disappeared. The Keplerian people were sinking into a spiral of decadence and pessimism. Disputes over power and control of the staves of command were constant. Chaos reigned.

"Shyunghi, one of my most illustrious ancestors, decided to take matters into his own hands. In a conclave like the one we find ourselves in now, it was decided, in order to achieve better cohesion of the villages, and—why not say it?—to control the masses, to endow the ancient prophecies with a little mysticism to make them more attractive, and even more credible."

"Are you suggesting that the cult of the Gaal-El is nothing but a lie?" Vaahur asked.

Waafdiv rejected this firmly. "No! I'm saying that they added a little decoration to the ancient prophecies, to save the Keplerians from the disaster looming before them."

"But that was followed by the great Revolt, which had such terrible consequences for our people," Vaahur said angrily.

"Yes, hundreds of years later. But if we ignore the disastrous end which unleashed the uprising against the Khol, those days were the result of an unprecedented collaboration between the Keplerians. That conclave gave way to a period of prosperity and growth for our people. And all that was the result of having sweetened the origin and the characteristics of our saviors.

"The only true thing here is that I have revisited everything my master was able to transmit to me before I took over this position. I've found no reference to the origin of our saviors in all the ancient writings.

All that was prophesized was that they would come from outside this planet"—he indicated Emily—"and that they would do so sheathed in metal suits."

Everyone turned to stare at her and Rakesh.

"The truth is," he went on, "I'm convinced that the humans are the ones our ancestors, in this very cave, prophesized would come to free us."

Once again the murmuring spread throughout the chamber. All the leaders wanted to make their positions clear, and most of them were unenthusiastic about what the high priest was suggesting.

"We can't believe any of this nonsense," Lajlab said.

"It's impossible," Khikhya's counselor added.

"What does the leader of the saviors have to say about all this?" Vaahur asked suddenly, giving a mocking emphasis to the word 'saviors'.

Suddenly Emily felt cornered. She had not prepared any speech. What can you say when you are introduced as the savior of a whole species?

"I…" she stammered. "Well, we… we haven't come to this planet to rescue anyone… or start a war with any alien race. Until we came here and met you, we'd never heard talk of the Keplerians or the Khol."

Once again, murmuring interrupted the conversation.

"They didn't even know about the prophesies," Khaaÿ's counselor said.

"It's obvious that they can't be the ones," Vaahur insisted.

Waafdiv raised his arms to quell the murmur. It was not easy.

"Brothers," he said confidently, "none of what the representative of the humans says changes by one iota the determination with which I assure this chamber that they are the ones our ancestors predicted would save us from our oppressors. More than that, I can state without fear of being proved wrong that she is the one chosen to lead our people."

"What!" Vaahur exploded. He banged the table and got up from his seat. "Has sanity completely abandoned this monastery and its worshipers? No foreigner is ever going to lead the Khaavahki, at least not as long as I'm alive!"

Khikhya condemned his attitude vehemently, and she was joined by Khaaÿ and his counselors. All the leaders and their counselors plunged into an argument which grew more and more heated, revealing all the quarrels and frictions of the past. Ancient attitudes, failed commercial agreements and abuses of power. The situation itself and the widespread disagreement made Waafdiv sink back in his seat, careworn and dejected, as his colleagues argued at the top of their voices.

Emily watched the situation with deep regret. Somehow they had deceived themselves into believing that arguments, selfishness, everything that had caused so much harm on Earth, had been left a thousand light-years behind them. Despite this, far from sinking down in her seat as Waafdiv had done, an irrepressible anger began to grow in her chest until it was burning her inside. She had no choice but to let it out. She got up with such determination that she knocked her chair over. Then she banged the table with her hands and shouted as loudly as she could:

"Silence!"

They were all left paralyzed, perhaps more from surprise than from the intensity of the shout, since though Ada was translating simultaneously, maintaining tone and volume, the restricted environment of the exosuit had muffled her real voice. Whatever the truth of it, she had managed to catch the attention of the four leaders and their counselors.

"I barely know your society," she said angrily. "We haven't been among you for very long. I don't know your history and your past quarrels, but I remember the history of my own people, and we behaved just as you're behaving now." She paused, but managed to keep their attention. "I don't know anything about prophesies, or about the Keplerian gods. I don't even know anything about the Khol. But a catastrophe threatened our people a very long time ago. The great rock which was heading for our planet was going to destroy everything we loved. If the leaders of my planet"—she pointed to the four Keplerians, who were staring at her in disbelief—"hadn't set their petty disputes aside, none of us would be here, trying to make a new home for ourselves.

"So I beg you to listen carefully to me. If some day one of you wants your people and his descendants to be free and to have a second chance, as we had, I beg you to open your eyes, to learn from past mistakes, and to think for once about the good of all Keplerians instead of your own interests."

Then she picked up the chair from the floor and sat down again, a little dizzy with the excess of adrenalin she had just generated. The Keplerian leaders were silent, exchanging meaningful glances. Waafdiv on the other hand was bright-eyed again and seemed euphoric.

"You see now?" he shouted. "She's the chosen one!"

Emily started in her seat. Her improvised speech had had the expected effect on the other leaders, but had caused an excess of enthusiasm in the high priest.

"N-no…" she stammered, "I didn't mean to…"

"All right," Khaäÿ said after the silence. "Suppose for a moment that everything the high priest says is true. What army do the humans have for dealing with the Khol? And who says they won't use it against us when the time comes?"

"We aren't here to be the leaders of any war," Emily said firmly.

The ancient leader was taken aback by this. "Do you mean to deal with the Khol without picking up a weapon?"

She did not know what to answer.

"How does the high priest expect us to trust a foreigner who knows nothing about the nature of the Khol?" Vaahur went on. "She doesn't even have any ideas about military tactics."

"The sacred scriptures are clear about this," Waafdiv said. "When our liberators arrive from outer space after their great journey in search of our planet, the sole command of our people will be handed over to them."

Vaahur gave a sarcastic laugh. "Just like that? And do we give them the keys to our city walls too?"

"The laws of our people are clear. If one of the village representatives wants to propose someone to lead all the Keplerians, as has been done on numerous occasions, he would only need a majority of the votes in this conclave."

"That doesn't change the fact that I don't intend to hand my staff of command to the first stranger who comes through the door."

"But our laws oblige us to," Waafdiv repeated wearily.

"Even if you manage to persuade that rabble," Vaahur said, referring to the two other leaders, "our laws also allow the departing leaders to set a test for the candidates so that they can establish their worth."

"Yes," the high priest agreed. "If the case were to arise, you'd have an absolute right to ensure that our laws were enforced."

"Excuse the interruption," Rakesh interrupted very quietly, "but could you explain what the sole command consists of?"

"In ancient times," Waafdiv began, "Keplerian society was a single one and was led by a single Keplerian, the high priest of the Gaal-El. It had four counselors, who were responsible for different aspects of society. Over time, and after centuries of pillage and suffering caused by the Khol, the successors of those five leaders, who were chosen by the Keplerians themselves, began to grow apart. Arguments and different ways of solving serious problems ended up breaking that unity. Thus were born the five factions, four of which are represented here.

"Despite following different paths, dealings between the factions were, and still are, almost always cordial. Each of them established its own traditions, its own culture, and of course its own laws. Nevertheless, all of them promised to obey a simple list of conditions which would prevail over any legal system of their own.

"Among them were some obvious ones, like the prohibition on stealing from, or killing, one another, whatever their origin. Others, such as that of sole command, obliges the leaders of each village to yield their staff of command should there appear a candidate we all agree on and should circumstances require it. In the same way we left our staff of command at the entrance to this conclave, each leader hands their own to the chosen one. However, the leaders reserve the right to test the candidates if they truly believe they are unsuitable.

"The last time this happened was thousands of years ago, at the time of the Great Revolt. A few centuries after the conclave I mentioned, and in all certainty spurred on by its consequences on society, the tribal leaders met in this same chamber and decided to give the sole command to an old Khaavahki leader named Faddub.

"The consequences were disastrous, I admit, but it achieved something no-one had ever done until then: the supremacy of the Khol was threatened. Faddub was a great military leader, and with the support of the entire Keplerian people he conceived the idea of a guerrilla war against the Khol. At first everything seemed to work, and the few contingents of Khol which visited the planet were taken by surprise by innumerable well-coordinated attacks. Those attacks, in spite of our obvious technological inferiority, were on the brink of destroying them. But Faddub was also too proud. Those small victories swelled his ego beyond reason, and he didn't hesitate to send the major part of his army against what remained of that of the Khol.

"Then Faddub, like all the other Keplerians, found out to his horror that the Khol who were visiting our planet were mere Kholvahki soldiers. Unfortunately we then met the Kholchach, the Khol military leaders. The firepower of the ships the Kholchach brought with them destroyed Faddub's entire army in only a few hours. The rest is history. The Khol made conditions harder in their subsequent visits, murdering many or our ancestors and kidnapping and enslaving the unluckiest.

"From that moment, when we tasted the most bitter of defeats and our villages were reduced to ashes, sole command has never again been suggested. Our people have gone their separate ways since then, with each faction following its own path. But now the situation is different, now at last we have with us the woman of metal, the one who was prophesied for us. At last we have the chosen one on our side."

"That's just your opinion," Vaahur muttered.

"It's what's written."

"And can the rest of us consult these scriptures?"

"You know full well that only the high priest and his disciples have access to the sacred scriptures," Waafdiv shot back. "And besides, they're written in the language of the ancients, which means you wouldn't understand anything, even if you wanted to."

"How convenient that you should be the only one who can understand what you're the only one defending in this conclave!"

"I'm merely defending what our ancestors left in writing, which is no more than the history of our people."

"Gentlemen," Khikhya interrupted, "I'm an aged Keplerian, and your rambling discussions are beginning to take their toll on me. I beg you to come to the point."

"The proposal of the high priest of the Gaal-El and the reason for this conclave," he said solemnly, "is to propose Emily Rhodes, leader of the foreign people known as the humans, as holder of the sole command of all Keplerian villages. The leaders and their counselors who are assembled here will now withdraw to meditate in their respective places of origin. The decision of each one of you will be given out at the next conclave. Until that moment, as is stated in our ancestral laws, they are not to communicate, directly or indirectly, with any of those who are here. May the spirits of our ancestors guide us on our way."

10
New Year's Eve

December 8, Year 0

Asimov Space Station, Kepler-442b

Three days had gone by since the conclave, and they were still waiting for the next one. The leaders of the various Keplerian villages and their counselors would stay incommunicado until then. However, Emily and Rakesh were not part of that select group, so that they could act with complete normality.

They had all gone back to the space station because that night, according to the new Keplerian calendar—which was already the one officially used in the project— was the last of the year. For this reason the deputy director and Captain Mei had decided to organize a small celebration with all those station staff who were available.

"Aren't you excited?" Chad said when he had taken his helmet off in the hangar. "Our first New Year's Eve on the planet!"

"Considering the Keplerian year only has a hundred and twelve Earth days and we're going to celebrate it three times more than on Earth," Taro replied, "not really."

"That's because you're lacking in the festive spirit."

"Will there be a countdown to celebrate the arrival of the New Year?" Paula asked excitedly.

Emily shrugged. "No idea. The deputy director just asked me if everyone could come."

"I'm sorry for the soldiers who've stayed on the base," said Chad.

"Someone had to take care of security," Sergeant Ferrara explained. "There was a draw, and they lost."

"Still, it's a pity they can't take part in the first New Year's Eve in the history of the planet."

"As Taro said, there'll be plenty more if we celebrate them all,"

Lieutenant Ortiz pointed out. "And anyway, they'll be following everything at the station remotely."

Emily was feeling quite excited. Not so much about enjoying a few moments of peace and celebration with her colleagues, but because going to the station meant being able to spend the night with Robert. Although they spoke frequently, his new responsibilities were keeping him very busy. In fact at that very moment he was in the other continent, inspecting the second site chosen for the installation of a new base. Not being able to be close to him was getting hard, harder than she had expected.

"When are we going to meet our new neighbors?" Kostas asked.

"Are you worried they'll walk on your garden?" Gorka teased him.

"I hope I won't have to put up a wire fence."

"To be honest, I don't know," Emily admitted. "This evening we won't talk about work, at least to start with. Though I suppose we might bump into some of them."

A familiar voice greeted them from the access ramp of the hangar. "Merry Christmas!" they heard the deputy director call.

"Merry Christmas!" Chad called back enthusiastically.

They all gave the deputy director and Captain Mei, who had joined him for this spontaneous reception, a fond welcome.

He and Emily hugged in a state of weightlessness. "Everything all right?" he asked.

"Yes, fine."

"Any news from the Keplerians?"

"Nope, nothing." They made their way toward the Centrifuge with the help of their electromagnetic boots. "Total silence. And how are things around here?"

"Fine. Everything normal, I guess. As you know, the building works for the enlargement are finished. The area where we want to set up the new base is being inspected as we speak."

"Any news of the rebels?" she asked.

"No, nothing there either. It's as if they'd vanished by magic. Our sensors and satellites aren't detecting any kind of human activity, apart from what's being directed from the station itself."

"Don't you find it strange that a dozen vehicles and ships, not to mention the equipment that was stolen, can't be detected in any way?"

"Yes, it's definitely odd," he admitted. "But maybe they're being wary and they've reduced their activity to the bare minimum."

"Coming from Captain Garth, all that caution seems very strange to me."

"Do you have any other theory?"

"Maybe," she said mysteriously. "I've been wondering for a long time how someone could bypass our detection systems."

"Can't you go any further than that?"

"We'll have to wait till we can do a bit of checking," she said. "And also, it might not be too safe to talk about it."

"I get you. We'll see where all this leads."

"Has the expedition to the second site come back yet?"

"No. Commander Bauer's coordinating operations from here. I think Captain Beaufort and his team'll be back in a couple of hours."

They came to the Centrifuge and once again were able to enjoy a much gentler gravity than on the surface.

"At the moment we seem to be floating," Paula said when she found that once again she weighed the same as she had on Earth.

"Be careful," Emily warned her. "When you get used to the gravity of the planet, this might make you a little dizzy."

"That's true," Chad admitted, "I feel a bit strange at the moment. I hope it goes away in time for the midnight celebrations."

"Don't worry, it's temporary." Emily reassured him. "The sensation passes quickly enough."

They still had several hours left before the New Year's Eve celebrations started. The deputy director had summoned all available staff of the station for a couple of hours before midnight. A small feast had been prepared in the atrium, and everyone would be able to enjoy a special evening. In addition, a small surprise had been announced as soon as it was New Year.

This gave Emily time for one or two other tasks. She could look into the idea she had been thinking about for some time: to try and find out what had become of the rebels. She had a conversation pending with Erik, the engineer who was going to form part of the expedition and to whom she had entrusted the job of checking the software of the surviving mule. She went to the engineering labs, where she expected to find him, but could not see anyone.

"Erik?"

A loud bump, followed by a moan, reached her from under one of the lab tables.

"Down here," she heard him say.

She followed the voice and found him under one of the tables amid a chaotic tangle of electronic boards and electric cables.

"Hi there."

"Hi." Carefully, he got up. "We've had one or two electrical problems this morning, and I'm trying to fix them before the celebrations this evening."

"Oh dear, is it serious?"

He was quick to reassure her. "No, no, it's just been a series of unpleasant coincidences caused by a slightly defective installation and a thousand years of travelling through space. Mind you, we can't complain, considering this ship at this moment is older than anything humans had ever created on Earth at the time we left."

She smiled. "You can say that again."

"I suppose you've come to ask about the software on that mule you left me."

"You suppose right. Did you manage to find anything?"

"Actually, yes." With a wave he invited her to follow him, and they sat down beside the other lab terminal. "I managed to take the code of the software version in the mule apart."

"And? What did you find?"

"That the code in this mule is not far short of a masterpiece."

She looked at him in surprise. "A masterpiece?"

"That's right, I have to say I'd never seen anything like it. I also compared it to the earlier version, 3.14.2."

"Were there many differences?"

"I'd rather say my problem was finding any similarities between the two versions."

"Wow, are they that different?"

"For some reason this new version has been built from scratch. It doesn't share a single line of code."

"Did you find anything that shouldn't be there?" she asked. "Something that could endanger the integrity of the mule, or its users?"

He shook his head. "Nothing at all. The code is absolutely perfect. It allows the mule to consider all kinds of situations which the prior version didn't even imagine, and what's more, it does it much more intelligently and efficiently. As I said, it's a work of art. In fact I've asked Ada to work out a version with the same characteristics from scratch— don't be offended, Ada—but it's a long way from that perfection."

"I'm not offended," they heard Ada say. "In fact I'd like to know who created the code too. That would allow me to improve my skills."

"I wasn't expecting any of this," Emily murmured. "I was afraid someone might have sabotaged the software in the mules. Do you know if it's only this mule that has this particular software, or are there others?"

The engineer shook his head. "No, it's just this mule that has this version. And apart for a couple of them, which had an earlier version because of some problem in the process of actualization, the others all have version 3.14.2, with no exception."

"How strange."

"But I've left the strangest thing of all till last."

"Something even stranger that having a software version that doesn't exist in our repositories?" she asked in surprise.

"Yes, I'm afraid so."

"So what is it?"

"It's about who compiled the version in June 2292."

"Who was it?"

"According to the compilation sequence, it was you, Emily."

"What?" she exclaimed. "That just isn't possible! I've never compiled a version of the software for the mules. I don't even know the specifications of their hardware. At the moment I wouldn't even know where to begin."

"For some reason I guessed you'd say that. I can't really see how this version could have got here, or who could have created it under your name. But I'm quite clear that it's digitally signed with your identification. And as far as I know, there's no way of faking those signatures."

"Thanks, Erik. You've done a great job. Although quite honestly, you've given me more questions than I had to start with."

"I know, and I'm sorry, but unfortunately I can't give you a logical explanation. If you weren't the one who created it, then someone else must have taken over your identity."

After this interesting talk with Erik, Emily left the lab with more questions than those she had brought with her, which was what was tending to happen every time anything was looked into. It had been clearly established that the terrorists who had organized the sabotage of the station had managed to obtain a copy of her identification chip while they were still on Earth. But she could not understand why those same terrorists who had conspired to destroy the project should have decided to install a much more advanced version of the mules' software than the one already there. What was the sense in that?

Ideas and questions churned and hammered ceaselessly in her mind. She was walking with her head down along the corridor of the Centrifuge when she heard a familiar voice.

"If you keep puzzling over that problem, Dr. Rhodes, you'll end up bumping into someone."

Emily spun round immediately. There he was, just arrived from his mission of exploration in the other continent.

"Robert!" She ran to him, and her look of worry was transformed into an enormous smile.

He took her in his arms, and both of them twirled for a couple of steps while their lips joined over and over in a series of passionate kisses.

"I thought you wouldn't be back for another hour," she said.

"We brought the return forward. Everyone was so thrilled about tonight's celebration I couldn't help but soften."

"That means we have an hour and a half before anyone misses

us," she said with a mischievous smile.

"Two, if we get there just in time for the ceremony."

"My room's a hundred meters from here."

She left her cabin late, for a change. She smoothed the improvised bun she had just put her hair up in and straightened the white shirt she had matched with a pair of jeans. What she could not do was erase the idiotic smile which appeared whenever she was with Robert. He meanwhile had gone to his own cabin twenty minutes earlier to take a quick shower and change his clothes. They wanted to avoid arriving at the celebration together, as there was enough gossip as it was without giving it any more to feed on.

The atrium was packed almost to overflowing when she arrived. She had never seen so many people there. It was noticeable that there were more newcomers in the different project teams. She had to make her way through the crowd almost as far as the other side of the hall to find her friends. On the way she had to stop to greet the acquaintances she met.

"Happy New Year, Emily!" Evelyn called when she saw her.

"Happy New Year, Emily!" her other colleagues chorused.

"Happy New Year to all!" she replied, smiling broadly.

"May the New Year never take away your tendency to arrive late everywhere!" Chad joked.

She laughed. "Don't worry! That'll never happen."

Many people there were wearing colored wreaths and paper hats.

"Where did you get all that stuff?" she asked.

"There are tables around the corners of the atrium," Paula explained. "They've left things there so that everyone can take whatever they want. There's food, drink and all these things."

A murmur, followed by a series of outbursts of applause, began to sound at the other end of the atrium. Something was happening. After a few minutes of uncertainty they saw the deputy director going up to the highest point of the stand beside the lectern. He made a shy gesture with his hands, but had to wait for a while until the crowd stopped applauding and cheering.

"I haven't prepared a speech," he said at last. "Today all of us here at the station are the important guests. We're all celebrating."

Fresh cheers and applause echoed through the atrium.

"The directors of the various sectors and I myself thought it would be a good idea if we were all able to enjoy a day as special as this, when we're entering Year 1 of the human presence on Kepler-442b."

More applause and shouts of support obliged him to interrupt his improvised speech.

"Enjoy everything we have here, eat, drink and be merry, and in just over an hour and a half we'll say a proper goodbye to this first year."

The more than five hundred men and women who were assembled there burst into applause to celebrate the deputy director's words as he left the stand and was lost in the crowd. At that moment, two human waves made their way to the sides of the atrium in search of something to eat and drink. In the center only a few absent-minded groups of people deep in conversation were left.

"Robert!" she heard Paula call. "How nice to see you again!"

Emily turned when she heard this. It was the first time since she had known him that she had seen him in civilian clothes. He was wearing plain blue jeans and a black T-shirt to go with his trainers.

How good he looks in civilian clothes, she thought.

She waited patiently for her turn, waiting until the others had greeted him. Once he had finished accepting all those welcomes and hugs he came to her side.

"Hi." He gave her a long kiss on the lips. "Did I take very long?"

"Longer than I did," she said with a smile as she stroked his newly-shaven cheek.

"My cabin's further away from here than yours is."

"I've never seen you in civilian clothes before. You look really good."

He blushed. "Thanks. You look great too."

Chad interrupted the conversation shamelessly, bringing paper wreaths and hats for everyone. These he placed on their shoulders and heads, keeping time to the rhythm of the music which sounded through the system. Emily excused herself and went over to the group of people who were with the deputy director.

"Happy New Year, David!"

He gave her a broad smile. "Emily!"

"Isn't it great to see everyone having such a good time!"

"It was high time we had the chance to relax and enjoy an evening without any responsibility whatever."

"You can tell people needed it." She indicated the overflowing enthusiasm of the crowd.

"Emily!" Captain Mei said suddenly.

Emily gave her a smile. "Captain! You look great!"

"We'd better make the most of the day!" the captain said as she took a sip of her champagne.

Emily would never have imagined the ever-professional and hard-working captain enjoying a party like this one. It was clear that she was releasing all the tension which had accumulated over the last few months.

She laughed inwardly. *I hope it doesn't take its toll tomorrow…*

She also greeted Commander Bauer and Director Patel, in addition to other council members and personnel who were in the group.

"Later it might be a good moment to meet the members of the expedition who'll be occupying the other building at the base," the deputy director told her before she went back to her friends. "For the moment, just enjoy yourself. Tonight there's no room for talk about work."

She went back to her friends, and they ate and drank, laughed and danced and talked. Tomorrow did not matter, only those moments. There would only be one first New Year's Eve on the planet, and it had to be enjoyed to the full. Everything was going perfectly normally and the groups were beginning to mingle. Maybe drink was impelling many to seek new people to talk with, or even approach people they had only seen in passing in the mess hall. Emily, for example, chatted with some of the medical team and even with several engineers who were colleagues of Erik's.

She and Paula were at one of the corner tables, laughing as they tried without much success to open a new bottle of champagne, when someone came over to them.

"Well, well, well," came a melodious voice. "What do we have here? Two lovely ladies in distress. Allow me."

And before Paula could say anything the man, who was in his mid-thirties, with tanned skin, short bleached hair and teeth so white they might have been made of ivory, took the bottle of French champagne from her hands.

"You see, champagne is a very delicate nectar," the man said in that deep yet soft voice. "And it needs to be treated with the utmost delicacy, otherwise it might be spoiled."

Very skillfully, the stranger began to turn the bottle, gripping the cork firmly at the same time. He was wearing white pleated pants, moccasins of the same color and a rather tacky shirt, unbuttoned at the top to reveal well-molded muscles.

"You see? You need to turn the bottle, not the cork. And it's important to control the sound as you uncork it." He removed the cork from the bottle with barely the trace of a sigh.

The stranger, who kept his eyes on them and never stopped smiling, delicately poured out the foaming, golden liquid.

"I've just spent thousands of years asleep, and nothing would make me happier than to start this weird New Year with a private party in my cabin. How would that seem to you?"

Paula was unable to believe what she had just heard. "Excuse me?"

"I noticed how you took the opportunity to come over to me. I guess my fame precedes me, even on this planet… James Coogan is irresistible in whatever corner of the universe. Well then? What time shall we meet?"

"Who the hell do you think you are?" Paula said fiercely. "I wouldn't come near you if you were the only man left on the planet."

"You'd better keep your crazy friend under control," he said to Emily without changing his seductive demeanor in the slightest, "or else you'll lose the opportunity of getting a taste of this…" He ran his hand over his chest.

Emily, who had stayed silent, without even moving her hands, could not resist the impulse to pour the contents of her glass of champagne over his head.

"Here, try this," she said.

Paula was surprised to see her do anything of the sort, but she could not help bursting out laughing when she saw his expression. Emily left the empty glass on the table and walked away before he could reply to the insult.

"I'm sure there'll be a towel waiting for you in your cabin," Paula said sarcastically before she followed Emily.

"Get out of here!" he shouted, trying to rescue some of his damaged ego. "I'll find someone else who knows how to appreciate the good things in life!"

"Who was that shouting at you?" Chad asked when they came back to the group.

"An imbecile," said Paula.

"An asshole, who unfortunately is one of our new neighbors," Emily added.

"What?" Paula exclaimed. "Is James Coogan going to be one of the new settlers?"

"Was that James Coogan?" Chad asked in surprise as he tried to find him in the crowd.

"Unfortunately I'm afraid he is," Emily said.

"I never liked him. I never understood how someone like him managed to make such a mark."

"Me neither," Paula muttered. "But if he thinks just because he bought a ticket he can do whatever he wants, he's got another thing coming. Next time I won't be so polite."

At last the hour came, the moment to say farewell to the year in which humans had reached Kepler-442b to be given a second chance. Only five minutes of it were left.

All the screens and projectors in the atrium began to show recordings of different iconic locations on Earth where the change of year had been celebrated: Times Square in New York, the Opera House in Sydney, the Great Wall in China, the River Thames in London, the

Brandenburg Gate in Berlin and the Eiffel Tower in Paris were some of the places whose images they were able to see.

Everyone held their breath. Emily saw more than one person with tears in their eyes as they watched those images of the Earth, of their own cities. They wondered whether they would still be the same as ever, whether Project Atlas had managed to succeed and whether humanity still existed on their planet of origin. These were deeply emotional moments.

Despite everything, an outburst of joy filled the station when the countdown on the screen reached zero. The staff had prepared cannons loaded with confetti for the occasion, which filled the hall with a synchronized outburst of color and joy.

"Happy new Year, Emily" Robert said.

"Happy New Year, Robert."

Clasped in one another's arms, and with a long kiss, they welcomed a new year which would be full of surprises and adventures.

11
The new settlers

January 2, year 1

Magellan base, Kepler-442b

Everyone at the station went back to their usual tasks on the second day of the new year, after a well-deserved and necessary break. Emily and her comrades had gone back to the base by now.

"What a drag," Kostas grumbled over breakfast, still looking sleepy. "Couldn't every day be a holiday like yesterday?"

"If it were, who'd look after your plants?" Gorka joked.

"The automatic system I've installed in the greenhouses will soon be giving us the first fruits and vegetables cultivated one hundred per cent on Kepler-442-b."

Emily was pouring herself a cup of coffee. Her interest was caught by this.

"I've been neglecting you a bit, Kostas," she said. "How are your experiments going?"

"A lot better than I expected. It's still rather early to put out the flags, but apart from the tubers, everything else has germinated outside, with no need for greenhouses."

"Hey!" she said delightedly. "Congratulations! That's really good news!"

He looked proud at this. "Thank you. Although I suppose the credit ought to go to the plants, which are better adapted to the environment than animals are. The atmospheric conditions here are very different, but they can germinate in almost any environment, however hostile. The best example would be those shoots of grass that always used to grow in concrete cracks on Earth."

"What about the ones in the greenhouses?" she asked.

"Well, it's rather odd, but for some reason there isn't very much difference from what I've been cultivating outside."

"Are they growing at the same speed?"

He laughed. "No, no. Plants always germinate a few days earlier in a greenhouse. But I was surprised to see that they took less time outside than expected."

"I see," said Emily. "Congratulations, it's great news, and it's going to give us some oxygen."

"Literally," Kostas joked.

That morning the new group of settlers was due to arrive at the base. Emily had arranged for the reception of the nine civilians who were going to join the expedition. Lieutenant Ortiz had already installed five soldiers in the newly-inaugurated extension.

She decided to go outside the base to check the premises before the newcomers arrived. The first thing she found, with some satisfaction, was that Director Patel had granted her request and set up a small module without either atmospheric control or decontamination chamber for Keplerian visitors. The module even boasted a room with four beds, full bathroom facilities and a common area.

It even looks cozy, she thought. *It's a pity we can't breathe the atmosphere.*

After looking around the guest area for a while, she paid a short visit to the greenhouses, where Kostas had already started work.

"Hi! Coming to check on the progress for yourself?"

"Actually, I'm just killing time till the newcomers arrive. But your plants were the second item on my list of priorities."

"I know, no-one can resist a good horticulture session."

"What do you have outside?"

"I've planted at least a couple of seeds of each kind," he explained. "Here we have lettuce, spinach, cabbage, kale… and all that area over there is cereals. We've got wheat, barley, oats and corn. We also have transgenic rice which was especially developed for the project and doesn't need paddy fields."

"Wow, I didn't know that."

"That's right, the project invested a fortune in making sure we had seeds that could put up with almost any kind of conditions."

"I can see that."

"Over there, almost at the end, we've got legumes: lentils, beans… and at the far end everything else: different kinds of tubers, peppers, pumpkins. And some fruits like tomatoes, melons and watermelons, among others."

"Wow! There's something of everything. And it looks as though most of them have already started growing."

"Yeah," he said happily. "Except that unfortunately we still won't be able to eat them. Before that we'll have to carry out a toxicological and nutritional analysis to understand how plants develop in this environment. We mustn't forget, it's strange and hostile for every living being born on Earth."

She followed him into one of the greenhouses.

"Here the distribution is the same," said Kostas. "That way it's easier to compare things at a glance."

"These have grown a bit more. But there's not much obvious difference."

He smiled. "That's right. It's great news. The project has the technology and materials to build thousands of greenhouses like this one, but it's always better not to depend on the station equipment."

"That makes sense."

She could see that the other greenhouse was doing slightly better than the first, but if Kostas had not warned her about it she would probably never have noticed. And after leaving him with his plants and checking that there was no news of the new settlers yet, she made a quick check of the new premises. They were all practically identical to those of the other building. The only differences were that Taro and Chad's laboratory had been replaced by an engineering workshop, and in place of the gym area and infirmary there was a small campaign hospital with a latest-generation operating theater. It was impossible to know what might happen, so that it was a good idea to make sure human technology worked on the surface. Inside the premises there were only a couple of soldiers she had seen around the station. These she greeted politely.

She took a tour inside the premises. As usual, Director Patel and the other engineers had done an excellent great job and everything was perfectly in order. Then she had coffee in the new mess hall. She would rather have had one of Rakesh's teas, but apart from the fact that he was in the other mess hall, she did not want to impose on him, especially considering that he had a very limited amount available.

It's 11:40 and no-one's arrived yet. I hope nothing's happened, she thought, frustrated and concerned at the same time.

"Ada, where's the transport that's bringing the new arrivals?"

"They're still at the station," the AI said. "They're having some trouble with one of the new settlers.

"Let me guess: James Coogan."

"Bingo."

"What's the matter with him?"

"He didn't arrive on time," Ada explained. "It seems he spent the night with someone and was still refusing to leave. Director Patel and Deputy Director Green are trying to resolve the problem. Do you want me to let you know when they leave the station?"

"Yes, please. At least I won't have to wait here dying of boredom.

I'll find something useful to do while I wait."

Almost two hours later, Ada warned her that the shuttle had left the station. They had just had lunch at the base, so Emily decided to go to the other building, together with the rest of the group, and make the introductions.

The transport did not take long to arrive, and they soon heard voices in the corridor beside the mess hall area.

"Hi there, Emily!" Director Patel greeted her. "We knew you were all here. All those exosuits parked at the entrance could only mean one thing."

The director looked tired, which was logical enough considering that he had had to deal with that idiot James Coogan. But even so, the veteran engineer never lost his cheerful smile.

"Right," he went on, "I think it's time to introduce both expeditions to each other."

Patel named the settlers who were to go to the first building one by one, specifying their functions and posts. They all greeted their new working colleagues hesitantly. Emily noticed a certain disappointment in James Coogan's face when Director Patel introduced Paula and Emily, but when he found out that she was the director of the whole base and that he was going to be under her command, a repulsively smug smile appeared on his face. Emily knew that sooner or later she would have to deal with him.

Next, Patel turned to the new arrivals and began to introduce them.

"I'll start with Melissa Hudgens, neurosurgeon. She'll work with the base medical staff, and in case you didn't know, this has a fully-equipped latest-generation operating theater just behind that other door."

A dark-skinned woman with very long frizzy jet-black hair, very tall and slender, gave an almost imperceptible wave, but her serious expression never changed.

"This young man here is Erik Johansen," the director went on with almost paternal pride. "Some of you already know him. He's spent some time in charge of drones and general robotics at the station."

The young man, who was also unusually tall, greeted the others with a wave without saying more than a shy hello.

"Next comes Mr. Alberto Mendoza. On Earth he was—"

"A businessman," the man said quickly in a strong Mexican accent. "But here my business skills aren't going to be any use, I'm afraid. Although you could say I have privileged hands, so I'll be at the disposal of anyone who might need my help."

The Mexican, whose arms were covered in tattoos, mostly religious ones, was wearing a light-blue short-sleeved shirt with large white lapels, not completely buttoned. In this way he could display the many golden chains which matched the sizeable rings on his callused fingers. Emily noticed the wedding ring among them and remembered the deputy director telling her that his whole family was on the station, even though he had asked to be awakened first.

"Yeah... well put," the director said. He shrugged at the new settler's spontaneity. "This is Marko Babic. Until now he was one of those responsible for medical and general equipment on the station. In fact he'll go on doing that, but he'll be working down here."

Marco greeted everyone, but his gaze stopped at Emily.

"Hello there!" he exclaimed.

"And this other young man here is Martin Karlsson," Director Patel went on. "I think when we embarked you were still studying, is that right?"

The young man, who was lanky and so pale-skinned that he looked almost sickly, nodded shyly,

"And what were you good at?"

"Dunno... playing video games?" he said hesitantly.

There was some laughter at the reply. Emily, on the other hand, remained serious. Her responsibility would be to find him a job, and by now she had some ideas about where he might be of some help.

"I guess that's not a lot of use here," Patel said. "But we'll find some way you can be useful. This lady here is Emma Martin, who was a welder at the station. She was part of the first groups who were involved with adapting the ship, then later with installing this very building, so if any problem crops up in the facilities, she'll fix it."

The woman, who was of average height, with golden hair and deep green eyes, raised her hand and greeted everyone.

"Next we have Dr. Yara Moreau. Together with Dr. Hudgens and Nurse Evelyn... where are you, Evelyn?"—the nurse raised her hand— "she'll join the medical team at the base. Let's hope no-one needs their services and skills."

The doctor had dark wavy hair. "Hello, everyone," she said with a smile.

"Right," the director went on, "we'll move on to Mr. Park Min-jun. Did I pronounce that correctly?"

Mr. Park was a smiling, elegant Korean in his mid-thirties. "Perfectly. But you can call me Min. That's what everyone used to call me."

"Great. Min was the owner of a leading robotics company, which in addition provided a great deal of technology for the project. He's spent his whole life in this business, which is why we have this amazing robotics laboratory at the entrance. I'm sure his work is going to be very useful here."

"I hope to be of service," he said humbly.

"And lastly—"

"I don't think I need introducing, director… whatever your name is," James Coogan interrupted him, stretching his tanned gym-arms and pointing to himself. "I'm sure everyone here knows perfectly well who James Coogan is."

Emily could not help a sigh, and she knew by the reaction of the other new settlers, especially the women, that no-one there was much of a fan of this character.

"I don't know who you are," Alberto said, "but pleased to meet you."

James returned the greeting with his index finger as if he were shooting an imaginary gun.

"I don't think I've forgotten anyone," Director Patel concluded. "So that if it's all right with all of you, we can go on with the tour."

"We'll go back to our work," said Emily. "I just wanted to say hello to you all."

"Perhaps you could say a few words to the new arrivals," Patel suggested unexpectedly.

"I hadn't really prepared anything," she admitted, "but welcome, all of you, to this base. I think I can speak on behalf of all those of us who are here and say we're delighted to have you joining our little community. I'm sure that together we'll do everything we set our minds to. I'm dying to work with every one of you, and though we're all newcomers to this business of colonizing planets, I think we'll be able to resolve any problem or doubt you might have. So don't hesitate to ask us whatever comes to mind."

"You don't want to know what's going through mine…" James whispered.

Emily let this problematic character's comment pass. She knew she was going to need a lot of patience to deal with someone like that.

If you agree," she went on, "we'll leave you to get settled in during the rest of the day. Acclimatizing to gravity and these surroundings can be rather complicated. Tomorrow, at first light, we'll assign tasks to each one of you so that we can go on with planning the project."

"Thank you, Emily," Director Patel said. "Now I'll show you the medical area, so follow me this way."

Most of the group followed him, while Emily's colleagues began to leave the corridor in the direction of the entrance. Marko came over her to say hello.

"So we're here at last," he said.

She smiled. "I'm glad there's at least one familiar face among the new arrivals."

"I can imagine, especially bearing in mind that the alternative is dealing with that idiot James Coogan."

"Ada's already updated me about the trouble you had getting here."

"I'd like to tell you his behavior from now on will be different," he admitted, "but I'm afraid this has only just begun."

"Yeah, I think so too," she said resignedly. "I fear we've only seen a small part of what he's capable of."

"We'll try to help you as much as possible," Marko said, "but just on the way here there were one or two strained moments between the two doctors and him."

"That doesn't surprise me in the least."

"Well, I guess I'd better listen to the director's explanations," he said with a wave toward the other settlers.

"Yeah, off you go. We'll talk later on."

"Yeah, maybe over a cup of coffee?"

She nodded. "Sure. Take it as read."

She gave him a wave when he turned once again to say goodbye.

"He's rather cute," she heard Evelyn say behind her.

She was startled to hear this. She had thought they were all outside the facilities by now.

"Um…. yeah," she admitted nervously, "I guess so."

"Take it easy," Evelyn said with a chuckle as she went toward to the exit. "It's natural to have a look at the menu, even if you're on a diet."

"He's just a friend," she said defensively.

"Well, I wouldn't in the least mind being his friend too," Evelyn said with a smile.

They went back to their daily tasks in the other building, leaving the new arrivals to get acclimatized in their new home. However, a couple of hours later Emily received an urgent message from Ada.

"The deputy director requests your immediate presence on the station bridge," the AI told her.

"What's happened?" she asked, taken aback by the vagueness of the message.

"The deputy director would rather tell you in person, with the other members of the council present, to avoid unwelcome leaks."

"Okay, tell him I'm on my way."

She left what she was doing immediately and asked Lieutenant Balakova to take her to the station. She was able to arrive at the command post less than an hour after receiving the call. Captain Mei, Deputy Director Green and Commander Bauer were waiting for her there.

"Hello," she said hastily. "What's the matter?"

"Hello," the deputy director replied, "Sit down, don't worry, we just want to tell you about something Ada's found, something we don't want to get any further than this."

This was unnerving. "What is it?"

"As you know, Ada's actively tracking all radio and laser frequencies in every direction," he began.

Emily swallowed, unable to hide her nerves.

"This afternoon she informed us of a strange discovery."

"What did she find?"

"We're receiving a signal at intervals of exactly thirty minutes."

"What kind of signal?" she asked, anxious at all this beating about the bush.

"Although we don't yet know the real situation exactly, as the signal is very weak and incomplete, Ada has no doubt it's an SOS from the Galileo."

Her heart skipped a beat at these words. Receiving a signal from the Galileo would be good news, except that it was incomplete and every half-hour. Thirty minutes was the interval of time during which SOS calls were sent when the ship requesting help did not have enough energy to keep them going continuously.

"We've got to go to the rescue!" she said.

"Of course," he said reassuringly. "Ada has traced all possible trajectories, based on the pulse-rate of the signals and the different sensors along our station."

"And?"

"Despite the fact that it should be detectable at a glance, at least going by the size of the Galileo, I haven't managed to see anything."

"And what does that mean?" She was beginning to fear the worst.

"That it might be a smaller ship, maybe an emergency pod. Unfortunately, as the signal is incomplete, we have no more information available."

"Still, we've got to go to its rescue. I volunteer to do that."

He sighed. "I guessed you'd say that, but the protocol's clear on this. If we don't have the exact position of the ship in distress, we need to send a probe."

"But what happens if they need to be rescued?"

"The moment we make a full evaluation of the situation we'll send someone in search of them."

"It might be too late by then…"

"Emily," the captain said very seriously, "I'm sorry to be so blunt, but it's been several years now since the Galileo should have arrived here. It's more than likely that it's too late by now."

"The captain's right," the deputy director put in. "We can't risk more human lives. We'll follow established procedure."

Emily was managing to remain composed, despite her tears. "How far away is the signal?"

"It's coming from a trajectory two weeks from here," Ada said. "Although it'll be necessary for the probe to correct its trajectory as we rule out possible points in it. It'll probably take us longer to reach whatever's emitting the signal."

"Do you need anything?" the deputy director asked.

Emily was doing her best to keep her composure. "No thanks, I'm fine. I just want us to find them."

12
The second base

January 2, year 1

Second location, Kepler-442b

Robert had gone back with his team, together with several members of Director Patel's, to the second of the sites Ada had confirmed when they had first arrived. They had already transported most of the habitat modules to the clearing where the Icarus had been struck by lightning. Since then, several weeks had gone by. The project had brought a dozen civilians, scientists and engineers out of cryo to settle in this zone of the planet. However, Robert was not worried about either electrical storms or the proximity to the camp of one of the obelisks, or at least not seriously. What was worrying him most was that Captain Garth's minions might make an appearance and ransack the facilities again. That was why he was there, to prevent any possible trouble.

"The last transport's just arrived, sir," one of his subordinates informed him.

"Thanks, Sergeant Cooper. I'm going to take three soldiers with me to patrol the surroundings. Make sure Director Patel's engineers have everything they need."

"Right, sir."

He went over to a group of three soldiers who were watching a bulldozer digging a huge hole in the ground to install some of the supplies the facilities were going to need.

"You three, come with me."

"Yes, sir."

"You," he said to one of them. "Fetch one of the drones and get it started."

"Right, Captain Beaufort."

He wanted to check whether the surroundings were still safe, or at least whether they were in the same condition as a few weeks before.

"Ada," he called, "how far are we from the alien obelisk?"

"About five kilometers in a straight line," the AI said. "I've worked out a route of about six and a half kilometers, to get there in half an hour."

"Right then. Let's go!"

With Robert in the lead, the four soldiers followed the route Ada had overprinted on their exosuit helmets. They left the clearing, where preparations went on, and followed a small wooded valley. The trees here were not as large as those he had seen elsewhere. There was not much variation in level; they were near the coast and the terrain was fairly flat.

They came to a small stream which ran through the valley, though there was not much water in it. They presumed that it must reach the sea, or else filter deep into the soil. Even so, there was enough moisture there to allow other kinds of flora to grow.

I bet Chad would really enjoy this, he thought. *It's a shame the storm didn't allow us to explore this area well enough. It seems to be quieter, and there's not so much vegetation.*

One of the soldiers gave a start when he saw movement in the water.

"There's something there!" he exclaimed.

"It'll be some kind of alien frog," another one joked.

"No," the first soldier insisted. "It was a lot bigger than a frog."

Robert was remembering what had happened in the past. "Be careful. There are some pretty dangerous creatures here."

The young soldier who had seen the splash in the water went over to the area where the noise had come from. On the surface of the water were plants which resembled water-lilies, floating algae and slender reeds, all of them reddish, which hid the stream-bed despite the crystal water. He adjusted his rifle behind his suit and bent down to get a better view.

The scream was hair-raising.

Something leapt from the bottom of the stream onto the helmet of the young soldier, who took several steps back, but unfortunately tripped over a stone and fell on his back.

"Help!" he shouted desperately. "Get it off me!"

Robert ran to him. On his helmet was a kind of worm, sixty centimeters long and ten wide. The soldier was struggling to get it off him, without success.

"Move your hands away!" Robert ordered.

The soldier obeyed immediately, and a shot split the creature in half. Robert picked up what was left of the front part of the worm. After checking that the soldier's helmet was intact, he looked closely at the creature.

"Ada," he called, "is this something like a leech?"

"Yes," the AI confirmed. "In general it has the features of a leech, although this one is much larger and has some odd longitudinal fins which I understand help the animal to leap out of the water and adhere to those animals which come to drink."

"Soldier, clean your visor and be more careful next time. You were lucky the exosuit helmet is tougher than that slug's teeth."

The soldier got up, still frightened, and his comrades helped him clean off the animal's remains.

"And now let's move on again," Robert ordered. "We're not halfway there yet."

A little further on they saw a large herd of *fhores* grazing in a small clearing. The soldiers, who had not yet seen any docile animals, were impressed by the size of the herbivores.

"It's as if a rhinoceros and Bigfoot had mated," one of them whispered.

Although they came across one or two other kinds of animal, it was obvious that on this continent there was much less activity. After crossing several forests and going up the occasional small hill, Robert was able to confirm that the variety of flora was much less. For some reason, the biodiversity in that other area was far greater. Even so, this did not make the place any less habitable, nor did it mean that there was not enough variety to make it interesting from a scientific point of view.

It did not take them long to reach the small clearing where they had landed the first time, near the obelisk. Everything there looked quiet.

"Ada, scan the area thoroughly with the drone," Robert asked.

"Right away, Captain."

The drone flew over the wooded surroundings, where the obelisk stood out prominently.

"Can you detect anything unusual?"

"No, nothing at all," the AI replied. "Everything seems to be quiet."

"Yeah, too quiet," Robert murmured. "This silence is rather disturbing."

"Don't forget, there are very few insects or birds on this continent."

"Yeah, that's pretty clear."

With great care, they went into a wooded area and approached the obelisk. Here everything seemed to be as they had left it. Robert passed his hand over the corner Taro and Gorka had managed to extract a sample of the material from.

"What's this, captain?" one of the soldiers asked.

"An alien artifact of unknown origin."

"And what's it supposed to do?" another asked.

"We haven't yet found out. All we know is that it expels some very complex molecules from the four nozzles at the top and spreads them across the planet. There are thousands of them, placed precisely all over the two largest continents."

"Wow," the soldier sighed. "That sounds ominous."

"Relax, private. As long as you don't take your helmet off or let a leech tear it off you, you'll be safe."

They checked the area cautiously, but did not come across any kind of strange activity, so Robert decided that this was enough.

"Ada, take us back by an alternative route."

"Right, Captain Beaufort."

This time the AI led them by a route which followed the coast. The landscape was rather more pleasant than the one they had traveled through on the way there. In the distance they could see the sea, and even hear the small waves lapping the rocks on the shoreline rather half-heartedly.

"Now this looks more like a quiet place," said the soldier who had had the confrontation with the leech.

Another of the soldiers laughed. "And there aren't any critters that jump up in your face here."

Barely fifteen minutes later Ada gave them a troubling message.

"I've lost communication with the base."

"Eh?" Robert cried. "What happened?"

"I don't know. All I know is that I can't see them any longer."

"D'you have visual coverage of the area?"

"No. As I have no connection with the base, we can't communicate with the station or request satellite images. I'm sorry to inform you that we're isolated."

Robert had left a contingent of ten soldiers in the area, but they were all inexperienced. It was possible that without anyone to lead a proper defense, the rebels had taken over the camp with barely any opposition.

"Quick! We need to move fast!"

They were still ten minutes away from the clearing, and at least they had a GPS signal. Once they were close to the spot, he gave the signal to keep quiet and move without making any noise. He could see the tension in their eyes. None of them had very much field experience.

He decided to take up a position amid a thick clump of ferns. These would not provide them with much cover, but would at least keep them hidden while they assessed the situation. From there, their worst fears were confirmed. All the soldiers and engineers from the base were kneeling in a group in the middle of the clearing. Five rebel soldiers were holding them captive, with their guns aimed at them. At the same time several transport ships were loading the equipment which was destined for the facilities.

He noticed that the rebel soldiers had made a significant modification to their exosuits: they had dyed them with a kind of reddish paint which enabled them to blend far better with the vegetation.

Very clever, he thought.

The important thing in the situation was to find out who was in charge. But however hard he looked, he could see no-one who fitted Captain Garth's profile. And yet someone must be directing the operation from the surface. He enlarged the image on his visor until he recognized Sergeant Cameron, who was giving instructions to the rebel engineers who were loading the material into the transports. On the other hand, she was too far away for him to hear her,.

"Ada," he whispered, "can you detect their comms channel?"

"No, Captain. I can't pick up any signal from their exosuits."

This was strange, but at that particular moment he had other priorities. He needed to come up with a plan to free the hostages and regain control of the facilities. It was not going to be an easy task, because there was a wide distance between the hostages and their own position, and the clearing was so open that any movement would be detected easily. If they had had the right equipment they might have been able to eliminate the five soldiers who were guarding the prisoners, but they did not have precision weapons, which meant that they would have to find some other way of doing it.

Activity in the transports was concentrated in the furthest extreme of their position. If they were to approach from the other side of the clearing, they might have a chance to get to one of the transports and seize it. Robert did not think that Captain Garth would be capable of killing any of the hostages, particularly as he had already captured them. But he was sure that if the captain was not in the clearing directing the operation, it was because he was looking for him.

It was time to move, but when he got up to turn and try to reach the far end, he heard a familiar voice.

"Well, well, well," Captain Garth said as he and four other soldiers aimed their guns at him. "Look who we've got here."

"I think it's that slimy worm Captain Beaufort," Sergeant Reynolds added scornfully.

"It looks like it. And look, Sergeant," the captain added, "he's brought three of his newbies with him. How disappointing, Captain… did you really think that group you deployed here was going to stop us? Doesn't that seem rather insulting to you, Sergeant Reynolds?"

"Certainly, sir."

"Drop your weapons very slowly, no heroics," Captain Garth

ordered.

Robert motioned his soldiers to do as they were told. "Why don't you leave us in peace once and for all!" he said furiously.

"And let you be the only ones free to enjoy all this magnificent technology and our livelihood? In your dreams!"

"Those supplies belong to the project. Without them we can't go on with our work here."

"Don't worry about that, Captain," Garth said. "I promise we'll make good use of it all. And now"—he indicated the clearing—"start walking. Slowly, and without any sudden movements."

Robert and the three soldiers were led to the center of the clearing, where the other hostages had been gathered together.

"Look who we've found, guys!" Reynolds shouted.

The other rebels raised their arms and celebrated the fact that the entire military contingent of the new base had been captured.

Garth pointed to the three soldiers who were with Robert, "You three, on your knees with the others. Captain Beaufort, you follow me."

The two soldiers moved away from the group and went to the small cliff from which they had gone down to the cove to get a closer view of the sea the last time they had been there.

"You know, captain… well, I find it strange to be calling you captain. But as that's the way things are, congratulations on your promotion. I have to admit I think it was too soon to promote you, but I also think you've earned it. Congratulations."

"Thanks," Robert replied coldly.

"I know we've had our differences, and maybe I was too tough on you sometimes. But I always did it in the belief that you could manage to put up with it, and that way you'd give your best."

"What's this leading to, captain?" Robert asked impatiently.

"Well, I'm not too proud of what I did, but I'm sure those faint-hearted fucking bureaucrats are going to lead us to make the same fucking mistakes that made our societies on Earth fall apart. Their fucking moral superiority and weakness when it comes to doing what has to be done to preserve the safety and freedom of the citizens is going to end up destroying what little we have left."

"Is all this because of the sentence that was passed on Mr. Wiśniewski?"

"And what else would it be about?" Captain Garth snapped. "Because of those rich fucking brats who've bought themselves a ticket to the asshole of the universe? Don't play the innocent, Beaufort. I could cope with waking up without an arsenal. I can cope with having to deal with those space tourists. But what I wasn't prepared to put up with is the fact that the bastard who meant to destroy us wasn't going to get his just deserts."

"Wisniewski was tried and served his time."

"Given a lukewarm trial as one more proof of the weakness of a system that was already falling apart when that fucking meteorite did what it did. And on top of everything else he gets given the chance to start over again. A chance which, by the way, Admiral O'Connell never had. A decorated soldier who gave his life for his country, with plenty of successful missions under his belt. A single nail on the Admiral's finger was worth more than a hundred terrorist scum. And what about your dear commander? Did you see him honor his superior who died during the journey? We honor terrorists and let heroes fall into oblivion. That, and nothing else, is the fucking problem with society. Wherever we are, politics is the cancer if societies."

Robert remembered Wiśniewski's terrible end. "But that doesn't give you the right to take justice into your own hands."

"The fact that the leaders did nothing gives me all the right in the world," Captain Garth said, very seriously. "An eye for an eye, a life for a life"

Robert had no desire to reply to his ex-superior. It was abundantly clear that their points of view were diametrically opposed.

"You know, Beaufort, even though you may not believe it, I respect you. You have principles, and I like that in a soldier. But ever since I started this operation months ago I've always wondered whether I might have acted differently, more the way you would. So you're only going to hear this offer once. I want you in my group. I can recognize a soldier the moment I see one, and with you I knew as soon as you were assigned to my command on the Copernicus. I know with you on our side it would just be a matter of time before the others saw reason."

Robert turned to look him in the eye.

"I'd never go back to being under your command," he spat, "not even if my life depended on it. "You're a sadist."

"Okay then," Garth said quite calmly. "In that case be very careful. From now on I'm afraid our encounters aren't going to be as friendly as today's was."

"I'll be careful."

"Let's go back to the others. And remember, don't try to follow us or locate us, or make no mistake, I'll retaliate. We'll finish in no time at all, don't despair, and soon your beloved commander'll send a transport to pick you all up. We chose a day without much cloud, and I'm sure they'll be keeping an eye on everything that's going on down here."

Robert went back to the other hostages.

"Give my regards to the rest of the team," Garth added, "including your beloved doctor."

120

Robert glared at him, his teeth clenched. He was bitter about the condescension Garth had just shown him. As the captain had promised, the operation did not take long. All the transports took off with the structures and equipment of the facilities hanging beneath them from sturdy steel cables. Very soon they had disappeared over the horizon.

Half an hour later a transport from the space station landed in the clearing. Commander Bauer was there to supervise the rescue in person.

"Is everybody all right, Captain?" he asked Robert as soon as he reached the hostages.

"Yes, Commander. There was no violence."

Then they moved away from the group.

"Everything okay?" the Commander asked in a lower voice.

"Yes, sir," Robert said with a broad smile on his face. "Everything went according to plan."

13

A small crisis

January 3, year 1

Magellan base, Kepler-442b

She was alone, floating inside an escape-pod like the ones scattered throughout the station. She had no idea how she had come to be in it or what had happened for her to have ended up inside one. But something was wrong. The intermittent red light in the pod left no room for doubt. She moved around and checked the small control terminal. There was barely any energy or oxygen. She did not have many hours left. Her nerves made her leg begin to twitch, as it always did.

Suddenly she noticed that something was tapping on the hull. She turned and looked in every direction, but was unable to determine the exact spot the tapping was coming from. She looked out of the hatchway porthole, but could not see much, only the immensity of space. The tapping went on from another part of the pod, but it seemed to be coming from outside.

"Who is it?" she tried to ask, but no sound came out of her throat.

More tapping. It was coming from one of the sides, but it was moving toward the hatchway. Emily tried to shout, but was unable to. The tapping had almost reached the hatchway area. Then she saw that the person who was tapping on the pod was her father, Steven Rhodes. He was not even wearing an exosuit, only street clothes: jeans and a checkered shirt. It was the one her grandmother had given him for one of his birthdays. She looked at him and begged him for help, as she had so many times before. Like when she had been little and had some problem. Like the time when she fell off her bike and he came to her aid. And yet he too was in danger.

"Help me!" she heard him say with absolute clarity. Then he banged the hatchway hard. "Help me!" he called again.

Emily tried to open the hatchway with all her strength, but she could barely move the long handle which allowed manual opening of the pod. In a state of weightlessness she found it hard to exert enough strength, so she decided to put both feet on the hatch to give herself a support which would allow her to exert the necessary force.

After three failed attempts she managed to get it open it at last, but by this time there was no-one outside. She tried calling her father, but once again no sound came out. There was no-one there, there was nothing.

She went back inside the pod. He was there, inert, sitting in one of the seats, in his checkered shirt and blue jeans. His arms seemed to be floating free in the absence of gravity. His skin had taken on an intense blue color, and the thousand tiny ice crystals which covered his face glinted intensely, giving him a macabre look. There was no red light any longer, there was no energy or oxygen left in the pod. But she was still there, alive, and her father was not.

A sound came from behind her. When she turned she saw that the Galileo was there. But this time what was behind her was not Kepler-442b but a gigantic metal structure in the form of a ring. There were eight devices distributed symmetrically over the surface of that alien construction, forming an octagon. From them there emanated an intense electric blue energy which seemed to surround the empty space of the interior. In the void was a dark mass with a bright halo around it which did not allow the light to escape. It was a black hole.

The circular structure stopped emitting that electrical pulse, then without warning it began to collapse on to the black hole, lose its shape and swallow up the devices and the gigantic ring. The Galileo was the next to disappear. It was on the point of being swallowed up by the black hole when she woke up.

This is becoming too much like a habit, she thought, startled, as she sat up on her bed in a cold sweat.

It was still early, but she got up and took a shower, because she needed to relax a little. This time there was no-one else awake, and she could not even see the two guards on watch duty. She presumed they would be outside, as inside the base there was only silence. She decided to have a cup of decaf coffee to see if she could manage to soothe her nerves a little. She would have to have a word with Evelyn and Dr. Moreau. Perhaps these nightmares were the result of some disorder, either hormonal or dietary.

After a few minutes of relaxation in the mess hall, she got down to work. She went into one of the lab rooms and checked the new settlers' files. She wanted to assign each of the civilians a job which would best suit their abilities.

Hours later, when the rest of the base got up, she called them all together in the first of the facilities.

"This is a rather special morning," she began. "I hope you all had a good night and that your batteries are..." She stopped. "One moment. Where's Mr. Coogan?"

"He was still asleep," Martin said with a touch of amusement.

"He must be very tired," Dr. Hudgens added sarcastically, "what with all the nonsense he comes out with and the way he flirts with anything that moves."

Emily gave a loud sigh of resignation. "I'll deal with that later. Let's go on. I think the medical team can organize their own tasks by themselves." She looked at the three health workers of the expedition, "Evelyn, perhaps you could start updating Dr. Hudgens and Dr. Moreau about conditions on the surface of the planet and the results of the analyses you've been doing for us."

"No problem," the nurse said. "I'll take care of it."

"And maybe, though he's not here at the moment, you could include Lieutenant Ortiz, as he's the military doctor responsible for the base."

"Of course, consider it done."

"Thanks. Right, Mr. Mendoza…"

"Oh, you can call me Alberto, miss."

"All right then, Alberto. While we're on the subject, and if no-one has any objections, I'd like to avoid formalities. Let's use our given names." She turned to Alberto. "You can call me Emily, in fact any of you can. The functioning of this base is based on mutual trust, on trying to be a small family of humans working for the common good. Of course, we're all free to ask to be addressed differently. This said, Alberto"—she smiled—"I think you'd team up well with Gorka, our engineering manager. Besides, you both speak Spanish, so you can practice if you like."

"That would be really *chido*," Alberto said in his mother-tongue.

"Min," Emily went on, "you were a leading businessman in the robotics sector. Thanks to you, we have a wonderful laboratory available. I don't think I need to tell you anything, except to get together with Erik to carry out research. Unfortunately our resources aren't unlimited, but I'm sure that with your ingenuity we'll be able to make plenty of progress."

He nodded. "No problem,"

Emily turned to the young Swede. "Martin, I'm not sure where to put you, but I think you might learn one or two useful things with Min and Erik."

The young man shrugged without saying a word.

"Marko," she went on, "you'll have to take care of maintaining the electronics of the medical equipment and the energy consumption of the base. I don't need to tell you very much about how to do your job."

"I guess I'll be carrying out periodical checks of the facilities, along with meeting the medical and engineering teams."

"That sounds great. Thanks, Marko. And finally, Emma." She turned to the welder. "We don't have any specific tasks for you, but you'll be working with all the other teams, apart from guaranteeing that the integrity of the facilities isn't breached. We're in your hands."

"No problem," she said.

"Right then, let's get down to work. Kostas, do you have a minute?" she added.

"Sure, what's up?"

"Well, I thought of assigning James Coogan to you so he can help you with your daily tasks. That way he might learn to look after the crops and greenhouses and make himself useful, but as he seems to be rather problematic, I wanted to have a word with you first,"

Kostas gave a little sigh and looked away thoughtfully.

"Well," he said, tugging his beard, "he's not the person I'd most look forward to working with, but I understand that someone has to try and lead him along the straight and narrow. So okay, I'll be that person."

"Thank you, Kostas," Emily said, considerably relieved. "I appreciate the effort."

"Don't worry, I guess deep down he'll turn out to be better than he looks. Let's hope we'll be able to make him cooperate, even though we've started on the wrong foot."

Emily put on her exosuit and changed buildings. There the other members of the expedition were busy with their tasks. She left the exosuit in the corridor and went to the dorms, where total quiet reigned.

"Ada, deactivate the noise cancelation," she said.

"Done."

A loud snore was heard across the whole area. James was still sleeping like a log, ignorant of the frantic activity of his comrades.

"Ada, broadcast the sound of a cargo transport horn at full blast, please."

"I need your permission to broadcast a sound above the pain threshold of a human being," the AI said.

"You have my permission," she replied, and covered her ears,

A powerful truck horn sounded in the hall. Even with her ears covered, Emily was startled by the uncontrolled volume level. But the fright James Coogan suffered was one for the record books. He sat up in his bed in panic.

"Shit! Fuck!" he muttered, still sleepy and not understanding what was going on.

Emily waited for a moment.

"This isn't a pleasure cruise, Mr. Coogan," she snapped. "If you want to stay in this expedition, you'll need to behave a lot more appropriately, follow an established schedule and obey instructions—"

"You scared me to death," he complained, ignoring what she was saying to him. "My balls nearly came out of my mouth."

"Did you hear anything I said to you, Mr. Coogan?"

"No, sorry, sweetheart, I still have to check everything's in place, you really scared the shit out of me. I was having such a wonderful dream, which unfortunately for you, you weren't part of. But you spoiled it for me with all that summer camp nonsense."

Emily went up to him.

"I won't tolerate you speaking to me in those terms," she said indignantly. "This is not a hotel. We work here for the survival of all mankind. Do you find that a laughing matter?"

"Yeah, whatever," he said vaguely. "Who do I have to ask for coffee?"

"We're nobody's servants here," she said even more angrily. "If you want anything you'll have to prepare it yourself. And now get your ass out of bed, take a shower and join Kostas outside to get started on your daily chores."

She left the room in a fury. She knew James Coogan was a real moron, but she had some lingering hope that his behavior was only a façade for the benefit of the audience. Everything seemed to indicate that it was nothing of the sort. Even so, she did not want to throw in the towel. It was almost a question of principle; she could not allow someone with that attitude to break the harmony they had managed to keep until that moment.

Suddenly she began to feel dizzy. She was having trouble breathing, her heart was beating too fast and she could feel a strong pressure in her chest.

"Ada," she said as she stopped in the corridor and sat down on the floor, "call Evelyn."

The nurse appeared a couple of minutes later, followed by Dr. Hudgens and Dr. Moreau.

"Emily!" she exclaimed when she saw her on the floor.

"Don't worry, I think I'm better now."

Evelyn bent over to check her. She had not even taken off her exosuit.

"Ada told me you were having a minor crisis. But don't worry, it's nothing. We're here and you're fine. It's only a small anxiety attack. D'you think you can stand up?"

"Yeah, I think so."

"We're going to take you to the infirmary and we'll do a checkup, okay? Just to be on the safe side."

Emily gave a slight nod. Once they were in the medical area, Evelyn checked her blood pressure.

"You have a hundred and forty over ninety," she said. "It's high, but it's normal, given your history. Don't worry, it must have been something specific that made your pressure go up."

Emily nodded.

"I won't ask whether you're going through stressful situations, because it's obvious you are. Everything you've been experiencing since we set foot on this planet could affect anyone. Are you sleeping well at night?"

Emily remembered the nightmares of the last few days which had wakened her early, soaking wet, but she decided not to attach too much importance to them for the time being.

"Yeah, I guess so," she said untruthfully.

"That's a good sign," Dr. Moreau said cheerfully. "It's important to have a good rest and a healthy diet to avoid these minor problems."

"We have a blood test of yours from a few days ago," Evelyn said, "but I'm going to take another one, all right? Just to be on the safe side."

"Fine."

The nurse took her syringe and pressed it against the inside fold of Emily's arm. After a click, the little vial filled with her blood.

"D'you want me to give you a sedative?"

"Won't that be too much?"

"They're natural. Is there anything you need to talk about?"

Emily shrugged. "I don't think so, but thanks. Quite honestly, I haven't felt overwhelmed at all. Maybe a little stressed sometimes because of the importance of what we're doing, but I haven't felt that it was too much."

"Often we're not aware of our true mood," said Dr. Moreau. "I guess you must be worried about all this business of being the chosen one. And what happened yesterday at the new base won't have helped either."

"What happened at the new base?" Emily asked, worried again.

"Haven't you talked to Robert?" Evelyn asked.

"No, we haven't talked for a couple of days. What happened? Are they all right?"

"Yes, don't worry," the nurse said, "they're all fine. Oh dear, I thought you'd have heard. It seems Captain Garth and his minions have come back on the scene, and they took all the equipment for the new base."

"What!"

"Yes, but don't worry, there was no fighting. All the engineers and soldiers came back safe and sound, it was only the equipment that was lost."

"Excuse me," Emily said apologetically, "I need to speak to Robert right away."

"Of course, but try to calm down a little."

She went back to the other building in search of privacy.

"When were you going to tell me about the attack yesterday?" she asked angrily the moment Robert took the call.

"In fact nothing happened," he said defensively. "And there's really not much to tell."

"But something might have happened."

"Emily, I'm a soldier. You know this job is going to involve complicated situations."

"But I like to know that my… whatever we are… is all right. And not having to find out from other people that a sadist has attacked the base where you happened to be."

"You're right," he admitted. "I guess I should have called. But I know you're knee-deep with the extension, and I didn't want to add to your worries."

Emily toned down her anger at the sound of what seemed to be a sincere apology.

"Well then, tell me about it now."

"In fact it wasn't really very much. Everything was going fine. I left with three soldiers to check the obelisk nearby, and Garth and his men seized their chance to attack the camp and capture the small garrison we'd left there."

"Is everyone okay?"

"Yeah, it didn't escalate," Robert said. "In fact I had an interesting conversation with Captain Garth."

"Really? And what did he have to say?"

"I'll tell you about it when we're together. I'm afraid at the moment I don't trust communications too much."

"Okay. I suppose it's not normal that they should have known your location and the exact moment to strike."

"Exactly. It's quite clear that we have a breach of some kind. We'd do better to talk about certain things in person. How did things go with the newbies?"

"Pretty well, in general. Most of them seem good competent workers. But there's one who's going to give me plenty of headaches."

"Don't tell me: James Coogan, right?"

"That was an easy one, so don't sing your own praises, Captain Obvious."

Robert burst out laughing. "Is he making trouble?"

"This morning I had to go and wake him up myself," Emily grumbled,

"Having someone like that can be exhausting," Robert said. "Are you all right?"

"Yeah, I'm fine." She avoided telling him about her recent crisis.

"Well, cheer up. I have to leave you now, I have a class. But be very patient down there, and also very careful. I miss you a lot."

"I miss you too."

14

An unexpected visit

January 4, year 1

Second location, Kepler-442b

She had taken one of the sedatives Evelyn had given her so that she could get a proper rest after her minor crisis the day before. And in spite of her reluctance, it worked. In fact according to the rest report Ada had shown her, she had slept for nearly ten hours. It had been weeks since she had slept so much and so well, which meant that now she was rested and in a very good mood. So much so that not even James Coogan's antics could wipe the smile from her face. Before breakfast Evelyn gave her another blood test and checked her blood pressure.

"The results of yesterday's tests didn't show anything significant," the nurse told her as she checked the pressure monitor. "You're as healthy as one of Kostas' lettuces."

"I told you I didn't feel ill. I should imagine it was things building up in my mind."

"Yeah, probably," the nurse agreed. "In fact your blood pressure's back to normal, even a tad low. Although I see you're genetically predisposed to hypertension, so I understand those values are normal."

"That could be, I suppose."

"How do you feel?"

"Wonderful," Emily said. "I slept like a log."

"I'm so glad," Evelyn said as she extracted the blood sample. "Those pills are amazing, though you mustn't abuse them. It's always better if your own body rests all by itself."

"That makes sense."

"Right, there you are," she said, stowing the sample away. "And if you feel all right now, I don't think we'll need to talk tomorrow,"

"That's great. Thank you, Evelyn."

After breakfast, she had a word with Kostas.

"How did it go yesterday, with James?" she asked him.

"How did it go?" he repeated sarcastically. "Well, considering he didn't show up and that he spent the whole day at the gym"—he pointed to the infirmary area, where there was a small but functional gym—"I'd say it went well."

"He didn't show up? All day?"

"Not even to say hello."

Emily wondered what to do to make the infamous James Coogan see reason and join in with the routine jobs on the base. She switched to another approach, trying to aim at less confrontation this time. She waited for him to wake up, then went to the other building and went to speak to him when he had finished having a wash.

"James, I'd like a word with you in private."

"Sure, honey pie," he replied with his usual swagger.

She summoned up all her patience to ignore the comment, and they both went into one of the small rooms of the new building.

"Sit down, please," she said. "I think we got off on the wrong foot."

"Yeah, no doubt about that."

"Let me finish, please. I know all of you have paid astronomical amounts of money to be here. I know you consider yourself entitled to certain rights, that no-one can force you to do anything you don't want to. I know that on Earth you were someone important, that you lived off that overbearing image you've been living up to ever since you were taken out of cryo. But I also know there's another James Coogan in there, a shy one, an insecure one, who needs to be valued for what he really is, who needs everyone else's constant approval. And who wants to be part of something bigger than himself."

Emily gazed at his eyes with such intensity that he had to look away. But that sudden shyness lasted for only a few moments.

"What are you talking about? I don't need anybody's approval. James Coogan is a lot stronger and more independent than all that."

"Your gaze is giving you away, James," she said. "Even the way you talk about yourself shows I'm right. But I want you to know that I have a lot more patience than most people, so I'm going to tell you what's going to happen from now on: I'll go on treating you kindly and properly and you'll go on with your childish behavior, with your repertoire of dated phrases and suggestive comments. But the time will come when you realize that no-one's going to laugh at your jokes, and then you'll feel lonely and you'll want to be part of all this. And when that day comes, we'll all welcome you with open arms."

He laughed. "Hey, I didn't know the fare included sessions with a shrink."

Emily felt real pity for him, seeing the way he resorted again and again to the same would-be humorous clichés.

"Before we end the session," she said, playing along with the game, "I need to remind you that this place is dangerous. There are creatures here that could cut you in half, even with an exosuit on. And I'm sure there are bigger threats we haven't faced yet. Once you come face to face with those dangers, you'll want to have someone covering your back. If we don't all work together, if we don't share the tasks we're assigned, people might die. And unfortunately for everyone, humankind, or what's left of it, is in danger of going extinct. It depends on you to be a plus or a minus in our survival. It depends on you whether or not anyone remembers us."

This time James was unable to brush off something as serious as this with a clever quip, so for the first time he was silent. Emily got up from her chair and patted his shoulder as she went out.

"Kostas is expecting you," she added. "I'd really like you to give him a chance. Who knows whether the James we all want to meet might come to the surface at last."

She left the room with a triumphant smile, but she was barely given time to savor what seemed like a small victory in that war which would involve many more battles. As soon as she left the hall, Ada told her that Shildii was about to arrive at the base.

She hastened toward the mess hall to welcome him with a slice of the chocolate cake the young Keplerian enjoyed so much.

When she came out of the other building with it in her hand, he was already crossing the final stretch to the base. She waited for him at their usual spot.

"Shildii!" she called eagerly. "How nice to see you!"

He narrowed his eyes happily. "Hello, Emily."

"How are you?"

"Fine, except you and Rakesh don't come to Wiikhaadiiz ofiz anymore."

"You're right," Emily said. "We've been very busy lately. I've barely even been here, in our own village."

Shildii could not help licking his lips when he saw the piece of cake in her hand.

"Come on, let's take advantage of the sun and sit under a tree," Emily said, and they went over to one of the enormous large-leaved trees which marked the limits of the clearing.

They sat down on the ground, leaning against the giant trunk of a thousand-year-old specimen. Emily still very much enjoyed watching him eat. In some way she was beginning to see him as the younger brother she had never had, despite the many times she had begged her parents for one when she was little. Her life would have been very different with a brother, there was no doubt about that.

"Is it good?" she asked.

"Mmm," he muttered almost without breathing, while he did full justice to his breakfast.

At that moment a small creature the size of a squirrel fell from the tree. After a few confusing moments the little animal stayed staring at them. It tilted its small head to either side, apparently watching them curiously. It had two dark eyes, bulging and enormous, and tiny ears like little trumpets. In addition it walked by hopping on its hind quarters like a miniature kangaroo. Its tiny front claws met at its chest where it was rubbing them in an endearing gesture. It seemed to be wondering what was going on there.

"Well, what's this we have here?" Emily said.

"It's a *jush*!" Shildii cried in surprise. "It's very difficult to see them in Wiikhaadiiz ofiz, they're very slippery. I haven't seen one for a long time."

"To judge by the way it's looking at you, I'd say it wants you to share your cake with it."

Shildii eyed her as if weighing up whether he would really have to share his precious breakfast with the little animal.

"My mother always tells me not to feed wild animals," he said by way of excuse. "In case they bite me."

"That's good advice," Emily agreed. "So don't offer it food and it'll go away."

"Would you like to give it a piece yourself?" He offered her half of what was left of the cake. He too was intrigued by the creature.

"Okay, I suppose with the suit on it won't be able to do anything to me."

The boy smiled. "It might hurt its little teeth."

Emily put a tiny piece of cake on the palm of her hand and leaned forward a little toward the small *jush*, taking care not to come too close to avoid frightening it. At first the animal hesitated, tilting its head to both sides again as though evaluating the situation. Its little hands had stopped rubbing themselves together and were ready to grab the juicy sample which this strange metallic creature was offering it. In the end it could not avoid giving in to hunger and curiosity. In three small hops it came over and grasped what Emily was offering it with its little hands. Then it moved away with another couple of hops, and without taking its disproportionately large eyeballs off them put the food into its mouth. This began to move very fast as its tiny teeth chewed the chocolate cake. Meanwhile the two small bumps on its chin, like a comical beard, moved ceaselessly. When it had finished it leaned back on its long tail, which ended in a crest of feathers, and rubbed its hands together again.

"I think it wants some more," Emily said.

Shildii chuckled. "It likes cake, like me."

She broke off another piece and once again put it on the palm of her hand. The little animal hesitated, but not for as long as it had before, and came over in a couple of hops. It seized the cake quickly, but this time it did not move back and stayed only a hand-span away from her.

"You look friendly," she said when it had finished. "But now I've only got this piece left, though there's some cream on it." She held the last piece out.

The creature grabbed it and enjoyed it, moving its jaws rhythmically up and down. When it had finished, she chuckled when she saw that there was cream on its hands.

"Look," she said, "the same thing happened to you the first time you tried it."

The boy narrowed his eyes in amusement. "Yes, I learned that the hard way."

The little creature tried to rub its hands again, but this only made the cream spread. Looking rather annoyed now, it began to lick them, then went on to an intense grooming session. Emily and Shildii watched the process in silence, enjoying the animal's movements.

When it had finished, it stood there staring at them again expectantly. Seeing that this did not cause the desired effect, it moved its arms rapidly as though begging her to stretch out the hand it must have thought the food came out of.

"There's no more left, little one," she said, showing it her hand.

The creature sniffed at it, looking for a crumb or two to put in its mouth. Emily tried to stroke it with her other hand. At first it was slightly startled, but it soon realized that her intentions were not hostile and allowed her to pet it. Very soon it was lying belly-up in her lap, delighting in the caresses she was giving it.

"Do you want to touch it?" she asked Shildii. "It seems quite calm."

The boy nodded. Gathering his courage, he stretched out his right arm and began to scratch its dark, furry belly. Shildii made a sound that seemed to suggest he too was enjoying making a fuss of their new friend. They spent a good time with the little animal, talking about his family, about how he regarded the Wiikhaadiiz ofiz, and also about his future. He was not sure what he wanted to do when he grew up, but he seemed very interested when they talked about the history of both civilizations. In fact, as he told Emily, his father used to tell him stories about ancient Keplerian heroes who had fought against the Khol.

When they stood up, she decided to show him the little building Director Patel had built especially without any life support.

"Come on, I'm sure you're going to love this. I got them to build this little place so that we can welcome any of you when you come visiting and you can stay sheltered from the rain."

Shildii seemed enthusiastic about the idea, or at least he showed it with the usual narrowing of his eyes. When they went in, he gave a moan and shaded his eyes with his hand.

"There's too much light," he complained.

Emily had not realized that with only a few exceptions all the structures, furniture and equipment of the expedition were in neutral white. If to these were added powerful lamps which gave off an intense but cold light, the result was that an alien would have trouble keeping his eyes open. The Keplerians were used to a low intensity star and used no source of artificial light in their buildings, as they had infrared vision. The excessive light was damaging Shildii's retinas.

Immediately she turned off the artificial lights so that only what came in through the glass would illuminate the hall.

"Much better this way," he said, "Although it's still very bright."

Emily could not help thinking about how many similarities there were between the two species, but also about the things that made them so different. The perception of light was certainly one of those differences.

Shildii looked carefully around the room with its white tables and plastic chairs, impressed by how delicate they were.

"What kind of wood is this?" he asked as he felt the back of one of the chairs.

"It's not wood," she explained. "It's a synthetic material, made by humans."

"It doesn't look very strong."

Emily showed him the bedroom in the small module. There were four beds in it, separated by cabinets for each visitor. Shildii stared at the four mattresses and could not resist sitting down on one of the beds.

"Wow," he said, beaming, "this is very comfortable."

"Lie down," she suggested.

He lay on the bed, putting his legs up on the mattress and testing its firmness.

"It's very hard," he said, "but very even and comfortable."

"Do you think you could sleep on it?"

"Yes, of course. This is much more comfortable than hay. Except that it smells a bit strange, like this whole place."

Emily realized that with the exosuit on she could not perceive the smells of the place. She presumed it would be like the smell of newness which the other facilities still had.

"Yeah, I guess the smell must be strange for you."

"Do you humans smell like this?"

"No," she said with a smile, "we humans smell different."

"It's a pity you can't come out of your shell."

"It certainly is," she admitted. "Hey, if you'd like to stay overnight some day, you can. Providing your parents give you permission."

Shildii's eyes lit up. "And can I eat cake?"

"Of course you can!"

Shildii came out of the small room hopping joyfully, happy to have a place where he could have his favorite breakfast. When they came out of the module they saw that the little *jush* was still there, waiting for them.

"Well, well," said Emily, "look who's followed us here."

Shildii laughed. "I think it wants more cake. It's a very smart animal."

She went into the main building while he waited at the door. As she had no idea what the diet of a *jush* consisted of, she fetched several small packets of different things, vegetables, nuts, and even a cereal bar made with synthetic honey.

When she came out of the building again Kostas and James, who had come in for equipment, were chatting with Shildii.

"Here's Emily," said Kostas. "A pleasure to meet you at last, Shildii."

"Yes, a pleasure," he replied, narrowing his big eyes.

Emily saw that her conversation with James had been successful and that he seemed to be cooperating with Kostas. Although at that particular moment the look of terror on his face and the way he was hiding behind Kostas indicated that he was having a hard time seeing a Keplerian for the first time. Once they were alone again she opened one of the small packets of cooked vegetables and offered some to Shildii so that he could try them as well. She found, with some surprise, that he liked them well enough.

Then she put a piece of carrot and a couple of peas on her hand and offered them to the little creature, which this time unabashedly hopped over and sniffed curiously at the colorful food it was being offered. It picked up the carrot with both hands and put it into its tiny mouth, chewing determinedly.

Next she took two half-walnuts and a couple of almonds and broke off a piece of the bar, giving the rest to Shildii. She repeated the operation, although on this occasion the creature left the energy bar to one side and decided on the four nuts, which it devoured in no time at all. Emily had no idea how much an animal that size could eat, but she assumed it was quite a lot, bearing in mind that the *jush* had presumably eaten that morning. Certainly by now it did not seem to be demanding the food quite so eagerly.

Shildii also preferred the nuts to the energy bar.

"This sticks to my mouth," he said. "It's a feeling I don't like."

She laughed. "Yeah, that's true."

"But I like these things. They're hard and dry, but they taste good. What are they?"

"They're a special kind of fruit, like the ones sold at the Wiikhaadiiz ofiz market, but they're either left to dry or roasted on a fire."

Shildii seemed to accept this explanation quite happily.

"I have to go," he announced a little later.

"All right, but you know you can come here whenever you want," she told him. "I'm very glad to see you again."

"Yes, me too."

Emily gave his head an affectionate stroke and hugged him goodbye. As he walked away she saw a couple of figures in the distance watching the scene. When Shildii was some distance away, they disappeared.

"Ada, who were those people at the edge of the clearing?" she asked uneasily.

"A Keplerian girl and boy. They followed Shildii without his knowledge, and they've been keeping an eye on the base from a distance."

"And why didn't you say anything about it?"

"They didn't seem threatening. And anyway, in your present mood I think you needed to enjoy a quiet time with Shildii. When you're with him your body relaxes a lot."

"I certainly enjoy these moments," she said, "but next time let me know. Even if there's no threat involved, I'd like to know if anyone comes anywhere near the base."

Something tells me Shildii's beginning to be famous among his people, she thought as she went back to the facilities. *Let's hope that won't cause trouble for him.*

When she reached the door, she remembered that she now had a new friend following her everywhere.

"What is it, little one? I've no more food left, so what is it you want?"

She watched it tilting its head inquisitively to either side.

"Would you like some water?"

She was about to go inside to fetch a small bowl of water when she remembered that Kostas had a couple of tanks there, beside his crops. She found stacks of small plastic pots, some with a germinating plant in them, others empty. She took one of the empty ones, put a pebble inside it and filled it from one of the tanks.

When she came out of the greenhouse she threw the pebble away and put the little pot of water beside the entrance door.

"Right then, here's some water for you."

She could see no trace of the little animal.

However, she soon realized where it was. The little *jush* was coming toward her in a series of small hops, carrying something in its paws. When it came up to her it dropped the pebble she had just thrown away at her feet.

"Hey!" she cried in surprise. "I wasn't expecting that. On earth it takes months for pets to learn that trick. You're a very clever little fellow."

She picked up the pebble, very pleased with what the little creature had done. Once its trade goods had been delivered, it took three big gulps of the rainwater Emily had brought it.

15
Rebel radio

January 4, year 1

Asimov Space Station, Kepler-442b

Ferrara arrived at the space station as the sole passenger on the transport. Captain Beaufort had ordered her to come there to carry out some kind of mission. But she had no more information, only that she was to report at eight in the morning to be given further orders. Robert was waiting for her at the hangar with his arms crossed behind his back. He was not wearing his exosuit.

She stood to attention in front of her superior. "Captain."

"Sergeant. Glad to see you."

"And I'm glad to be here," she said, still with her exosuit on.

"Right, let's not waste time, we're leaving soon. Come with me."

"What's the mission about, Captain?"

"I'll let you know in due course," he said. "But not yet."

"Understood, sir."

They went across to another hangar, considerably smaller and more isolated, with a hall next to it. It was a small multipurpose room which as yet had no specific use and which was deep in shadow. The light came on as they went in. There, standing ready, were two exosuits.

Ferrara could not understand why the color had been changed. "What's this, then?"

"Don't you like the red, sergeant?" Robert asked. He had been amused by her reaction.

"I'd imagine it'll make us less visible on the surface," she said.

Robert thought very highly of Ferrara. Ever since she had come under his command there had been a good rapport between them. He only had to look at her eyes to let her understand what they were going to do and why he had not yet told her where they were going.

They put on the exosuits, which were painted in different shades of red and brown following a kind of camouflage pattern. After this they went back to the small hangar, where there was only one transport shuttle, which was ready to leave. Once they were on board, the pilot took off without even asking permission from the station control post.

"These suits and this ship have no communications," Robert explained as they approached the planet, speaking very loudly, "but they have the coordinates of the place we're going to. I don't need to explain how this works, do I?" He indicated a yellow ring which poked out above his left shoulder.

"No, sir. It's very clear. And I think I know where we're going now."

The transport they were traveling in was slightly different from the others. It was smaller and more robust, built for another set of tasks such as spreading gas or other compounds through the upper layers of the atmosphere. It was not designed for passenger transport. Even so, it was a non-military vehicle which was suitable for what Robert had in mind, which was no less than parachuting from it.

"We're going to do a HALO jump, which stands for High Altitude Low Opening. We'll be taking the plunge from around thirty-five thousand feet, a little over ten kilometers, and we won't open our parachutes till we're down to three thousand feet, less than a kilometer from the surface. When we reach our destination I'll give you more details of the mission."

"Understood, sir," she said with a smile. "At last, some action!"

It was not long before they were crossing the outer layers of the atmosphere, which meant that they could hear the friction on the ship's hull from inside. They spent some time in silence, enjoying the lively swaying caused by the different densities of Kepler-442b's atmosphere. It was not long before they began to feel some stability in the ship. A red light began to blink in the cargo bay, where they were. The pilot opened the small door which separated both areas.

"We'll be at the launch area in five minutes," he called.

"Okay. Thanks, Lieutenant."

Robert unstrapped himself from the seat and got up. They had gravity once again.

"We'd better get ready," he told her.

They both went to stand close to the hatch of the cargo bay, which would open in the next few moments. They secured themselves with harnesses to the structure of the bay itself. At last, the door began to open. A deafening noise engulfed the inside of the transport, and they both felt the strength of the wind when it came into the space. The light was still red, but both of them knew it would very soon change color.

The light turned green.

First Robert, then Ferrara, jumped out without hesitation. Both of them took up an aerodynamic position to be able to get as close as possible to the landing-site. Robert checked his visor, which was showing him their exact position, and Ada, even with only the GPS communication at its disposal, marked the optimum course as they went. In little more than two minutes they were at an altitude of a thousand meters. Robert made sure Ferrara was following behind, as they had planned.

The visor informed them when they arrived at the right point that it was now time to open their parachutes. Robert pulled the yellow ring, but nothing happened. Nine hundred meters. He pulled again, with the same result. Eight hundred meters. He pulled a third time, and it still failed to unfold. Seven hundred meters. The tops of the trees on the other side of the range, where the Magellan base was, were coming closer and closer. He felt for the red ring of the emergency parachute. Six hundred meters Ferrara was no longer behind him. He guessed that her parachute had worked properly and that by now she was sailing calmly over the landing-area. Five hundred meters. He tugged at the red ring, and finally a parachute emerged from the back of his suit. Four hundred and thirty-five meters left before touchdown.

As he steered the parachute, apart from relaxing his heart-rate, he took a moment to check how far he had deviated from the intended landing-site. He was almost five kilometers away, which meant that he would have to walk quite a way to rejoin Ferrara. At least the absence of wind allowed him to maneuver to try and get closer while he was still in the air. What he was not going to be able to do was search for some area clear of trees to land on. He would have to go through the tops before he reached the surface.

The impact against the first branches was not too violent, but then he came down to a height where they were already substantial. In addition, the wood on the trees on this planet was quite a lot harder than on Earth, so he ended up hanging fifteen meters or so above the ground.

He looked up. The parachute was now stuck in the upper branches. Luckily the suit had saved him from multiple scratches and dislocated joints.

When at last he stopped swaying, he tried to work out how to get down from there. The suits were not meant for a jump from a height like that, so he thought of using its thrusters to soften the fall. He reached for the knife on the side of his right leg, then with great care began to cut the taut lines which joined the parachute to his suit and were keeping him hanging from the crown of the tree.

He cut the first two cautiously, in case this unbalanced him. The others tensed even more, and he spun round on himself at least ninety degrees. For the moment he seemed stable. He went on with two other lines, and this time the parachute fabric felt the effect, as all its weight was now resting on a smaller surface. He slid a little further down to the ground, but stopped before he had gone a meter. When he felt stable again he got ready to cut two more lines, but at that moment he heard worrying sounds from below.

He could see six quadrupeds, each the size of a large dog, prowling around the area. Their maws, divided into three jaws, reminded him of the creatures which had attacked them a few weeks back, taken the life of one of the soldiers and injured anther seriously. Even though these were smaller, they looked equally fearsome. Little by little they were coming closer to his position. They gave guttural growls as they came which were definitely threatening.

"Great, as if I didn't have enough trouble getting down from here as it is," he told himself.

He considered his options. He could use his gun and try to finish them off. As long as they could not reach him, there was no danger. But that would reveal his position. If there were any rebels in the area, they would know he was there and the mission would be compromised. He could wait for Ferrara to get him out of this tight spot, but unless he dealt with them first, the sergeant might have problems with all six of the creatures. He remembered clearly what their big brothers' claws were capable of doing to the exosuits. No, he had to do something, because if not he would be putting Ferrara in danger.

He reached for an object on the side of his suit which was shaped like a small extended cylinder. After going over his plan in his mind and heaving a long sigh, he operated something on the object and threw it to the ground. While the creatures were looking at the object, he grasped the remaining lines joining him to the tree and cut them as quickly as he could. He shut his eyes when he began to fall. Everything happened in an instant.

A powerful flash of light, which stunned the creatures, flooded the place. Robert activated the suit thrusters to cushion his fall and allow him to land on the ground with his knees flexed. The edge of his commando knife gleamed in his right hand. He opened his eyes and took advantage of the creatures' confusion to run toward the one which seemed to be the biggest of them all. It failed to see him coming and he was able to plunge the blade, almost twenty-five centimeters of it, into its neck, then use the resistance given by the suit to run the knife along the rest of the beast's throat. It fell lifeless to the ground with a desperate moan.

Now for the next, he thought.

With a powerful leap he hurled himself at the second creature, which was about five meters from the first. Same attack. This time he did it from below, so violently that he almost slashed the beast's throat from side to side. From the animal's neck there began to gush a blackish liquid which almost covered both his hand and his knife. This time he pushed to the right to widen the laceration. The movement ended with the creature on the ground.

One less, he said to himself.

He repeated the operation against the third animal, which by now seemed to be regaining its sight and managed to attempt a few defensive bites. But it was no rival for someone trained, like Robert, and it met the same fate as its two companions. By the time he turned toward the three remaining animals they could see him and were watching what had just happened in horror. Far from offering resistance, they were hesitating. They knew he was dangerous, that he had just killed their leader and two other members of the pack as if by magic.

He set off running toward them, knife in hand, and gave a threatening shout which also served to release some of the adrenaline his body was generating. None of the three animals stayed to see the result, they fled the way they had come.

"That's right," he said, his adrenaline still running high, "Away you go!"

He checked the state of the parachute in the tree. Leaving the evidence of his presence up there was not an ideal plan, but there was nothing much else he could do. If anyone found it, he would be a long way away by then. He wiped the blade of his knife on the pelt of one of the creatures and stowed it away again in the small compartment in his suit. He checked his visor; he still had a fair way to go to join Ferrara at the landing-point.

I hope she had more luck than I did, he thought as he set off.

A while later he reached the clearing where he should have landed in the first place. He found no trace of the three surviving animals on his way. However, Ferrara was there waiting for him, with her parachute folded and hidden under a clump of ferns.

"I thought I'd have to go in search of you, captain," she said. "Are you in one piece?"

He nodded. "Yeah, I'm fine. But I almost didn't live to tell the tale."

"What happened?"

"What didn't happen, you mean. My parachute refused to open, and I had to use the reserve. And unfortunately for me, this whole area to the north"—he pointed behind him—"is dense forest, so I was left hanging from the trees for quite a while."

"Oh, my God. I wondered whether to go in search of you, but as we don't have comms we might have crossed paths without realizing, so I waited."

"You did well, sergeant," Robert said. "If you'd come looking for me you'd have come across six dangerous animals that did their best to include me on their menu."

"I don't like the sound of that."

"I was lucky. I remembered the Keplerians have such good sight that they don't need to put lights in their rooms, so I used a blinding grenade."

"Well done, captain."

"Yeah, if not for that I'd have had to reveal our position by using the rifle."

"And what became of them?" the sergeant asked.

"I killed three of them. I think one was the leader of the pack, and the other three ran away when they got over the flash."

"That's quite a way to start the day, sir."

"You can't afford to get distracted for a second on this planet," he said. "Well, we'd better get going, sergeant. The place we're heading for is almost forty kilometers to the south."

"Right, sir. Do I understand we're heading for a possible base of the rebel army?"

"Bull's eye," Robert said. "I'll bring you up to date during the first ten kilometers, then after that we'll go on in silence. We don't want to attract the attention of any undesirables."

They set off on their private excursion, following the edge of the clearing where Ferrara had landed. The day was partly cloudy, so that the light was not very bright, and even less so once they went into the wooded area which extended to the south.

"Right," he began. "Commander Bauer ordered me to try and find the location of the rebels. Not with any clear intention of attacking their facilities, but to monitor the area on a permanent basis with a new satellite. With the station fixed on the area of the Magellan base, the satellites can't cover much more territory. As we've always taken it for granted that the station comms were compromised, apart from the fact that we're sure they've infiltrated someone who could warn them about what's happening on the station, all this was organized using very low-tech espionage methods."

"Low tech?" she repeated.

"That's right, the whole operation was organized in spots where there were no surveillance cameras, and planned without saying a single word aloud."

"And how was that?"

"We did it the old-fashioned way, using paper and pencil."

Ferrara stopped for a moment.

"Are you telling me you planned a military espionage operation using a piece of paper and a pencil?"

He nodded. "Yes, sergeant. That's exactly what I'm telling you. In fact it wasn't easy. There's not a lot of paper in the station. I had someone in the store moving containers and boxes around till we found something to write on the way they did in the twentieth century."

"And that way you avoided any chance of someone listening in," she said, impressed. "Intelligent. Simple, but very intelligent."

"The thing is that we organized the settlement of the second base, setting a trap for the rebels. We took advantage of the fact that they knew the original plans of the project beforehand to check how compromised our comms were. We pretended to be setting up a permanent base at the second site and acted as if we were really going to follow through with it."

"And that wasn't true?"

"Yes and no," Robert said. "Everything was a genuine effort, the engineers thought they were working according to plan, and in a way that was true. The plan being that if Captain Garth didn't know about our movements or didn't intend to play the same trick as he did with the enlargement of the Magellan, the base would be installed genuinely and the scientists would begin to carry out their research there. But if, on the other hand, our comms were compromised and they were aware of when we were going to settle in the other continent, Captain Garth was going to try and carry off everything we planned to set up on the surface."

"But how does that benefit us?"

"We put a high-frequency transmitter in one of the habitat modules."

The sergeant thought about the plan the captain and her commander had worked out for a few moments, then began to unravel it.

"The suits and satellites communications don't use high frequency signals, which means they'll be harder to detect. But how did you know they wouldn't turn up with guns blazing?"

"Captain Garth is a madman, but above all else he's a soldier in the classic sense of the word. Although it might not look like it, he operates by a strict military code. He only acts wildly when he thinks there's been some action against that military ideal he has in his mind. Concepts of treachery and terrorism are meaningless to him. He wouldn't be capable of killing innocent soldiers or engineers, however much they might oppose his goals."

"Still, suppose one of the soldiers had opened fire on the rebels?"

"Well, I made sure that didn't happen. All the soldiers who came with me were straight out of the academy. I gave them explicit orders to hold their fire no matter what might happen, and I made sure I was absent for quite a while so that Garth would have free range to burst into the camp."

"You opened the door for him."

"And not only that," Robert added. "When I went back to the area I made sure I approached from his less vulnerable flank, so that they'd spot us easily and overwhelm us without firing a single shot."

"Are you telling me you surrendered on purpose?"

Robert smiled broadly. "That's exactly what I did. I let him think he'd won. I guessed the captain's ego would make him lower his guard and never even dream he'd just fallen into a trap that had been set up to trick him."

"Well done, Captain!" Ferrara exclaimed. "I have to congratulate you. It sounds a magnificent plan."

"Once he took the bait, all we had to do was release a drone without any communication with the station to make a high-altitude flight over the different areas of the planet in search of some signal that would match the five megahertz of the transmitter we installed in one of the modules they took."

"And that drone has given us the location we're heading for right now," she guessed.

"Correct."

"But even so, I have a doubt. How have they been able to hide all the equipment they stole from the satellites?"

"That's a good question," Robert said. "We think they've set up their bases following the same strategies the Keplerians use to hide from the Khol."

"You mean they hide it under the trees?"

"That's right. And they move with the transports on cloudy days or in the dark, at night, to avoid Ada being able to track them in plain sight."

"As there's no moon to reflect the light of the star, the darkness is almost absolute."

"Exactly, and unfortunately the infrared optics aren't powerful enough to track their movements from the satellites."

"But moving in the dark without GPS could be very dangerous."

"Yeah, that's the only part we haven't been able to explain as yet. Flying and making blind approaches by night without having any satellite help is suicide, and it's not easy to predict the weather so that you can organize so many operations to be carried out only during cloudy days. So another of the more feasible hypotheses is that they've sabotaged something at the station, so that they can go on using our infrastructures without our knowledge, escaping from Ada's control."

"And now we're about to find out where they're hiding," said Ferrara.

"That's right." He checked their position. "And we'd better go on

146

in silence from now on. We don't know what range they're able to keep an eye on from their position. Be careful where you step, sergeant, we might stumble on some kind of hidden trap."

"I'll be very careful, Captain."

They moved on in silence, taking every precaution as they moved through the vegetation. There was little light, as the day was cloudy, but there was enough to allow them to move fast. Although she was incommunicado, Ada was able to go on showing them the way on their visors. These were some tense moments, because any noise coming from an animal, even the movement of the branches in the wind, forced them to stop for a moment or two to verify its source. What in normal conditions would have taken only a couple of hours was taking them twice as long.

When they were less than a kilometer from the place the hidden signal was coming from, they began to move on one by one, with synchronized movements, keeping hidden behind the trees, from one to the next, carefully checking their surroundings as they tried to find something that could indicate the presence of the rebels in the area. There was no trail; they had not even found footprints or anything to tell them they were close to their destination.

And then they saw it. Two hundred meters away, behind a large tree. It was one of the habitat modules the rebels had taken after that recent scuffle. Robert peered out from the safety of the tree they were hiding behind. There seemed to be no activity, or anything else, in the surroundings, only the module. A slight shiver ran down his spine, and the shadow of disappointment began to be reflected on his face.

"I think they've detected the transmitter," he said.

"Yeah, I don't think there's anyone here."

"Still, we'd better be careful. We could be the prey ourselves now."

Ferrara nodded. They checked the area with extreme care, paying special attention to the ground. Only when they were close to the module did they see one or two traces of human activity. There were prints, but whoever had made them must only have been passing through.

They went to one end of the module. The door was open wide and a few dry leaves had drifted inside, but otherwise it was empty except for a chair. Robert went to it very carefully. On it there was a working terminal with a message: Turn me on.

Ferrara examined it. It did not appear to have been interfered with.

"Doesn't look dangerous," she said.

Robert did what the message said and turned it on. Garth had left them a message.

Hi there, Captain. I have to congratulate you on this attempt. You were very close to achieving your aim. If not for a lucky coincidence, we'd never have been aware of the transmitter hidden in this module. I'm glad to know there's someone worth locking swords with in the project. So you can rest easy, captain. This time we haven't loaded the module with explosives.

But be careful. You're getting too close, and that goes against our little agreement: you don't try to track us down and we don't retaliate against the station. Bear that very much in mind, captain. Try not to let this dispute between the two of us try my patience too far. I don't want thousands of innocent deaths on your shoulders.

Captain Tyson Garth.

Over and out.

The communication ended there. Robert and Ferrara looked at one another in disappointment.

"It was a good idea, Captain," the sergeant said, to encourage him.

"But not good enough," Robert said.

16
The discovery

January 5, year 1

Magellan Base, Kepler-442b

Emily wanted to find out what progress Chad and Taro had made in their research using cloned mice and other small animals. It would play an important part in establishing the impact of the different alien molecules on complex organisms. But when she arrived at the lab after breakfast, the only person she found was Taro.

"Where's Chad?" she asked. "I wanted you to tell me what progress you've made."

"He's looking after those two *fhores* outside," Taro said. "He feeds them, walks then around, talks to them..."

"Anybody would think you were jealous."

"If he ever paid as much attention to me as he does to them, then maybe," Taro said indifferently.

She called the biologist on the radio. "Chad."

"Yes, Emily?" she heard from the other end.

"I'd like you to bring me up to date about what you've been doing these last few days."

"Sure. I'll be in straight away. Although... it might be best if you were to come out. There's someone here I'd say is expecting something."

"Who?"

"I'm not sure what it is, you'd better come out."

Emily got into her exosuit to see what he wanted her to see. As soon as she came out of the base she knew what it was. There, almost in the same spot she had left it, was the little *jush* she had shared some food and water with. The creature gave little cries of joy at seeing her again and came to her with little hops, moving its tiny claws rapidly.

"Well, well, well," she said in surprise as she bent down to pick the little animal up and pet it. "You again? Hungry, are you?"

The creature showed its appreciation of her stroking it with several moans of pleasure. Then it stood up in her hands and began to scamper over her arms, neck and back. She could hear its minute but sharp claws as it ran them over the metallic material of her exosuit.

"You seem to have picked up a pet," Chad said when he came to her side.

"D'you think so? All I did was give him something to eat yesterday."

"Well," the biologist speculated, "maybe this species doesn't have any natural predators, and that's why it's not afraid of coming close."

"What do you think it is?"

"By the looks of it I'd say it's something like a squirrel. It reminds me of some kind of Earth lemur."

"Shildii says it's a species called *jush*."

Chad gave a shrug. "He'll certainly know a lot more about the local species than we do."

"D'you think it's dangerous?"

"I don't think so. To judge by its size it looks like a fruit-eating or omnivorous species. The greatest danger it could pose, which would be true of any other animal species on the planet, is that it might infect us with some unknown kind of disease. Or that we ourselves might infect them. As long as we go on using the suits and don't bring them into the base, I don't think there's any risk."

Emily brought out some food in a bowl and refilled the small plastic pot with water. The little animal appeared delighted to be given these supplies by its new friend.

"You'll have to give it a name," Chad pointed out.

"A name?"

"Well, of course, if you're going to feed it every day, then it becomes your pet." You'll have to give it a name."

"Hmm, I hadn't thought of that. I never had pets at home. I've no idea what to call an alien squirrel."

Chad thought for a moment. "How about Lemy?"

"Lemy?" she repeated hesitantly. "What kind of a name is that?"

He shrugged. "Well, it looks rather like a lemur, right?"

Emily thought for a moment. She liked the idea.

"All right then, little one," she said as she stroked its back. "I'm going to call you Lemy."

They left it there to enjoy its little banquet. Taro was waiting for them inside the lab, analyzing a mineral sample Emily herself had brought from her last trip.

"Okay, bring me up to speed. How are the tests going?"

150

Chad sat down in his chair again.

"It's still early to draw conclusions, but we've made a few discoveries. To start with, we've exposed several of the mouse clones"—he indicated the terrarium, where there were a dozen mice in individual units—"to the different alien molecules, in different quantities and conditions. The main thing is that all of them are fine, just as Ada's previous simulations showed. Exposure to the molecules doesn't seem to have any harmful effect. The results were mostly harmless or imperceptible."

"Mostly?"

"There've been some very interesting cases from the biological point of view," he began.

"Get to the point, Chad," Taro said reproachfully. "You like to spin too many words."

"Let me enjoy my moment of glory!" he protested.

"You're wasting Emily's time."

"Okay, I'll get to the point. The thing is that in subjects where there was a greater concentration of one, and only one, of the types of molecule, we've noticed an obvious physiological change. Right now we have a subject that's generated an additional thirty per cent of bone matter."

"Do you mean one of the mice has strengthened its bones?"

"That's right, we took several x-rays of all of them and there's a significant difference. So to make sure, we did a bone densitometry reading as well. The results are very enlightening." He showed her the data on his screen. "The subjects which were more exposed have experienced a greater strengthening, at both bone and muscular levels."

"So does the molecule create super mice?" Emily asked.

"Not exactly," Chad said. "Taro has a theory about that."

"We think the molecule makes the subjects adapt to the environment around them," Taro explained. "If you look at the data, this proportion of bone and muscle growth coincides with the difference of gravity between Earth and Kepler-442b."

"Thirty per cent," Emily murmured.

"Exactly," Chad said.

"So why are there some of them that haven't evolved in that way?"

"Because we've given them another type of molecule," said Chad. "We think each of them has a series of different properties, and so they affect different types of living beings. To validate this theory, we're going to do a test with a plant Kostas is going to help us grow inside here, in a controlled environment which resembles that of Earth."

Emily was thoughtful for a few moments.

"Chad, I'm going to ask you a personal question," she said suddenly. "You don't have to answer, because it's a medical issue and it's sensitive information. D'you remember when we came out of quarantine, and Dr. Schmidt did those analyses for us?"

"Yes," he said with a smile. "And I think you're on the right track. When we were exposed to the molecules after that fateful accident, our bodies reacted in the same way."

"The doctor told me I had an abnormal amount of calcium," Emily said, "and she gave all of us the same tests you gave the mice."

"My bone density was higher than normal too," Chad said. "I suspected that, but I had no way of corroborating it."

"But why did it only affect some people?" Taro asked.

"It was a pretty chaotic day," Emily pointed out. "But Chad, Robert, Ferrara, Lieutenant Balakova and I were the only ones who weren't on watch-duty."

He realized what this meant. "And you all took off your suits in the emergency tent."

"Exactly," said Chad. "We were exposed to the molecules that came in with the suits themselves, even though very briefly, because the tent wasn't equipped to decontaminate on entry."

"That's a great discovery, Chad," said Emily. "So now what?"

"Now we have to confirm the theory that different molecules affect different types of living beings."

"We have four types of molecules," Taro explained. "One of the things we'll have to establish is that if there's a molecule that specializes in the animal kingdom and another in the vegetable one, what are the other two for?"

"That's a good question," Emily said thoughtfully. "Keep at it, guys. You're doing a great job."

"Something else," Taro said. "I wanted to talk to you about those two stones you brought from that lake."

"Did you find anything?"

"Yes. Ada was right, they're almandine garnets. They're also found on Earth. There's nothing special about them, they were used in jewelry and also to make jewels and abrasives. Nothing mystical or supernatural, I'm afraid."

"Oh dear," she said with a touch of disappointment. "That's what I was expecting, but I still hoped they might have something magical about them."

That same afternoon she went to the station and briefed the deputy director about all the news at the base. The cooperation of the new members, progress in the research and everything about the future conclave were some of the issues they talked about. But in reality she had gone to the Asimov for other reasons which she did not discuss with anyone. She suspected that the rebels had manipulated something in Ada's control room which allowed them to know at every moment what was happening on the station. Her idea was to go over the place thoroughly, to see whether there were any grounds for this suspicion.

She went alone, and did her best to pass unnoticed until she reached Ada's control room. She tied her hair up in a bun and put on electromagnetic boots at the axis of the Centrifuge. She was going to need her hands free and some point of support so that she could operate the console freely and check Ada's hardware cabinets. The lack of gravity made everything more complicated. After the brief walk, she went into Ada's control room.

I don't think anyone's seen me, she thought, feeling like the central character of a spy novel.

She took out various tools and devices from her backpack which would allow her to carry out a number of tests in the hall, then put them all on the desk which housed the AI's private access terminal.

"Hello, Ada," she said.

"Hello, Emily," came the AI's reply. "To what do I owe the honor of your visit?"

"Just a simple routine check," she said untruthfully, trying to appear calm.

"Do you want me to carry out a full analysis of my present state?"

"Not at the moment."

"Okay, I'll wait for your instructions."

At least for the time being, Emily did not want Ada to get involved in her own diagnosis. If she herself had been unable to find anything strange in her core, it probably meant that Captain Garth's engineers had managed to hide their tracks.

Her first suspicion had to do with the room itself. Ada's hall was isolated from the rest of the station. No kind of electromagnetic signal could either enter or leave the place through its walls. The main reason was that an electromagnetic signal could affect her quantum processor, but it was also a good system for preventing an external attacker from trying to access Ada from outside. Any communication with the AI was made through a complex system of wiring which crossed the door via the ceiling. Everything came here via wires and cabling which enabled her to receive information from the millions of devices which made up the station.

Hence it should be impossible to detect any kind of wireless transmission inside that hall. Emily operated one of the devices she had brought with her, and which she had prepared over the last few days in her free time. This device scanned all possible frequencies in order to detect any kind of wireless emission within the room. If anyone had altered the insulation of the walls in any way, this device would detect it. She waited patiently for the five minutes it took to detect signals across all the possible spectrum. The result was negative.

Well, that really doesn't surprise me. It would have been too easy.

But this was not her chief asset. She knew that Captain Garth's men might have a copy of her own identification chip to gain access to this place. They could have done anything to Ada on the spot, instead of doing it wirelessly.

Let's move on to the next point.

"Ada, show me the plans of this room."

"Right away."

The AI showed her a diagram which showed every one of the systems that made up its brain, together with their interconnections. On the one hand were the cabinets containing the processors and the memory, which unfortunately she had already had to manipulate once. On the other hand was the complex tangle of data cables which connected all the cabinets and then converged at the terminal where she herself was at that moment, then went on to the top of the exit door. And finally, a series of power cables connected Ada's hall with the one next door which contained the three nuclear fusion generators which fed the entire facility.

"Why are there three generators, Ada?" she asked.

"All three are isolated from the others in the station. They were designed to feed me at only ten per cent of their capacity, so that if two of them failed, the system would go on working with a small percentage of the capacity of one of the generators. In the case of a catastrophic failure of all three, there's an auxiliary entrance which would allow me to connect to the general electrical system of the station."

"I see."

Emily was thoughtful for a while. She went over the plan several times, wondering over and over again how dozens of ships, habitat modules and stolen exosuits could have passed unnoticed by Ada.

Someone's installed something somewhere that means not all the information gets as far as Ada, she thought. *But where? There are thousands of kilometers of wire converging in this room.*

And that was when she realized.

"Ada, do you have information about your electrical consumption?"

"Yes. What do you need to know?"

"I want to know the consumption of your cabinets in detail, and within each one of them, of all its components."

"Fine, I have all that."

"Can you compare your consumption with what it was a few

months back?"

"Yes, I have data from… well, from the incident. What would you like me to look for, specifically?"

"Any very subtle variation. We're talking about a few watts of consumption."

"I'm afraid there are a lot of variations over time. The consumption of all my processors depends on the load and the tasks I have to perform at any moment. Could you be more specific in your request?"

Emily thought about how to express what she wanted to find without mentioning the rebels. If she was right, that rabble might have access to all the conversations and information in the station, but without Ada's help to filter them they would have to do it themselves, manually. Hence she decided not to use any key words, such as any mention of Captain Garth or the rebels.

"I'm looking for a new device which might have been connected to any of your sources of supply and which wasn't there when we left Earth," she said at last.

"Let me search all the information I have. It'll take me a while."

Emily went on trying to establish how the rebels might have managed two things: to avoid being detected, and to have firsthand knowledge of everything that was going on in the station. There must be some device which filtered everything before the information reached Ada, and also a transmitter which would pass on whatever they needed to know.

But the transmitter has got to be outside here. I've just established that there's nothing in here that either transmits or receives a signal.

"I have the results now," Ada said.

"Did you find anything?"

"One of my cabinets in the center row registered an increase in power consumption that doesn't match the load of work I had at that particular moment. And from that same moment, the cabinet's consumption is just over a hundred watts higher than it should be."

"Show me this cabinet."

Ada indicated the place in the terminal, and Emily went over to it. She remembered the last time she had had to access Ada's cabinets. She had just woken up from her cryo phase, and the space station had been in danger of being swallowed up by a black hole. The mere memory gave her a shiver that ran up and down her spine. When she reached the cabinet in question, she opened it without hesitation. At first sight everything seemed to be in order, with the memory blocks lined up along the lower part of the column. In the upper part, one of the gigantic and complex quantum processors rested in a small aquarium, submerged in liquid nitrogen.

"The feeding for the blocks is at the back of the column," Ada told her.

Emily turned the column round and examined the back.

"Oh my god!" She stepped back and put her hands to her head.

"What is it, Emily? What did you see?"

"Nothing, don't worry, Ada," she said, trying to show a confidence she did not feel.

She gathered her courage and came closer to get a clearer view of what to all appearances looked like an explosive. It was not very large, the size of a hand-grenade. But detonating it there, inside Ada's brain, would cause irreparable damage to her. They would lose her forever. And without the AI, the station would be ungovernable. Captain Garth had chosen well where to strike. A small explosion would not make any breach in the ship's hull, but would leave them without ears and eyes. And over time the whole station might stop working, leaving all the equipment inside it at the mercy of someone like him.

She had to deactivate this bomb. And she had to do it without allowing the rebels to realize what had happened. She studied it in detail. It was set in a small motherboard with two groups of wires connected to it: one for the power supply, the other for data transmission. She presumed that if she disconnected either of them, the bomb would explode.

I must find out where this data cable goes, she thought.

The wire went down to the floor, then was lost in a tube which other wires passed through. She went back to the terminal, where she checked Ada's diagram again. Each of the columns of the processor included two electrical points, one pipe for the refrigeration circuit for the processors, and two data cables which converged in Ada's access terminal, which was where she was now standing.

Right, this third wire doesn't appear in the plan. Now all I have to do is find the other end.

She stared at the square metal plate on the floor in front of Ada's terminal. There were some tiny marks on the metal, as if someone had handled it. She presumed that the connections would pass under it on their way to the terminal. The plates were screwed to the floor, so she took the screwdriver from her backpack and began to take out the screws. Underneath the plate were all the data cables for Ada's processors, arranged in perfect order and fixed in place by small clamps. But apart from those cables, there was another which caught her attention because it was floating weightlessly on its way out of the room. It was loose; someone had added it rather carelessly.

She could not see where the cables ended, as the rows were lost when they passed through the terminal. She followed the trail and noticed that the metal plate immediately before the terminal had also been handled. She repeated the same process and took out all the screws that fixed it to the floor. Here there were not so many cables, only eight of them, but they were all clearly arranged and fixed to the floor in the same way. According to the diagram, all of them went outside to connect Ada with other systems of the ship. And there was the extra cable, not fixed, connected to something that should not have been there. In that stretch of cabling was a device which did not appear in the diagram. It was a small board, rather rudimentary and slightly larger than the one connected to the bomb. In addition to this, the device was connected to another cable which pointed outside the hall. Presumably this would allow someone to work on this device without needing to go inside. But what drew her attention above all was the rest of the device.

Each of the eight wires of the floor was clamped together in two places. By way of the first clamp it received all information from outside. The second allowed them to send to Ada only what the device wanted her to see.

A vampire-type connection, so that a 'man in the middle' attack could be carried out. *Hell, why didn't I think of this earlier?* she reproached herself.

She left the control room as though the devil were after her, leaving everything in a mess. She needed to speak to Deputy Director Green, urgently.

17

Countermeasures

January 5, year 1

Asimov Space Station, Kepler-442b

Emily was nervous as she went into the deputy director's office. She was not at all sure how to hide her tension and urgency when she spoke, but it was vital that it should not be intercepted by the rebels.

"What's the matter?" the director asked. "You look as if you'd seen a ghost."

She stopped short and frowned.

"Wait," she said suddenly. "Give me a few minutes."

She left the office at top speed and took one of the pods. Without gravity once again, she passed the modules which housed the hydroponic crops, the silo and the farm until she reached the huge module which housed the warehouse. Here everything the project had brought from Earth was stored. It was the largest of the ones which remained. She went over to the worker who was in charge of dealing with requests from the other station crew members. For some of these the deputy director's approval was necessary, but she hoped not in this case.

He gave her a friendly smile. "Hello!"

"Hi there!" she replied, in something of a hurry. "I'm going to make a rather odd request. I hope it won't be a problem."

He looked curiously at her. "Go ahead."

"I need some paper and a pencil."

He looked suddenly serious. "You're kidding, right?"

"Not in the least. I need a few sheets of paper and a couple of pencils." She could not understand the manager's reaction.

"What are the chances of two different people asking me for paper and pencil in less than a week?" he said aloud. "Are you all going to start learning to write this late in the day?"

"Has someone else has asked you for paper and pencil?" she asked in surprise.

"Yeah, a few days ago. That young captain. He came here and asked for the same things."

Emily smiled. It was certainly odd that Robert should have used the same technique to avoid being overheard by unwanted ears. But she supposed it made sense. The use of tools for writing was not usual, unless you were a five-year-old whose parents had enrolled you in extracurricular classes to learn calligraphy. For over a century everyone had been using computers to write and communicate with other people.

"Right, in that case I need some more."

"Thank goodness I went through all this the other day." He sounded relieved. "I had to look in three stores to find everything, and the system had to move all sorts of bundles to get as far as those damn pencils."

She heard the machinery moving inside the enormous warehouse. After a while the worker vanished behind one of the doors. When he came back he was holding a stack of A4 paper and a couple of well-sharpened pencils.

"Here you are. I'll register them in your name, shall I?"

"Yes, of course. Thanks very much."

She hastened back to the deputy director's office and rushed in. She was perspiring, but now she had what she needed in her hands.

"Wow, now you really have surprised me," David said when he saw her.

She put her finger to her lips and sat down in one of the chairs the office kept for guests. Then with great difficulty, as she had never done so before, she began to write.

I found the bomb, she wrote, more or less legibly.

"This is more difficult than I expected," she said aloud.

I also know how the rebels stay hidden, she went on to write, *and what they do to make sure they know everything that goes on in the station.*

She handed the piece of paper to the deputy director, who read it and looked up at her in surprise. But he ended up asking for the pencil with a gesture.

Can you defuse it? he wrote, slightly more skillfully.

She shook her head.

No, I'll need an explosives expert.

The deputy director nodded and went on writing on his sheet of paper.

What would be the result of the explosion?

Ada would be put out of action forever, the station would be unmanageable. The project would be in serious danger.

The deputy director closed his eyes and sighed, then sank back thoughtfully into his chair.

So what do you suggest we do? he wrote,

I know how to disconnect the device they're using to spy on us, but I'll need someone to check the bomb before I touch anything,

We can't do that. If the information stops getting to them they'll know we've found it.

This time it was Emily who paused to think before picking up the pencil again.

We might be able to do something like what they did themselves, she wrote. *If I can manage to divert the information the device is sending and receiving so that it goes to Ada instead, we'll have everything we need to dupe the device, and maybe then we can disconnect the bomb.*

I'll talk to Commander Bauer so that he gets an explosives expert in touch with you, the deputy director wrote. *In the meantime you can work on a solution that will give us the advantage over Captain Garth without blowing ourselves up.*

"All right. I'll be at the engineering lab," she said as she tore up the sheet of paper they had been writing on.

From the office she went straight to one of the station engineering labs. Erik was at the Magellan base, which meant that there was no-one there. She took some motherboards, several clamps to allow her to create a bypass for the data cables in the hall and a soldering iron. Then she got down to work. In little over an hour she had two prototypes of a device for doing to the rebels something very much like what they were currently doing to the station. Ada would be able to see all the information about them and would make them believe they were still receiving everything they wanted to see and hear.

But what was worrying Emily most was the bomb. Any decision wrongly taken, any wrong step, would set it off. That would ruin all the efforts which had been made to date, and for all anyone knew might doom humanity to extinction.

You're not doing much to help if all you can think about is catastrophes, she told her own brain.

Next she began to test the two devices. She connected several wires to a terminal and left it to establish that the signal was coming through. She prepared to clamp each of the wires at different points to make sure that the flow of data was not cut off at any moment. Once she had clamped all the wires she was able to verify that the information passed through the device just before reaching the terminal. And the good news was that for the terminal there was no cut-off at all.

Right. Now all I have to do is program the board so that Ada can filter out what we don't want them to see.

She sat down and began searching in the data base for the

160

station's source code. She had access to millions of code repositories, which meant that she could do whatever she wanted. In a normal situation Ada would have done it all in the blink of an eye, but in as things were she was afraid that the rebels might be able to monitor what she was doing. Hence she had no choice but to do it the old-fashioned way. However, and thanks to Ada's modular construction, she was able to use her programming routines to make the job easier.

She realized that she would need many hours to get everything ready. *I'm going to need some coffee,* she decided, and her brain was delighted by the thought.

Resigned, but very focused and with a sense of urgency because of the situation, she went to the mess hall. It was still early for dinnertime, with only a couple of groups chatting in complete ignorance of the crisis she was trying to sort out. There was a microwave oven in the lab, so she took three large cups of coffee.

I'll heat it up later if it gets cold, she thought. *It'll need to last me all night.*

When she went back to the lab she heard a noise inside. She went in carefully, very alert. It was beginning to be rather late for anyone to have come to work. She heard things being moved around inside the room where she had been working. She was practically certain that she had shut down her session on the terminal before she had come out, to stop anyone nosing about into what she was doing.

She went into the room, sill balancing the three hot coffees in her hands. There was someone messing about in a closet, but the door prevented her from seeing who it was. She realized that carrying three cups of coffee was not ideal if she needed to defend herself against a possible attacker, so she looked for somewhere to put them down. She turned, saw an empty spot on one of the work desks and left them there carefully. But the intruder saw her before she could turn round.

"Emily!" Director Patel exclaimed.

She screamed.

"Oh, did I scare you? Sorry, I didn't know you were here. I thought you were at the base."

She sighed with relief. "My heart's galloping like a wild horse."

"I'm really sorry, I didn't think there was anyone here. Today we've been working in the hangar and we needed some shears." He picked up the enormous metal tool with an air of satisfaction. "I knew Erik had some here, and I came to get them. And if it hadn't been for the obvious smell of coffee that came wafting in, I'm afraid I'd have been the one who got the fright."

"Yes, it was a coincidence," Emily said as she got her breath back. "What are you doing here?"

She did her best not to tell an untruth. "I had to come for a meeting, and I decided to stay."

"Oh, right, I see. And I suppose here it's harder for you to stop working."

"Yeah, that's right."

"Okay. But try not to make it a routine. Rest is important too."

"I'll keep that in mind, Director Patel."

"In that case I'll let you go on. I have what I wanted now."
Proudly, he showed her the shears once again.

Once he had left, she went back to the terminal and saw that it was still switched on.

Is it possible that I never signed off? she wondered, without remembering clearly. But she could not stop mistrusting the coincidence that Patel should have come in just when she herself was not there. *You're getting paranoid,* she told herself when she remembered she was talking about Director Patel, someone she had known for a very long time and who had even been there for the presentation of her doctorate. *It's impossible,* she told herself firmly.

She took the coffees and put them on the terminal desk, then worked non-stop for hours. She wanted to have it all done and available for the next day. What she was doing was enabling Ada, through those two devices, to trick the other device the rebels were using, and the bomb itself, so that they would all think the situation was unchanged. Hence she needed to define exactly what she wanted to hide from them and what not. For the first time, they would be two steps ahead of their opponents.

But what was worrying her most was the bomb. Several hours later, when she had both devices nearly ready, she got up from her seat and began to pace the room, thinking of a solution.

I'm sure the device is sending signals to the bomb practically all the time, she thought. *That way the bomb's own board would make it explode if the power were cut off, or if it stopped receiving the signal from the other device.*

She came to the conclusion that to trick the bomb she would need to keep it connected to the current and go on sending the same signal. *If I can manage to replicate thirty minutes of the signal that reaches it in a new battery-fed device, and if we can connect the bomb's power supply to the batteries, we might be able to take it out of the cabinet without letting it realize we're moving it.*

She liked the plan. She took a new board, connected it to a portable battery and got ready to add the data and power clamps to create the bypass. Once the new device was assembled she programmed its routine: to receive the signal from the main device for half an hour, find the pattern and then repeat the same signal until the explosives expert the deputy director was sending her either deactivated it or subjected it to a controlled explosion.

One cup of hot coffee and two cold ones later, she had

completed everything they needed to eliminate the threat. She was exhausted.

She stowed away everything she had prepared in her backpack and took a walk around the station. When she reached the mess hall she realized that she had not eaten anything for hours. She fetched herself another cup of coffee, an orange juice and two slices of carrot cake. While she was trying to relax, someone came into the mess and kissed her on the top of her head.

"I didn't know you were here," Robert said.

"Hi," she replied vaguely, in a tired voice.

"Is anything wrong?" He sounded worried.

"Yeah... well, no..." She did not know what to say. "I'll tell you later, maybe with pencil and paper."

His face turned more serious.

"I see," he said. "I guess we both have a lot of things to talk about."

"Yeah, so I've heard."

"Right then, we'll talk. What's this feast you're having?"

"I didn't have any supper last night," she explained, "so I'm giving myself a treat."

"I see."

"I'm going to have a pretty hectic morning, but would you like us to spend the afternoon together?"

Robert was thoughtful, running through his schedule.

"Of course I'd like to. I'll try to put some of the day's tasks forward to the morning. Shall we talk later?"

"Sure, call me in the evening. *If we're still here,* she added mentally.

"Right." He kissed her on the lips and left her there to go on with his daily routine.

When it seemed the right moment, she went to the deputy director's office once again to tell him about the progress she had made during the night. All of it, of course, using pencil and paper.

"Are we ready to begin the operation?" he asked when she had finished her explanation.

She nodded, and immediately he called the commander.

"Timo," he said, "we're ready."

When he had hung up, he turned to her.

Join the expert the commander is sending at the door to Ada's control room, he wrote. She nodded again, but before leaving the office the deputy director said aloud: "Be careful."

"Don't worry, I will be," she promised him confidently.

When she reached the control room there was already one person waiting at the entrance: a middle-aged man, in his forties, but with plenty of white hair. He was carrying a large trunk and a huge blue metal device in the form of a sphere which looked like a huge pot with a lid on top. Without the lack of gravity, the equipment must have been extremely heavy.

"Morning," she said. "I hope they've brought you up to date and we won't have to talk too much."

"Yes, don't you worry about that. I've been briefed."

"Okay then."

They entered hurriedly in before anyone saw them. Once they were inside, Emily took out the devices she was carrying in her backpack and put them on the floor near where they needed to be assembled. The bomb-disposal expert, who was wearing the colors of the military sector of the project, left the trunk in one of the corners.

"I suggest you put this on," he said. "I'll give you a hand."

He had just taken two bomb or EOD (explosive ordnance disposal) suits out of the trunk, padded and very tough, capable of withstanding the impact of a much larger bomb than this one. Emily hesitated. The suit looked as if it would be uncomfortable for doing the delicate work she needed to do. But immediately she realized that handling a bomb was an even more delicate business, and the experts used them. Hence she did not stop to argue with the order and put it on with his help.

While he too put on his suit, she began to work on the device the rebels had installed. First she had to connect one of her own to the eight entry cables. One by one, she clamped the corresponding stretch of the highway of cables which came in from outside the room. When she had finished, the device itself confirmed the fact via a small integral terminal. She went on to repeat the process with the exit socket of her device, then to connect everything with Ada, so that she would have all the information again.

"All done," she said with a sigh. "Now we can modify the data that goes to the rebels as much as we like."

Despite the low temperature in the hall, she began to sweat inside the bomb suit. It might be very safe, but transpiration was not one of its strong points. She gave a long sigh to calm her nerves and went on to the next stretch of wires, the one which came out of the rebel device. She repeated the same process with the clamps of her own, cable by cable. Everything looked perfectly all right now, and by now Ada would be able to know what the rebels were hiding from them.

"Ada," she said aloud, "are you receiving everything I've just sent?"

"Yes, Emily. And I have to say they've been very intelligent."

"Yeah, except that now we have another priority. After this you can bring me up to date with what you can see. Keep up the flow of information so that they only receive whatever you think convenient," she added. She turned to the bomb expert. "I think we can get on with the important thing now."

"Show me where it is."

They went to the back of Ada's cabinet where the bomb was, and she showed him. The expert looked at it through his helmet, then took out a torchlight and a small mirror so that he could check it from all angles. He did not speak, to avoid revealing anything that might be important, but it was obvious that he had something to say.

"Oh, sorry!" she said. "You can speak normally. There's no risk of anyone listening now."

"That's good," he said, sounding relieved, "because otherwise it was going to be very difficult to do this. The commander told me you have a signal replicator."

"That's right." She showed him the third of the devices she had prepared. "It's programmed to clamp onto the data cable, recognize the communication patterns for the next half-hour and then repeat the same pattern."

"And what about power?"

"It has a battery," she said, and showed it to him.

"Great," he said as he took it. "We begin with the data cable, then wait half an hour, right?"

"That's right."

"Although it doesn't seem to have much of a charge," he warned her, "to be on the safe side stay beside the wall, behind the last column."

Emily did as she was told without a single complaint and hid behind one of Ada's cabinets, though she could not help peeping out round a corner to see how the expert would defuse the bomb.

With a precise movement, he fastened the clamp of Emily's improvised arrangement onto the data cable which sent information to the device. Nothing happened.

"That's it," he said. "Now we just have to wait."

"Right."

She came out of her improvised hiding-place.

"Where did you learn the way a bomb works?" he asked. "By the way, my name's First Sergeant James Scott of the bomb-disposal squad." He held out his gloved hand.

"Pleased to meet you, Sergeant Scott. My name's Dr. Emily Rhodes. And I don't understand your question. I've no idea how a bomb works."

"But you've done an amazing job with this," he said, pointing to her creation. "Even I wouldn't have managed it in such a short time."

She tried to shrug as best she could with all the paraphernalia she was wearing. "What I really understand is how digital communication works, and that bomb is stuck to a motherboard and gets fed like any other device."

They talked for some time longer while they waited for Emily's device to finish gathering the information they needed to generate a signal that would trick the bomb. Sergeant Scott used those moments to lift up one of the metal floor plates. He placed the round metallic pot he had brought with him in the space and began to fix it to the structure of Ada's control room.

"I need to fix the restriction chamber to the floor," he explained. "Otherwise in a gravity-free environment like this it could end up being hurled in any direction and could cause unwanted damage."

He fixed the chamber to the floor with four large bolts, which he secured with two enormous nuts and a hydraulic pistol. Once Emily's device had finished its sampling work, he asked her to move back again.

"We're going to get the bomb out of here," he announced.

He picked up the clamp of the device which was going to feed the motherboard of the bomb via the battery. Any miscalculation, any cut in supply, would be catastrophic for Ada and hence for the entire station. Emily felt her heart galloping in her throat. Next he fastened the clamp onto the cable which fed the bomb. Nothing happened; everything seemed still to be working. The moment he took off the fixtures which joined it to Ada's cabinet they would be able to get it out of there at last.

The bomb disposal expert got down to work. The bomb was fixed via its board to the structure of the cabinet with four screws, which he now began to loosen. When he had finished freeing the last of them, he picked up the combined battery and bomb with great care. Everything seemed to be going well, but then suddenly something started beeping in the bomb board. The beeping grew faster. The sergeant put it into the restriction chamber as fast as he could and shut the lid in a flash.

A loud explosion sounded suddenly from inside the pot. Emily, who had instinctively put her hands to her head and shut her eyes, was still wearing her electromagnetic boots, so that she felt the structure of the room vibrating from the explosion. When she opened her eyes again and dared to peer out of her hiding-place, she saw that the restriction chamber was still in place, though the solid bars of the underfloor were rather deformed after the explosion. Sergeant Scott took off his helmet, and the drops of perspiration from his head clustered together to form small transparent balls which floated at random through the air.

"Done," he said. "It's all over."

18

The telephone

January 6, year 1

Space Station Asimov, Kepler-442b

Emily woke up in her cabin and looked at the time. She was still very tired and drowsy, even though she had been able to rest for quite a long time. She sat up, still under the warmth of the blankets, and tried to remember what she had done before going to bed the day before.

"Robert!" she exclaimed suddenly.

But Robert was not there any longer. They had agreed to meet in the afternoon, and he had been a little late because of some last-minute hitch. They had been talking about trivialities and things outside the world of work, then they had decided to spend the night together. But she did not remember much apart from that.

"Hell!" she muttered. "I think I must have fallen asleep too soon. Ada, what time did I fall asleep last night?"

"At 19:28, Emily."

"Was Robert with me?"

"I can't store information about the whereabouts of the military team," the AI reminded her.

"That's true."

"However, you have a message from him in your inbox."

"Play it."

Good morning, sleepyhead, the transcription began. *You'll be wondering why you're waking up by yourself, but yesterday when I came out of the shower you were sound asleep. I don't know what you'd been up to the night before, but it obviously left you exhausted. So after spending some time thinking how beautiful you look when you're asleep, I decided to let you rest in peace. We'll talk some other time. Robert.*

She got up and dressed. Her back ached from sleeping for so long. She had spent nearly fourteen hours in the same position, and that had ended up taking its toll. She had an important meeting coming up with the administration board, but it was still very early, so she decided to have breakfast. Having fallen asleep so early had its drawbacks, and it meant that she had had no supper the night before.

"Ada, any news from the base?" she asked when she had sat down by herself at a table in the mess hall.

"Nothing noteworthy. Although Shildii was there yesterday with Rakesh."

She sighed. "Oh dear, what a shame I can't get in touch with him so he doesn't come all this way for nothing."

"Well, he was entertained very well by Professor Kumar," Ada said. "If you're worried about someone needing to play host to him, it seems that everything's under control."

"You're right, I'm sure he'll be all right with Rakesh."

"What's beginning to worry me a little," Ada added, "is that more and more Keplerians are crossing the river and coming close to the base to nose about."

"Those two kids who came last time. Have they come back?"

"Yes, but this time they didn't come by themselves, they came with three others."

"It looks as though Shildii's beginning to be popular," Emily said. "That might be a problem. We'll have to think of something. I don't think it's in our interests to have a bunch of Keplerians hanging around the doors of the base."

"All I can do is keep you informed."

"Yes, thanks. Anything else?"

"Kostas has spent a couple of days working on his own," Ada went on. "James Coogan has given up the tasks you assigned him."

Emily gave a long sigh of resignation. It was not going to be quite so easy to make that individual toe the line and transform himself into an asset to the project. She would need to have another talk with him.

"And also he's had some more confrontations with his comrades," the AI added. "I'm afraid they want to talk to you about it."

She sighed again. She had known it would be just a matter of time before something like that happened. But she still had hopes that the group itself would manage the situation and make the former influencer start to behave properly. But everything seemed to indicate that she was going to have to take the matter into her own hands.

She finished her breakfast and put her tray away. It was still early, so she wandered aimlessly around the Centrifuge. She thought about all the things that were keeping her awake: the SOS from the Galileo, the second conclave, the rebels, the Yokai... and though all these things troubled her, for some reason she found herself thinking of a more distant future. Was that planet really humanity's future home? How were they going to manage to make its conditions compatible with human life? What would happen to the Keplerians? Did they themselves have the right to modify those conditions, bearing in mind that the planet did not belong to them?

They had spent a long time avoiding all these questions, and no-one in the project was prepared to claim the responsibility for starting an open debate. But sooner or later she feared that they would have to make a decision about it: either the Keplerians, or humanity. Her legs trembled at the mere thought.

By the time she went back to the mess hall, it was time to go to the command post. This time, for a change, she was the first to get there. She was soon followed by the other three, who sat down after greeting her.

"Did you manage to get some rest?" the deputy director asked.

"Yeah," she said proudly. "I slept for nearly fourteen hours."

"That's not surprising," Captain Mei said. "You must have been exhausted, especially after all that tension."

"Sergeant Scott told me you did an excellent job yesterday, Dr. Rhodes," the commander added.

"He's the one who was really risking his life," Emily admitted. "I was always in the background."

"One way or another," the deputy director said, "with what you did and what you found out, you saved the station again. You've no idea how much debt the station's getting into with you."

"I do what I have to do, Deputy Director."

"Of course, and we thank you for it. But we'd better get down to business. I think we're all up to date about what's happened over these last few hours. But just so we don't miss any detail, please give us a summary of the station's current state."

"Well," she began, "as you know, yesterday we took out the bomb which had been put in Ada's control room. In addition, two devices were installed which will let us turn the tables on the rebels. Now we can control what they see and hear and what they don't."

"How had they managed to deceive Ada?" Captain Mei asked.

"Their gadget was put in just before the information from the station reached the AI," she explained. "All the equipment that communicates with the station or the satellites has a unique identifier, a kind of identity card. The gadget stopped the information from certain devices from reaching Ada's centers. And in addition to that they used our communication antennae to send the information they regarded as relevant through our own satellites."

"What kind of information?" the deputy director asked.

"In effect, everything to do with the military and with this administration board."

"But I don't understand," Captain Mei said. "Isn't Ada forbidden to store information which concerns the army?"

"Yes, but there are shades of grey involved," Emily said. "Ada doesn't read the contents or analyze anything that involves military matters, but the information reaches her just like any other kind. She stores the sensitive data in ciphered databases without even reading it. Because it was installed before the information could reach her, this gadget included all that sensitive information which once Ada had stored it can only be accessed via the order of a high-ranking officer."

"I see. That means they had virtual access to everything that was going on in the station."

Emily nodded. "Exactly, though as they lacked Ada's processing capacity I presume they were only able to watch the activities of particular elements or particular people. Hence the device would filter only what they thought was of interest."

"And how are we supposed to act from now on?" Commander Bauer asked.

"Quite normally," Emily said. "We won't need pencils or any other kind of ancient mechanism to communicate any longer."

"But they'll go on thinking they have the advantage," the deputy director said. "We need to make use of that fact."

"That's right. Ada will share with the rebels what we want them to see. This meeting, for example, will never have taken place as far as they're concerned. But we need to be intelligent about that, seeing that they're used to us acting in a specific way, doing what's dictated by protocol. I propose that every meeting which takes place in this hall, or among those members of this council who make decisions that could affect the rebels, has a second meeting, either before or after, to establish the genuine strategy. We'll decide what we want them to know at any given time, and Ada will send it via the devices."

"And we'll all have to act as if we hadn't found anything yet," the deputy director added.

"The covert operations must go on being exactly that," the commander added.

"And we can install the second base whenever we want to," the captain pointed out.

"Right," Emily said, "as long as those imaginary meetings all fit together."

"And will Ada take charge of everything?" the captain asked.

"That's right. We'll just need to involve her in the decisions and strategies we want her to follow with regard to the rebels."

"I'm ready to play this game of espionage," Ada put in.

The deputy director looked satisfied at this. "Good. So what do we know about the situation of the rebels?"

"Not much, in fact," the AI admitted. "I still can't receive the geolocation of either their exosuits or their comms. Nor have I received any signal from the lost ships, at least for the moment."

"They have some very experienced engineers with them," Emily pointed out. "It's more than likely that they've deactivated certain elements of the equipment."

"I think they're using analog systems to communicate among themselves," the commander said.

"How can you be so sure of that?" Captain Mei asked.

"From something Captain Beaufort told me."

Emily tensed when she heard the commander mention Robert's name. It was days since they had heard from one another, and something told her that she was now about to find out what he had been doing.

"The operation to set up the second base was a decoy," the commander said.

Everyone in the room was silent. Apparently no-one had known this before.

"Captain Beaufort hid a long-wave transmitter in one of the modules," the commander went on, "the kind that aren't used nowadays. The idea was to be able to detect the position of the rebel base once they'd set up the module. However, Captain Garth found the decoy, and they took this module to an isolated spot. But he left a message in which he explained that they'd found out the deceit as a result of a 'lucky coincidence'. What probably happened was that the signal itself somehow interfered with their communications."

"That makes sense," Emily said.

"But there's something very strange about that," Ada put in, "because I'm picking up the signal from some of the structures they took away."

"Good," the deputy director said. "At least that's something. What's strange about it?"

"The fact that they're scattered across a number of locations," she explained, showing them the locations on the map.

The deputy director gave a long whistle.

"They'll be decoys too."

"It certainly looks it," Captain Mei agreed.

"The only thing we can do is wait for them to move during the night," the commander said. "Captain Beaufort thinks the reason we can't see the ships from the satellites is because they move them in the dark."

"But without any kind of light," the captain added, "they'd need to use the satellites."

The deputy director nodded. "And now Ada can track where the transports are coming from and where they're going. We seem to have the basis of a plan. Let's hope this'll let us find that damn leech Garth. Until then we'll have to play this game of espionage."

Emily wanted to eat on the base, so once the meeting had ended she looked for a transport. As soon as she had landed, Ada brought her up to date.

"Today all we have is four Keplerians waiting in the distance."

"Where are they?"

"About a hundred meters to the north." She marked the spot on the visor of Emily's suit.

"I see them," Emily said, then suddenly stopped.

She did not know whether approaching them would be a good idea. Giving them something to eat, as she had with Shildii, could be interesting. But if there were four today, tomorrow there might be more, and that would be a problem. Despite this, she decided to get close to them.

"They seem to be children."

"They are," Ada said. "None of them are older than Shildii. According to the Keplerian calendar, today is free for the young ones. There's no school."

Emily gave a start when out of the corner of her eye she saw something approaching her. A proximity alert appeared on her suit visor. She bent down and saw a little bundle moving toward her at top speed.

"You really gave me a start there, Lemy!"

She bent down and stretched out her arm toward the animal, palm up.

"Sorry, little one, but I don't have any food. I've only just got here from the station."

The little *jush*, which seemed to have lost all fear of humans, came closer with its usual hops. And before Emily could react it climbed up the arm of her exosuit with its little claws, twirled a couple of times around her neck and settled on her right shoulder.

"Hey! Where d'you think you're going? D'you like being up high?"

She smiled and decided to go over to the little feeder she had put beside the entrance to the facilities. She bent down, careful that the little one would not lose its balance on its privileged position, and picked up some of the food one of her comrades had left for it there that morning.

She held out a few puffed grains of cereal left over from breakfast. "Here you are, little one."

While the little creature picked up the food with its paws and prepared to devour it, Emily turned to look once again at the visitors who were still watching her attentively from some way away. She set off toward them, careful that little Lemy did not fall, although it seemed to be managing to keep its balance very well with its hindquarters and its muscular tail. When she was half-way there the children took fright and ran off, first the two who seemed to be the eldest, then the smaller ones.

"Don't worry!" she called, not very hopefully. "I'm not going to hurt you!"

"I fear it's too late now," Ada said. "They're going back the way they came."

"Yeah, I think I scared them. But I guess they'll be back."

Back at the entrance to the facilities, it occurred to her that she would like to keep in touch with the Keplerians. Despite the fact that their leaders must be isolated according to the laws that governed the conclaves, she missed the conversations with Shildii and Yisht. She had not seen the girl again since she had brought her the invitation for that first conclave.

Hence with the problem of the rebels apparently resolved, she thought about remotely enabling the communicator she had given the girl. It was quite a simple thing to do, but she was afraid of someone finding out that she was speaking remotely. Even Yisht herself might be frightened if what she thought to be an electronic brain started speaking in Emily's name.

"Ada, could you establish communication with Yisht's backpack and explain how long-range communications work, to stop her being afraid?"

"Sure," she said. "Would you like me to do it now?"

"Yeah. But try not to frighten her, and be discreet, so that no-one in the building will find out that she's talking to us."

The last thing she wanted was for the girl to be accused of treason, as had almost happened not long before. She went into the decontamination chamber, not realizing that Lemy was still perched on her shoulder. But the alert reminded her of the fact with stroboscopic lights and a shrill sound which must have scared the little creature, because it shifted nervously on its improvised lookout on her shoulder.

She picked it up in her arms to take it outside. "Don't worry, Lemy, it's only the alarm, to remind me you have to stay out here."

She was sorry to leave it as she watched it shaking its little arms in the air, demanding more attention from its new friend.

"I'm sorry," she said as once again she crossed the control threshold.

"I've established communication with Yisht's device," Ada announced. "At the moment she's not in her room. I'll try to explain how remote communication works when she's back."

"Perfect. Thanks, Ada."

Later on, just after dinnertime, a timid greeting came from the other end.

"Emily?" a familiar voice asked. "Are you there?"

"Yisht!" she said eagerly. "How lovely to be able to speak to you! How are you?"

"I'm fine. Ada's just explained how this business of talking at a distance works. Are you really in your village?"

"Yes, that's right. I'm a few kilometers away from you."

"Wow," she exclaimed. "This is amazing. If only we had a technology that would allow us to speak remotely. I mean, we have messenger-birds, but this is something the Khapabir engineers certainly ought to see. Think of the number of journeys and dangers this would save the rulers."

Emily smiled at her reaction.

"Tell me, how are you and Rakesh? I suppose that now you'll have so many urgent things to do, you won't be able to keep our little morning meetings."

"We're fine. But yes, I'm afraid you're right. Everything that happened at the conclave means we can't go on learning about your culture and your customs."

"Well, actually, the situation here isn't making it easy to have peaceful meetings either."

"Is everything going all right?" Emily could tell that she was worried.

"I guess so," she whispered. "But ever since the conclave, the place is full of strange people I've never seen before. And… I don't know whether I ought to tell you… but Khikhya barely leaves her office now, and there are meetings with these Keplerians all the time."

"But, aren't the leaders supposed to be isolated from any contact with the outside world?"

"Yes," Yisht said, "but Khikhya has been acting very strangely for some time. She's trying to make us think these Keplerians are her counselors, but here we all know that's not true. And also she never seems to like what they tell her. You can often hear her shouting from outside her office."

"But if they're not her counselors, then who are they?"

"No-one knows. They've come out of nowhere, you could say. They don't have any kind of badge, and they don't talk to anyone outside their circle. All I know is that one of them, a young one who always looks completely impassive, seems to be the leader of the group."

"Young and impassive?" Emily asked.

"Yes, he hardly looks at the others, he always walks in an arrogant way, as if we didn't exist, and I've never heard him speak to anyone, he just listens to what the others say and his expression never changes. He's rather sinister."

Emily had a sudden hunch when she heard this description of the Keplerian.

"Wait a moment, Yisht." She began to operate her terminal. "Ada, can you find me the image that shows the face of the young soldier who was with the Khaavahki delegation at the conclave?"

"Sure."

A little later she saw a video which showed the young man turning to look behind him. And yet she found that gesture very strange, as she had had her eyes on that young man during almost the entire conclave. And she could not remember him moving from his position at any moment. Not even when his other two superiors had got up from the bench and paced around the temple to talk between themselves. He had always stayed isolated, impassive. That was what had most attracted her attention. It was odd that Yisht should have chosen the same word to describe him as she had herself.

"Is that the only time he turned round during the whole ceremony?"

"Yes," Ada said. "He didn't make any other gesture the whole time, not even during the conclave. He only got up to go to the dining hall, and I haven't even registered a single image which shows him exchanging a word with the rest of the Khaavahki delegation."

"How interesting," Emily murmured, "What was happening when he turned round?"

"I'm afraid you know the answer," Ada said.

"Khikhya was getting up from her seat to go into the conclave hall."

"Exactly."

Emily showed Yisht the image of the young soldier. "Is this the young man you're talking about?" she asked.

"Yes! That's him! Do you know him?"

"No, in fact I don't know who he is," Emily admitted. "But I do know he's a high-ranking soldier under Vaahur's command. He's a Khaavahki."

Yisht muffled a cry as she realized what must be happening. "What damn intrigue is Khikhya involved in?" she wondered in a whisper.

"I've no idea," Emily said. "But if the Khaavahki are involved, that sounds ominous."

"I'll try to find out everything I can."

"Yisht, you know too much as it is, and you might be in danger. Be very careful about the questions you ask and where you go. Something strange is going on with Khikhya, and I don't want anything bad to happen to you."

"Yes, I don't like the sound of all this," Yisht said in the ghost of a voice.

"Be careful," Emily repeated.

"I will be."

19
The second invitation

February 1, year 1

Magellan base, Kepler-442b

"Ada tells me James Coogan isn't cooperating with you, is that true?" Emily asked Kostas as they finished their breakfast.

"Yeah, that's right. He was very keen when he started, and he even seemed to like what we were doing, but he soon slackened off. He told me he was getting bored and that this wasn't for him."

"So what's he been doing these last few days?"

"I've seen him in the gym every morning," said Paula, who was listening to the conversation.

"I honestly don't know," Kostas said. "If he doesn't appear when we start work, I have no authority to tell him what he has to do or doesn't have to do."

"Yeah, that's all right, don't worry, Kostas," said Emily. "It's not your responsibility. Unfortunately, it's mine. You just get on with what you know how to do."

"You'll have to have a word with him," Gorka added. "Do you need us to intimidate him?"

Emily knew Gorka was perfectly capable of doing that, as he had been a semi-pro boxer before leaving Earth. But she did not want to descend to the level of being a bully, she still believed that it was far better if people joined forces in the project out of conviction rather than because they were being forced to. She had to find some way of making James Coogan change his way of thinking without needing to resort to drastic methods.

And to understand the new settlers' needs and attitudes, she had planned to interview all of them. She had set the whole morning aside for that. She began with Min, the robotics genius, who at the time was beside

177

Erik in the tech lab in the other building. Emily knew he had barely moved from there ever since they had arrived at the base.

"Min?" she called from the door. "Could we have a word for a few minutes?"

"Sure, no trouble."

They both went into one of the halls to talk in a quieter environment.

"I just wanted to know how you're acclimatizing to the base," she began. "If you think you need anything, or if the people you're working with are the right ones. I can understand that there are a lot of things you'll need to adapt to, and it might be a complicated business dealing with everything. That's something I know from experience."

He smiled when he realized what the meeting was about. "Oh, thanks! So far I'm delighted. The equipment we have isn't perfect, but it's suitable for our current needs. And I get on very well with Erik. He's very intelligent. It's a pity I didn't find him earlier, so that I could have brought him into some of my company's projects."

"He certainly is very intelligent. And also he's always willing, it's a pleasure to work with him. I'm glad you're working well together. And what about Martin?"

"Well, Martin… is a young man in a special position," he said awkwardly.

"Don't worry, Min," she said. "Martin has no formal education. He hasn't shown any interest in anything in his whole life. This may not be the right place for him. If you think it's too much for him, the best thing might be to find him something else to do."

"Yes, that could be true, of course…" He obviously appreciated the help.

"I'll have a word with him," she promised. "And depending on his point of view, we'll make a decision about whether this is the best place for him to contribute to the project. Don't worry."

"Thank you," he said more calmly.

"Anything more to add?"

"Well… I don't like doing this kind of thing," he began hesitantly, "but I think James Coogan is generating a very bad atmosphere among the people here."

Emily's eyes narrowed, aware of what was coming.

"What kind of behavior?" she asked, wondering whether she really wanted to know.

"Well, he makes misogynistic comments and he treats everyone as if he were the owner of all this. Personally I haven't had any confrontation with him, but Dr. Hudgens isn't exactly reluctant to talk… And I think Alberto's often on the point of blowing up, even though he manages to keep his nerves under control, but sooner or later that could change, and Alberto doesn't seem the kind who'd stop for anything or anyone. I think it could turn into something serious."

Emily realized that the building was a potential bomb. If she failed to take the necessary measures, the situation could easily get out of hand.

"Thanks for your honesty, Min," she said with a forced smile. "Let's hope we can all do something to sort out the situation.

Once again an intense worry began to grow inside her, but she tried to stay calm and avoid falling into the spiral of anguish and frustration which had flooded her a few days before. She called Alberto Mendoza, the multimillionaire with the dubious fortune.

He greeted her with a hearty handshake which nearly dislocated her shoulder.

"How nice to see you here!"

"Hello, Alberto. It's wonderful to see you in such a good mood. I just wanted to have a word with you about how you feel, whether you like it here, about your tasks."

"Oh yes!" he said enthusiastically. "I like it very much, thanks for asking. All this is fascinating, this place, this planet. I never imagined when I was a little *chamaquito* that I'd ever come as far as this. And although you can feel the extra gravity when we're here, I see it as something positive. I hope it helps me to lose some of this belly." He laughed uproariously as his tattooed hands pounded his prominent midriff.

"I'm glad to see you're so positive," Emily said. She was a little overwhelmed by the Mexican's limitless energy.

"Life is celebration," he replied with conviction. "We'll have time to be serious in our graves."

"You're absolutely right. Is there anything you'd like to tell me that could improve things for you?"

"Oh no," he said very seriously, "I'm very happy here. This is better than I could ever have imagined. You see, I think everyone here is aware that I haven't been an exemplary person in the past." He showed her his many tattoos. "I've done some very bad things, I've committed atrocities that would make any of you throw up, and more than that, I don't regret anything. But I don't want to hide any more, for me this journey is my way of trying to tilt the scales a little.

"You know my wife and children are still frozen on the station. I said farewell to everyone when we left Earth. My penance will be to prepare this world so that they won't have to commit the same atrocities I had to do just to survive. It's something I feel I have to do, not just for them, but for the children of all those of us who've searched for a new starting-point. And it's a task I've accepted proudly and humbly. I'll do whatever is necessary, even if that means shoveling manure for the rest of my life."

Emily had listened to Alberto's words attentively. She did not want to know what kind of atrocities he had been talking about, but although he had put his lack of contrition into words, his eyes were saying just the opposite. He was here to redeem himself for his actions, but mostly for the sake of his family. And it went without saying that at least as far as that was concerned, she could not have agreed more with him.

"Wow…" she said. "I'm not sure what to add to all that."

"You don't have to say anything. But if you need me for anything, however crazy it might sound, I'm your man"

"I really appreciate that, Alberto, and if there's anything I can do to make your stay here easier, please let me know."

"Of course. So far everything's *chido*."

"Is there anyone you consider is behaving negatively?" she asked.

"If you mean that individual James, I don't intend to create any trouble. But I'd be lying if I told you I'd have put up with his behavior on Earth the same way. But as I said, I decided to start again and I'm not that person any longer. Unless you ask me to."

She was taken aback by this. "Oh, no! I want to change his behavior, but in a peaceful way, making him understand that we all need to cooperate on the project for the common good."

"Well, anyway…" He shrugged. "I'm ready to help in any way necessary."

"Thank you, Alberto. Although I hope I don't need to go to those extremes."

"Thank you!" he said, smiling from ear to ear.

Next Emily called Dr. Moreau. She was deliberately postponing her interview with Dr. Hudgens so that she could get an idea of how the others felt about the problem of Coogan's behavior. But when she came into the hall where Emily was waiting, she was not alone. Both Dr. Hudgens and Emma, the welder in charge of general maintenance, were with her.

"Hello, Emily," they said.

She was rather surprised.

"But… these were supposed to be personal interviews."

"We know," Dr. Hudgens said. "But the three of us are going to tell you the same thing, so this way we won't waste time."

"All right, then." She accepted what she could see coming. "Sit down, please."

Dr. Hudgens took the initiative.

"I think I can speak on behalf of my colleagues, and I can definitely say that the three of us are very excited to be part of this project. We know it's something of historic significance. But what none of us are ready to tolerate is constant misogynistic comments and behavior from that brainless troglodyte with the IQ of an amoeba. And who in addition is incapable of keeping his testosterone level below that of an ape."

"I'm aware of all the damage and annoyance Mr. Coogan's presence on the base means to you," she said very seriously. "Believe me, I've suffered from it too. And you can believe me as well when I tell you I have the power to take drastic measures. All I'd have to do would be make one call, and our problems would disappear. But I don't want to do that. Or at least, not without trying to make him understand that there's no room for his behavior here. Not without trying to turn him into someone who could be useful to us all.

"You see, there were a little over twenty thousand people in the project. Some of them—too many, unfortunately—died without even getting as far as where we are. We have several dozen people who've decided to follow a different path to ours because of disagreements about how to manage the colonization of the planet. I don't want to… I don't think we can afford to dispense with anyone else. I'm asking for a little patience while I try to make him reconsider. I know I'm asking a lot from you, but I really believe we can get through that odious shell he lives inside and get the real, insecure James out of it."

The three women were silent.

"I have to admit, this wasn't the conclusion we hoped to get out of this conversation." Dr. Hudgens glanced at her two colleagues, rather taken aback. "But I understand your point of view and I guess we can try to put up with it a little longer. What do you both say?"

"We'll wait and see whether there's any development," Dr. Moreau said.

"I guess I can put up with it," the welder added.

After talking a little more with the three women, Emily was able to confirm that, like Min and Alberto, they were excited to be there and had the same feeling as everyone else of being engaged in writing a new chapter in the history of humanity. Only the problems with James needed to be resolved. Despite this, she decided to speak to Martin, the young son of a Swedish multimillionaire.

He greeted Emily shyly, sat down in one of the chairs and waited for her to take the initiative.

"How's everything?" she asked. "How are you adjusting to your new life?"

"Well, I suppose."

Emily knew she was going to have trouble getting information out of someone as shy as this.

"Have you acclimatized well to planetary conditions?"

"Yeah."

"And how do you find your new colleagues?"

The young man shrugged.

"Okay, I'll take that as a positive answer," Emily said. "How are you getting on with your work? Do you think you have a future in robotics or general engineering?"

"Dunno."

"Well, you must have some ideas, surely?" she insisted. "Where do you see yourself in a few years' time?"

"Dunno. Here?"

"Yes, of course, but what I mean is, what do you want to do with your professional life?"

"I don't know," he said again.

Emily summoned all her patience and tried to find a new approach.

"Do you find you can understand what Erik and Min are doing?"

"Not really."

"Okay, no problem. That's understandable. I have a degree in another branch of engineering and I think I'd have trouble keeping up with them too. What did you do on Earth when you weren't playing video games?"

"Dunno. Sleep?"

"Didn't you want to be anything when you grew up, when you were little? For instance, I wanted to be an astronaut, like my father."

He spent a little time considering his reply. Suddenly his face lit up.

"When I was little I used to spend a lot of time with the family gardener, making holes in the soil to plant flowers and plants," he said. "Except that my father never let me play with him, he used to say that wasn't a job for someone like me."

Emily smiled. "That's interesting. We might have a solution that would let you do something you like."

"Oh, yeah?" he asked in surprise.

"Tomorrow you'll start working with Kostas," Emily announced.

"Who's Kostas?"

"He's the botanist of the colony. You'll be able to work with plants there, if that's what you prefer."

"Okay." He shrugged, without showing much enthusiasm at the prospect.

Emily decided to deal with the main course when she had sent Martin away. She called James Coogan, but there was no answer.

"Ada, where's James?" she asked.

"In the other building, in the gym."

She put on her exosuit again, ready to leave, but a red pilot light came on in her helmet. There was something wrong.

"I can detect that the air filtration system Director Patel's engineers designed isn't working correctly," Ada informed her. "It might need adjustment."

"But it still has the oxygen tank, right?"

"Yes, but it's less full than usual, it doesn't even last twelve hours."

"I see." She took off her helmet. "I'll tell Erik to have a look at it."

She went back to the robotics lab, where Min and Erik himself were still at work on a prototype. Both of them looked up as she went in.

"Sorry to bother you," she said, "but my suit's alerting me that the air filter isn't working properly. Could you take a look?"

"Sure." Erik came over to her. "Although I wasn't on that particular project, it might need to be taken back to the Asimov. Where's the suit?"

She pointed back. "In the loading corridor."

He was thoughtful for a moment.

"You'll need another one while we check this. Take one of the spare ones in the storage room. I think there's one your size."

"Yeah, don't worry about that, I'll look for one and ask Director Patel to send us a spare, if we need one."

She and Erik left the lab. The engineer went straight to fetch Emily's suit from the loading corridor while she went into the store, where there were a couple of suits in different sizes, ready to use. She was checking the smaller of the two when she heard a familiar voice.

"Hello, Emily," Marko said. "What is it? D'you need anything?"

"Hi!" she said, rather startled.

"Sorry, I scared you."

"You did a little, to be honest. I didn't think there was anyone here."

He scratched his head. "I'm looking for a device that's listed in the inventory, but I can't find it. Are you having trouble with your suit?"

"Yeah. Director Patel gave me a prototype that didn't need an oxygen tank, but something's gone wrong with it."

"Right." Marko went over to one of the exosuits. "I think this one's your size." He looked at her, estimating the size of the suit.

Emily was able to smell his cologne as he passed in front of her. Somehow this made her nervous.

"I'll try to get inside," she joked as she tried unsuccessfully to turn it on.

She pressed the button several times until Marko, amused by her clumsiness, explained her mistake.

"These outlets don't allow the suits to be turned on while they're connected to the power." He passed his arm behind the suit. "You have to disconnect them manually before you can get into them."

The moment he had disconnected the terminals Emily was able to activate the suit, which split wide open to allow her to step in.

"Thanks, Marko."

"You're welcome, but there's a price."

"A price?"

"Yup," he said with a broad smile on his face. "Now we'll have to have two coffees instead of one."

"Yes… of course," she said as the suit closed on her body.

Both of them moved for the helmet at the same time, but their arms bumped and their faces ended up a few centimeters from one another.

"Sorry," Marko said. "I was going to… hand you your helmet."

"Yeah… thanks, helmet… I mean Marko," she said clumsily. "I… um... I think I'd better go."

And putting the helmet on, she left the store as fast as she could.

What a fool you are. What d'you think you're playing at? she asked herself as her heart regained its usual rate.

She left the building to face up to what she did not have the slightest desire to do: to have an adult conversation with James Coogan. Out there was Kostas, throwing something away from him. Lemy, the little creature, ran off after it, picked it up in its tiny hands and went back to Kostas hop by hop.

"Look, Emily," he said when he saw her. "This little thing brings back anything I throw for him."

He repeated the operation, and little Lemy hopped away after the pebble which had just been thrown for him. But this time, and to Kostas' surprise, instead of bringing it back to him the little creature put it in its mouth and climbed up Emily's suit to her forearm. She opened her palm and Lemy deposited the pebble in it, making gestures of delight with its funny little arms.

"What the—" Kostas put his hands on his hips and pretended to be indignant. "What a treacherous little animal! So that's the way it's going to be, eh, little Judas? Okay then, don't complain if there's no water in your bowl."

Emily burst out laughing.

"Very good, Lemy." She stroked it a couple of times. "Let the world know who's boss around here."

Then she had no choice but to come back to reality. She set off to the gym, where she expected to find the infamous James Coogan. She passed behind Evelyn, who shook her head to show her weariness. She found him on a treadmill, listening to music at full volume.

"Mr. Coogan!" she called. But he went on with his exercises, with the music still deafening. "James!" she shouted, but got no reply. "Ada, turn off the music and stop the treadmill."

Ada did so, and at once a lament came from his throat.

"Hey! I had a good rhythm going there!"

"I couldn't care less what rhythm you had going," Emily said angrily. "This isn't a pleasure cruise, James. We have duties here, we all have to work to get—"

"Okay, don't bother me, sweetie-pie," he said as he wiped the sweat from his face.

She had to make a titanic effort to keep herself under control.

"I'm going to put an end to your nonsense," she went on, suddenly very calm. "And though I have the power to order you to be detained for some time in the space station…"

"What?" he cried, scandalized. "Are you threatening me? That'd be illegal! I have rights!"

She stopped and gestured to him to keep quiet.

"James," she went on, "you're alone here. None of your followers on Earth are here to applaud your antics. Do you really think any of us here would mind if you were taken to a cell in the station? Do you think I can't do it? My advice to you would be to think about how utterly alone you are and whether it's really in your best interest to be like that when the Yokai or the Khol attack us… it's quite possible that you might prefer to be in a cell for the rest of your life."

James was silent for a moment, but then immediately regained his swagger.

"I don't care about your company, I don't care about those Yokai and the Khol or whatever they're called, whatever they happen to be."

"What the hell did you come to this planet for?" she asked him.

She got no answer.

"I'll tell you," she said. "You're afraid. You're afraid of dying, you're afraid of being alone, you're afraid of yourself. But don't worry," she added, "I told you that last time. I don't intend to throw up the towel with you, you'll end up realizing how useless your behavior is, I can guarantee that."

James did not seem to be listening to anything she was saying.

"For the moment, and as you're behaving like those teenagers who adored you on earth, we're going to treat you as one. Ada, revoke James' access to the gym till further notice."

"What? Are you crazy?"

"No, I'm not, I'm just taking steps to give you the education you need. If you want to enjoy your privileges again there are two things you're going to have to do: carry out your duties, like everybody else on the base, and apologize to your colleagues for the thoughtless things you've said and done."

"Hah!" he said. "Think again if you imagine James Coogan's going to apologize."

"You will," Emily insisted, with an unexpected confidence in her gaze.

At that moment Ada interrupted her again.

"Emily, three figures are approaching. One of them is Yisht, and the other two, to judge by their clothes, look like Khaavahki soldiers."

Emily gave a start.

"Soldiers?" she asked aloud.

"Yes, I fear so."

"What can have happened?" she murmured as she went to the entrance.

She went out to meet the three visitors and waited for them to cover the last stretch of the way. Just as Ada had told her, Yisht was coming, escorted by two intimidating Keplerians in heavy clothes, armed with huge halberds. On their chests they bore the badge of the Keplerian army, a stone tower and two crossed swords.

"Are you Emily Rhodes?" one of these unknown Keplerians asked.

"Yes, what is it?"

With a cat-like motion of his hand which surprised even Emily herself, he took out a letter from his leather jerkin. Then he handed it to her, and she read it once she had broken the wax seal which bore the badge of the Khaavahki.

Cordial greetings:

By the present letter I, Vaahur, leader of the Khaavahki people, summon you to the conclave which is to take place in the temple of Khormak, in the heart of the Gaal-El village. The conclave will be conducted according to our ancestral traditions, and its sole purpose will be to consider the fate of the one proclaimed Metal Woman, *of the human people.*

The conclave will take place on the second of February. You are requested to confirm your attendance to the emissary who is the bearer of this invitation.

Vaahur, leader of the Khaavahki people

"What does this mean?" Emily asked, taken aback. "Can any of the leaders summon a conclave?"

"Yes," Yisht said, much less freely than usual.

"But that's tomorrow."

"Vaahur has summoned a new conclave urgently."

"At the same place as the one before?"

"That's right."

"Do you confirm your attendance?" asked the soldier who had handed her the message.

"It doesn't say here whether I can bring a companion with me."

"Do you confirm your attendance?" the soldier asked again, sounding more like an automaton than a soldier.

"Yes," Emily said. "I confirm my attendance."

The soldiers turned and set off on their journey back. Yisht did the same with her head bowed, without even looking her in the face. Except that as they were moving away she turned for a single moment, and their gazes met. She looked frightened.

20

On the road again

Someone was trying to communicate with her in whispers.

"Emily?"

"Yisht!" she exclaimed. "You had me worried. How are you?"

"Fine, fine. I'm not sure how much time I have. I wanted to talk to you yesterday, but they had me watched."

"What's going on, Yisht?"

"I don't really know. The atmosphere here is very rarified. Khikhya is behaving very improperly. She spends the day shouting at everyone, even over the tiniest detail. Yesterday a garrison of Khaavahki soldiers arrived, and they handed her the same message as they did to you. Then they made me go with those two soldiers to give you the invitation, but I didn't dare tell you anything."

"Don't worry, the important thing is that you're all right. You must have been very scared."

"I was, quite honestly. I couldn't even say hello to you properly, and you must have had all sorts of questions."

"I did, actually. I don't even know whether it's normal for another of the leaders to be calling the conclave again."

"It's possible," Yisht explained. "And I thought it was strange too, but it seems that Waafdiv had talked about it with all the leaders in the previous conclave."

"Have you seen any signs of the mysterious soldier who met with her?"

"No, at least not for the past couple of days. But there's something about all this that seems even stranger to me. Why would a high-ranking officer of the army stay in Wiikhaadiiz ofiz, then disappear before

188

the garrison could arrive?"

"Do you think Vaahur and Khikhya are in cahoots?"

"I don't know," Yisht said, "though seeing how angrily she talks about him, I find it hard to believe. But after seeing how strangely she's been behaving lately, I don't know what to believe."

"Have you spoken to her?" Emily asked.

"Very little lately, in fact. But I've had to do her bidding, however strange it might seem to me."

"Such as?"

"A couple of weeks ago she ordered us to equip one of the rooms in her residence with all kinds of luxuries. And she also ordered a couple of lads to go and find some strange flowers to decorate the room. But it turns out that those flowers don't grow in Wiikhaadiiz ofiz, so they had to travel to the mountains to get them."

"She sent someone to the mountains, just for some flowers?" Emily asked in surprise.

"Yes, some that only grow quite high up. The poor things had to go even further than Haagar's cabin to get hold of them. They came back exhausted."

"How strange," Emily said. "And who stayed in that room?"

"That's another strange thing. When the visitors arrived, she ordered us not to go near the room under any circumstances."

"Do you think it was our mysterious soldier who stayed there?"

"I'd say so. At least that's what the servants are saying among themselves. The rest of the delegation stayed somewhere else, somewhere outside Khikhya's residence."

"She seems to have taken entertaining her guest very seriously," said Emily. "Has she ever welcomed a guest like that?"

"No, or at least not since I've been here. They usually equip a nearby building so that they can have their own security and all the comforts they need. As far as I know she's always done it like that, but unfortunately I never met my predecessor, so I don't know whether it was done the same way before."

"How strange," Emily said again.

"It certainly is. I've been talking a lot with the servants these past few days, and they tell me this isn't the first time Khikhya's behaved in this odd way."

"Really?"

"It seems that many years ago, after a spell of constant shouting and mysterious visits, she was very ill and spent four years without carrying out her duties."

"Oh, I thought Keplerians never fell ill."

"That's quite true. But the most curious thing is that no-one saw her during those four years. No healer came to visit her, no-one prepared food for her. It was as if she weren't there."

"This is beginning to sound very bad to me, Yisht."

"Yes, I know. I have the same impression, that something very serious is going on here. Especially because of the way the other servant told off the one who told me about it. She looked scared, as if something could happen to them for gossiping."

"Why are you telling me about all this, Yisht?"

"Because I don't know who I can trust. One or two Keplerians have been looking at me in a strange way over the past couple of days. But also because I fear this conclave might turn out to be a Khaavahki trap. Emily, I think you're in danger. Take precautions against it."

"Don't worry. I'll be careful."

"I'm going to try and find out what's going on here."

"And you be very careful too, Yisht," Emily said. "You seem to be getting close to something that someone is taking a lot of trouble to keep hidden."

Emily was sitting in silence in the deputy director's office chair. She could not stop moving her leg. She had to make a decision as soon as possible.

"I don't think you ought to attend," he said.

"You've made your position very clear. But personally I feel I have to go."

"At least let the commander arrange a small contingent to go with you."

"No. If anything happened, Keplerians would die, and maybe humans too. I don't want to be the cause of our going into a war against them."

"Well, in that case the solution is not to go." Green insisted.

"But I think it's our duty to attend," she argued. "We don't even know whether there's any basis for these suspicions. I don't want to risk all the progress we've made through diplomacy just because of a slight suspicion."

"Right, let's suppose you attend the conclave and it turns out to be a trap. They capture you, or worse still, something happens to you. What are we supposed to do then?"

"Nothing."

"Nothing?" he repeated in disbelief. "One of our most important assets is captured, and you're saying we should do nothing?"

"That's right," Emily said. "I don't want to be the trigger for any kind of retaliation or act of violence. Not in my name."

"Emily, are you aware that you could be going into the lion's den?"

"Yes, David, I know that."

"You know I've always supported you. And believe me, I've seen how much you've grown up since that black hole forced us to come out of cryo. But I don't understand you."

"I've already made my decision, and I'm a hundred per cent convinced, David," she said confidently. "I don't want to provoke a massacre in my name. And nor do I want to run away from my responsibility."

"But it's a responsibility that's been imposed on you by the drunken leader of a decayed religious cult."

"You don't understand, David. In some way I can't explain, I feel their faith is real."

"You're not telling me you believe in those old legends of an underdeveloped alien species, surely?"

"No, I'm not that naïve. But I know they trust me so that they can have an opportunity to escape from slavery. The Keplerians have spent millennia bearing a burden that won't let them advance, either as a society or as a species. They need us to defeat the Khol, and they believe I'm the key to gaining the support of the humans."

"They might be taking advantage of you to fight their own internal battles and settle unfinished business between the different tribes."

"I don't deny that," she admitted. "But neither can I ignore the fact that if we want to stay on this planet, then sooner or later we're going to have to confront the Khol. And to do that without our arsenal, we're going to need all possible support. Not to mention all the information the Keplerians have about them. I think an asset, however important, is a fair exchange if we can manage to move forward in that direction."

"You could be right," David said, "but what I don't like is that you're the one being sacrificed."

"That's how things have turned out. But we have a lot at stake. We need to bear in mind that the Khol almost certainly won't be as casual with a race that's able to travel among the stars. What's at stake is human survival. I think we have to take risks if they can give us a chance of survival, however slight."

The deputy director considered all this for a long time.

"All right, then," he said at last. "I hope you know what you're doing. If not, I'll never forgive myself."

"It's not your decision to make, David. I'm the only one who can do that."

Once again he was silent.

"Your father would be proud of the woman in front of me," he said at last. "He knew one day you'd become a great leader. But quite honestly, I never expected it to be so soon," he added proudly.

"He would have made the same decision as I have," she said with conviction.

"I know, Emily. I sometimes worry about how much you're like him."

She began her preparations for her new journey immediately. This time she was going to go alone, without anyone accompanying her. She did not want anyone else to risk their life for a decision she herself had made.

"Gorka," she asked, "can you check the rover's in perfect condition?"

"Yes, of course, Emily. Going on an excursion?"

"Yeah, something like that."

He saw that she was looking troubled. "Is there a problem?"

"No, don't worry," she said, forcing a smile.

"You know you can count on us, right?"

"Yeah, I know, thanks, I really appreciate it."

"Okay then, I'll check the rover."

She intended to follow the same agenda as for the previous conclave: leaving the base in the afternoon and arriving before nightfall. She presumed that Liikmi would be waiting for her below in the Gaal-El village, so that she could spend the night there. After lunch she took a shower and got ready for her solitary adventure, perhaps for the last time.

But when she came out to load the vehicle with the supplies which would be needed for three or four days, she was surprised to find that someone had done it for her. And not just that: several weeks-worth of supplies had been loaded. Taken aback, she got off the vehicle and found herself facing three of her comrades.

"What's going on here?" she asked.

"That's exactly what we were wondering," said Paula.

"So we decided to speak to Rakesh," Gorka added.

"And I told them what I knew," the anthropologist explained.

"So we've decided that this time all three of us are coming with you," Paula said, to complete the ambush.

"Go back to the base, all of you," Emily said. "I've made the decision to go by myself. This time I'm afraid it's too dangerous."

Gorka shook his head. "With all due respect, Emily, we're not going to change our minds."

"We're coming with you, whether you like it or not," said Rakesh.

"But I've made my decision to go alone. You can't…"

"We can't what?" Paula asked her. "Make our own decisions, the way you do?"

"We don't want to leave you all by yourself, Emily," said Rakesh.

"But it might be very dangerous…"

Paula interrupted her "Yeah, yeah, we've talked about it all. And all three of us are willing to take the risk."

"But you don't understand…"

"Yes, we do, Emily, we understand the risks we're taking perfectly well," Rakesh pointed out. "You're not the only one who can speak to Yisht."

Emily took a deep breath and looked at them one by one. She saw determination in them, and though she was worried about what might happen at the conclave, in a way she felt relieved to have her friends with her, even if it would not make much of a difference if things were to go wrong.

"Okay," she said. "I suppose I can't make you stay here."

Paula smiled. "Nope, you don't have a chance."

And so once again the four of them began the journey to the Gaal-El village, where the second conclave was to take place the following day. This time Emily let Gorka do the driving, because he insisted that he wanted to see how powerful the rover was, so Ada gave him full control.

One of Emily's concerns was the Khaavahki military checkpoint at the halfway point. The last time a maximum of two people had been permitted to pass. This time they were twice as many of them, and there was no saying how the soldiers would react. The journey proceeded more or less in silence. She had plenty to think about, and did not feel much like talking. But she answered the questions they asked as they went: about the conclave, or about the Keplerian political situation in general.

"Slow down," Emily said abruptly to Gorka. "We're coming to the checkpoint."

Gorka slowed down noticeably. However, there did not seem to be much activity in the area.

"That's very strange," she said. "There doesn't seem to be anyone in the sentry-box."

Rakesh was looking out from the row of seats at the back. "I can't see anyone at the barracks either."

"What do I do?" Gorka asked. "Keep going?"

"Yes," Emily said. "Though it's very strange that there's no-one manning this."

Paula shrugged. "They might have had to leave the area."

Or maybe they've opened the gate to the lion's den so that we walk into it all by ourselves, Emily thought.

It did not take them long to reach the village, where as usual the ever-polite Liikmi was waiting for them. He welcomed Emily and her companions with a deep bow.

"I've prepared the usual rooms," he said as he led them to the old inn where they had stayed before.

"Perfect, Liikmi," Emily said. "Thank you very much."

He gave her a nod. "There's no need. Is there anything else I can do for you?"

"Actually, yes," she said. "I'd like to ask you a couple of questions, if you're able to answer them."

"Of course, whatever you like."

"Has there been any kind of unusual activity in the area?"

"Unusual activity?" he repeated blankly.

"Yes, anything out of the ordinary. For example, a sudden increase in the number of Keplerians passing through the village, or someone turning up at the monastery unexpectedly. Something that would be unusual on a normal day."

Liikmi was thoughtful for a few moments, then broke his silence with a monosyllable:

"No."

"And is it normal that we didn't find anyone at the military checkpoint on the way here?"

At this question, on the other hand, they noticed that Liikmi's eyes opened wide.

"Was there no-one at the post?"

"No, not a soul," Gorka said.

"Now that really is strange. I remember times when the allocation was smaller or larger, but there's always been someone there. How very strange. Although I don't really understand what's behind the movements of the soldiers. They might have had to leave the area." He shrugged.

"That's what I said myself," Paula pointed out.

"Is there anything else you need to know?"

Emily shook her head. "No, Liikmi. Well, actually, yes. I gather the conclave will be held at the same time as the previous one, and in the same conditions, is that right?"

"Yes, that's right. Tomorrow I'll come up with you to the monastery, as once again I have the honor of acting as usher to the chosen one."

Liikmi bowed so deeply that Emily wanted to beg him to stop. At the same time Paula and Gorka watched this display of devotion with some amusement.

"He seems very nice," Paula said when the Keplerian had left the ancient inn.

Rakesh nodded. "So he is."

Gorka smiled. "But I'm afraid he's too correct in his manners. I can't see myself taking him out for a beer any time soon."

"Well then," Paula asked, "what do we do till tomorrow?"

Rakesh sighed. "We wait."

"Wait and keep our eyes open," Emily corrected him.

"Are you still wondering about why there were no soldiers at the checkpoint?" Paula asked her. "Are you worried that they let us through, just like that?"

She nodded reluctantly.

"Do you really think they'd risk setting off a war against humans," Rakesh asked her, "just because your name's been put forward as a candidate to lead the Keplerian people?"

"Of course. Human history's full of events where one faction rises up against the others."

"Of course. But in none of those cases was the aggressor fighting a much more advanced civilization. If human history has taught us anything, it's that the more advanced civilization has always annihilated the weaker one. They're not in a suitable position to take any action against you. Or at least, not without some compelling reason behind them."

"A compelling reason?" Paula asked.

"Yes, something even humans can't deny," Rakesh explained. "Something that leaves the advanced civilization without any logical argument for making a counterattack."

"Something like what?"

"At the beginning of the twentieth century, in what was still called the former United States, there was a mafia boss called Al Capone. Like any self-respecting mafia boss, he did all sorts illegal things which the law was determined to prevent. However, the police could never manage to capture him. And when at last they did, they couldn't gather enough evidence to prove his offences. Until a federal agent called Elliot Ness decided to look into the tax returns for his whole illicitly-acquired fortune.

"After a massive amount of fieldwork, Elliot Ness and his team managed to have Al Capone arrested and sentenced to eleven years in prison for tax evasion. They couldn't prove even a single one of his illicit business dealings, but he was sentenced for what he should have paid if those dealings had been legal."

"I'm not sure I quite get the moral of this story," Gorka complained,

"What Rakesh means," said Emily as she looked out the window of the inn, "is that as long as we don't do anything that their laws can show to be illegal, those who are opposed to the humans won't be able to take any direct action."

21
The last farewell

Unknown date

Unknown location, Kepler-442b

A cart pulled by a single *fhore* was approaching the edge of the village. It was noon, and though the weather was fairly mild for that time of year, Shyiich was wearing warm clothes. He had been very weak and did not want to do anything to threaten the recovery of his leg wound. When he had woken two weeks before, he had not even been able to remember how he had got to Khaavahki. There had been moments of great confusion. All he knew was that the healer had poked around in his bleeding wound, but he had fainted again from the pain and not woken up until two days later.

However much the doctors might want to prevent his death, he felt that he was dead already. He had no-one and nothing to stay alive for, he felt dead in the middle of life. That foreigner had torn away from him everything he had once had. And however much he might try to forget, those small eyes still stared at him in his nightmares from within that strange armor. There had not been so much as a single night since that day when he had not woken in the small hours, afraid and drenched in sweat. The echoes of the desperate cries of his wife and his son echoed over and over in his mind after they had been being murdered by that ruthless intruder.

He stopped the cart before going into the village and looked at his house in the distance, but he did not dare go a single meter further. Looking again at what had been his home for the last few years, where he had known so many moments of joy and such happiness, was like a powerful blow on his chest. He did not feel he was capable of visiting the place where his loved ones had been murdered. Instead of following the path into the village, he decided to turn his cart toward the west. He shook the *fhore's* reins, and it moved on obediently.

That particular path was not much frequented. In fact it had only been used a couple of times since he and his neighbors had settled there. Despite this, there were fresh tracks on the earth. He knew that the Khaavahki soldiers had been there to recover the bodies. He went a few meters further on until he came to a clearing, not a very large one. In the center he found a small mound of ashes. He stopped the cart so that the rear faced the burnt remains of the funeral pyres which the soldiers had set up a few days before.

He heaved a sigh and got off the cart, with difficulty. The wound in his leg was still recent, and the healers who had treated him had put on bulky bandages which made it hard for him to bend his joints comfortably. Apart from that, the physical pain was still too intense to ignore, and every move that required the use of the affected area brought a frown to his face.

He limped to the rear of the cart and began to unload the logs. With great effort he arranged them to form two rectangles of different sizes on the ground. It took him far longer than he had expected to empty the cart. The wound in his leg hurt with every movement he made, either when he got on and off the cart or when he had to arrange the different layers of wood. He remembered the numerous offers the army lieutenant had made, but this was something he had to do for himself, alone.

Once the two rectangles had been built, he unloaded the leaves and branches he was carrying at the front of the cart and used these to fill the empty space between the piled-up logs in both structures. Now only the last part of his plan was left, but for some reason his mind wanted to delay it for a while longer. It was noon, so he went to the front and took down the skin full of fresh water and the satchel he was carrying with him. He leaned his back against one of the wheels of the cart and took a long draught. When he had quenched his thirst, he stood there bitterly contemplating the work he had just completed. It was something he had never thought he would ever have to do.

He opened the satchel and took out some strips of dried meat, a piece of cheese and a chunk of grayish bread. The lieutenant had insisted on giving him all this so that he would have enough for the day. He tasted the meat, which he tore with the sides of his two molars, and began to chew without enthusiasm. It was tasty, but food had ceased to give him pleasure; everything was insipid, lacking in appeal. He cut a piece of bread and put it in his mouth, then cut a slice of that yellow cheese with his knife and chewed it with his gaze distant. It was bitter.

And yet the bite managed to embitter something more than his tastebuds. Yiïÿa, his dead wife, had enjoyed that cheese far more than he did. She loved it. She had made her own cheese with *tür* milk and the rennet which Laankhol, the farmer of the village, gave her. Just because of this he had eaten it, even though it was not much to his liking. The tears he had managed to keep at bay began to slide down his cheeks. The cheese had reminded him of the way Yiiÿa had taken great pains to mix the milk with the rennet. He saw her in his mind's eye straining, then draining the whey through cloths, then putting it into round molds which would give them their final shape. He had never told her he did not like it, even though she always made sure there was a piece in his satchel.

   He wept for some time in his loneliness, held there by memories and by the freshness of his loss. But he had to get on with his task and push all that out of his mind. He leaned against the spokes of the wheel to get up from the ground and went once again to the back of the cart, where there were two bundles of different sizes wrapped in white cloth. He picked up the smaller, which was a little over ten kilos, and cuddled it in his lap for one last time while his tears flowed uncontrollably. With extreme care, ignoring the pain in his leg, he placed it on top of the smaller of the structures he had made with the wood.

   Then he picked up the larger of the bundles. It took him much longer to set it in place. And yet it was not his leg which was hurting him the most. He left it very gently on top of the wooden structure and leaned his head against it. With tears in his eyes, he laid his hand on top of the bundle and uttered a few words, between sobs. Then he went back to the cart and fetched the last thing left in it, an enormous skin. He took out the bung and poured the thick, golden liquid on top of the two structures.

   From his satchel he took a piece of metal and a white stone and rubbed them together quickly until sparks flew out, but the oil he had just poured out failed to catch fire. He tried three times more, until at last one of the sparks fell on it with enough heat to make it burn. He took a couple of steps back and watched the fire devouring the two funerary pyres in which his wife and son were soon consumed for ever. After watching the smoke which rose from the orange flames for a long time, he wiped his eyes with a corner of his waistcoat and left the place, never to return.

22

Following the trail

February 2, year 1

Unknown place, Kepler-442b

Robert and Ferrara left the aerial transport on a rover the captain had painted in tones of red and brown, like their suits, so that they could pass unnoticed while they were traveling through the dense forests of the planet. As soon as they had landed, the transport rose again on its way back to the station. There was no communication of any kind between the two vehicles. Robert had made sure that neither the transports nor the equipment used in the mission had any active communications installed, to escape detection by the rebels.

They were two hundred kilometers or so north of the base, on the far side of the two mountain ranges which formed the huge crater located halfway between them: some fifty kilometers to the northeast of the spot where they had landed a few days before.

"Right," Ferrara said, "what's the plan this time, Captain?"

"After Dr. Rhodes found the devices the rebels were using to spy on us," he explained, "we were able to turn the tables on them. And now they're the ones thinking they've got us under control, when the situation is exactly reversed. We know where they are, but they're not receiving anything about what we're doing and Ada's sending them reports of false activity."

"Do we know where they are?"

"Well, more or less," Robert admitted. "That's why we're here, Sergeant."

"How can we know their position 'more or less'?"

"As soon as Dr. Rhodes managed to get rid of the device that was hiding their trail, we started to receive GPS signals from some of the modules of the facilities they'd stolen. On the other hand, for some reason we're still not receiving any kind of communication from the rebels themselves."

"And how's that?"

"We don't think they're using our satellites to communicate among themselves."

"Right."

"The problem is that we have five different locations, with dozens of kilometers between them, but at the same time a steady and disturbing radio silence."

"That's strange, right?" she asked.

"Yes. Very suspicious, in fact."

"D'you think they could have established more than one base?" she asked.

"In fact I don't think any of those locators are at the rebel base."

"They're decoys…"

"Yeah, I think so," he said. "Captain Garth is an old dog. He knows that sooner or later we're going to try and locate them. Spreading little bits of bait across a wide area seems a good way of detecting whether we're getting too close to the real base."

"It's certainly rather suspicious," she said. "Is that why we're still doing without comms?"

"Yeah. We can't risk them monitoring our frequencies, which is why we have to speak at the tops of our voices. And the last time he managed to find the decoy we'd hidden in one of the modules they stole. That decoy used high-frequency signals, and Captain Garth congratulated us on the attempt. Remember he said, literally: *if it hadn't been for a lucky coincidence we wouldn't have been aware of the transmitter hidden in this module.*"

"What do you think he meant by that?" Ferrara asked.

"I think he made a mistake. By revealing it was a lucky coincidence, he as good as said that they don't use that frequency for their comms. And yet they detected it by chance."

"Which means they're using others which are affected by the one the decoy was using," she deduced.

"That's right. With Ada I investigated wave-dispersion on this planet. On Earth, low-, medium- and high-frequency waves would bounce off the ionosphere, so that the signals would be received many kilometers away with no need for repeaters. In comparison, on this planet that layer doesn't seem to be as dense as it was on Earth, which means that the radio waves on this frequency only reach a few kilometers from the transmitter."

"What makes them perfect for short-range communication with no risk of detection," Ferrara concluded.

"Exactly. And in some way the rebels found the transmitter, because it was interfering with their communications."

"And now we know that."

"Still, we'd better move very carefully," Robert said. "They might have prepared an unpleasant surprise for us."

"And do we have any idea where their real base could be?" she asked.

"In fact we don't. Until they move one of their vehicles and need to use GPS, we can't be sure. And unfortunately I'm assuming they only move the ships when they decide to attack one of our bases."

"I get you," Ferrara said. "So we're just going to check that those transponders which have been detected are just decoys."

"Yeah, for the time being I'm afraid that's it."

"Oh, hell," she protested bitterly. "And here was I thinking we were going to have a spot of action!"

"Be careful of what you wish for, Sergeant. On this planet there are all kinds of animals that can split us in half."

They made their way on through the dense forest of that area. It was still quite early, and a dense fog filtered through the treetops, hindering their vision. Ada had memorized and pre-calculated a route before they set off on their mission, so she was guiding them as they moved on through the vegetation.

"How are we going to know whether we're near a trap?" Ferrara asked.

"Ada prepared this rover to detect emissions on all frequencies. If we come near anything that's emitting any kind of signal, we'll find out about it and go on foot. We could also release some of the drones we're carrying in the back."

"And suppose what they've done is set isolated traps, or explosive ones?" she asked.

"They took some of our military equipment," Robert explained, "but let's hope the captain might have decided it was worth keeping the limited arsenal he has available intact, and not waste it setting traditional traps that could easily be activated by some wild animal."

Although they came across one or two isolated animals, they had no other encounter worth mentioning. They came to an area which by then was close enough to the first of the signals to suggest the possibility of going on foot. They left the rover in a reasonably secluded spot, away from indiscreet eyes, and got out of it. Robert opened the rear door and put on a sort of backpack on his chest. Both of them took their guns and some extra ammunition.

"Right," he said once they were ready, "the signal's coming from the northeast. We'd better try not to slip, so that Ada can guide us accurately without the GPS."

"Understood, sir."

"We'll move on in silence," he added. "At least for the moment. Keep an eye on where you're putting your feet."

Ferrara gave him an OK sign with her fingers, and they set off along the road Ada was indicating for them on their visors. They tried to walk very carefully, avoiding tripping over anything and making as little noise as possible. When they had covered a few meters, Robert made a sign with his fist and they both stopped on the spot. He opened the pack he was carrying in front of him and took out three of the small exploration drones. He connected these to his suit through a small cable, then maneuvered them so that they would track and scan whatever he wanted them to. When he had finished setting up the third, he released each of them in a different direction.

"We'll wait here," he whispered.

In not much more than ten minutes the drones appeared again, one after the other. Robert fetched them and once again connected them to his suit terminal, which showed the results of their little excursions on its screen.

"There's nothing around the point indicated. No radio transmitters, no movement sensors, no human structures. I don't think it's worth going anywhere near, there might be some kind of mechanical trap and we'd only find a GPS locator in the underbrush."

"Okay then, let's go on to the next point," Ferrara said. "How far is it?"

"A little over twenty kilometers to the east. Let's go back to the rover."

They took the route Ada was recommending, but before they had even covered half the distance between the two locators, Robert stopped the vehicle again.

He pointed ahead. "There are some structures there, in front of us."

"Where?"

"At around a hundred and fifty meters, at eleven thirty. I'd say it seems to be two wood cabins."

Ferrara nodded. "Yeah, I can see them. "And it looks as though there are more behind. Can you see them?"

"Could be. Let's get out and approach on foot. Get ready for anything."

They repeated the ritual of the previous stop, but this time Robert launched the drones from the rover itself.

"That's odd," he said when he had checked the images they were sending back.

"What is it?"

"It looks like a small Keplerian village, with no more than ten or twelve houses. But though it looks as though the buildings are in a perfect state and there's an occasional vegetable garden, there's no sign of activity."

"It certainly looks strange," she agreed. "We'd better be careful."

"Yeah, I don't know what's going on here, but I don't like the look of it."

"Could be a trap,"

"That's possible."

"Off we go," Ferrara said, smiling mischievously.

In total silence, moving with great care, they approached the back of one of the first visible houses. They walked in short steps, leaning a little sideways to avoid making any noise. They did this with their movements synchronized, each of them watching one flank. Ferrara was the first to lean against one of the back walls of the house, which completely surrounded an enormous tree-trunk. On it in turn there rested a small roof made of wood and dry leaves which leaned against the walls of the structure. All the wood looked more or less new. Robert moved on past her without a word while she peered around the corner, aiming her rifle to cover her superior.

When he reached the nearest corner of the building, she moved forward just behind him and put her left hand on his right shoulder. Both of them covered all the areas of the avenue which now opened in front of them. At least four other houses could be seen from where they were, on the other side of the avenue.

"Clear," Robert said.

"Clear," Ferrara repeated.

"Seems to be no-one in sight. Let's go to the other side."

Both of them peered out with coordinated movements, then crossed the space which separated the two cabins on the edge of the forest from the four in front. They crossed the path which divided the porch of the two first ones. Here there were gardens with strange flowers and plants, and also a small vegetable patch of odd vegetables neither of them had ever seen before. But all of these looked rather unkempt. They spun round, aiming their guns in every direction, as if this were some complicated ballroom dance.

When they came to the gap between the cabins on the other side of the avenue, they separated once again and went on in single file to the next row of trees, where they could catch a glimpse of five other cabins in a row, leaning against five trees.

"Nobody here either," Ferrara whispered.

"The gardens look as though they've been neglected for a couple of weeks," Robert said, looking at the state of some of the plants.

"It's as if the inhabitants had vanished."

"And yet some of the doors are open," he pointed out. "Let's go into this one."

He went through a small wooden gate which separated the avenue from the property. He soon stopped. Something had attracted his attention. He bent down when he came to a small garden of flowers at the entrance.

"What is it, Captain?"

"Someone attacked this place a few days ago. Look, someone bled here. The flowers are crushed, and there's a large dark stain on the ground."

Ferrara stopped scanning the area, aiming her gun as she did so, then turned and bent down beside her superior, who went on examining what he had found.

"Who could have wiped out an entire Keplerian village?" she asked.

"I'll give you two guesses, but I bet your first one's correct," Robert said. He was holding a bullet-casing the same caliber as those in their own weapons.

"Garth!" she exclaimed.

"I told you you'd guess right."

"The bastard!" she shouted. "Why would he do a thing like that?"

"Because of xenophobia, or because he doesn't want any Keplerians near his operations base, or for fun…"

"To wipe out an entire village for fun…" Ferrara said, nauseated. "Just thinking about it makes me want to throw up."

"Let's check the rest of the place. We might find some clue to help us find out what happened here."

One by one, they went through the wooden cabins of the village. In all of them they found marks of blood and signs of violence. They took a particularly close look at one particular dwelling on a corner of the avenue.

"Someone was left here badly wounded but alive," Robert said. He was examining the faint trail of blood which seemed to lead out of the cabin as far as the gate which separated the garden from the avenue.

"Do you think someone got away from the captain alive?"

"Looks like it. But it seems strange to me, because he's very meticulous about everything he does. Leaving a loose end would be an unpardonable mistake on his part, something unworthy of a soldier like him."

"Perhaps all this was done by his minions…"

"So that he missed the entertainment?" Robert asked sarcastically. "He always leads the missions. I don't suppose it was any different this time."

"In that case, it can only mean he did it on purpose."

"Yeah, I fear so. But that brings me back to the same question."

"Why did Captain Garth decide to attack a village of farmers, leaving one person alive?"

"Exactly."

"Maybe to set the Keplerians against us?"

He nodded. "Could be. But what would he get out of a confrontation between Keplerians and humans?"

"Sowing chaos to stop us taking a closer look at what they're doing?"

Robert did not answer this time. It was very strange that Captain Garth should have massacred a whole village without any apparent reason. Something was going on, and his instinct told him that this massacre was going to play an important role in their diplomatic dealings with the Keplerians. They went into the cabin, following the trail of blood.

"My God!" he exclaimed as he looked around the main room.

"What is it?"

"Here's where the survivor took the shot that wounded him." He pointed to a larger stain of dried blood. "But there were two more people here: one sitting in that rocking chair and another in the corner, and judging by the wooden toys on the floor, it was a child."

"What sort of son of a bitch would murder a child in cold blood?" she asked, feeling nauseated.

"A very unscrupulous one."

He examined both spots carefully.

"I think they both bled to death," he said. "But the one who escaped did it by dragging himself along the floor to start with. Then he managed to get up by leaning on the door and the gate of the fence by the porch." He went out again. "He managed to stagger as far the edge of the property, dragging his left leg. Then he went on down the avenue and turned."

They followed the trail of blood, almost imperceptible by now, which went on through the space which separated the survivor's cabin from the one beside it and came to the next avenue of trees. In front of the only cabin on this avenue was an enormous stable with space for a number of animals. But it was empty, with only a couple of dead animals. There were no apparent signs of violence on them.

"Our survivor took a mount from this sable and fled," Robert said.

"It looks as though there were plenty of cattle." She pointed to the many prints inside.

Robert calculated as he examined the flattened land by the stable entrance. "Someone took them away not long ago."

"After the attack?"

He nodded. "Yeah, maybe. The trail of blood fades away just at the area where there are most prints. I'm not sure how fast dead bodies decompose on this planet, but judging by the state of these two animals I'd say they've been dead around a week."

"That means someone came back days after the attack and took the rest of the cattle away."

"That's right. Otherwise they'd have taken these two as well."

"Our leading actor came back a few days later."

"Him, or else someone who knew what had happened here," Robert said. "Don't forget, we haven't found a single dead body. What probably happened is that someone came back to bury them."

23
The second conclave

February 2, year 1

Gaal-El village, Kepler-442b

After the first hesitant rays of light began to filter in through the windows of the room they were staying in, Emily and the others woke up feeling sleepy and still rather tired. The discomfort of their suits and their doubts about what was going to happen had taken their toll on them during the night. But tiredness was not going to spare them the need to climb the steep ramps which led up to the Gaal-El temple. Liikmi came to the inn when he saw that his guests were up.

"Did you sleep well?" he asked.

"Yes, very well," Emily said untruthfully. "Thanks for asking."

He nodded. "Good. I understand you don't need me to prepare breakfast for you."

She shook her head. "We've already done that ourselves."

"Right, in that case we can set off whenever you like."

She turned to her companions. "Are you all ready?"

"Yes," Paula said, "all ready."

"As ready as we can be after sleeping inside these wretched sardine cans," Gorka complained. It looked as though he was not coping very well with the lack of sleep.

Both he and Paula, who had never been there before, enjoyed the climb to the temple immensely. As soon as they reached the more sparsely-vegetated zone and were above the height of most of the trees in the village, they were able to look out at the spectacular views offered by the enormous, red-tinged sea of leaves which extended as far as the eye could see. The wind ruffled the massed crowns of the trees, offering an unforgettable image.

When they reached the apron of flat land which surrounded the monastery, neither of them was able to contain their admiration at what the Keplerians had built there. They went up the wide steps with their accompanying marble busts, and finally came to the temple entrance. There, as at the previous conclave, hundreds of cult-members were waiting, armed with their wooden staves and assembled in orderly rows. They were all waiting attentively for the arrival of the guests.

"Wow!" Paula cried. "This is really impressive!"

"Well, you're going to love what's on its way now," Rakesh warned her.

As they went along the corridor formed by the cult-members, these began to strike the floor sharply, creating the same effect they had experienced on their previous visit. Each row began striking as the visitors made their way toward the temple door.

This time they found the interior well lit. In addition to the two cauldrons, the cracks where the fire had been lit at the previous conclave were still burning. Paula and Gorka were able to see all the details of the interior in all their splendor without any help from their exosuits.

"Hey!" Gorka exclaimed as he looked in every direction. "This is unbelievable!"

Paula's mouth was hanging open from pure awe. "That's right. From outside it doesn't give any hint of this. Look at those frescoes on the ceiling."

Rakesh nodded. "This whole place is a true work of art."

Once again they were the first to arrive, and Liikmi urged them to sit down on the same bench as before. Emily noticed that the flowers on the bench in front had been changed. Now she knew that they were in honor of the Wiijof jikhaashyush, the Keplerian faction which had disappeared. And in the same posture as before, in the same place, was Waafdiv: still and impassive, taking no notice of the minor outbreak of noise his fellow-cult-members had just created in the stillness. Emily realized that though they themselves were the only ones there, the staves belonging to the Keplerian village leaders were still standing where they had been left when the leaders themselves had gone into the small room behind the reredos.

They haven't taken them away, she thought. *It must be a way of showing that the sole duty of the leaders is to resolve the issues that came up in the conclave.*

One by one, and in the same order, the various Keplerian delegations began to make their appearance. The first to arrive was that of the Wiikhaadiiz ofiz with their leader Khikhya, clumsy without her staff, leaning on the arm of one of her counselors. A few minutes later the Khaavahki appeared, led by Vaahur, who this time was only accompanied by the two high-ranking officers, Lajlab and the other, older and more senior Keplerian. There was no trace of the mysterious young man who seemed to have had a meeting with Khikhya during the previous few days.

Perhaps Khikhya was in cahoots somehow with the young soldier from the Khaavahki, and Vaahur's found them out, Emily wondered when she saw that the Khaavahki delegation was not the same as before.

Then, and after the appropriate announcement from the cult-members outside, came the turn of the representatives of the Khapabir village, whose delegation was led by Khaaÿ, their old leader. The five members of this final faction took longer than expected to take their seats. As with Khikhya, age weighed heavily on the old man's shoulders by now, but unlike his colleague he did not accept the help of any of his four counselors, which delayed his progress.

Despite the fact that everyone was now seated in their respective places, Waafdiv stayed immobile for a few more minutes, ignoring everyone there. As before, he got up without warning and went to the wooden reredos which adorned the front of the temple. Once again he appeared bearing the huge and ancient book which contained all the liturgical knowledge of the Gaal-El. With extreme care he placed it on the altar, then raised his arms and turned to the audience.

"My Keplerian brothers and sisters," he began solemnly, "once again I welcome you and thank you for your presence in this sacred temple of the Gaal-El. Our people are now deep in meditation and in the hope that they will see their leaders concluding the deliberations which arose from the first session of the conclave, a meeting which was once again celebrated after so many years and which once again links us with our most ancient traditions."

He paused for a moment, then began again: "Today, however, we are not gathered here to conclude what we began a few days ago but in answer to a request for clarification by the Khaavahki people. Hence, without further delay, the leaders of the free Keplerian peoples will now enter the conclave hall to consider the said request."

After a few moments of silence, he repeated the entry ritual for the conclave chamber.

He raised his arms, "I, Waafdiv, high priest of the Gaal-El, invoke the ancestral and sacred conclave of the Keplerian peoples. And for the moment I leave my command here at the disposition of the conclave while the future of our society is being determined. And to seal my commitment to the Keplerian people, I offer my own blood in symbol of submission."

As he had done the time before, he cut his hand with the ceremonial dagger and poured a few drops of his blood into a bowl. One by one, the other three leaders repeated the same liturgy and shed their own blood into the same bowl. Once the first part of the ceremony was over Waafdiv took the bowl and poured its contents into the stone sink in one corner. This done, the four leaders went into the conclave chamber once again, and with a metallic sound the door shut behind them.

"Now we have to wait," said Rakesh.

"So far it doesn't look as though anything out of the ordinary's happening, wouldn't you say?" Paula asked optimistically.

Emily was looking around uneasily. "No, everything seems quiet."

They all waited, bored, while inside the chamber some kind of amendment to the Gaal-El proposals was presumably under discussion. Vaahur had not seemed too keen to give up his command staff at the previous conclave and must have decided to dig in his heels. Emily relaxed a little when she realized that at least for the time being, the path of diplomacy seemed to be working when it came to resolving disputes between the various peoples.

Both Paula and Gorka got up from the bench to look more closely at the many inscriptions and carvings in the hall. Some of the counselors decided to go outside to stretch their legs and get some fresh air. The two Khaavahki soldiers, on the other hand, were much quieter than usual today and barely moved. Perhaps they had a better idea than the others of what was being discussed in the chamber. This began to make Emily nervous.

Suddenly, and despite the thick walls which separated them, a growing murmur from inside the chamber began to be audible. A heated argument had begun in the midst of the conclave, Whatever Vaahur might have brought with him, it did not seem to have pleased the other leaders.

The noise went on for several intense and interminable minutes. At last, when almost an hour had gone by since the beginning of the conclave, the sound of the key in the door of the chamber announced that something was about to happen. The four cult-members who were acting as guides to the delegations hastened to it. Waafdiv conversed with them in a whisper. At that exact moment, something unusual happened in Emily's suit and those of her companions, a small warning appeared in their helmet visors: *Connection lost.*

Liikmi came up to her.

"The leaders request your presence inside the chamber."

She and Rakesh got up from the bench, but Liikmi made a gesture to him.

"I'm afraid that this time they've only asked for the presence of the chosen one."

Paula grasped her arm. "Something's happening here. We have no connection with either the Asimov or the rover."

Emily stopped for a moment and thought about the situation.

"Try to recover comms," she said. "I can't make them wait."

She gave her three companions a reassuring wave and went across to the entrance to the chamber. Inside it the four leaders were seated, looking serious and concerned. Whatever they might have been discussing until that moment, the tension was palpable. Waafdiv proceeded to shut the door once again; it was clear that he was noticeably dissatisfied, even a little downcast.

Emily sat down in the vacant chair, but nobody addressed her. Their heads were all bowed, except for Vaahur, who was looking at her defiantly with a grimace which was clearly intended to be a triumphant smile.

"Well, Miss Rhodes," the leader of the Khaavahki began. "I understand that's what the humans call one another, am I right? They use their father's name."

"Yes, that's right."

She did not like the tone the conversation was beginning to take.

"All right, Miss Rhodes," he repeated. "You must be wondering why I've called this conclave. You must believe that our people don't want a foreigner in sole command of the Keplerians. And in fact you're not altogether wrong. The Khaavahki people don't want you here. But that isn't really the reason why I called this conclave."

He got up from his chair, passed behind Khaaÿ, the leader of the Khapabir people and came up to her.

"Would you be able to tell me what this is?" he asked. As he spoke, he laid several small plastic cylinders on the table.

Emily stared at them closely. She knew perfectly well what they were.

"They're... bullet-cases."

"Forgive us, but I don't think we're familiar with human technology. Where do these small pieces come from?"

"They're the remains that fall to the ground when our weapons are fired."

Vaahur pointed at the other leaders there, who were listening carefully. But he did so more forcefully when he came to Waafdiv.

"You see? She herself has just confirmed what I told you. They feel they're so superior they don't even try to hide their barbarity."

"What's going on here?" Emily asked. "Where did these cases come from?"

"There's no need for you to pretend, you know perfectly well we're talking about the atrocious crime you and your people committed three weeks ago."

She was completely taken aback by this. "What? What are you talking about?"

"You know perfectly well. Three weeks ago, you and a group of humans dressed in that same armor"—he pointed to her exosuit— "massacred a village of nomadic farmers, putting an end to nineteen

Keplerian lives, including a pregnant female and her little son."

"What!" she repeated, still not understanding. "We haven't done anything as horrible as that!"

"There's no point in your denying it," Vaahur said. "We have witnesses who can confirm this. And you're going to have to pay for your crimes."

"But this can't be true," she insisted. "We've never attacked Keplerians."

Vaahur banged the table hard. "You're lying again!"

"We'd better stay calm," Waafdiv put in. "I'm sure there must be a mistake and that there's some logical explanation for all this."

"What explanation can there be?" Vaahur shouted furiously. "The humans you so worship have massacred nineteen innocent Keplerians. What else do you need before you accept the evidence?"

"What motive would they have for committing an atrocity like that?"

"Isn't it obvious? They want our land! And to get hold of that, they know they'll have to exterminate all of us. They've begun with this one small village, and if we don't act decisively they'll gain control of all our other villages."

"I think the human has the right to defend herself," said Khikhya, who until that moment had not opened her mouth.

The four of them stared at Emily, whose brain was racing furiously. If all this was true, it was clear that it bore Captain Garth's signature. But it was also obvious that Vaahur would never believe her. She could tell from a league away that he had no intention of doing that. And in any case, whether or not Garth had been responsible for the massacre, it was still an attack on Keplerians by humans, with nineteen casualties. It was going to be incredibly difficult to manage this situation, and the trust of the Keplerian peoples had now been lost forever.

"I can promise you that neither I nor any of my allies have attacked any of your people," she said after considering her reply.

"I think you're going to have to give us something more than a promise," Khikhya said very seriously.

"At the moment it's all I can give you. I've only just found out that a terrible attack has taken place. If you grant me time to look into it more deeply—"

"Time?" Vaahur broke in. "I don't know how justice works among humans, but here delinquents and criminals are punished decisively."

"By all the stars in heaven, how the devil do you expect her to prove her innocence if you won't let her investigate what happened?" Waafdiv asked. Like Emily, he seemed not to understand anything of what was happening.

"Your absurd creed and your hopes are clouding your judgment, Waafdiv. The humans have come all the way here to put an end to us all. No foreigner is to be trusted."

"They deserve a fair trial!"

"I'd be lying if I said I'm particularly sorry," Vaahur said, "but I have no choice but to put her under arrest."

"What?" Waafdiv shouted. "This is ridiculous! You can't do that!"

Vaahur laughed. "Can't I? I'm the highest military authority among all Keplerians. Of course I can! And I that's what I'm going to do!"

Waafdiv turned to the two other leaders. "I can't believe we're allowing the people who are destined to save us from the Khol to be treated in this way. Khaaÿ, you haven't said a word in all this time. Help me stop this nonsense."

The old man looked up from the table, and after thinking about it for a moment he said: "I'm trying to make sense of all this confusion, Waafdiv, I'm really trying. But unfortunately at this moment everything points to the fact that it was a human attack."

Waafdiv turned to Khikhya.

"Khikhya, you know this human better than anyone. Do you really believe her capable of doing a thing like that?"

"Quite honestly, I don't know what to believe any longer," she said. "Of course if it were true it would certainly make me feel very stupid. I've welcomed them into my own home, thinking about the good of my people… and… and then…"

She seemed to crumple at the thought of the atrocities which had been committed in the village.

"You haven't been able to convince anyone, you sanctimonious fool," Vaahur said mockingly. "At least have the dignity to admit your defeat. But don't you worry in the slightest, your jar of drink is waiting for you and you'll be able to go back to your previous life, before all this pantomime ever began."

Waafdiv lunged at him in fury and launched a powerful right hook to his chin, which took the Khaavahki leader by surprise. The force of the blow made him trip and topple backwards, and he fell against the wooden floor with some force.

"This is all your idea, Vaahur!" Waafdiv cried, beside himself with anger. "Don't think I haven't realized that, you despicable rat!"

Vaahur got up from the floor with difficulty, but he laughed maliciously as he became aware of the high priest's reaction.

"I admit you have a good punch, for a damned sanctimonious drunkard," he said as he rubbed his jaw. "But what you've just done was sign the death sentence of your beloved and useless cult."

An endless series of forceful footsteps seemed to be approaching the entrance to the chamber from outside. There were shouts and scuffles which ended up with the unmistakable and desperate scream of a woman.

"Paula!" Emily shouted.

"You'd better all get away from the door," Vaahur said.

"This is a sacred place!" Waafdiv cried.

"I warned you that a foreigner couldn't take on sole command of the Keplerian peoples. Foreigners aren't trustworthy. These are the first consequences of that."

A powerful impact struck the massive wooden door, which withstood the first blow. A second snapped one of the huge metal hinges which supported its weight, but it could not withstand a third and collapsed with a deafening crash. The door, which was of incalculable value, splintered in several places and its beautiful carvings were destroyed.

Immediately a dozen soldiers armed with enormous halberds and wearing heavy breastplates burst into the chamber. They surrounded Emily and aimed their weapons at her. Lajlab entered with them with his usual evil smile.

"If I were you I wouldn't try anything stupid," Vaahur's minion said calmly. "We have your friends. Although I have to admit, it was harder than I'd expected to deal with the big one."

"I won't resist," Emily assured him. "I'll come with you, but I'm the one responsible for the human base. They have nothing to do with this."

"Unfortunately," Vaahur said, "you aren't the one who decides. Take her, all of you!"

Two of the soldiers pulled her arms behind her back and attached a couple of rudimentary but solid handcuffs of cast metal.

"Take her away!" Lajlab ordered.

The soldiers obeyed the orders swiftly, and Emily was able to see the state of her companions as she came out of the chamber. Paula and Rakesh seemed to be all right. Paula was weeping beside Gorka, who was lying on the floor surrounded by a crowd of Keplerian soldiers. However, the ex-boxer had not gone down without a fight. Emily could count eight injured and three unconscious.

"Are you all right?" she asked as they were taken out of the temple.

Paula was still sobbing. "Yes. But Gorka…"

"What happened?"

"They came without warning and tried to arrest us," Rakesh explained. "Gorka managed to get free of several of them, but then one of them used a kind of Taser to bring him down. What happened in there?"

"Garth, that's what happened," said Emily as they were taken out to the open area in front of the temple.

24
The eye of the mountain

February 2, year 1

Unknown location, Kepler-442b

Robert and Ferrara went back to the rover and left the scene of the massacre. They skirted it to the south, where the land was beginning to slope upward as it approached the mountain range. On the way they passed a wooden cart containing a few tools which looked as though it had been abandoned hastily. They assumed it must have belonged to some inhabitant of the village who had fled at the sound of gunfire.

"I guess we go on to the next signal," Ferrara said wearily.

"Yeah, though my stomach's upset. Still, we have to go on with our mission, and we still have four other possible locations left. We need to find them before we can put an end to all this."

She nodded. "Especially knowing they're capable of attacking innocents."

They moved on through the vegetation in silence for a few minutes. On several occasions Robert had to maneuver the rover to avoid rocks, tangles of thorns, or else some deep dip in the ground.

"Can I ask you a question, captain?"

"Sure, sergeant, though I don't want us to get distracted talking. We could be close to our goal by now, and we need to be more alert than ever."

"Yeah, of course. It's just that what we've found has got me thinking."

"I don't blame you. We've just seen the remains of a barbarity that's completely unprecedented. I'd be telling you a lie if I pretended that what we've just seen isn't going round and round in my head."

"Well, it's like this," she said. "Human history is full of cases where the more powerful, or more advanced, civilization ends up

216

subjugating the weaker. And often that ended in total extermination of the race that was less well-prepared. It happened with the Australopithecines, who succumbed when they were confronted with Homo habilis, along with other reasons. But also with a lot of native people in the Americas, or in Africa, and all sorts of other places on Earth throughout our history."

"Are you worried we might end up doing the same to the Keplerians?" Robert asked.

"Yes."

"I can't give you an answer to that. But if it's any consolation, I ask myself the same thing every time I think of the Keplerians and their civilization, and the fact that they're the true settlers of these lands, not us."

"Do you think we'll end up exterminating them, the way Garth intends to?" Ferrara asked.

"If it were up to me," Robert said, "you can be sure that would never happen. I'd rather live the rest of my life in a space station, or even die, than take part in genocide. For better or worse, this planet is enormous, and if the Keplerians aren't populating the other continents, then we might get to share it in relative harmony. But whatever happens in generations to come… I'm afraid that's beyond our reach."

"We've no right to do it," she said adamantly. "And it really gets to me that people, for lack of a better word, like Captain Garth, could even dream of doing anything like what we've just seen."

"Captain Garth isn't a representative of the morality the founders of the project followed to establish all this."

"Yeah, but I have the feeling that sooner or later we'll end up doing just that. And what's more, the Khol might do the same with us."

"That's quite true," Robert said. "How can we even think about creating a family and settling down anywhere on this planet, with all the uncertainty around us?"

They were both silent. They were aware that they were living through difficult moments for humanity. The battle was being fought on many fronts, and ethics and morals needed to take precedence in those initial moments. It made no sense for either of them to establish the foundations of a new civilization on the same atrocities as the one before.

"Perhaps our fate's to go extinct," Ferrara said thoughtfully.

There were still a few kilometers left to the next signal, but though the conversation could have gone on for much longer, both of them made the decision to be silent. They had nothing positive to say, so they decided to concentrate on the task which had brought them there. Several animals crossed their path in the course of this stretch: a flying insect, worryingly large and dangerous-looking; the occasional evasive animal which fled as soon as it became aware of the rover's presence; and they even caught a glimpse out of the corner of their eye of one or two animals leaping from the branch of a tree to catch their prey on the ground.

Once they were close to the signal, but still a safe distance away, both of them got down from the vehicle and went through the same routine as before. Robert launched the drones, and they got ready to start walking if they found any signal which would indicate the location of the rebel base.

The drones came back, and the captain checked the results one by one.

"Negative, there doesn't seem to be anything here either. We'll take a break and stretch our legs. We can take the opportunity to have something to eat."

"I don't feel much like eating, quite honestly," she admitted.

"Do it. We never know when it might turn out to be the last mush we ever get the chance to eat. In fact we ought to charge our suits too while we're on the move in the rover."

"Understood, captain. Shouldn't we say something about what we found?"

Robert nodded. "I thought about it, but it's too late for the villagers now. And it seems to have happened several days ago, so I don't really think reporting immediately would make much of a difference. Especially knowing that it would give our position away. If the rebels detect us, they'll know we're getting closer. Then we'd lose the surprise factor, and they'd know we'd found the device they were hiding in the station."

"That's true. This is getting to be very hard to manage."

Both of them had something to eat and rested for some time, contemplating the red immensity which stretched away in front of them. They had found no trace of the rebels yet, and they had to finish the mission before the day was over. Though they did not think it probable, there might be Yokai anywhere around. It did not seem particularly intelligent to stay there overnight to find out whether or not there really were.

"On we go," Robert said. He headed the vehicle toward the next point.

They had not even traveled a couple of kilometers when the radio system began working. All they could hear was static, but every now and then they would make out other tones, which vanished amid the white sound generated by the analogue radio receiver they had installed.

"D'you think it's them?" Ferrara asked.

"It's got to be. I programmed the radio to make a continuous scan of the whole frequency range."

She indicated the terminal. "There seems to be something between two point two and two point seven megahertz."

"The decoy we put in the other base was five megahertz, so they might just have stumbled on it by chance."

"We used a frequency just double the frequency of theirs," Ferrara pointed out. "That might have generated harmonics, which is why one signal might have cancelled the other."

"Yeah, that makes sense. I'll release the drones again."

He operated the three devices, which vanished through the treetops, each in a different direction.

"Keep on the alert," he said. "We're only a few kilometers away, but there might just be some surprise waiting in the surroundings."

It was not long before the devices returned. Robert studied them one by one while Ferrara kept watch. His eyes widened when he saw the place the drones had flown over.

"Have they found anything, captain?" she asked eagerly.

"Yeah. But it's really strange."

"Why?"

"See for yourself,"

He showed her the images one of the drones had recorded during its brief foray. In them the lie of the land was growing steeper. The increasing frequency of rocks and almost vertical walls gave the impression that the range was turning predominantly rocky, though there were still a few trees and bushes here and there.

But then the device came to a location some ten kilometers from their own position, and here the lower slopes of the mountain vanished. In their place was a huge square hollow which continued into the mountain itself. Those stone walls formed an enormous void a kilometer or so wide and went on into the mountain as if this were an enormous cubic cave, several hundred meters high. It was too perfect to be a cave.

Ferrara looked at her superior in disbelief. "How can this be possible?"

"I've no idea. But I'm quite sure that cave isn't natural."

He pointed to the edges of the crevice, which had been carved out of the stone itself. Their surface was completely smooth.

"Look at this: the walls are practically flat. There are only a few areas where you can see impurities and parts where the stone looks more worn."

"But this can't be the work of Captain Garth and the rebels," she said. "They don't have the machinery to make an excavation on this scale."

"I doubt very much whether there's any machinery in the Asimov that's even remotely capable of doing anything like this."

"Are you suggesting it's the work of aliens?"

"Well, it certainly isn't human. There's no rubble anywhere, and besides, the walls themselves look as though they're eroded. And they've been damaged by landslides."

"So it's a very ancient construction."

"Yeah, thousands of years old, maybe."

"Do you think the ones who built the obelisks made this?" Ferrara asked.

"It's a possibility. I doubt very much whether the Keplerians could have managed this with the technology they have available."

They watched the rest of the recording from Robert's terminal and saw that all along that crevice, in a fairly flat and secluded area, a dozen or so transport ships lay on the stone floor, unaware that a small drone was watching them from afar. Near that improvised hangar a number of interconnected habitat modules made up the rebel base they had been in search of for so long.

"There they are!" exclaimed cried triumphantly. "We've got them!"

"Yes, at last."

"So now what? Do we inform the Asimov and come back with the cavalry?"

"No, not yet. We're going to get a bit closer. From here it looks as though this was some kind of hangar once upon a time. Maybe from closer to it we might be able to see some kind of building or sign that could give us a clue. And also I want to see how complicated it would be to get to them without being detected."

"Action at last!" Ferrara said cheerfully.

Robert put the pack containing the drones on his chest, and Ferrara loaded herself with all the equipment she could carry. They left the rover well-hidden in a clump of vegetation and set off to the east, toward the hollow. They walked in single file and without a word, both of them knowing what they had to do at any given moment. Gun in hand, each of them in charge of one flank, they covered the distance that separated them from the beginning of the hollow. By the time they got there they had already travelled nearly six kilometers. They found no sign of activity whatever, nothing more than the occasional small animal, or else clouds of insects which fed on the resins which oozed from some of the species of trees there.

They came to an area where the land descended in what seemed an unnatural way: a descent too pronounced and regular to be natural and which continued inside the mountain. Robert gestured to Ferrara to be on the alert; they had now reached the part where the colossal excavation began to enter the range. If their calculations were correct, this was something like a ramp which would lead them to the rebel base. What in the distant past must have been a waste-land was now a dense forest which prevented the occupants of the cave from keeping watch on the entrance from their artificial lookout.

Ferrara got ready to descend the ramp, which was inclined about forty-five degrees and was almost thirty meters high. But before she could take two steps, Robert stopped her with a gesture. He pointed to his own eyes with two fingers, then to an area five meters away. He approached this area very slowly. Just before he got there, he stopped and crouched down so that he could get a closer look. Once he had found what he was looking for, he beckoned her to his side. He showed her where a small device had been camouflaged between two trees.

He lowered his voice to a whisper. "Activate the infrared, with a daylight filter."

Ferrara did so by operating her terminal, to avoid giving Ada the order.

"Movement-detector lasers," she muttered under her breath.

Robert stood up and prepared one of the drones. He specified a course along all the edges of the crevice, so that it would start on their side and come back along the other. He adjusted its lenses so that it would detect the lasers the rebels had set around the perimeter, then sent it to gather information. After a little while it came back again, silent as a raptor. He examined the information the drone had gathered and pointed toward the south, following the edge of the crevice.

"We'll skirt this area," he whispered. "Further on there are two turrets keeping watch on the front of the base. If we go round it'll be more complicated, but that way we'll avoid their sensors."

They began the ascent toward the mountain, skirting the crevice which burrowed further and further into the innards of the land. There were fewer and fewer trees as they went on, and those which managed to grow were progressively smaller. It was obvious that this area was rockier, with less soil to put down roots in. Everything was going well, with both of them making sure there were no surprises on the way. Until Robert peered over one of the edges and slipped on a loose pebble. His left foot sank toward the abyss, so that the rest of his body lost its balance and began to slide helplessly toward the bottom of that ancient structure.

It seemed to him that the fall lasted an eternity. He tried to cling onto something, but he had fallen on his back and however hard he tried, the angle was too steep for any of the bushes on his way to stop his uncontrolled fall. Then he thought of activating his suit thrusters, and this slowed him down, allowing him to cling to a bush without breaking it. At last he came to a halt.

A quantity of earth and stones of various sizes went on sliding down the steep slope. He had caused quite a disturbance. He realized that this unfortunate slip could easily have revealed his presence to the rebels. He stayed there without moving for several moments with his heart in his mouth, waiting for a warning shot or an alarm which never sounded. He had no idea how far away the turrets were, but he knew they could have detected the tremendous blunder he had just committed.

He gathered his courage together and at last got to his feet. He decided to stay crouching and observe the area cautiously while he was hidden behind the bush which had helped break his fall. Without warning, something moved on his left. In the visor of his exosuit a small yellow square was blinking, and this indicated that there was something unknown on one side. Luckily the suit had allowed him to keep his gun in his hand, and at once he aimed at the area superimposed on his visor. He hesitated for a few moments because he could not see what had moved, but whatever it was had stopped by now. Maybe it had just been a pebble. Then something like a six-legged lizard with a tiny tail emerged from another bush; it too must have been frightened by his slip. The creature ran to hide behind a clump of dense ferns.

Robert heaved a deep sigh and set off up to the edge of the crevice again. Ferrara was waiting there, lying on the ledge and aiming her gun to give him cover.

"You all right, sir?"

"Yeah, don't worry. I hope I haven't given our position away with my clumsiness."

"Don't worry, sir. Except for that thing you saw, not a soul's moved."

"Let's go on, then. And we'd better hope I don't cause a landslide this time."

It did not take them long to reach a stretch of wasteland which was beginning to take on a pronounced angle. By now the crevice, instead of rising at forty-five degrees, was now entirely vertical down to the ground, which was more than two hundred meters away. They did not approach the edge until Robert was sure they could not be spotted from there with the naked eye. They both crawled to the edge and looked down into the abyss, taking great care not to make the same mistake again.

"We're very high up," Ferrara whispered.

"Be careful, sergeant."

Both of them looked to their right, toward the interior of the mountain, where a hundred and fifty meters below and two hundred more toward the interior they could see the transports and structures of the rebel base. Robert used the optical capabilities of the suit to get the best possible view of the way Captain Garth and his engineers had installed the habitats. Although it was not very different from the Magellan base, the rebels had managed to take the equivalent of two complexes like the one Emily and her colleagues were now living in, so that they had more modules interconnected.

The floor seemed to be of living rock, so that instead of burying the tanks for water and air, or the fusion reactors, these were distributed among the other habitats. There was hardly any natural light, but spotlights allowed them to see normally, although at that particular moment they were turned off. There was no specialist botanist among the rebels, so Robert guessed that their food would come mostly from the local fauna. And in fact it looked as though something was roasting on a huge bonfire at the front of the base. At that particular moment one or two embers were shining weakly, perhaps what was left from lunchtime.

"I think they're preparing some animal for roasting," Ferrara pointed out. "Look there, the side of the module nearest the ships."

Two rebels in their red-painted exosuits were skinning an animal the size of a boar.

"They won't have anything else to eat," Robert said. "They've got mash, but they're probably saving that for long-range military operations. And as they don't have access to the Asimov greenhouses, they have to resort to hunting."

"But is it safe to eat the things that grow here, or live here?" she asked.

"I'm no expert, but it could be. Dr. Murakami and Dr. Williams are studying the long-range effects the food of the planet could have on our organism. But in the short term it might have no obvious effect, apart from a bit of discomfort or mild diarrhea."

"What is it you want to find?" Ferrara asked, changing the subject.

"Above all, the defenses they have available."

She shook her head. "Apart from the two automatic turrets you can see below and what little firepower the transports have, I can't see anything worth mentioning. You could say it's not very well-defended."

"Their greatest asset is the site they've chosen. Without an adequate arsenal at their disposal, it's all they could manage. They're protected from behind by the mountain." He pointed to the darkness, which deepened toward the interior. "And that forces any attacker to make a frontal approach. They could defend it easily with very little manpower. They've chosen the best possible place for avoiding an attack. Even if we were to let ourselves fall on them from up here, we'd touch down in a dangerous spot."

"Do we intend to attack?" Ferrara asked.

"No, at least for the time being. But in the future, who knows… Now let's go. We've got what we wanted, and we can go back to the rover."

They went down the mountain toward where they had hidden the vehicle, then left the area. Now they had to get back to the pickup point and report on everything they had found.

25
Quick trial

February 2, year 1

Khaavahki prison, Kepler-442b

It took them several hours to take the four detainees away from the temple. Emily could not see anything during the journey, because the Khaavahki soldiers had put something like a cloth bag over their heads. She was sharing the cart with her friends, but the soldiers with them would not allow them to talk and hit their helmets every time they spoke a couple of words. She imagined that all of them had their hands tied behind their backs. She was reluctant even to test the strength of the Keplerian handcuffs, as some soldier might use his Taser on her.

As far as she knew from the few words they had managed to exchange among themselves Gorka was all right: unconscious, but alive. If they had used a Taser as they had on her when she herself had been kidnapped, it was quite possible that his suit might have a problem now. They would have to wait until he woke up to find out for sure. Their comms were still not working, so there was no way they could warn the station of what had happened. She presumed that when they were confronted with a prolonged lack of communication, someone would go to the Gaal-El temple to find out what had happened. But they themselves would be a long way away from there by now. She trusted that everything would be cleared up and that this would not start a violent escalation of violence between humans and Keplerians.

When they reached their destination they were pushed off the cart they had travelled in and taken in different directions, first to the left, then to the right, then again to the left, until she had lost count. The only thing she knew for sure was that they were in a building with stone floors and that they were going down into the depths, at least two floors below the ground.

After going through several doors, they came at last to a place where the soldiers, who had led her there without any pretense at gentleness, stopped dead. For the whole journey she had been forced to put up with the jubilation of her captors at having caught the foreigners who were guilty of the massacre, all of it spiced with unflattering adjectives and one or two additional jokes.

A very recognizable metallic sound announced the opening of some kind of ancient lock. After the screeching of the hinges, one of the soldiers took off the cloth bag which had kept her in half-light during the journey, and she was shoved into a dark cell. Then her jailers shut the door behind her again, and darkness returned.

"Ada, infrared," she whispered.

The cell was tiny, barely two by three meters. Everything was of stone and there was no other opening, only the enormous wooden door, reinforced with metal, which separated her from her captors. In one of the corners a small pile of unhealthy-looking hay seemed to be doing duty as a mattress. In the opposite one, excrement and urine made her give thanks that she still had oxygen in her suit.

The oxygen, she thought suddenly.

She checked the state of her suit. She still had thirteen hours of oxygen supply and thirty-nine of battery, though these were relative numbers based on average consumption so far. She would have to save oxygen. The situation did not look in the least hopeful, but despite that, it was vital that she should stay calm. She found herself regretting the fact that the experimental suit had failed just before they had come to the second conclave, although that would not have helped her colleagues. By now it was some time since she had heard from them. She did not even know where they were, or when they had been separated.

"Paula?" she asked aloud, hoping for an answer.

The only reply she got was from a Keplerian soldier, who slid back a tiny peephole in the door and looked in.

"Shut up, you foreign rat!" he spat viciously.

"Ada, can you pick up any sound that might belong to a human?"

"No, Emily," her suit's AI replied. "All I can hear is moans and conversations between Keplerians."

"Do you have any idea where I am?"

"No, Emily, I'm sorry. My functions are limited now I have no connection to the Asimov station."

She tried to get rid of the metal handcuffs she was still wearing. The suit was able to generate considerable force, but even so, the effort was in vain. The handcuffs were very strong. If Captain Garth was behind this detention, it was clear that he had taken the capacities of the suits into account.

"Put the suit on resource-saving mode," she said after she had taken a sip of water and some mash.

Her visor went out completely, leaving her in the dark and showing only the meters for energy and supplies to one side.

I've got to think of something

However much she went over the situation, she could not come up with anything which looked like a feasible plan. She could try to bring down the door, but as with the handcuffs, it seemed logical to think that their captors were prepared to keep the humans imprisoned. Quite apart from that, she would risk having a Taser end up ruining everything. As long as she was conscious, she might just manage to come up with some idea, however unlikely.

Emily came out of her lethargy an hour later when she heard the lock opening. The darkness was complete, both within the cell and without. There was no doubt that the Keplerians' night vision gave them a strategic advantage in those conditions.

"Up!" came a cruel voice from the doorway.

She turned on her infrared vision and saw a Khaavahki soldier wearing slightly more elegant clothes than those of the two soldiers who were guarding her cell. He had covered his face with a scarf, a sign that the stench was not to his liking.

"Come out of there!"

She obeyed and followed the Keplerian, although she was never free from the two huge soldiers who were guarding her a few steps behind. They were now in a corridor full of cells. They turned right, then right again at the end. From here they moved on to a wider area with a spiral staircase leading to the upper levels. She could count at least six other guards in the course of that short walk, and she also heard Keplerian voices laughing and shouting from a room she could not place. But though she tried, she could see no sign that indicated where her friends might be locked up.

They went up the narrow stairs for two floors, with the two guards forced to go in single file, one in front of her and one behind. The officer led her along a couple of corridors to an enormous double door. She could see more light than usual, so she guessed that they were above the surface.

He opened both doors, and she went into a large rectangular hall with numerous stained-glass windows and semicircular arches which allowed in a faint light. However, far from looking majestic, they produced a rather dismal effect. A worn khaki carpet started at the entrance and ended thirty meters ahead, where after avoiding several steps it reached the foot of an old wooden throne on which someone she recognized immediately was seated. The walls were covered with threadbare tapestries and ancient shields, revealing that the place had seen better times.

Vaahur was waiting impatiently. He was wearing full uniform, the same khaki as the carpet, and on either side of him were his two counselors, Lajlab and the more senior soldier who had also been at the conclave. On either side at the far end of the hall several officers of the military high command were watching the scene curiously, following Emily with their gaze as she went forward to the front of the hall. Another lower-ranking officer wearing a black stole was standing waiting for the group in front of the steps. If she had not known that she was light years from Earth, she might have thought she had just used a time machine to travel to medieval England.

When they came to the end of the hall, the officer who had come to fetch her bowed.

"The prisoner, your honor," he announced.

"Thank you, lieutenant," said the Keplerian who was waiting at the foot of the steps.

The officer stood to attention and went back the way he had come, but the two guards stayed a few steps behind Emily to keep an eye on her. Standing at strategic points along the hall were several more soldiers wearing heavy breastplates and armed with halberds three meters long.

"Leader Vaahur," began the soldier, who seemed to be a kind of prosecutor, "counselors, members of the tribunal"—here he turned to the Keplerians sitting on the benches on either side—"we find ourselves dealing with one of the most controversial cases our beloved society has known until today.

"As you all know, a few days ago a nomadic carpenter reached our walls from a small village to the northwest of here. Shyiich, for that is his name, was mortally wounded. Luckily, and despite his very serious wound, he was able to survive. However, his good luck in managing to travel the hundred kilometers which separate the heart of the mountains from our village was not shared by the other Keplerians who inhabited that humble village, and whose worst sin was that of cultivating their fields and tending their cattle.

He pointed forcefully at Emily. "Here, in this very place, in front of you all, is the author of this shameful act. And thanks to the shrewdness of our revered leader, she has been apprehended along with the other foreigners who took part in the barbarities on trial here."

"But that's a lie!" she protested. "We haven't committed any crime!"

"Silence, foreigner!" Vaahur shouted. "I won't tolerate any insolence!"

"But everything he's said is false! Neither I nor any of my friends have even been in any nomad village!"

The guards hit the back of her knees sharply, and she fell to the floor despite her exosuit.

"Miss Rhodes," Vaahur said patronizingly, "I recommend you not to interrupt the judge's allegation, because that might complicate your situation even further."

"Your problem is only with me!" Emily shouted. "Release my friends!"

"Continue!" he urged the judge with a wave of his hand, ignoring her completely.

The judge nodded. "Thank you, sir. As I was saying, young Shyiich appeared at the gates of Khaavahki badly wounded, almost dead and apparently delirious, or so we believed at first. To start with, all he could do was mumble incoherently about some strange creatures which had killed his family. But as the hours went by, once he had received medical attention, he began to describe with great detail what he had experienced in his own village. According to this brave Keplerian, at least two foreigners, wearing strange metal armor and carrying diabolical devices which spit small arrows, killed the nineteen inhabitants of the village one by one, including his pregnant wife and his seven-year-old son."

A murmur rose in the hall, while the judge stopped his address for several moments to encourage the indignation of the assembled crowd.

"The foreign humans arrived here several rotations ago," he went on, "and although they deceived other leaders by making them believe they had come without any warlike intention, reality has shown that they were lying. In the course of this hearing you will be able to listen to various testimonies which reveal the lies which have defined the acts committed by the humans. With our leader's permission"—he turned to Vaahur—"I would now like to summon Hionerf, an elder from the Wiikhaadiiz ofiz village."

Vaahur waved his hand reluctantly, inviting him to proceed. One of the sentries on guard at the entrance opened the doors wide to admit an old man, who hobbled in toward the front of the hall. When he came alongside the others, the judge told him where he had to stand so that he could address the people attending the hearing. The man did as he was told without a word.

"Could you tell us your name and what you do?"

"I'm Hionerf, of the Wiikhaadiiz ofiz village. I'm a fisherman, and I'm occupied chiefly with fishing and food."

"Thank you, Hionerf. Tell us what happened the day you and your grandson came across the humans."

"Certainly," the old man said. "My grandson is thirty-six years old, he's still a little fish, and though he still has some time left to decide his future profession, I like to take him fishing with me from time to time so that he knows his origins. My grandfather did this with me and I do the same with him. I suppose I look forward to my grandson following in the same steps as the sixth generation of our family, who are dedicated in body and soul to this noble art."

"Tell us what happened that afternoon."

"*Huuros* are best caught in the last hour of the day," the old man went on. "They like to take advantage of the last rays of light to look for food among the reeds and water-lilies in waters that are quiet, almost stagnant."

"Please be brief," the judge interrupted him. "What happened then?"

"I was just providing a little context for those listening. You young ones nowadays are always in a hurry." This reproach, addressed to the judge, caused a minor outbreak of giggles on the benches. "What happened was that my grandson and I were on our way to the river at the end of the day. We were carrying our usual fishing gear, rod, bait and a basket, which my missus makes by hand, to carry our catch. And that's when we saw them, on the other side of the river. There were at least a dozen of them. My grandson was the first to notice them. Unfortunately I have some kind of ailment of the eyes and I can't see too well out of this one." He indicated his right eye.

"My grandson warned me that there was someone on the other side. By the time I realized, we heard a loud noise which frightened us so much that we ran away. We thought those beings wanted to put an end to us."

"Did they attack you?"

"I think so," the old man said, "but we didn't stay to find out. We were so frightened that we had to wait twenty rotations before we dared go back to that place."

"And tell us," the judge asked him, "is this being here one of those who attacked you?"

The old man looked Emily up and down. "Yes, it might be. It was certainly dressed in the same way. Except that I seem to remember one or two of them were wearing green armor."

Vaahur, who seemed rather bored on his throne, waved his hand disdainfully to order the man to be taken away. Two of the guards went with him to the door as he muttered something about how rude they were being. Meanwhile the judge, who was pacing the hall thoughtfully, addressed the hearing again:

"Now I would like to call soldiers Kihrgutz and Lamdhol, further witnesses to the human atrocity."

Vaahur waved his hand, and the door opened again. Two privates entered the hall and came forward to the front. Emily could not see them very clearly, but something about them looked familiar.

"Do you know this human?" the judge asked.

Both of them turned to look at her, and at that moment she knew who they were: two of her kidnappers.

"Yes, sir," one of them replied.

"And can you give us any further information?" the judge asked. By now he seemed to be in a hurry to get all this over.

"Several days ago we heard that there'd been a massacre in a small nomad village," the soldier said. "We heard that the perpetrators of it all were the foreigners from another planet everyone was talking about."

"And what did you do then?"

"We decided to investigate the foreigners' activity. Everybody knew they'd had contact with the Keplerians of Wiikhaadiiz ofiz, and we found a boy who seemed to have this foreigner's trust. We managed to set a trap using this boy and arrested her, always with the intention of bringing her to trial."

"And what happened?"

"At least a dozen humans came, armed to the teeth with far superior technology, and after a bloody battle we were forced to retreat because there were too many of them. Miraculously we managed to escape thanks to the bravery of the rest of our unit, but we had no choice but to leave the prisoner there."

"Not a word of that is true," Emily muttered. "All this is a farce."

The judge ignored her completely. "Well now, that's a very troubling story. It looks as though these foreigners are a dangerous people."

"They certainly are, your honor."

"Thank you very much," the judge told them after seeing a gesture of agreement from Vaahur. "You may withdraw." His voice turned solemn. "I would now like to call one of the bravest Keplerians I have ever met, to give testimony. I call Shyiich to give his evidence, the sole survivor of the massacre perpetrated by the humans near the heart of the mountain."

The doors opened again and a Keplerian appeared: young, but mature-looking. Under his left arm was a crutch, which he leaned on as he walked. The sound of the wood striking the floor at each step echoed across the whole room.

"I would like to begin by thanking you for your fortitude, and for letting us know at firsthand what happened in your village," the judge said. "You're very brave. I wouldn't even like to imagine what this must mean for you, on every level."

Young Shyiich bowed his head in gratitude for these words.

"Would you be so kind as to explain to everyone here what happened on that fateful day?"

The young man was silent for a few moments. He seemed to be gathering all his strength together to face what was clearly a traumatic situation for him. After a short pause he swallowed, cleared his throat and began to tell of his experience.

"As I did on many mornings, I had breakfast with my little boy. Yiïya, my wife, was expecting, and our family was due to grow in a few weeks' time. Years ago we decided to join a nomadic village to escape from the bustle of city life. My life… our life," he corrected himself, "was perfect, we loved each other. We loved our son. No-one could have wished for anything more.

He went on, after sighing with genuine sorrow. "That day I had work to do. My job involves clearing tree-trunks and building cabins for anyone who asks for them, and that morning I had to go a few blocks from our home. I can still remember saying goodbye to my wife." He closed his eyes. "She was sitting in the rocking chair I'd made the winter before, when we found out we were going to have another baby. I… I told her I loved her as I left the cabin."

A murmur spread through the hall, while Shyiich paused to wipe away the tears that were running down his cheeks.

"Take your time," the judge said sympathetically.

"As I was saying," he went on, after a long sigh, "I went to get on with clearing the trunk of one of the ancient trees. One of our neighbors wanted to move his stable to an area further away from the village, so I had some work to do getting the site ready before building could begin. The morning went by uneventfully, then suddenly I heard the strangest sound, like thunder. But though it was cloudy that day, I didn't think it foretold a storm. Other sounds like the first one followed, and soon I realized that they were coming from the village and that they weren't natural.

"Then I heard someone screaming… it was agonizing, desperate. I knew at once that something very serious was happening in the village. So I left everything I was doing and ran back toward my house."

He paused again to gather his courage so that he could go on with his story. The pain was obvious in his voice.

"By the time I passed my neighbors' door, it was too late. All I found were dead bodies. But I… I couldn't even stop to do anything for them. He began to sob. "All I wanted to do was get to my home and make sure Yiïya and our son were safe and sound. But I was also late…" He seemed to be blaming himself for this. "There was nothing I could do… it was too late… they were both dead…"

He paused again to regain his composure. But his sobs were now accompanied by the murmurs of some of those listening. All of them seemed to be deeply sympathetic toward the carpenter.

"I'm deeply sorry to hear that," the judge said. "And I know that it's very painful for you, but would you be able to describe what you found there? Take all the time you need."

He nodded. "Yes… I'll try."

He did his best to recover his composure, but burst out weeping again. They were obliged to wait a few minutes for the disconsolate man, and also for some of those in the audience, to calm down.

"Can you go on?" the judge asked. "Do you want some water?"

"No, sir, I'm better now," he said, sounding more composed. "I found my wife sitting in the rocking-chair, but she had a small wound which had put an end to her life, and there was an enormous puddle of blood staining the floor of the cabin. My son… had suffered the same fate…"

"What kind of weapon could have caused a brutal act like that?"

"I didn't know then. But I was sure the sounds I'd heard must have had something to do with it."

"What happened then?"

"I collapsed on the floor, overcome by grief. But I soon realized that I wasn't alone."

"The attackers were there?"

"Yes."

"And what happened next?"

"I saw a creature which had come from hell itself."

"Could you describe it to the audience?" the judge asked.

"Of course," he said with overwhelming hatred, and at the same time he pointed to Emily. "It was wearing that same strange armor."

A murmur spread through the audience, who began to whisper and murmur in response to the witness's determination. Emily could only shrink in shame at the story the poor Keplerian had told. At the same time she could see Vaahur's smile of satisfaction.

"What happened after that?"

"The creature said something in a strange language I didn't understand and aimed one of those devices directly at me. I heard that deafening noise again, the noise that had made me leave my work, I felt a sudden, horrible pain in my left leg. I soon found there was a hole in it which wouldn't stop bleeding, but I couldn't find what had caused it."

"But you survived," the judge pointed out.

"Yes. I fainted, and I presume the creature must have thought I'd died. But I woke up some time later, drenched in sweat and blood."

"And what did you do then?"

"I dragged myself to my neighbor's stable, got onto a *fhore* as best I could and came to Khaavahki as fast as I was able."

"Thank you, Shyiich," the judge said. "That's more than enough. I think I can speak in the name of everyone here in thanking you for your efforts and the fortitude you've shown in testifying before this hearing. We share your pain at your loss and wish you speedy recovery from your wounds."

The young man nodded and left.

"We've listened to the testimonies of four good Keplerians who've told us how the humans have lied to our peoples, have conspired to exterminate us and dominate these lands which are ours by right. That is why I ask our commander-in-chief to punish these acts with a strong hand and with all possible speed. If we're not firm now, we may regret the fact in the future when the humans have put an end to all of us."

A fresh murmuring began to be heard throughout the hall. Vaahur, who had exchanged his perverse smile for an expression of arrogant sternness, raised his hands to quieten the murmur and spoke with determination.

"I have listened to all those voices which have spoken here. I have considered all the options open to the Khaavahki people, and unlike other Keplerian leaders I believe that we should not show any weakness before these foreigners. We must show that our determination is strong and that our will is to be respected. That is why I have decided to sentence the four prisoners to death for the genocide committed against our people. The sentence will be carried out tomorrow, at dawn."

Emily gave a start. She had not thought Vaahur would be capable of going so far. But she had been wrong. Captain Garth and the leader of the Khaavahki himself had set a trap, and that trap was going to cost the life of four innocents.

26
Desperate

Robert and Sergeant Ferrara went back to the rover and set off for the pickup point the captain had agreed with the pilot who had flown them there. They were pleased with the success of the mission, but what they had found in the village had relegated the location of the rebel base to the background.

"And now what d'you think they'll do with the rebels, Captain?" Ferrara asked.

"Quite honestly, I have no idea. We'll report to the commander, and I'd imagine that he, Deputy Director Green and Captain Mei will make the appropriate decisions."

"D'you think they'll just let things be?"

"It's possible. I can't see them going for a fratricidal frontal attack, quite honestly."

"But we can't just let them go on attacking our bases and stealing our equipment."

"No, of course not. Although at least now we have them under control. I'd like to think they'd try to find some diplomatic way out."

"I don't suppose Captain Garth would ever admit a defeat on that scale," she pointed out.

"No, he won't," Robert agreed, "but if they try for a deal that lets them carry on with their lives while we do the same with ours, I don't think there'll be a crisis."

"And how do we manage that? They'll be sure to need supplies and equipment."

"Mutual exchange," said Robert. "If the project decides to provide the rebels with everything they need in exchange for them staying on the margin of official activities, it could be sold as a fair deal. Maybe Captain Garth's more pragmatic than we think."

"Especially as they no longer have the asset of being able to destroy the station."

Robert smiled. "Except that they don't know that yet. But we have to bear in mind that we don't know whether they have allies inside."

"And what about what we saw in that village?" the sergeant asked after a brief pause.

"I can't stop thinking about it," he admitted. "And I'm afraid that's going to be a serious obstacle. If the Keplerians find out that a human carried out a massacre on that scale, I suppose they'll want to see justice done."

"And then we'll have plenty of problems."

"Something tells me these are going to be difficult times for diplomacy," Robert said uneasily.

"Do you think that could affect Dr. Rhodes? Isn't she attending a conclave at the moment?"

He thought about this for a moment. "I hope not. Otherwise it would be a very complicated business to handle. The Keplerians themselves could easily imagine any one of us committed that atrocity."

"I suppose for them we're all the same."

"Yeah, and it's going to be difficult to prove it was Captain Garth who committed the murders."

There was not much light left by the time they came to the pickup point. The weather had changed; it was beginning to rain, and a slight wind had risen. It looked as if bad weather was on its way. They had to wait for some time until the transport appeared.

The pilot landed, emerged from the cockpit and saluted. "Captain. I guess you don't know…"

"Don't know what, lieutenant?"

"Dr. Rhodes, Dr. Kumar and Engineers Martinez and Gonçalves have disappeared."

"What?" Robert exclaimed. "What happened?"

"Afraid I don't know, captain," the lieutenant said apologetically. "They've only just informed me about what I just told you."

"Turn on the ship's comms, lieutenant," Robert said sharply.

"What about the rebels? Won't they intercept the signal and find out our position?"

"We know the rebels aren't anywhere near our position," Ferrara said.

"Right," the lieutenant said, and rushed back to the cockpit.

After a couple of operations on the ship's terminal he leaned out once again.

"Comms reactivated!"

Robert sat down in the rover's driving-seat and called the commander.

"Captain," came Commander Bauer's voice at the other end. "I presume from your call that you're already up to speed with the latest events."

"Yes, sir. What happened?"

"We don't know for sure, but this morning we lost all four signals simultaneously."

"How could that be possible?"

"We think someone's used a frequency inhibitor," the commander said.

"But what happened?"

"All four of them were at the Gaal-El temple waiting to be granted access to the conclave, and all of a sudden we lost all their signals at once."

"What was going on at the time?"

"That's the strange thing. Nothing at all was going on."

"Has anyone gone there?" Robert asked.

"No. The deputy director thought it might be a better idea to wait a little and see if communication could be re-established and we could find out what had happened."

"He thought?" Robert repeated. "Doesn't he think that any longer?"

"We've just received some news."

"Have they communicated with you?"

"No, not them. But Yisht, the assistant to the Wiikhaadiiz ofiz leader, contacted us to warn us about what had happened."

The captain waited tensely for his superior to go on.

"They've been taken prisoners, we don't know where to," the commander went on. "Apparently they've been accused of carrying out a massacre in a small Keplerian village."

"What!" Robert exclaimed. "But that's impossible! We found that village, and everything points to Captain Garth."

"Yes, we're aware of that, captain."

"Who detained them? And when exactly were comms lost?"

"It was the Khaavahki. It was all orchestrated by their leader Vaahur," the commander said. "We lost communication nearly nine hours ago. The deputy director's on his way to the Gaal-El village as we speak, to try and meet with the high priest of the cult."

"And who's he appointed to lead the rescue team?"

"We haven't yet decided whether to send anyone…"

"Eh?" he said in puzzlement. "But we've got to send someone as soon as possible, to follow the trail."

"The deputy director says Dr. Rhodes herself gave instructions that no-one should go to her rescue if anything were to happen."

Robert stopped to think about the reasons which might have led Emily to make that request and the chances they had of doing anything by now. Ferrara, who had been listening to the argument from the other front seat of the rover, gave him a conspiratorial glance.

"Are you still there, captain?" they heard the commander say. "I hope you're not thinking of doing anything stupid, anything that could unleash an escalation of violence…"

Robert did not answer.

"Captain?" the commander called again. "I absolutely forbid you to make any kind of incursion into Keplerian territory."

"… sorry… cut off… commun… fog…" Robert mumbled. Immediately he cut off communication.

He leaned back in his seat, deciding what to do. If he went to rescue their friends he risked being court-martialed for disobeying a direct order. But nor was not doing it an option. Emily was in trouble. He could not stay there doing nothing and simply waiting for things to sort themselves out. He knew perfectly well that there was some kind of tie between Vaahur and Garth and that all this was part of a strategy to take control of Keplerian society. And at the same time, of course, to weaken the project.

"I've got to find them," he said at last.

"And I'm coming with you, captain," Ferrara said determinedly.

"No. I'm about to disobey a direct order. I'm risking a court-martial. I can't let you be dragged into the same mess because of my own irresponsibility. Go back to the station in the transport. I'll take the rover."

"With all due respect, captain," she said, "if you think that after listening to your little song-and-dance routine with the commander I'm going to stay put while friends are in danger, you can go to hell… sir."

Despite the seriousness of the situation, Robert could not help but smile at the sergeant's reaction.

"Okay then, sergeant. In that case we'd better get a move on. We've got to find out where they've been taken to."

He ordered the pilot to go back to the station without them. He justified himself by saying that they still had things to check about the rebel base and that he should come back to pick them up at the same time the following day. He hoped to have solved the problem by then. They had more than enough supplies in the armed vehicle to spend another two whole days on the planet. Robert had been feeling a little tired a few minutes before, but thinking about the danger Emily and their friends might be in was enough to enable him to find strength in himself when he had thought he had none left.

"Ada," he called, "keep comms operative."

"Are you sure, captain?" Ferrara asked. "If we go anywhere near them we'll give our position away."

"Yes. We'll stay as far away as possible from the rebel base to avoid detection. And in any case, the activity of both the rover and our exosuits is being filtered by Ada, who's sending information to deceive the device they planted there."

"But we don't have a clue where they are. How are we going to find them?"

"If it was the Khaavahki, I'd imagine they'll have taken them either to their village or to some military post that's equipped to hold four human prisoners."

"Do you think they'll have used Tasers against them, the way they did last time?"

"It's quite possible," Robert said, "and I've activated comms so that we can ask questions like that. Ada, show us the last images from their visors."

"Right, captain."

"They've used some kind of inhibitor," she said after she had checked them.

"How d'you know that?"

"Because the four signals from their suits were cut off at the same time. Either the attackers are perfectly synchronized, or else they've used some device to isolate all four of them at the same time."

"Ada," Robert asked, "where's the rover they took?"

"They left it at the foot of the range where the temple is, in the Gaal-El village, behind the place where both of you spent a night."

"Do you have a connection?"

"I do," the AI replied. "Do you want me to do anything?"

"Did you lose communication with the rover at any moment during the day?" he asked.

"Yes, this morning, forty minutes or so after losing communication with Emily and the others."

"Fast-forward the images from the moment you lost communication to the moment you lost connection with the rover."

Ada did this until he found what he was looking for.

"Stop!" he called. "Now play it back at normal speed."

In the images from one of the cameras on the rover he saw dozens of Keplerian infantry soldiers passing in front of it, armed with halberds and wearing chainmail. With them they were leading a couple of covered carriages, together with one or two unidentifiable wooden devices. Bringing up the rear was a cavalry platoon and a couple of campaign officers mounted on *fhores*.

"My God!" Ferrara exclaimed. "Looks as though someone's taken plenty of trouble in this operation!"

"An entire company, just to arrest four people,"

"It's going to be hard to get through," she pointed out.

"We'll just have to be more intelligent than they are. Ada, can you talk to Yisht?"

"Sure, captain."

"Yes?" came Yisht's voice from the other end. She was speaking in whispers to avoid attracting attention.

"Hi, Yisht. Unfortunately we don't have much time to be polite or make small-talk. You'll have guessed why we're calling."

"Of course, captain," she said, understanding exactly what he meant. "I managed to speak to one of your leaders just a while ago."

"We know, but I need to ask you whether you know where they could have been taken."

"I'm sorry, I don't," she said ruefully. "The news arrived by messenger bird, and unfortunately I don't have much more information than I gave Mr. Green."

"But you must know what the usual proceedings would be in a case like this. When the Khaavahki arrest someone, where do they take them?"

"To the Watch Tower, I guess," she said after thinking about it for a moment.

"Watch Tower?" Ferrara repeated.

"Yes. It's an enormous stone tower. They call it that because it's several meters taller than the treetops. From there they can check the arrival of the Khol. It has the reputation of being a secure fastness within the Khaavahki village, which is practically unassailable to start with."

"That doesn't sound like good news," Ferrara said.

"If that beast Vaahur has kidnapped Emily and Rakesh," Yisht said angrily, "I presume he'll have taken them to his lands to hold one of those imitation trials where he controls everything that happens."

"Do you know the tower?" Robert asked. "How many soldiers there are, I mean, or where the cells are?"

"I've only been there once, so I can't tell you much about it. All I know is that it's Vaahur's own residence, and if I remember correctly none of the high command live there. Although now I come to think about it, the cells might be in the tower itself. But not on the upper floors, underground."

"Well, I think that could be a great help," Robert said. "Thank you for everything, Yisht."

"Be very careful," she pleaded. "That place is very dangerous."

239

Robert set the rover's electric motor to maximum, and more than once they very nearly toppled down a precipice or crashed into a tree-trunk. Ferrara begged him to slow down in case they had an accident and all their efforts were in vain.

"Ada, can you locate Captain Garth?"

"No, captain, I'm sorry. His exosuit hasn't made use of the Asimov's infrastructure for some time."

"I guessed as much, but I had to try."

"However, you may be interested to know that a rebel rover used the GPS signal a couple of hours ago to find its way to the Khaavahki village."

"That's very interesting," Ferrara said. "It can't be just coincidence."

"Has any other vehicle traveled there?"

"No," Ada said, "only that one."

"Right, let us know of any movement they make."

"Of course, captain."

They went on at a good speed, and though the terrain and the abundant vegetation prevented them from reaching very high speeds, Robert made every effort to get there as quickly as possible. They had to go around the entire mountain range and reach the Khaavahki village from the north. On top of that, they had to keep as far away from the mountain as they could to stop the rebels detecting their comms, so that the journey was a hard and worrying one.

Once they had passed the site of the rebel base and calculated that by now there was no danger of anyone spotting them, Ada showed them the route the rebel rover had taken and Robert followed the trail as far as the entrance gate of the Khaavahki village.

Before reaching the fortress they began to see the small, humble cabins of those less fortunate Keplerians who could not afford to live in the most affluent area of the city. It was night by now and everything was dark, with not a soul in the street. The infrared vision allowed them to see the first barrier in their path.

"Yisht didn't say anything about a palisade," he whispered.

"It's at least twelve meters high," Ferrara said. "We can't manage that with our suit thrusters."

"We need a more panoramic view of the place."

He released the drones once again, this time with comms open so that they could watch everything in real time. The city was larger than it had looked at first; apart from the scattered cabins outside the palisade, which were very small, the interior was crammed with buildings of different sizes and heights, catwalks between the trees and other wooden structures. And, as was to be expected, a strong military presence, especially at the palisade which surrounded the settlement.

A small river crossed the city, and here the palisade came to an end, although it went on into the riverbed to keep out any intruder. There was more of a military presence here, with two sentry-posts.

There were three main entrances to the city: one in the north, another in the southeast and a third in the southwest. As with the riverside, there were sentry-posts at each. In the northwest was an enormous stone structure which—just as Yisht had told them—by far surpassed the height of the treetops, which were tall enough to begin with. Other stone buildings which adjoined it appeared to be army barracks. This meant that the surroundings of the tower, which was sited between four massive trees, was heavily guarded.

"Yisht wasn't exaggerating," the captain whispered. "The city's well-protected and the military presence there is very strong. They've probably strengthened it because of the arrests."

The sergeant nodded. "That makes sense."

The drones came back without being detected, and Robert put them away in his pack.

"So how are we going to get in?" Ferrara asked. "Following the river seems the most suitable way of doing it, but the area's closely-watched."

"And don't forget, the Keplerians have excellent night vision. Much better than ours. They might be able to detect us even if we went underwater."

"What about climbing a tree and jumping onto the palisade?" she suggested.

He shook his head. "No, that'd be too complicated. I think I know how we'll manage it."

"How?"

"Through the main gate," Robert said, and began walking determinedly toward the north gate.

27
Time is running out

February 3, year 1

Khaavahki Prison, Kepler-442b

Emily woke up abruptly. She had heard a noise. It had come from below, from a lower level. She was in her own bed, back in Orlando. The light of her room was on, but outside it was completely dark. She got out of bed, feeing strange. Something did not fit: she was wearing her exosuit. She left her room and looked out into the corridor of the family home. There was no-one there. Once again she heard a noise from downstairs. It was a metallic sound, like that of an old-fashioned lock. She leant out to look down the stairs, but there was only darkness below.

Suddenly the door opened and light flooded the lower level, dazzling her. Once her eyes had got used to the light again she saw what had caused all this disturbance. It was her father Steven, and his eyes were fixed on her. He was carrying a gray Orpheus Project suitcase and was dressed in the same clothes she had seen him in last time, an eternity ago. And yet there was something strange about his face. His eyes were not human, they were dark and too large. She had seen that look at other times. They were the eyes of a Keplerian.

Her father left the house without saying a word. He slammed the door behind him and everything was once again submerged in the most absolute darkness. Emily tried to turn on the lights, but nothing happened. She tried to use her exosuit to see, but everything stayed dark. She found the banisters and went down slowly, groping, afraid of tripping and falling. Downstairs, she stretched out her arms as she moved forward blindly across the floor. She found the door, hastily felt for the handle and opened it. Outside, everything was equally dark. Without warning, two trails of fire flared up on the floor and extended onward, showing her a narrow stone corridor which stretched away until it was lost on the horizon.

Emily went along that path, illuminated thanks to those golden flames which reminded her of the ones Waafdiv had lit in the Gaal-El temple. She walked for some time until she came to a bend to the left. She saw the mysterious figure vanishing at the end of the corridor into another bend, this time to the right. She had to walk faster to keep up with the pace of that shadow, which she could barely glimpse in the distance. When she reached the next bend she saw that the two trails of fire, like the tunnel, came to an end a few meters ahead. On the other side vacancy was waiting for her, the immensity of space. Suddenly she began to float uncontrollably. Gravity had disappeared once again.

The tiny figure seemed to be fleeing from her, far away, in outer space by now. Once again she found herself in the middle of the firmament. She turned, but now there was no longer any corridor behind her. Her attention was caught by a group of stars which shone more brightly than the others, even seeming to follow a kind of pattern. She could not recognize any particular constellation, but then astronomy had never been her strong point.

Suddenly, just as on other occasions, she felt the presence of something colossal which was drawing her irresistibly toward it. She recognized the overwhelming rounded shape of the black hole and could not resist the attraction. The gravitational force of the hole began to draw her inside it, and she felt her body stretching until it had turned into a long, thin strand of spaghetti.

Then she really woke up, once again back in the dark cell Vaahur had locked her up in.

Emily sat up on the filthy floor of the cell and leaned against the wall. She had fallen asleep while she had been thinking about her situation. She had no idea how long it had been since they had come to that ominous place. She did not know where her friends were or what state they were in. They might not even be aware that they had been sentenced to death. Were these really the last hours of their lives?

So is this really how it all ends? she thought, without shedding a tear. *We cross the immensity of space only to find the journey comes to an end like this, millions of kilometers from our home? It's not fair.*

A sudden metallic sound brought her out of her introspection. Someone opened the door of the cell, even though everything was still dark.

"Emily," came a whisper.

She had to turn on her suit visor before she could see a familiar face on the other side of the door. It was Liikmi, the assistant to the Gaal-El high priest.

"Liikmi!" she exclaimed. "What on earth are you doing here?"

"I've come to get you out of here," he whispered. "But there's no time to lose, you'll have all the explanations as soon as we're outside."

She did not waste a single moment, but got up from the floor and hastened out of the cell. She was surprised to see a Keplerian soldier with him.

"Don't worry, this is Avmup, he's one of our own. He's helped us prepare this whole operation."

"Get a move on," his companion said urgently. "We don't have much time before someone finds out what we're doing,"

"And what about my friends?"

"What friends?" Avmup asked.

"I came with three other humans."

"That wasn't in the plan." The soldier turned to Liikmi, "We don't have time for any more, we're risking enough as it is."

Emily stopped abruptly. "I'm not leaving without my friends."

"What?" the soldier said. "Are you crazy? Don't forget, there are only a few hours left before you're executed."

She was adamant. "I don't care, I'm not leaving them here. If the four of us don't go, you'd better leave me here."

Liikmi saw that she was serious. He turned to the soldier.

"We have to do it, Avmup."

Avmup weighed up the risk, but seeing that there was no chance of persuading them he gave up. He shook his head, sighing heavily.

"This is going to be very dangerous. And it's going to mean my cover being blown, so I'll have to come with you."

"Where are the other prisoners?" Liikmi asked.

"I don't know."

Liikmi turned to Emily. "Can your technology find them?"

She glanced at her visor to check. "No, someone or something is blocking our suits."

"In that case," Avmup said, "we have no choice but to check all the cells on this floor, one by one."

"But what about the guards?" she asked.

"Let's just say someone brought them a few barrels of tree-honey with a secret narcotic ingredient," Avmup said with a smile. "At the moment we're safe, but only on this floor and not for very long. You two check the cells while I stay on watch here in case anyone comes sniffing around."

Emily and Liikmi left him beside the spiral staircase and went to check all the cells on that the floor. They separated to go down the two corridors, opening the peepholes as they went. Most of them were empty, but in some there was a sleeping Keplerian, oblivious to the plan which was being hatched outside.

She turned down one of the corridors; there were far more cells than she had expected. The place was huge. She had almost lost hope of finding anyone when she saw a figure which seemed to be wearing an exosuit.

"Avmup!" she whispered.

The soldier did not hear her, so she memorized the route and went back to the staircase. As she raced round the corner she did not have time to see that Avmup was chatting to another soldier, who stared at her blankly, unable to understand what was going on. When he realized that one of the prisoners had escaped he opened his mouth ready to give the alarm, but at that precise moment a sharp blow echoed along the corridor. Avmup had cracked a length of wood on his head, and he collapsed onto the floor.

They were both petrified at the noise they had just made. They stood there without moving for a couple of minutes, expecting to hear footsteps on the stairs or the sound of the alarm. But nothing of the kind happened, and they were both able to breathe freely again. With the keys in her hand, Emily went back to the cell where she had caught a glimpse of one of her friends. She opened it. It was Rakesh, huddled in a corner, apparently asleep.

She called his name, keeping her voice low.

Seeing that he was not reacting, she went over to him and shook him.

"What is it?" he said sleepily.

"Rakesh, we've come to get you out of here."

"Emily!" he cried. "How good to see you! What's happened?"

"Come on, there'll be time for explanations later."

They checked the remaining cells, but found no trace of Paula or Gorka. They went back to Liikmi and Avmup, who had managed to hide the Keplerian's body and were cleaning up the smears of blood on the floor.

"We haven't found our two other friends," Emily said. "Have you any idea where they could be?"

"They must be on the upper level," Avmup said. "And that's a problem, because it's still manned."

"Can't you get rid of the guards the same way?"

"We haven't any more alcohol left, or any more narcotics. I'm afraid we'll have to improvise something if we're to get your friends out."

"The first thing we have to do is find out how many guards there are and where they're posted," Liikmi said.

"I fear I'm the one who's going to have to do that," Avmup said.

He raced up the stairs and came back very soon afterward, looking calm.

"There are two guards outside a couple of cells that are almost

245

next to each other. I presume that's where your friends are."

"Only two?" Liikmi asked. "That's good news."

Avmup shook his head. "Yes, but it's not going to be that easy. The bad news is that the guards' barracks are on the same floor, which means there'll be at least a dozen soldiers asleep there. The one we just took out was the sergeant in charge of the whole upper floor. The two guards who are awake might start wondering what's happened to him."

"Right then, so how do we get rid of them?" Liikmi asked.

"I don't know. Those two are almost twice as big as I am."

"Do you know whether there's any human technology down here?" Rakesh asked. "Gorka was immobilized with a device that fires electrical discharges. We could use it on the guards without making too much noise."

"Good thinking," Emily said. "Someone's sure to have kept a Taser in case we overstepped the mark."

Avmup shrugged. "I don't know. What does it look like?"

"It's a small yellow device," Emily explained. "You hold it in your hand, and it's more or less this size." She demonstrated with her hands.

His face lit up suddenly. He went into one of the rooms to one side and came out triumphantly holding a Taser.

"Is this it?"

"Yes, that's it! How did you find it so quickly?"

"I noticed it when we hid the sergeant's body. I thought it was a strange color."

"Right, so what happens now?" Liikmi asked.

"Suppose Avmup takes me upstairs as if I were still a captive," Emily suggested. "You could say the sergeant ordered you to move the two prisoners from downstairs."

Avmup stopped to think.

"And while I deal with one guard, you deal with the other. It might work."

"And what about us?" Rakesh asked.

"You wait here," Emily said. "Liikmi, you could put on a uniform, in case someone else decides to come down."

She and Avmup set off upstairs. Emily was holding her hands behind her back, although they were free, hiding the Taser. Avmup took a careful look into the barracks to check that no-one had woken up. When he saw that everything was quiet, he beckoned her to come up.

She moved in front of him and they made their way to the corridor, where two solidly-built guards were deep in conversation. When Emily and Avmup appeared around the corner they both turned in surprise at the sight of someone at that hour of the night. One even put his hand on the handle of his mace ready to use it, but when he saw Avmup behind her he seemed to relax.

"I have orders to move the two prisoners to this floor," Avmup announced. "Which cells are free?"

"Let me see. I think there's one here."

Emily was nervous. Although she was taller than the two guards, the breadth of their shoulders was intimidating.

"Keep an eye on the foreigner," Avmup said to the first guard as he went up to the second.

The soldier gave Emily a hostile glare, assessing the limited threat she posed.

"What the devil are you looking at?" he spat out as he hit out at the exosuit helmet.

Emily, who had barely felt the blow, waited patiently for Avmup to come up to the other guard.

"This one looks empty," the soldier said.

"Right, could you open it?"

Everything happened in a single moment. The guard opened the door and Avmup pushed him with all his might inside the empty cell. The soldier, who had not been expecting this, fell inside and hit the floor with a loud bump. Emily brought her hands from behind her back, put the Taser to the guard's right arm and pressed the button. Nothing happened. Taken aback, she pressed the button again with the same result. The guard stared back at her in disbelief.

The reaction was not long in coming. The guard, who was considerably more solidly-built than Avmup, pushed Emily away so that she tripped backwards and struck the wall sharply, so that she was forced to drop the Taser. Then he hurled himself at Avmup, who was trying to lock the cell door. He had such a head start that he threw him into the air. The blow was sharp and the fall painful.

Emily, who had been left lying there stunned by the violence of the blow, looked at the Taser, which was lying on the stone floor of the corridor. Then she noticed the small notch on the device and realized her mistake. *You didn't switch it on, you idiot!*

She got up quickly, picked up the Taser and switched it on. While the guard was seizing poor Avmup, who had not yet recovered from the violent impact, she ran and hurled herself on him. The impact made the guard lose his balance and fall, rolling over a stunned Avmup. Emily managed to keep her own balance, and managed to keep hold of the Taser. The buzz she could hear indicated that it was ready to use, so she went up to the solidly-built Keplerian and fired. The guard began to have spasms as the electric current went through his body.

At the same time the imprisoned guard began to yell.

"Get me out of here! You bloody traitor!"

"What do we do with this one?" Emily asked as she helped Avmup to his feet. "He's going to wake the others."

"I just wanted to gain time, and I improvised," he said as he rubbed his bruises. "Can this device be fired more than once?"

"I think so."

"Right." He took it from her. "We'll get you out of here," he called, "but keep still, okay?"

"Okay," they heard from inside.

Avmup opened the cell again, and before the guard could say or do anything he pulled the trigger of the Taser, causing him to suffer the same spasms as his comrade.

"Your technology seems to work very well." He looked down in satisfaction at the small yellow device.

"We don't have much time before these two get on their feet again," she warned him. "Let's open the cells."

First they brought Paula out, and she nearly threw herself into Emily's arms.

"Get Gorka out!" she said the moment she found she was free.

Avmup opened Gorka's cell, but he did not come out as quickly as his comrade. Paula herself did nothing to help by pushing her way in front of the others to see how he was.

"How are you? Does anything hurt?"

"I'm fine," he assured her, "but my head's about to burst."

"And what about your suit?" Emily asked.

He was moving with some difficulty. "The servos aren't working, and right now I can't see anything. I think what happened to you must have happened to me too."

"Do you have oxygen?" Emily asked.

"Yes," Paula said.

"Yes," Gorka said, "but I don't know how much I have left."

"Sorry to interrupt," Avmup said, "but we need to get out of here."

"Yeah, let's do that," Emily agreed. "Rakesh and Liikmi are waiting upstairs."

They had to help Gorka to move his inert suit. The distance between the cell and the stairs seemed too far for the hurry they were in. At any moment a soldier might wake up, or one of the fallen guards begin to call for help. And they were beginning to hear the voices of other prisoners, who must have guessed that something was going on.

"Emily," Paula said, "help me carry him piggyback."

"How are we going to get out of here?" Emily asked.

"By the floor below," Avmup explained.

"Below?"

"That's right."

Meanwhile the lack of energy in his suit was keeping Gorka incommunicado. "Am I the only one who doesn't understand what he's saying and has no idea who you're talking to?" he protested.

Between the two of them, and thanks to the help of the exosuits, they were able to carry him relatively easily. In no more than a minute they were on the spiral staircase. Liikmi and Rakesh were waiting for them below, without any news.

"Follow me this way," Avmup said.

He led them along a corridor to a small chamber where instruments for torture were kept, along with equipment appropriate for an executioner and other items which made the hair on the backs of the newly-freed prisoners' necks stand on end. The stains of Keplerian blood and entrails told them stories of the pain and suffering the prisoners in that fortress had suffered over centuries. Avmup went up to the only wall where there were no instruments of torture. Everything there was dark, so that no-one had noticed three small holes in one of the stones. Avmup inserted three of his four claws into them, and there was a loud crack.

He pushed what turned out to be a door, and an enormous stone passage was revealed before them. One after the other they went into that dark passage, which was barely wide enough to let them go in single file. Liikmi took the lead, while Avmup stayed behind so that he could close the passage after them. Emily, who had saved some energy, switched on the light of her visor. At last Gorka was able to see and to establish that his eyes were all right, because he had not been able to see a thing since he had fainted in the Gaal-El temple.

Avmup was surprised by the artificial light. "What's that?"

"We humans can't see in the dark," Emily explained. "We need artificial light."

He seemed to be impressed by this.

"We have a few kilometers to walk until we're outside," Liikmi said. "I hope none of you are afraid of enclosed spaces. Can you move normally?"

"Not very well," Gorka admitted faintly after Paula had translated the question.

"All right, we'll all try to go at your pace," Liikmi said. "That'll slow our progress, but I guess it's better to stay together so that we don't get lost."

"Lost?" Rakesh repeated. He was second in the line. "But this is just a passage."

"After this we come out into a complicated series of caves which go on to connect to others."

Emily was unable to repress a feeling of déjà vu. This corridor was very much like the one in the nightmare she had woken from only a short while ago. Still, she tried to put it out of her mind and pay attention to what was happening ahead of her.

"Why is there a secret passage in a Khaavahki fortress?" Rakesh asked.

"The watch-tower is thousands of years old. It was built before the Great Revolt," Liikmi explained. "The architect was a notorious Khapabir who professed a deep faith in the Gaal-El cult. When he designed the fortress, the then Khaavahki leader asked him for a secret escape-route. In this way they would be able to evacuate the inhabitants in the case of an attack by the Khol. But the Khaavahki leader died before the fortress was finished. Over time the fortress and the tower were enlarged more than once, but by then no-one knew of the passage's existence."

"And how is it that you do?" Rakesh asked.

"As you know, we Gaal-El are the guardians of Keplerian knowledge. And as I told you, the architect professed a great faith in our cult. Hence he himself made sure that the plans for the original design were kept in the Gaal-El library. Luckily for all of you, the later rebuilding of the fortress only affected the upper part, which means that the dungeons and this escape-tunnel have stayed unmodified since their construction."

"I'm very sorry to interrupt your history lesson," said Paula, "but I'm beginning to worry about the amount of oxygen left in our suits."

"How much do you have left?" Emily asked.

"Twenty per cent. About four hours."

"I have eighteen per cent left."

"I don't even know how much I have left," Gorka said, sounding worried.

Rakesh was silent.

"And what about you, Rakesh?" Emily asked.

"Don't worry about me," he said calmly. "Let's keep going. The important thing is to get out of here."

Emily knew that he must have barely any reserve left. A middle-aged man like him would consume more oxygen than someone Paula's size. They had to get out of there whatever it cost them, and they had to do it as soon as possible.

They went on for many minutes, during which time they realized that the passage they were travelling through, instead of being entirely straight, twisted a little and from time to time turned left. After this it came to an end. They had come to a huge cave with a huge opening on its right, forty or fifty meters high, far beyond their reach. Through the opening came the faint light of the stars, indicating that it was still night. A small stream, which must surely have played a part in the cave's formation, zigzagged through the center.

The terrain became more irregular in that area, to the point where they had to help Gorka to keep going, even though he was doing everything he could to move on with a suit which lacked any electrical supply. But the extra effort this was costing him was going to increase his oxygen intake, so Emily and Paula arranged between themselves to carry him on their shoulders every now and then so that he could rest a little and save some oxygen. They crossed the cave and reached the other side of the hollow, where dozens of small cavities began. They followed Liikmi and Avmup's directions, as they seemed to know the place well and had taken the lead.

"How far is it before we come out into the open?" Rakesh asked.

"We still have a stretch ahead of us," Avmup said.

Rakesh was silent, but suddenly he stopped until Emily had drawn level with him.

"Whatever may happen," he said, "I'd like you to know that it's been an honor to work with you."

She looked at him uneasily. "What are you talking about, Rakesh?"

He ignored the question. "I don't want you to blame yourself for anything that's happened. You've always done the right thing, and you have to go on working hard, just as we've been doing these past few weeks. These have been the best days of my life."

"Rakesh…" Her eyes moistened. "We've still got time to get out of here and ask for help."

But the next moment his suit split open completely, leaving him exposed to the planet's atmosphere. He opened his mouth very wide so that he could breathe. To everyone's surprise, including his own, he took in a mouthful of air. He felt something in his throat and cleared it.

"I think I'm all right," he said with difficulty. "It's harder to breathe… but I think… I can go on."

Emily sighed with relief. Perhaps conditions were not as dangerous as Chad and Taro had thought at first.

"Do you want me to give you a piggyback?" she asked.

"No… no…" he coughed. "I can go on."

Rakesh had just experienced the change in atmosphere, but he had also lost the assistance of the exosuit, so they decided to slow their pace so that he would not have to make such an effort. And as if that were not enough, he had also been left without anything on his feet, as the black skin-tight suit they wore underneath was never intended for walking outside.

"How do you feel?" Emily asked.

"Actually… I feel very well," he said with difficulty, coughing as he spoke. "I thought… it would be worse. In fact, this place smells… clean."

"What about you, Gorka?" Paula asked.

"Fine," he said laconically.

After traveling several hundred meters between rocks and stalagmites, they came to a place with only a single exit. This required them to enter a tunnel much like the one they had come from, but in this case excavated out of the living rock. The ancient Keplerians must have invested a lot of time and effort in digging out that narrow passage. At first there was a great deal of damp on the walls, but as they advanced this grew less and the scars which the primitive tools of the Keplerians had left on the mountain became more noticeable. Rakesh was still breathing with difficulty, to the point that his snore was now constant. Emily took a closer look at him by the light of her visor.

"I'm... fine," he said with something of an effort. "I can... go on."

But his pupils were dilated and his gaze distant.

She picked him up and slung him over her shoulder. "Quick! We've got to get out of here!"

They all tried to go faster, but Gorka could not keep up with the pace.

"You go on!" Liikmi said. He had stayed with Paula and Gorka.

They went on as fast as they could along that difficult terrain. Emily did her best to keep Rakesh from losing consciousness.

"Don't fall asleep, Rakesh," she told him desperately. "Stay with me!"

A few minutes later she realized that he was no longer coughing, nor was he able to hold his head up any longer. She laid him on the floor and checked his vital signs. They were weak, but he was still breathing. She slung him over her shoulder again, but a few meters ahead she was forced to stop. His body was inert, and she was finding it increasingly hard to carry him. She checked his vital signs again.

It was too late.

"No... Rakesh..." she sobbed, holding her friend's head in her arms. "It was all my fault. I should never have let you come with me. And now... you're gone..."

"I'm really sorry," Avmup said. "I wasn't aware of this problem. If I'd known, I could have brought some medicinal plants with me."

She thought of trying to resuscitate him, but what sense did it make to prolong the inevitable? Without enough oxygen, the possibility of hypoxia was too great. If they did not get out of there soon, this would be the fate which awaited all of them, including her. They had managed to get out of the frying-pan, but they had fallen straight into the fire.

"We can't breathe this air," she said with tears in her eyes. "I don't think your plants would have helped very much."

"Well, it seemed he didn't have enough air. I think the Wiikhaadiiz ofiz know certain leaves that enable us to climb high mountains where the air's different."

"Still, it's too late for him," she whispered. "And perhaps for all of us as well."

"Anyway," Avmup said, "I'm really sorry. He seemed a good man."

"He was," she said disconsolately. "He was an extraordinary being."

A few minutes later the others appeared, with Liikmi in the lead and Paula a few meters behind giving Gorka whatever help she could.

"What happened?" Liikmi asked when he came up to them.

Avmup gestured to him in explanation.

"I'm very sorry," he said. "I know what it's like to lose a friend and comrade."

"Thank you, Liikmi," Emily said, "but we'd better get a move on if we don't want this to be repeated."

Paula broke down as soon as she realized what had happened. But for all the sadness of the moment, they all understood the urgency. They had to get out of there as soon as possible, so without spending more time mourning their friend they went on. Emily picked up Rakesh's body, while Paula gave Gorka some support so that he too could go on.

Emily checked the amount of oxygen left in her suit: less than five per cent. This meant that Paula would have a little more, but Gorka's situation was a mystery. He had spent some time unconscious and his breathing had presumably been slower during that time. But she feared that the extra effort involved in moving the suit without artificial assistance meant that he might have been forced to use up much of his reserves. Unfortunately it was not long before they found out the answer. His suit split completely open.

"No, no!" Paula cried as she helped him to stay on his feet. "Gorka… no…"

"Don't worry…" he said breathing with difficulty. "I'm not afraid… of whatever's coming."

"Don't speak," Emily said. "Save energy. We've got to get out of here as soon as possible."

They went on, this time much faster. Paula lifted Gorka onto her back, but he began to cough and become aware of problems in his throat.

"Not much left now," Avmup said. "Keep going."

Emily could not stop thinking that even if they were to get out of there, they still had to make an attempt to contact the Asimov. By the time they were picked up it would probably be too late. She only had one per cent of oxygen left.

"Ada," she called, as she went on after Avmup, "I want to record a message for the deputy director."

"Whenever you want."

"David, if you're listening to this it'll mean we didn't make it, but I don't want you to feel sad, and nor do I want you to blame yourself for what's happened. We got as far as we could, but I don't regret any of the decisions I've made. What I do regret most is not having been able to find a place where we could all begin again. Perhaps the most sensible thing would be to re-start the mission a long away from the Keplerians, without any interference. Maybe we were too arrogant, thinking we could manage Keplerian politics all by ourselves. I wish you the best of luck in your work.

"I don't think I've ever thanked you for everything you've done for me ever since my father left. I know you promised you'd never lose another Rhodes, but I don't want this to trouble you. I'll leave here at peace with myself and with everything I'm leaving behind. You've always been like a father to me, and I want to thank you for all your advice and for all the help you gave my grandmother and me. Thank you, from the bottom of my heart."

She was silent for a few moments.

"Ada," she went on, "I want to record a message for Robert."

"Go ahead."

"Robert," she began with tears in her eyes, "I never thought I'd have to record a message like this. I'm afraid I'll never be able to see that farm of yours. But don't be sad on my account, I hope that you at least will see it come true. The Keplerians have shown that they're a free people, even if they live under the constant threat from a superior race. I don't want anyone to start an escalation of violence in my name. I can see a lot of us in them, and I think they have every right to doubt us and to defend themselves against us. More than that, I know for sure that both species have no choice but to understand each other. It's the Khol who ought to be the target of our anger.

"I go in peace, sad because I never achieved what we needed to, because I was never able to share more time with you, my love. But I also go in happiness because I knew you, because I shared part of my heart with you. Take care, Robert, and take care of all the others. I'll always have you in my heart. I love you."

Her tears were running down her cheeks. The farewells were over, and she decided to fight for her life one last time.

"Ada," she said serenely, "send these messages if you manage to recover comms and I'm not here any longer."

"All right, Emily."

Her meter reached zero. She was able to leave Rakesh's body on the ground before her suit could open completely.

"Emily…" Paula murmured.

"It's all right," she said, breathing with some difficulty. "Let's try… to get out of here. At least I'd like to breathe a bit of the outside air before hypoxia takes over."

"We're there now," Avmup announced, though Emily was unable to understand what he was saying.

"Liikmi…" she said, coughing and breathing with difficulty, "promise me… you'll come back for Rakesh… and the equipment we're leaving behind."

Paula did the translation for her.

"I promise," he said with a heartfelt bow. He was obviously distressed at seeing her in such a fragile state.

"Take it all… to our people."

Liikmi nodded at this final request.

"And now… let's get out of here. I want to… feel the breeze one last time."

By the time they realized, Avmup had vanished. But it was all the same now, because their time was up. Liikmi helped Emily as best he could, but soon Paula too had to shed the protection of her suit.

It was at that moment, with all their hopes lost, that at last they saw the first light of the morning peeping through a small hole in the rock. They had just seen the way out of that ill-omened place. They came out through the opening and Emily was able to see the beauty of the planet for the first time with her own eyes, without any kind of filter or barrier. The purple of dawn soon turned to beautiful shades of blue and green, almost as though this were an aurora borealis.

"Wow!" Gorka cried as he struggled to breathe.

"It's beautiful!" Paula whispered with tears in her eyes.

For the first time the air of the planet was filling their lungs. The scent of the place reminded her of the moment immediately after an electrical storm. That feeling of cleanness Rakesh had mentioned was the result of the greater concentration of ozone in the air. Emily began to feel her mind drifting away, but she was not afraid, she had accepted her fate. She looked at her two friends. And despite the fact that she regretted with all her heart having dragged them along with her on this suicidal mission, she was glad that she was not alone. She hugged them both. She was aware that Gorka's ragged breathing and Paula's sobs were fading further away from her as she closed her eyes and lost consciousness.

28
Old enemies

Robert and Ferrara strode determinedly up to the north gate of the Khaavahki village. If they played their cards well, they could probably go through it easily enough. Outside the wall a multitude of small huts were piled against the wooden palisade which protected the settlement. Activity at this time of the night was non-existent. All the Keplerians were resting inside their homes.

"Follow my lead, Sergeant," Robert said. "Keep your gun at the ready, but don't show it."

"Understood, captain."

Beside the gate a small sentry-box allowed the two soldiers there to shelter from the rain when this was too heavy even for the dense crowns of the age-old trees under whose shade the settlement had been built. On the top of the palisade several soldiers had become aware of their presence and were watching them closely as they approached the entrance to the city.

Two of the four soldiers below started back in shock when they saw the newcomers and tensed in their positions as if they were bamboo stems.

One of them brandished his halberd at them. "Stop! Don't come any closer!"

Despite Ferrara's doubts, Robert did not slow down in the least. Determination was vital if his plan was to work. All the same, he decided to raise his hands to reassure the soldiers.

They look young, he thought. *Good, that should help us.*

"Who are you?" another of the soldiers asked.

"Out captain is inside the tower with your leader. We come bearing urgent news."

"No-one's warned us of any visit," said another.

"We're bringing urgent news," Ferrara insisted, "As a rule urgent news tends to be unexpected, wouldn't you say?"

"But we have orders not to let anyone through," the first soldier argued.

"And we have orders to warn our captain of everything that could change the course of our mission," Robert said. "We have to come in."

The first soldier turned to his comrade. "I'll have a word with the lieutenant." They heard him add in a whisper: "But he's going to be angry, he hates being woken up."

"I don't think I explained myself properly," Robert interrupted them. "We have to come in right away. It's either that or wait till our captain gets angry because he couldn't be given the news immediately. I dare say if that were to happen, your leader wouldn't be very happy if he found out you two were the cause of the delay."

The two soldiers were thoughtful for a moment. Certainly Vaahur would not be as indulgent with his two privates as their lieutenant, even after they had woken him up from his rest.

"Would you rather it was left to your leader to decide?"

"No, no," the first soldier said nervously. "You can come through."

"Thanks, private," Robert said, and he and Ferrara went in.

Once they were through the gate he looked in the rear-facing camera of his suit and saw the sentries following them carefully as they went down the avenue which led into the city.

"How did you know the soldiers weren't going to ask why we didn't just use our comms to talk to each other?" Ferrara asked.

Robert shrugged. "I didn't. I just tried to think like a rookie Keplerian soldier who doesn't know anything about human technology. But this was only the first stumbling-block, and I don't suppose it'll work again. I don't think we're going to get into the fortress just like that. We'll have to think of something different."

It took them a few minutes to reach the vicinity of the fortress. When they reached the halfway point and had left the palisade behind, he decided to take an alternative route between the cabins to avoid being seen. Security would be more intense the closer they came to the tower.

They came to an avenue of elegant buildings on several floors which hugged the tree-trunks. It was obvious that the ones in this zone had been built with far more care. From there they could see the fortress some distance away without exposing themselves too much. They had spotted several soldiers patrolling the main entrance and the first floors. The Watchtower was a square structure which rose imposingly above the treetops which hid the sky. It did not offer many openings or windows an intruder could slip in through, apart from the arrow-slits which ran along the various levels and which enabled defense against an attacker from outside. This gave it a solid, impenetrable look and made things harder for the two intruders.

It was obviously a very ancient construction, particularly in its lower levels, to judge by the general wear and tear of the stonework. It also seemed to have been enlarged and modified many times, as was shown by the contrasting tones and sizes of the stone which had been used in the upper levels.

Ferrara gave a whistle of admiration as she looked up. "I have to say, this is a pretty impressive building."

"It certainly is. It's going to be a complicated business getting into it without being seen."

"Especially seeing that we don't know where we have to go."

Robert had spotted an elegant balcony on the lower part of the tower, twenty meters or so from the ground. By this height the tower began to reveal itself as distinct from the other buildings nearby. Apart from the richness of the detail in the masonry, which contrasted with the sobriety of the remainder of the building, there was one thing which distinguished it from any other part of the fortress; an orange light lit up the room framed by the balcony.

"See that?" he said.

"Right."

"That's where we need to go."

"How d'you know?"

"The Keplerians don't need light to see in the dark, and it's not a particularly cold evening. And yet they have a fire lit. There are guests in there."

"And also it looks quite luxurious," she pointed out. "Do you think they're the Khaavahki leader's quarters?"

"Or a hall where he can receive his allies."

"That's where Garth must be," she said.

"We have to work out a plan for getting to that balcony."

Ferrara was looking at the stairway at the base of the tower, just below the illuminated balcony. "There are a lot of guards around the main entrance," she pointed out.

"We might be able to use the suit's thrusters to jump from the roof of the building beside it."

"But there are guards on the rooftop too."

"Then we'll have to neutralize them."

They approached the building beside the tower, which seemed to be something like barracks where the soldiers rested and trained. In the aerial images the drones had sent, they had seen that it was built around an inner, rectangular courtyard. In it there were different training tracks, equipment and weapons for the troops who were training the new recruits. The building was tall enough to mean that there was no way of reaching it with their suit drives. At the top, four guards were doing the rounds of the battlements. Each pair was in charge of their own part of the perimeter.

"I think we need to go up to that other building first." He pointed to a luxurious construction of stone nearby. "Then from there we can climb onto the elevated platform on that tree."

Ferrara looked at the platform he was pointing to.

"But that's twenty meters above the building!"

"If we gain momentum and then activate the suit drive before we land, I think we can cover the distance easily enough."

"We'll make a noise."

He shook his head. "Not if we activate the suit's stealth system. And what's more, let's do it now."

"Do you think it'll be enough to camouflage the noise of the thrusters?"

"It ought to. In theory the system emits sound waves that are the opposite to everything the suit itself is able to generate, footsteps, propulsion, and even shots. It works the same way as the noise-cancellation Ada uses in the dorms back at the bases to stop us hearing other people snoring. It should work with the thrusters."

"I guess we'll find out soon enough."

They approached the building from the side. The guards of the Khaavahki fortress were concentrated at the front of the tower, so that side access would be easier. They reached one of the corners of the building without making any sound, then with a powerful leap they activated the thrusters to get onto the roof. But as soon as they landed on the stone, they realized something they had not taken into account.

"Hell!" Ferrara muttered. "The thrusters give out light."

"Some of the guards have seen the flash," Robert said. He had crouched down and was watching some of the soldiers searching for the light source which had disturbed their watch-duty.

"Now what do we do?" she asked.

"We'll both have to jump at the same time, then hide as fast as we can to avoid detection."

As soon as the soldier had given up and gone back to his position, both of them used the wooden platforms in the nearby trees to climb to the highest of them. This was the one which was high enough to cover the distance which separated them from the roof of the barracks.

"Have you ever made a jump like that, captain?" Ferrara asked.

"Nope, but I saw someone do it once. Don't tell me you're starting to have doubts now, sergeant."

"No, no," she assured him, "it's just that if we brake too soon we could fall into the inner courtyard and create a commotion not even the stealth system could hide."

"We'll just have to make the perfect jump, I'm afraid."

"Both at the same time?"

"Yeah, I think that would be best. The guard probably thought there was a storm brewing in the distance. Doing it at the same time should minimize the risk."

"Okay."

"We'll count to three, then jump."

"Okay." Ferrara took a breath.

"One… two…"

"Wait a moment!" she exclaimed suddenly. "Do we move on the count of three, or do we do it when you count three and then say *now*?"

"No, we move on the count of three."

"That means one, two, then we move when you say three."

"That's it."

"Okay, just wanted to make sure."

"One…" Robert began again, "two… three!"

They made their run-up and jumped from the wooden platform of the tree the moment they reached the edge. The suit gave them the power they needed to cover the horizontal distance between platform and building. Adrenalin took over. Luckily the jump had been well-calculated and they were heading to the side of the rooftop, where the guards were keeping watch, but in a spot which was clear at that moment.

Ferrara activated her thrusters two meters from the stone of the building. and with an accurate movement managed to land with very little difficulty on a suitable spot so that she could hide behind the inner wall.

Robert tried to do the same, but his leap was not so perfect because he had leaned too far forward. He activated his thrusters two meters from the ground, but he knew his aim was wrong. This, added to his incorrect landing angle, made him trip and roll uncontrollably forward. He was unable to grasp a handhold anywhere and ended up falling into the inner courtyard of the barracks. The stealth system of the suit did its best to muffle the commotion he had created, and though it succeeded to some extent, the dull blow, combined with the flashes of the thrusters, alerted two of the guards. He got up from the floor as quickly as he could and hid behind a pile of wood the soldiers presumably used for target practice.

"What was that?" he heard from the upper level.

"It looked like lightning," came another voice. "I think there must be a storm somewhere, but the noise came from down there."

"I'm going to see what it was," the first soldier said, and set off to the stairs which connected the inner courtyard to the battlements.

He came downstairs with a spear in his hands, aiming at the spot where Robert had landed. He had fallen on a kind of trestle with various wooden weapons hanging from it. The soldier came closer, with Robert watching all his movements from his hiding-place.

"Who's there?" the soldier asked, sounding rather unsure of himself.

Robert stayed silent, hidden, waiting for him to come closer. The soldier took a step forward, turning his head from side to side, seeking some explanation of the commotion.

When Robert saw that he was coming too close, he gave a leap and ran toward him at full tilt. The soldier saw him in time, but all he could manage to do was swipe sideways with his spear. Robert stopped the attack with an accurate punch. The soldier, confused, realized that the blow had been a silent one, and Robert seized the moment to get closer. He pushed the soldier to make him lose his balance, but failed in his attempt, and the soldier thrust his solid spear of Keplerian wood between them. They grasped it simultaneously: Robert by the middle, the soldier by both ends. He was surprised by the strength of the Keplerian, who was not prepared to give way despite the strength his own suit was giving him.

Both of them kept up the struggle for a few seconds which seemed endless, until the Keplerian moved his feet a few steps back. Then Robert used the thrusters in his heels and leapt over him without letting go of the spear. The somersault gave him the opportunity to stand back to back with the soldier. Keeping his hold on the spear, he pressed it with all the strength his suit could give him against his opponent's neck.

The Keplerian began to gasp for air. With another slight movement forward he made him lose his ground, increasing the pressure on his back. A few seconds later he realized that the soldier had stopped trying to get free, and he loosened his hold. The soldier fell to the ground unconscious. Immediately Robert looked up to locate the soldier's partner, who seemed to have been following their movements from above. But the figure he saw was not that of a Keplerian soldier but Ferrara, who had synchronized her own actions with those of her superior and neutralized the other guard silently.

The two guards on the other side of the courtyard still seemed to be unaware of what had just happened. He hid the body as best he could and went up the stairs which led to the front of the fortress. From this area it was ten meters or so to the balcony, a complicated jump even with the assistance of the thrusters. He leaned out over the battlements to assess the threat posed by the soldiers guarding the main entrance to the tower. So far everything seemed to be in order, and no-one was the wiser about their presence there.

"This is going to be even harder, sir," Ferrara said. "Do you think you'll be able to do it properly this time?"

"Very funny, sergeant." The slight smile Robert tried to make looked more like a grimace.

"Do we make a run-up from back there, then grip the battlements for a last push?"

He nodded. "Yeah, that seems feasible."

They went to stand at the corner of the building and set off at a run along the ramparts. The moment Robert judged their speed and distance to be optimum, he said:

"Now!"

As if the movement had been choreographed, both of them turned to the right in a perfect exercise of coordination. Both gathered a little momentum, enough to let them lean their dominant leg on the battlements. At the ideal moment they activated their thrusters to gather force and propel them into the air, emitting a momentary flash which carried them as far as the stone columns on the side of the balcony. Barely wasting a moment, and as soon as they had grasped the stone columns, both of them leapt over it and hid inside the balcony, far from the astonished eyes of the guards on the lower level, who spun around, trying to work out where the flashes had come from.

Robert assessed the situation as he waited there without moving so much as a muscle. Everything seemed to suggest that no-one had seen them. All he could hear was his own heartbeat, which was racing now after what they had just done. Once they had got their breath back, they approached the balcony door with great caution. It was decorated with delicate, intricately detailed carvings. Soon he had to wrench his mind back to the reason they were there in the first place. He heard a voice shouting inside, so they went as close as they dared.

"You promised me access to human technology!" a Keplerian was saying. "So keep your damn word!"

"I told you there'd be a deal if you could get rid of Dr. Rhodes, but you haven't been able to meet your side of it," a voice replied very calmly. It sounded familiar to Robert. "We've complied with every single part of the plan, including that little massacre we had to carry out in that village. But you're the one who was required to make sure you sentenced her and put her to death. And yet what you've done is let four scientists, with no military experience whatever, escape from this fortress that you yourself called… unassailable? Was that the word you used?"

Robert glanced aside at Ferrara.

"They escaped," she whispered in relief.

He put a finger to his lips. For him too it was a relief to know that Emily had been able to escape. But if they were not there, where could they be?

"I've risked everything I have by collaborating with you," the man talking to Captain Garth went on loudly. Do you know what the other leaders'll do to me if they ever find out about all this? The deal was that I'd ruin that leech Khikhya's plans to ally herself with your equals and then you'd give me human technology so that I could take power."

"Make no mistake, Vaahur," Garth said, very seriously, "you know perfectly well: if I'm to hand over our technology, then first I have to gain control of the human ship and then, with our support, no-one among the Keplerians will dare to stand up to you. But if I'm to carry out this operation I need that slippery rat out of the equation, the slippery rat your men have allowed to escape."

"We don't know how they escaped," the Keplerian assured him, rather more calmly than before. "We think they've used some kind of technology to get out of here without being seen. I've ordered a perimeter to be set around the city to catch them."

"I hope for your own good that you find them," Garth said. "We're both risking a lot. In fact I'll order two of my best soldiers to accompany your troops to catch them."

The conversation went on more cordially after that small outburst on the part of the Khaavahki leader. Minutes later Garth left the room, leaving him alone.

They decided to leave the balcony and follow Captain Garth. Going back to their starting point was a lot easier, and very soon they were following the captain's footsteps. As usual he was accompanied by his ever-faithful Sergeant Cameron. To avoid passing through the entrance, this time they managed to cross the wooden palisade through a neglected spot.

"What do we do now?" Ferrara asked.

"We put an end to all this. We're going after them!"

She smiled. "I like the way you think, captain. "They'll have to answer for what they did."

They moved on more quickly and followed the two rebels stealthily as they left the northern entrance behind on their way to their transport. Robert and Ferrara went up to them, guns in hands, until they were immediately behind them.

"Freeze!" Robert shouted as he aimed at Captain Garth's head.

"Well, well, Sergeant Cameron! Look who we have here."

"Looks as though your old pupil has learned a few tricks, sir," the sergeant said mockingly.

"Don't move!" Ferrara shouted. "And put your hands up!"

"And he's brought his good friend the unbreakable Sergeant Ferrara! You surprise me, Captain Beaufort. I thought I'd made myself clear the last time we saw each other when I said our next encounter wouldn't be so friendly."

"And as you can see, I took your word for it. Now turn around slowly, and no surprises."

The rebels turned as he had told them to, with their hands up. Sergeant Cameron looked serious, almost angry, which on the other hand was the way she usually looked. But something in Captain Garth's expression made Robert think that something was not right; his smile was not that of someone who has lost control of the situation.

"What's so funny?" he asked. "You almost caused the death of four innocent people."

"I admit it's a setback to find out that your beloved doctor has escaped from this dunghill those animals call a fortress," he said without losing his smile. "It looks as though this little kitten of yours has innumerable lives. However, her time will come, and obviously I'll have to deal with her myself."

"You killed the inhabitants of a Keplerian village in cold blood, and who knows how many more crimes you've committed since you've been here," Ferrara spat at him.

"Come on, sergeant," the captain said very calmly, "surely you'd have enjoyed yourself as much as we did watching all those bastards dying one by one, begging for their lives. Especially that pregnant sow. How she cried for her little son's life!"

"That's enough!" She aimed at the captain. "You're a monster!"

"Now, Sergeant Reynolds!" Garth shouted. His smile turned suddenly to a threatening scowl.

Everything happened very quickly. The drone which had been flying over the area fired a projectile which impacted among the four of them. A small explosion generated a bright flash in front of Robert and Ferrara which was visible hundreds of meters away and blinded both of them. Sergeant Cameron hurled herself on Ferrara and knocked her down. Captain Garth took a step forward and seized Robert's gun with his left hand, then with a powerful right punch split it in half.

Ferrara tried to get up, but Sergeant Cameron grappled with her in an attempt to seize the gun she was still holding. Both of them struggled, but Ferrara had not yet recovered her sight and was an easy prey for the experienced Sergeant Cameron, who managed to disarm her.

Robert too was blinded. Captain Garth gave him a tremendous shove which made him lose his balance and roll helplessly on the ground. He ended up falling on his stomach a few meters further back. Garth came up to him and began to kick the back of his suit, exactly where the oxygen tank was. Robert, still stunned by the flash, was only able to roll onto his back to avoid the blows, to avoid damage to his suit's life-support.

"I'm going to enjoy this very much, Captain Beaufort," Garth said as he tried to strike him again, but without success.

Sergeant Cameron straddled Ferrara to try to immobilize her now that she was disarmed, but she was fighting back with tooth and nail. Faced with the difficulty of loosening her attacker's grip, Ferrara decided to use her suit thrusters. She moved a few meters away, then made her opponent fall and hit her back hard against the ground. Ferrara, who was beginning to get her sight back, got to her feet more quickly than her rival and went for her. When she was close she jumped with her feet held out and struck Cameron in the chest so that once again she rolled helplessly backwards again.

Robert tried to get to his feet several times, but Garth was always ahead of him. A strong kick made him roll over again.

"Do you really think you can beat me? You had your chance to join our cause… but now it's too late, captain, I'm afraid everything's over as from today."

He kicked him again, and although Robert rolled over, he could see well enough to react. In a swift movement he grasped the rebel's leg with both hands. Once he had him blocked he activated his thrusters, jumped several meters up and threw the captain into the air, Garth made two full turns before hitting the ground with a loud thud. Robert on the other hand managed to land without any trouble.

"You're right, captain, everything's over today," he said. "But not the way you think."

He ran forward to hit Garth, but with a swift, agile movement his opponent got to his feet and dodged the attack. He also hit the back of Robert's helmet hard, so that he almost lost his balance. Robert turned in time and managed to deflect a hook with a swift move of his hand. Garth tried again, this time with a left hook, but Robert was alert and managed to avoid it by hurling his body to one side.

Once again Ferrara lunged at Sergeant Cameron and began to batter her helmet. She managed to crack the resistant material of the visor, but this time it was Cameron who used her thrusters. She aimed the two on her hands at Ferrara, hurling her backwards. Despite this she did not fall to the ground, and by the time Sergeant Cameron got up, Ferrara lunged at her again. After the impact both of them rolled as far as a downhill slope, and they tumbled helplessly down this. Ferrara managed to stop short after cannoning into a tree, while Cameron went on down.

Robert pulled himself together after Captain Garth's quick reaction and managed to avoid all his attacks. The captain was basing his training on brute force. This might have made sense on Earth, but here, with the exosuits in the way, force lost the advantage and skill became the only thing that mattered. By now Robert had managed to annoy Captain Garth with his greater agility.

"Don't dodge the fight!" Garth shouted in an attempt to

intimidate him. "You cowardly rat!"

What he wanted was hand-to-hand combat so that they could fight on equal terms, but Robert dodged his attacks over and over again, and even managed to hit his helmet once or twice. If he could manage to keep his opponent at a distance he might have a chance. But sooner or later he would have to go on the attack if he wanted to defeat him.

"You'll end up paying for your crimes," he told him.

He took advantage of one of Garth's unsuccessful attacks to launch an upward punch straight at the rebel captain's chin. The sharp blow sounded clearly against the helmet, testing the strength of the joints of his suit. He took advantage of Garth's confusion to launch another right hook straight to the cheek. A crack zigzagged down the visor of Garth's helmet. Robert tried a third blow with his left fist, but his rival reacted in time and managed to seize him with both hands.

Ferrara meanwhile got up, stunned, after striking a huge tree. Using the cover provided by the trunk, she looked for her rival downhill. The thickness of the foliage and undergrowth made it difficult to see, and not even the suit's motion sensors were able to detect anything.

By the time she realized, her opponent was already on her. Sergeant Cameron had taken a small detour uphill and now threw herself on her with a powerful jump so that she could use gravity to help her. Ferrara, unable to avoid the blow, felt dents forming in her suit: first in the chest area, then on the top of her helmet. However, Sergeant Cameron had not fully calculated her maneuver, and once again both of them rolled downhill. This time Ferrara's progress was blocked by a huge rock and the impact, despite the protection her suit gave her, left her gasping.

Captain Garth reacted quickly and agilely to Robert's new attack. He gripped his free arm and began to hit his visor violently with the metal part of his own helmet. At the third blow Robert's visor cracked in turn. Before Garth could deliver his fourth headbutt, which would have compromised the structure of the suit, he set his feet at an oblique angle and activated his thrusters, forcing Garth to let go of him. He used his momentum to deliver a powerful blow with his knee to the head of his former superior officer, making him lose his balance and fall backwards.

Robert hurled himself on him again, but before he could reach him the drone, which was still flying over the area, fired another projectile, which blinded him again. Garth seized the opportunity to launch a powerful right hook at his helmet. The strength of the blow knocked him to the ground, and his suit visor, unable to take any more attacks, ended up shattering. The oxygen-rich air began to escape and mix with that of the outside. Robert was left breathless and began to gasp from the effort on top of the tension of the fight. Soon he began to feel an irritation in his throat, then to cough and writhe in panic. He knew what was happening to him.

Evil laughter sounded a few meters away, and though his eyes could not see clearly he managed to make out a sinister figure coming toward him.

"I told you this would all end today, captain," he heard Garth say. "It's a pity, because you and I would have made a good team. But you insist on following the same absurd moral rules as the leaders of the project. They're all too short-sighted. Now relax, because if the hypoxia doesn't kill you, the rest of the filth in the air of this infected planet will finish the job. And don't worry, I'll make sure personally that your busybody girlfriend joins you in hell as soon as possible. *C'est la vie! Au revoir,* captain," he finished mockingly as he left him to his fate.

Robert knew he had very little chance of getting out of there unless he got to the rover quickly and asked for help, but he was still stunned and the lack of oxygen was doing nothing to help. He tried to calm down. He remembered what his mother had taught him when he had attended her yoga classes as a child back in his native Marseilles. He slowed his heartbeat and controlled his breathing, and in a little while he felt better. Captain Garth was no longer there, but he had to find his sergeant as soon as possible.

"Ferrara?" he managed to call,

There was no answer.

The blow against the rock had left her stunned. When at last she reacted, there was no trace of Sergeant Cameron. She climbed the hill with some difficulty and found traces of the fights, but not a single clue to the rebel's whereabouts.

Fucking coward, she thought. *She's run away.*

She went back to the starting-point, but could not find either of the other two combatants. But she saw a body a few meters ahead, lying immobile. She hastened to his side. He was lying face down.

"Captain!" she cried in horror when she turned him over. "No, no! Not you!"

She saw the state of his battered helmet and realized that he had been exposed to the air of the planet. When she checked his vital signs he was still breathing. There was a chance of saving him. She slung him over her shoulder and began the journey back to the rover, while at the same time she tried to contact the station.

29
The new awakening

Date unknown

Location unknown

Everything was happening in slow motion. She was in a museum, all by herself. The echo of her footsteps on the pale wooden floor echoed off the walls with their endless works of art, then came back to her ears in sudden bursts. Every step she took seemed to last an eternity. She recognized the place from one of her few visits to Europe when she had been with her father on one of his many working trips.

She was in the Louvre.

She gazed all around. She did not like being alone there, but all she could see was her own reflection in the glass of one of the security booths. It was her, but fifteen years younger, more or less the age she had been on that trip to Paris. And yet there was something different about that reflection, something troubling: something that did not fit. The girl's eyes were not human, they were those of a Keplerian. She put her hands to her face, and though the movement took a lot longer than she had expected, she was able to see them. She studied them closely, turned them in every direction, but they were still human.

A noise startled her. It had come from one side of the hall. She turned her head very slowly, but there was no-one and nothing there. She went to the corner with a slow, heavy tread. It was too difficult to move, or else the air was too dense, or else time passed at a different speed there. It took her an eternity to reach the other end. Here she found a series of golden metal posts, like the ones used to fence off a work of art. A red velvet ribbon joined them, blocking access to the public when the museum was open.

She looked around carefully. The spot where Leonardo da Vinci's *Giaconda* ought to have been was empty. In its place there was only a dark, very delicate wooden reredos, which looked very old. She tried to get closer, but the velvet ribbon blocked her way. Once again she looked around. She was alone, so she decided to squeeze under the ribbon and go up to the reredos. On its surface were very detailed engravings of bucolic Keplerian scenes: draft animals, farmers and miners dominated most of the pictures. She had seen those images before, in the Gaal-El temple. She turned around again, but now she was no longer in the Louvre but in the conclave chamber. The table, which was the same color as the four walls, was surrounded by five chairs, one for each of the Keplerian leaders.

Suddenly she heard a noise. She turned slowly, but there was nothing. The sound seemed to be coming from beyond one of the walls. She looked for the entrance door, but the sound was coming from behind the wall in front of her. She ran her fingers over the area it was coming from, and as soon as she touched the wall a door opened. There was no light on the other side. She pushed gently. When it opened, she was confronted by the Galileo Station. In the midst of all that infinite darkness there rose, splendidly, the space station her father had travelled in. Kepler-442b loomed behind, and something very familiar to her completed the scene: the black hole.

She took a step forward. Her body began to float amid that dark immensity. She knew what was about to happen, because she had experienced it several times before and knew that she was about to wake up. But in the clarity of her dream she needed to find out the meaning of it all. Unfortunately she was given no time for anything more. Kepler-442b began to narrow and vanish under the influx of the black hole. Next the space station followed it, and at last she began to open her eyes.

She was drowsy. She felt dizzy and was beginning to feel a growing pain throughout her body. The light was soft, but she could manage to make something out, although she did not really know where she was. She was lying on her left arm on a bed of hay covered with a grayish cloth, rough-looking and very coarse to the touch. The smell was far from pleasant, and this helped her to come to her senses. From that position she could only see two other empty mattresses, but there seemed to be more on the other side of the aisle she could see at her feet. It looked like a kind of barracks. A place where the wounded and convalescent were treated.

She tried to turn over, but her body would not respond. She could feel that it was stiff, as though she had just finished running a marathon. Swallowing was hard, and her throat was very swollen. She became aware that her body was giving a faint moan which she was not aware of having ordered in her mind. She was having trouble breathing, the air felt like fire in her lungs, but she was no longer aware of that sense of suffocation she had felt in the cave when her suit had used up all its oxygen. Suddenly she became aware of movement behind her. Someone else was moving.

"Emily?" came a faint voice.

With difficulty she managed to turn over onto her back, and an unwell-looking Paula appeared in her field of vision. She was getting up from another bed, and was wearing a kind of nightgown of threadbare white cloth.

"Paula…" Emily tried to say. She had to be careful not to hurt her throat.

"I'm so happy," Paula said with tears in her eyes. She knelt on Emily's mattress and hugged her.

They stayed locked in the embrace for a long time. Despite the battered state of their bodies, each appreciated the other's warmth.

"What about Gorka?" Emily whispered.

Paula pointed to the other side of the room. "Unconscious, but breathing."

"And Rakesh…"

Paula shook her head. There was no-one else there.

"How long have we been here?" Emily asked.

"I don't know. I woke up yesterday afternoon."

"Do you know where we are?"

"I don't know that either," Paula said. "I've tried to talk to them, but I can't understand a word they say, and they don't understand me either."

"The suits," Emily said. "Without the suits, Ada can't translate Keplerian for us."

"I know. I need to speak to the station so that they can come and get us. Gorka needs help."

"He'll come out of this," Emily said as she tried to sit up. "He's much tougher than the two of us put together."

She realized that she was wearing a nightgown like Paula's. The environment was heavy with smells, most of them unpleasant, but there was something which felt familiar. She turned and saw a kind of incense-burner which was giving off a shy wisp of smoke. She also saw lengths of gauze and bowls of water on a table beside the entrance door. Wherever they might be, it looked as though at least someone was taking the trouble to try to look after them.

"Have you seen Liikmi or Avmup?" she asked.

Paula shook her head. "No, only one of the ones who seem to have been looking after us. This morning he came back to light the incense burner."

Without warning, the door opened. Two Keplerians entered rather absent-mindedly. The first was carrying a water-skin on his shoulder and a kind of bowl from which a thin steam was issuing. When he saw that they were awake and chatting to one another he stopped in his tracks, so that the one behind him bumped into him.

He turned back toward his companion. "Laph, *pii* Liikmi *wid poph yo daaz.*"

The younger one nodded and looked at them, then turned and ran out of the room.

"*Ayö taa iip a daaz,*" the Keplerian said, and bowed as he came forward to them.

All Emily could do was nod, as she did not understand a word of what he was saying. He filled a couple of bowls with the contents of the skin, then left them beside their beds.

"*Ombiw,*" he explained.

Then he did the same with the hot bowl he had brought. Inside was a reddish, viscous liquid. He poured some of this concoction into two smaller bowls and left them in the same place, beside the ones he had filled with water.

"*Jiilov tiiw,*" he said as he put the bowls down.

Seeing their reaction, the Keplerian indicated by a gesture that it was hot and that they should eat it. He seemed to be explaining to them that it would do them good. Then he went to the bed where Gorka was resting and examined him, with Paula's observant eyes following every movement. He opened his eyelids, took his pulse, checked his breathing and seemed to be pleased with everything. He turned him over to give him a change of posture, then gave another slight bow and left the room.

"I think we're in the Gaal-El temple," Emily said.

"How do you know?"

"He's dressed like a cult-member." Her throat was still painful. "And I think I caught Liikmi's name in that snatch of conversation."

"In that case we could go down to the rover and get in touch with the station," Paula suggested. "D'you think they'll be looking for us?"

"I'm sure they are, but I imagine they'd have come here in the first place, while we were being held in Khaavahki. We need to have a word with Liikmi, to get some answers."

"I guess we'd better have something to eat," Paula said. She was looking at the bowl out of the corner of her eye. "In fact they brought me the same thing yesterday when I woke up, and it's not bad at all. It's some kind of vegetable purée."

"If it didn't hurt so much," Emily said, "I'd say I was hungry."

Then she sat up on the uncomfortable mattress and began by picking up the small bowl of water. She was very thirsty. She took a draught, but it tasted strange, slightly metallic. She thought that her maltreated throat might be modifying the flavors, but then she realized that the Keplerians must take their water straight from the rivers and springs

271

without subjecting it to any kind of filtering or purification. She decided that when all was said and done it was water, and she was very thirsty.

Then she took the bowl of vegetable purée, which like everything else on that planet was red, almost purple, rather than the green of plant life on Earth. She blew with difficulty across the surface of the thick liquid, then took a small sip. She tasted the food curiously and swallowed carefully, to avoid hurting her throat any further.

"Well, I have to admit it's quite tasty," she said at last. "I mean, they're vegetables, and I'd almost say they taste like the ones back on Earth, except that they leave a bitter aftertaste."

"Yeah, it's not bad, is it?" Paula agreed. She was equally surprised. "I suppose vegetables are going to be much the same on planets with similar characteristics."

When they had finished half their bowlfuls, the door opened again and Waafdiv and Liikmi came in, as ceremonious as usual when they were dealing with Emily.

"*Nak taa ghishbik a li tii*," Waafdiv said, spreading his arms wide and raising his staff of command as he came over to them. "*Lu li numma.*"

Emily was grateful for his words, but more because of his body language than because of anything she had actually understood. He seemed to be genuinely worried about them. But she had to stop the conversation before he began to assume that she understood what he was saying to her.

"*Ju wok Kophy*," she said. "I don't speak your language," she added to emphasize the point, repeating the same thing in another language so that he would understand the translation problem.

Waafdiv stopped dead in surprise. It was Liikmi who whispered something neither of them understood. Whatever it might have been, Waafdiv seemed to understand the problem and asked him a question. Liikmi replied in the affirmative and left, but not without bowing to Emily before he did so.

"*Jiiilov tiiw wubrrik am*," Waafdiv said shyly, pointing to one of the bowls of purée. He even took the liberty of mimicking taking an imaginary bowl and rubbing his stomach.

Emily remembered those first moments with Shildii, when Ada had still been unable to translate her words into the Keplerian language, so she decided to imitate the gestures the boy had made when he had eaten the chocolate cake. The high priest seemed to be pleased with her facial expression, and both of them twined the fingers of their hands together to show that they understood each other.

Waafdiv became aware that Gorka was still unconscious, in that lethargic state she and Paula had now woken up from. The high priest noticed the tense concern in Paula's eyes when he went over to Gorka to check how he was. After examining him, he turned to her and made a reassuring gesture which both women understood. She was grateful for the information, which until that moment no-one had been able to give her. Tears burst from her eyes like a waterfall.

"*Niiw ghod tii*," he added gently as he handed her a piece of cloth.

Paula wiped away her tears on his handkerchief and showed her gratitude for the gesture by twining her fingers.

A few moments later Liikmi reappeared, together with another cult-member. Between them they were carrying one of the suits. To judge by its size it seemed to be Paula's, which was the smallest of all. They put it in a corner. Liikmi thanked his colleague for his help and motioned him to leave the room. Waafdiv pointed out the suit to Paula and gestured to them to use it. Emily tried to get up, but she needed the help of both Waafdiv and Liikmi. She felt the contact with them directly, on her skin. It was warm, much like human contact, but their skin felt rougher and thicker. Between the three of them they managed to reach the suit, and she activated it by placing her finger on the chest plate. The suit reacted by opening fully.

"Can you understand me now?" she asked.

"Yes," Waafdiv replied delightedly, "now I can!"

She smiled. "Perfect! At last we'll be able to talk properly," she added as she went back to her cot

"How do you feel?"

"Pretty well, considering everything we've been through."

"That's good news," Waafdiv said. "When Liikmi and Avmup brought you here there was only a trace of life left in you. If it hadn't been for Iwshaj, our master healer, you almost certainly wouldn't have made it."

"How long have we been here?"

"This is the dawn of the fourth day since you came here."

Emily indicated Gorka. "How's our friend?"

"I'm afraid he spent the longest time breathing our air without appropriate treatment," Liikmi said. "When he came, he was in a worse state than you two. But he's very strong, and everything seems to indicate that he'll survive. Iwshaj is keeping him in a state of hibernation so that his body will accustom itself to the new situation. With you two, he considered that you were ready to wake up."

"But how's that possible?" Emily said. "Our bodies aren't adapted to breathe this air."

Waafdiv shrugged. "Iwshaj knows what he's doing very well. He's very old, and he's treated many cases of poisoning and mountain sickness in his life."

"Still, we'd like to take our friend to our village."

"I'm afraid that's not advisable in his state. Iwshaj will decide when it's safe."

"Are we in the Gaal-El temple?"

"Yes."

"And our village. Have any of our people been in contact with you?"

"Yes, they were here a few hours after you were taken prisoner."

"Does that mean they know we're here?"

Waafdiv shook his head. "We knew a group of humans was collaborating with the Khaavahki, so I wasn't sure whether it might be a trap to prevent the rescue operation we'd organized. After all, it looked as though Vaahur's soldiers had human arms at their disposal. Perhaps I acted wrongly, but I thought that carrying out the operation as discreetly as possible would make it more likely to succeed."

"Do you remember the names of the people who came?"

He cast his memory back. "Someone called Green, if I remember correctly. He was quite tall, and the color of his skin was different from yours, darker."

"Yes, that's the deputy director, David Green. He's our leader."

"But that's not all," he went on. "A couple of days ago, when you were already here, your leader came back. He asked us about you again and told us you'd escaped. I lied to him again when I told him I didn't know where you were. I didn't want to risk you falling into the hands of your enemies. If humans are half as twisted as we Keplerians are, I could see that it might have been a trap."

Emily was thoughtful. This meant that no-one in the station knew they were there. But at least they had learned that they had managed to escape from the fortress.

"You did well, Waafdiv," she said. "Though in this case it wasn't a trap."

"We'd need to be able to get to our vehicle so that we can communicate with our people," Paula put in. "Please don't be offended, but I'd like one of our own healers to examine our friend."

Waafdiv smiled. "We're not offended. But I'm afraid I don't understand. What vehicle are you talking about?"

"The one we left down there in the village," Paula explained. "That's how we came all the way here."

Waafdiv turned inquiringly to Liikmi.

"The humans left a vehicle behind the old inn," he explained. "But I haven't been down there since we came back."

"Right," Waafdiv said, "but how are we supposed to bring it up here? You're still too weak to walk all that way."

Emily thought about this carefully. They were the only ones who could start the vehicle, because without the localization chip in the backs of their necks there was no way to open the rover.

"When you're beside the vehicle, speak to it," she said. "Tell it Emily and Paula are up here, that we're all right. And tell it to report our situation to the station."

Liikmi grimaced. "Do you want me to speak to your cart?"

"Yes, that's what I'd like you to do." She smiled. "But it might not believe what you say, so you'll have to give it some piece of information only she and I know. Tell her that when I was thinking of a name for her, my first idea was to call her Emma, like my mother."

30
The legend of the Gaal-El

February 6, year 1

Temple of the Gaal-El, Kepler-442b

While Liikmi was trying to bring the rover back, Waafdiv summoned the healer to assess the state of the three convalescents. Iwshaj appeared promptly. He was a very old Keplerian, much older than Khikhya and Khaaÿ, the Khapabir leader. His gait was tired and clumsy because of his age, but he moved with determination. Emily saw that his right eye, instead of being black like his left, looked whitish, as if he had some problem or affliction with his sight.

"Well, well, this young lady's awake now," he said. He was startled to hear the simultaneous translation which came from Paula's suit.

He went up to Emily, left his staff on one side and examined her closely with his good eye. He made her open her mouth, then put his ear to her back to listen to her breathing.

"Good," he said, sounding satisfied, "the swelling's going down slowly. You've been very lucky, both of you. If you'd come a little later I probably couldn't have done anything to keep you alive."

"How did you know what you had to do to help us?" Emily asked. "We're not Keplerian."

"Keplerians, Khol, Humans… it's all the same thing. All creatures are made of the same things: muscles, organs and blood. And we need the same air to breathe. And also Keplerians only fall ill when conditions around them change abruptly, such as when you climb very high mountains."

"Don't Keplerians ever fall ill?" Paula asked.

"Not if they stay still," the elder said with an air of amusement. "But there's always some young man who's too daring and wants to prove he can climb the highest mountain, or someone reckless who thinks he can eat everything nature offers us."

"Aren't there such things as contagious illnesses?"

"Contag… I don't know what that word means, young lady."

Ada had not even translated it but simply pronounced it literally, just as Paula had said it, so there seemed to be no word in Keplerian for *contagion.*

The old healer also examined Paula and came to the conclusion that everything was going as expected. Then came Gorka's turn. The elder studied him where he was lying there unconscious and said 'oh'. Then he checked his pulse and said 'ah', then finally listened to his breathing and gave a satisfied nod.

"Well?" Paula said impatiently. "How is he?"

The elder looked at her with his good eye. "He's doing well. There's no need for you to worry, young lady, he'll recover. He's just a little weak, so I'll carry on with his medication for one more day."

He took a kind of phial from one of the wide sleeves of his robe and emptied it down Gorka's throat, then did the same with a little water. Despite the elder's fragile appearance he moved very easily and was perfectly able to change Gorka's position on his bed all by himself.

"He'll wake up tomorrow, just as you both did," he told them.

"Master Iwshaj," Waafdiv interrupted him, "can the guests start to walk?"

He waved his hand. "Yes, they can if they wish to, but make sure they go slowly, because their lungs are still a little swollen. At the slightest trace of dizziness or feeling of tiredness, they'll need to stop and rest."

When the healer had finished his work and left the hall, Emily turned to Waafdiv.

"What about the body of our friend?"

"We recovered it. We don't know what human customs are with regard to the deceased, so we embalmed the body so that you can decide what to do with him."

"Thank you, Waafdiv," Emily said sadly. "That was really thoughtful of you."

"It's the least we could do. I suppose in a way we feel responsible for everything that's happening."

She shook her head firmly. "None of this is the responsibility of the Gaal-El. It's that scum Vaahur who's to blame for everything that's happened."

"Well," Waafdiv said, changing the subject, "there's something I'd like to show you, if you feel like getting up and having a little walk. It's not very far."

"If you'll excuse me, I'd rather stay with Gorka," Paula said.

"Of course, there's no problem, you can do whatever you like."

"A bit of movement will do me good," Emily said. "My whole body's stiff."

She managed to sit up by herself on the uncomfortable mattress, but she needed Waafdiv's help to get to her feet.

"Off we go, then," he said as he walked with her to the door.

"But we'll need the suit so that we can communicate, and this one isn't my size."

"I'll take you to where the others are," he said.

He led her to a small alcove, where she found the three other exosuits. This time, however, she did not put on the helmet. With no oxygen in the tank there was not much point. Once she was inside the suit, both of them went out to an inner courtyard where there was a small fountain and a large tree in the middle. After this Waafdiv led her inside another building, where as they went along corridors they passed a number of cult-members who greeted them, bowing to the one who was called to be the chosen. Emily's steps were very slow and heavy, even though she was inside the suit. She felt clumsy and very weak, and noticed she had lost some muscle tone during her stay there. On the other hand, she was sure it was less of an effort to breathe than it had been in the cave, and this raised many questions in her mind. At last they came to the temple forecourt through one of the side doors of the nearby buildings.

It was cloudy, with not much light coming in, but the touch of the breeze on her face and hair was very pleasant. She moved a little away from Waafdiv, closed her eyes and filled her lungs with a mouthful of air. It was cool, and just as Rakesh had said, it was reminiscent of the moments just before an electric storm. And though she knew that this feeling was a result of the high ozone content in the air, the scent and the freshness of the place made her feel alive, comforted, as if she were back on Earth. Waafdiv meanwhile waited patiently until she had taken enough time to enjoy the sensation of freshness the mountain gave her.

"Come this way," he said when he saw that she was relaxed. "I think you've earned the right to come to know the true heart of our cult."

When they went through the temple door, Emily could now pick up the smell of mustiness and old wood. She found the scent quite familiar, as it had been normal in the ancient temples of Earth.

"Very few among us have ever seen what you're about to see now," her guide said mysteriously.

They crossed the temple and stopped in front of the wooden reredos which gave access to the conclave chamber. Emily realized that the staves of command belonging to the leaders were no longer on the altar, a sign that by now the conclave had ended. Waafdiv, with something like a conjuror's skill, took a huge metal key out of one of his sleeves and inserted it in the lock. He opened the door and motioned Emily to enter. Someone had devoted their time to restoring the door after the violent entry of Vaahur's soldiers into the conclave, and though they had done a good job the damage was still visible, particularly in those places where the door joined the hinges. There was almost complete darkness inside the hall, and she hesitated before going in. Without the helmet she could see nothing.

"It's dark," she explained.

"Oh!" Waafdiv exclaimed. "That's right, humans can't see in the dark."

"Don't worry, some of us have an eye implant which lets us improve our vision," she explained. "Infrared," she said immediately.

"You humans never cease to amaze me," he said.

They went into the conclave chamber, and Waafdiv went across to the wall opposite. He stroked one of the areas and introduced his claws into a cluster of small holes which were camouflaged in the wood. A hidden door opened in the wall itself. Emily could not help feeling a sense of déjà vu, as though she had experienced that moment before.

Leaning on his staff, Waafdiv went through the mysterious door and beckoned her to follow him.

"Here's where everything began," he said when they were in the original cave the Gaal-El temple had been built within.

The cave was wide and fairly high, but there was less space than in the temple area. Emily could not see how deep it was, as the implant did not allow her to make out so much detail, but she had the impression that it went on into the depths of the mountain. Waafdiv stopped to look at the wall on the left and pointed to an image painted on the stone. It was simple and rather worn and seemed to be very ancient, far more so than the temple itself.

That pictograph, which was rather naïve in style and barely used a dozen different tones, had nothing to do with the delicate, realistic frescoes of the temple. In it one of the obelisks was shown lying fallen on the ground, while beings of fearsome appearance seemed to be accusing several other, smaller, individuals of responsibility for this. In the sky dozens of flying ships looked down on what seemed to be the first appearance of the Khol on the planet.

"Our people paid for the affront of attempting to destroy the artifacts of the Khol," said Waafdiv.

"Did Keplerians really destroy an obelisk?"

"Yes, and though we have no writings which say so, I think this may have been the reason the Khol began to take an interest in the people of Kepler. This painting might represent the day the Khol began to visit the planet regularly."

"Why did they do it? Why did they pull down an obelisk?"

"I would imagine, out of curiosity," Waafdiv suggested. "Even I, who am aware of the importance those artifacts seem to have for the Khol, have always been curious to know what they are and what they're for. But the thing that's always intrigued me is to know why, despite the fact that they don't seem to care about them at all when they've come, the destruction of one of them seemed to be the trigger of our slavery."

"Have none of you ever shown any interest in them?"

"No, at least according to the writings we have available. When they visit us all they do is collect the minerals that have been extracted from the mines, and if the amount isn't to their liking, or if the Keplerian population has grown too much, they punish us harshly, decimate our population and take many of our people away with them."

"How horrible!"

"Most of us have learned to coexist with the fear," he explained. "But that doesn't make it any less unfair and horrible."

She pointed to the artifact shown in the painting. "Was this obelisk between the villages of Wiikhaadiiz ofiz and Khapabir?"

"How do you know that?" His facial expression hardened, so much so that she was a little scared.

"From our ship up there in space," she explained, "we can see the whole planet. There are thousands of obelisks like that one all over it. In fact their distribution follows a very clear pattern. They're separated from one another by the same distance, so that they form something like a very precise web."

"Well, well," Waafdiv murmured in surprise, though his expression was kindly once again. "I had no idea there were so many of them."

"We know they release a series of molecules into the atmosphere, though we're still not very clear about their function."

"Mo…lecules?" he repeated when he saw that there was no translation for the word.

"They're very small things, invisible to our eyes, but which are present in the air you breathe. Well, that we breathe."

"I see." He took a few steps forward.

On that same wall, but a little further away from the conclave chamber, was another painting. In it she saw Waafdiv's ancestors making their way to something like a cave, while the dozens of Khol ships appeared slightly smaller than they had in the previous picture, as if they were moving away. On the path a huge number of individuals had been represented lying on the ground, dead.

"My people sought shelter in the mountain caves and fled from the atrocities of the Khol," Waafdiv went on. "It's thought that this very cave was one of the first ones we hid ourselves in."

"And that's why the temple was built here."

"That's right. And that's why this place is sacred to us." He indicated the surrounding walls with a wave of his hand.

"When were these paintings made?"

"I don't know," he admitted. "All I know is that they're very ancient, far more so than the temple itself. This building was built thousands of years ago, but these paintings are much, much older."

"It seems there was a leader," said Emily. Her attention had been caught by the Keplerian who was closest to the cave. He appeared to be pointing to the entrance.

"Yes, he's the first of the Gaal-El, the founder of the cult. It was said that he could talk to spirits, and that he could do supernatural things we other Keplerians can't even dream of."

"What kind of things?"

"He could see the future," the high priest said. "It was he who predicted the advent of our saviors. He said that you would come from very far away to free us from the Khol."

Emily felt a shiver run down her spine as she looked at the imprecise figure of the supposed founder of the cult. Waafdiv moved on to a third painting. In this one the supposed leader appeared beside a more or less trapezoidal structure from which there issued something like rays, or irregular lines, toward either the sky of the planet or space. At the same time the other Keplerians worshiped their leader.

"What's this rectangle?"

"We've never known," Waafdiv replied. He sounded disappointed. "We have writings which are very ancient, some of them in languages no-one knows how to interpret nowadays, but none of them mentions anything that could even remotely explain what this painting represents. I had the absurd hope that you'd be able to help us understand it."

"Well, I'm really sorry, but I haven't the slightest idea."

Waafdiv contemplated the picture again for a few moments, then turned to the one on the opposite wall. This new painting gave the impression that the leader was lying on a kind of altar. His followers looked saddened, with their heads bowed, so that it was logical to think he had died. Another Keplerian, standing a little apart from the center of the scene but almost at the same level as the deceased, held a staff.

"Our prophet died after a long life in the service of others," Waafdiv explained. "The other Keplerians honored him for hundreds, thousands of years, but life went on and others, either better or worse, took his place."

"He seems to have been someone who was well-loved."

"Yes, at least so the scriptures say. He was the one who led us after the first visit of the Khol, but most of all it was he who gave us hope, who made us believe that one day our nightmare would come to an end."

They went on, once again in the direction of the conclave chamber, to the next painting. In it the new leader from the previous image, or perhaps one of his successors, seemed to be talking to four other important-looking Keplerians. Each of them carried a staff, which apparently gave them power over the remainder of the people, who stayed on a lower level obediently and accommodatingly.

"Many years later the other clans were founded, and new leaders arose to govern them. Together they would eventually form the Keplerian Council, which you yourself have witnessed."

Emily noticed that despite the obvious wear and the fact that the infrared vision did not allow her to see very much detail, each of the staves was painted in a different color. Presumably these would correspond to those she had seen in the heraldic emblems or in the wood of the leaders' staves: gray for the Gaal-El, blue for the Wiikhaadiiz ofiz, green for the Khaavahki and orange for the Khapabir. And yet there was another, which she supposed must belong to the tribe which had vanished: the Wiijof jikhaashyush.

She pointed to the leaders. "One of these four I presume would be the representative of your brothers, long gone."

"That's right," he replied, bowing his head.

"It's a pity an entire population should have disappeared,"

"Well… they haven't really done that," Waafdiv said.

"What? I understood they didn't exist any longer. But in that case why haven't they attended the conclaves?"

"Well now… what I'm about to tell you is known to only four Keplerians. The history we teach in our schools about our people isn't entirely correct. It's true that there was a serious problem with the Wiijof jikhaashyush, but that wasn't what led to their disappearance."

Emily listened carefully. Waafdiv seemed very troubled, as though he were talking about ancient ghosts.

"The Wiijof jikhaashyush were a formidable people, made up of individuals of all kinds, with a range of skills. They were very much loved and considered very worthy by the other clans. But one of their leaders became obsessed with the Khol to an exaggerated extent. He believed that if we exposed ourselves too much, we'd all end up dead. The rest of us learned to live with the threat, we left the shelters in the rocks and began to build villages using the forests as natural protective barriers. That kept us away from the eyes of our enemies. But they didn't do that, they stayed deep in the mountains.

"At first everything went well, trade began to flourish between all the villages. Each faction focused on specific jobs and provided the others with specialist workers, as we still do today. But at some point in history the

Wiijof jikhaashyush stopped taking part in the exchange and became elusive and shy. Time went by, and at some indeterminate moment things began to happen which horrified the population. Keplerians from the other clans began to disappear. We discovered, to our horror, that the few workers the Wiijof jikhaashyush sent to our villages were practicing cannibalism with our own neighbors."

"Good heavens!" Emily said, covering her mouth.

"Yes, indeed," Waafdiv admitted. "It seems that the Wiijof jikhaashyush, in their spiral of madness, began to carry out rituals and sacrifices worthy of the darkest shamanism. Hence we others turned our backs on them. We know they still exist, but we avoid going anywhere near their settlements at all costs. I seem to remember that you gave them a name: Yokai."

Emily's eyes opened wide. "What?" she exclaimed. "Are you telling me the Yokai were once Keplerians?"

"Yes, that's right."

She put her hands to her head, unable to believe this. An entire Keplerian village becoming creatures of the night who had then somehow turned into horrible monsters.

"But how could anything like that happen?"

"We don't know," he admitted. "All we know is that they began by carrying out sacrifices and adopting very dark practices which led them first to madness, then to becoming what they are now."

"Wow…I don't know what to say," she murmured in horror.

"It's something which saddens me and makes me a little ashamed at the attitude of my ancestors. They were unable to see what our brothers were turning into, and they left them to their fate."

"But I don't think it could just have happened from one day to the next. It must have been very difficult to deal with a situation like that."

"Perhaps if you'd been here the situation might have been different. And this brings us to the last of the pictures."

He went up to the wall of the conclave chamber. In the painting the five leaders were welcoming a mysterious figure which looked humanoid, but with certain differences from the Keplerians. It seemed to be descending from a long structure reminiscent of a spaceship. A great crowd of similar, smaller, figures were worshiping the new arrival.

"I don't think this picture needs any explanation," Waafdiv said. "You're the ones we've been waiting for." He pointed to the main figure. "And you're our chosen one," he added.

Emily felt suddenly overwhelmed by everything she had just been looking at. Up to that point the prophecies and beliefs of the Gaal-El had seemed to her no more than mystical superstitions without any kind of logic. As usually happens with human religions, everything seemed to have been the result of words or facts which had been either misinterpreted or magnified over time. But whatever the truth of it, what she had just seen had led the Keplerians to expect the advent of an alien race which would save them. She herself had to admit that even the ship in the picture was an extended structure divided into different modules, very much like the Asimov station. How could they fail to believe that humans might be their saviors if even she herself was beginning to have doubts after seeing an abstract drawing made by a Keplerian thousands of years before?

"But it doesn't make any sense," she protested. "The mere suggestion that someone could predict the future is absurd. It's completely impossible."

"I can't claim to understand it either," Waafdiv admitted, "but our ancestors were very different from us, much wiser in certain aspects. They knew the way the universe is intertwined. Unfortunately for us, none of this knowledge has reached our own times. It's been lost over time and with the demands of the Khol."

When they had finished looking at the paintings, he suggested leaving the temple and going back to the buildings nearby.

"We have a great library of thousands of ancient scrolls and parchments, which some day I would very much like you to be able to look at. I'm sure that with your help we'll be able to understand what happened to my ancestors and the origin of the cult of the Gaal-El."

"That would be wonderful," Emily said as they left the temple.

A voice she knew very well interrupted the conversation.

"Emily?" Ada called. "Do you copy?"

"I copy, Ada."

"What a relief! You had me very worried."

"You've no idea how glad I am to hear your voice," Emily said.

31
The return

February 6, year 1

Unknown location, Kepler-442b

Waafdiv and Emily saw Liikmi coming toward them. He had come out of the rover, which Ada had just parked in front of the stairs which gave access to the temple forecourt.

"This machine of yours is amazing," Liikmi exclaimed when he came up to them. "And also she's very kind and considerate. We had a lively conversation on the way up here."

"Thank you," Ada said from Emily's suit. "I enjoyed the conversation very much too. I'd love to go on with it some other time, because I find your culture and society extremely interesting. But I'm afraid that now I have other, more urgent matters to talk about with Emily."

"Of course," he said with a slight bow.

"I've warned Deputy Director Green," the AI went on. "They've sent a ship to pick you up, and it'll be here shortly."

"Thank you, Ada."

"I presume you'll want to take your convalescent friend, and also the body of your other comrade," Waafdiv said at once. "Liikmi, could you see that everything's ready?"

Liikmi bowed. "Of course, master."

"What are you planning to do from now on?" Emily asked.

"You mean about the conclave?"

"Yes. I'm afraid nothing's come out the way any of us would have wanted."

"In fact I underestimated Vaahur's determination to gain power," Waafdiv said. "I never thought he'd go so far, and because of me one of your companions has died. I'm really sorry. It's going to be something that'll haunt me for the rest of my days."

He seemed to be genuinely moved by Rakesh's death.

She did her best to reassure him. "It wasn't your fault. There's only one person to blame for everything that's happened."

"I know this was all Vaahur's doing, but I can't stop thinking that if we'd acted differently he'd still be alive. I still believe we did the right thing, but we may have to be more intelligent from now on."

"What do you want to do?"

"I need to consider that carefully, but there are other ways of gaining sole command."

"I suppose I need to start thinking about our next steps too," Emily said. "I'd imagine Vaahur won't be happy about the way we were able to get out of his fortress."

"True. He'll spend days trying to find the security failures that let it happen."

"What worries me is that he might take it out on somebody innocent."

"Coming from him, I wouldn't be surprised by anything," Waafdiv said. "Be careful, all of you."

The evacuation ship appeared through the clouds and landed on the forecourt without any trouble. Several medical staff, carrying isolation stretchers, came down the cargo ramp. With them came Deputy Director Green, looking agitated.

"Emily!" he called. "Thank God you're all right…. but where's your helmet?"

"I don't need it anymore."

"How's that possible?"

"I'll bring you up to speed very soon, Deputy Director," Emily said. "For the moment the most important thing is to evacuate Gorka as soon as possible."

Iwshaj, the old Gaal-El healer, suddenly came out of one of the buildings, agitated and muttering under his breath.

"Excuse me young lady," he said, "how can you possibly be taking the convalescent human? This is completely irregular, and it would be very dangerous for him."

Emily smiled. "Don't worry, Iwshaj, our doctors will take over now."

"But it's important that he shouldn't be moved and that he spends the next few hours in complete inactivity. That's the only way his body will adapt to the changes."

"We'll let our doctors know," she reassured him.

The elder accepted the decision reluctantly. He did not seem convinced that he should allow them to take Gorka away, but soon his face regained its earlier affable expression. He produced a couple of phials and a handkerchief with something wrapped in it and handed them to Emily,

"In that case, take this. These phials contain the medicine that needs to be administered to your friend if he gets worse, together with these dried medicinal herbs." He showed her what was in the handkerchief. "Remember: one phial per day, and the inhalations from burning these leaves."

"Thank you, Iwshaj, you're very kind. I'm really grateful for everything you've done for all of us over these last few days."

"Not at all, young lady. I'm glad to have been of service. At my age I never thought I'd get to meet the chosen one. After all I've lived through, I think I can die in peace now."

"Don't say that, Iwshaj. You look in excellent health."

"Don't you believe that. I'm finding it harder and harder to get up in the morning, even though I'm grateful for the white lie."

Liikmi took the medical staff to the room where Paula and Gorka were, and a little later they brought them out inside the isolation stretchers. Ahead of them was a long period of quarantine. At the same time the cult-members delivered the shrouded body of Rakesh. Several of the soldiers who had come with the rescue mission made sure they bore it away with the honors the anthropologist deserved.

"Waafdiv," Emily said, "thank you for everything, from the bottom of my heart."

He smiled. "We'll be in touch."

She was thoughtful for a few moments, then before she even sat down on a stretcher she went across to the rover, which was still parked at the end of the ramps which led up to the forecourt. She fetched a communications backpack and gave it to Waafdiv, with a few brief instructions on what he would need to do to use it.

"With this device you won't just be able to speak to Ada, our artificial intelligence, you'll be able to ask to speak to any of us. Even with Khikhya's assistant Yisht, though please keep that last piece of information secret. No-one in Wiikhaadiiz ofiz knows she has a similar device, and I don't want her being accused of high treason. Which is something that after what we've seen could very well happen."

"Don't worry," he reassured her, "I'll guard it like a treasure."

Emily took her leave of Waafdiv and Liikmi and asked them to thank Avmup, whom they had not been able to see, for everything he had done and the risks he had taken to save them. She also asked to have the phials Iwshaj had given her sealed, then at last she climbed into the stretcher. As soon as the oxygen supply inside it was connected she felt revitalized, as though a stimulant was being administered. Very soon after this the ship took off from the forecourt and set course for the station. They were going home at last.

All three of them were put in the same quarantine room as before, and although at first they did not realize it there was one more person there, intubated and fitted with a complicated respirator. Deputy Director Green, who had accompanied them all the way there and had even gone with them into the quarantine area, stayed for a word with Emily after she had gone into her cubicle.

"Sit down," he said very seriously.

"What is it, David? You're scaring me."

"It's about Captain Beaufort."

"What is it? Is anything wrong with Robert?"

"When he found out you'd been captured, he and Sergeant Ferrara decided to go to the fortress where you were being held."

She listened with growing tension to what he was telling her, but she knew by his tone of voice that something bad had happened.

"They had an encounter with Captain Garth and Sergeant Cameron there, and it looks as though Captain Beaufort's suit suffered considerable damage."

"Where is he?" she asked abruptly.

The deputy director looked aside at the quarantine area, where the unknown patient was. Emily got up at once to look through the glass wall which separated the small isolation cells.

"He's in a coma," the deputy director said. "They don't really know how to reverse it. They think he spent too much time breathing the outside air."

"How long's he been like this?"

"Four days. Apparently they reached the Khaavahki fortress just after you'd all escaped."

"I want to speak to Dr. Schmidt," Emily said. "I need to see him."

"They've tried everything, Emily."

"No, not everything." She showed him the two phials the Gaal-El healer had given her.

He was taken aback. "What? Do you expect the shamanism of a Keplerian healer to bring the captain out of his coma?"

She pointed to Paula. "He managed it with us, didn't he? And if he's right, Gorka'll wake up tomorrow. I think it's worth trying."

"I don't know whether it's such a good idea."

"All I'm asking is for them to analyze what they gave us, then depending on what they find in these phials we'll see what we can do."

Deputy Director Green thought about what she was suggesting. He knew how persuasive and tenacious she was, so she would probably end up getting what she wanted, one way or another.

He sighed. "All right, I'll see what I can do."

"Thanks, David. But even so, I'd like to talk to Dr. Schmidt. I… I need to see her."

"I'll have a word with her."

He left them alone in the quarantine room, waiting for the station medical staff to carry out all the relevant tests and checkups.

"What are you planning to do, Emily?" Paula asked from the cell opposite.

"I don't know," she said thoughtfully as she watched Robert in the distance. "But there's got to be something in these phials and the leaves Iwshaj gave us that would explain why you and I are fine and Robert's in a coma."

"What do you think those phials do?"

"I haven't the faintest idea, but it looks as though it helped us to breathe down there."

"I mean, how are we able to breathe in an environment like Kepler-442b? I'm no expert in biology, but as far as I know we ought to have died of hypoxia, or failing that, from the other components of the air."

"Yeah, I'm asking myself the same question," Emily admitted. "And I'm hoping the answer is in these small containers."

She sat down on the bed again. Her mind was racing, and nothing made sense to her. And the fact that Robert was in danger just a few meters away was doing nothing to calm her nerves. Her leg began to shake rapidly, as it always did when she was nervous.

Dr. Schmidt brought her out of her thoughts. With her was Nurse Conte, who was pushing a small cart full of equipment. They came into Emily's cubicle first.

"Hi there," she said. "How are you feeling?"

"Quite well," Emily said, "a little tired, but quite well. Now the important thing is to get Captain Beaufort out of his coma."

"He's stable," the nurse assured her. "We're doing everything we can."

"That's obviously not enough," she said sharply.

"Emily," Dr. Schmidt went on restrainedly, "I'm going to ignore your tone of voice and bear in mind that you've been through a very complicated situation over these last few days. I'm also aware that you and the captain had a very close relationship and it's natural that you should be worried. But be careful, I'm not going to tolerate anyone in this station calling into question my work or that of any of my colleagues."

To Emily the doctor's words felt like a slap of reality. Immediately she felt guilty and ashamed at having allowed herself to be carried away by despair.

"I… I'm really sorry," she said. "I don't know why I said that. Forgive me. Forgive me, both of you. I guess we've been through a critical situation, and finding Robert like that… it's hard."

"I accept your apologies," the doctor said, "and I'm truly sorry about what you've had to go through, first with Dr. Kumar and now with Captain Beaufort, but we're doing everything possible so that the captain recovers."

"I know. I'm truly sorry. I don't know what came over me."

"Let's leave it there. How do you feel?"

"Quite well," she repeated. "I think we're both well. But we don't really understand why we survived."

"That's what we're trying to find out here. We're going to carry out some tests to see how it is that suddenly you're able to breathe normally in an environment which by definition isn't compatible with human life."

The doctor examined her before focusing on her respiratory system, which included an exhaustive auscultation together with several palpations of her torso. After these preliminary examinations were finished, and seeing the changing expressions on the doctor's face, each more serious than the last, Emily asked:

"Is something wrong? The expression on your face isn't very reassuring."

"Your vitals are rather strange, to say the least," the doctor said. "We're going to check your blood pressure."

Nurse Conte, who had said nothing all this time, made the preparations for this, then asked Emily to sit up and stretch out her arm.

"Your blood pressure's very low," the doctor said. "Too low in fact."

"And is that bad?"

"It would be in normal circumstances," she said thoughtfully. "But… it doesn't make sense."

"What doesn't make sense?"

"Your pulse is too weak as well. It was a fairly common condition on Earth, when someone used to living at high altitude came down to sea level."

"So if cases like this were common, what's the problem?"

"The problem is that it takes our bodies months to produce this kind of response. If you were only exposed to such extreme conditions for a few days, it makes no sense for you to be presenting such acute symptomatic conditions now."

"I see. So what could be causing it?"

"I don't know, that's what we're trying to find out. We're going to do some blood tests, but I'm sorry, I'm afraid you'll have to stay under observation for a few days."

"The Keplerian healer gave us this." Emily showed her the phials she had brought with her.

The doctor looked at them in surprise. "What is it?"

"I haven't the faintest idea. But this is what Paula, Gorka and I were given so that we could survive over these past few days."

"But Gorka's still unconscious," the doctor pointed out.

"According to what the healer told us, he ought to wake up from his lethargy tomorrow, just as we did. Maybe you could analyze the chemical components to find out what's in it."

"And don't forget the leaves they burned," Paula added from her cubicle.

"That's right, I almost forgot." Emily searched in her bag. "They also burned these leaves in a kind of incense burner."

"I'll have a word with the lab to see what they can tell us about all this."

"Thank you, doctor, perhaps this'll help Gorka, Robert or anyone else who goes through what we had to."

"Let's hope you all recover as quickly as possible."

"Um… if you'll allow me one more thing, doctor," Emily added before they left. "Could I have access to Captain Beaufort's cell?"

Dr. Schmidt considered this request.

"I realize these are very difficult moments," she said at last, "But I'm afraid you'll have to stay in your own cell, You three"—she indicated Gorka and Paula's cubicles—"have had a deep interaction with the Keplerians and with the atmosphere of the planet, quite apart from having ingested Keplerian food and medicines. We don't yet know the consequences all this might have on your bodies in the short and medium term. I'm sorry, but I can't let you infect another patient with some unknown pathogen."

Emily nodded sadly, but the argument made all the sense in the world. The medical staff went on to check Paula and Gorka, then Robert himself. They took blood and tissue samples from all the patients, then left the quarantine area.

"Do you think what was in the phials was what saved us?" Paula asked.

"I don't really know what to think right now," Emily admitted. "This very morning I saw some paintings in a cave from thousands of years ago which seemed to prove the Keplerians are waiting for someone to come from another planet to save them. I don't know what the hell's in these phials, or why we're healthy and Gorka's still unconscious. But by this stage we're going to have to consider all the possibilities we're faced with, however unlikely."

"Weren't Taro and Chad doing some tests on animals?" Paula

recalled after a few seconds.

"You're right! They might have come to some conclusion while we were away."

Emily called the two scientists, who were still at the Magellan base, oblivious to everything their colleagues had been through.

"Emily! Paula!" came Chad's voice. "Thank God you're both all right!"

"Yeah, it's so good to see you again!" Taro added.

"Hi, guys." Emily managed a timid smile. "We're glad to see you too."

"How are you?" Chad asked. "Ada told us everything. We were shattered to hear about Rakesh."

"We still haven't got used to the idea that he isn't with us any longer," she admitted sadly.

"We're all knocked sideways," Taro agreed.

"How's Gorka?" Chad asked.

"Still unconscious," Paula said. "The Keplerians gave us a kind of medicine, and we think it's helped us get over it."

"And that's what we wanted to talk to you about," Emily said. "How far have you got in those experiments of yours using living beings?"

"Well, we've inoculated several of the lab mice with different amounts of the molecules."

"Well? Anything worth mentioning?"

"Nope, they're all in perfect condition," Chad said.

Emily hesitated for a few seconds over whether to put what was going through her mind into words.

"What are you thinking, Emily?" Taro asked.

"I know it's not going to sound very ethical, but I'd like you to take some of those mice outside."

Chad looked at her in surprise. "Outside? That could kill them."

"That's what we have to avoid at all costs. Whether Gorka and Robert live might just depend on whether you're successful."

She explained to them how they had been left without any air in their exosuits during their escape from the Khaavahki fortress. She told them that Rakesh had been the first, and how the others had gone through the same situation one by one. After this Paula told them about how the Keplerians had looked after them and given them medicines, and that Gorka was due to wake up the following day.

"You all seem to have come back to normality in reverse order," Chad commented.

Emily looked at him in surprise. "What do you mean?"

"I mean that according to what you told us, you've come back to normality in the reverse order to the length of time you were exposed to the planet's atmosphere."

"And how are we supposed to interpret that?"

"I think what you were given was just a tranquilizer, or something that lets the molecules do their work."

"Their work? What work?"

"Haven't you put two and two together yet?" Taro said impatiently.

Paula shook her head. "No…"

Chad took up the story. "Ever since we started investigating the alien molecules, the pattern's repeated itself over and over again, with every single one of the organisms we've exposed to them: earth bacteria, yeast and fungi. Some of the molecules—though not all of them—modified our subjects' genetic information, but far from destroying them, as a virus would have done, they improved it, making them more efficient.

"A while ago we talked about far more complex organisms: small rodents, frogs and toads. And even though we haven't seen any great differences between them, we've realized that there's a relationship between the length of time and quantity of molecules the subjects have been exposed to on the one hand, and their improved adaptation to the environment on the other."

"Cut to the chase…" Emily urged him.

"The thing that's allowed you to breathe on Kepler-442b isn't what's inside those phials, nor is it in the smoke from burning those leaves. It's the molecules, Emily. The answer to our problems with adapting to the planet's atmosphere is those alien molecules themselves."

32
Echoes of the past

February 7, year 1

Unknown location, Kepler-442b

Emily was still asleep when Dr. Schmidt came into the quarantine area. Her body was so depleted that she needed many more hours of rest than usual. She was woken by the sound of the trolley the doctor herself was pushing.

"Were you still asleep?" Dr. Schmidt asked in surprise.

"Uh…. yeah…" she admitted, still drowsy.

"Sorry to wake you up, but its past nine o'clock. You've slept for over fourteen hours."

"I was very tired. I needed it."

"You were asleep by the time the nurse came to take the remains of your supper away yesterday."

"Yup. I was very hungry, but all of a sudden my body said *enough*."

"I see. Well, at least you finished the food, which is what matters. All three of you have lost quite a bit of muscle in this business. How do you feel?"

"Half-asleep still," Emily admitted. "I need a coffee."

"Breakfast's on its way," the doctor said. "Don't give up hope."

"Has there been any change in Captain Beaufort's condition?"

"No, he's stable. But what I've come to do is take another blood sample."

"What about the results of yesterday's analyses?" Emily asked.

The doctor was silent for a few moments.

"Is there anything strange about them?" she insisted. "If there's anything wrong I'd like to know."

"It's not that we've found anything bad," the doctor said, "it's just that it's got me rather confused."

"What have you picked up?"

"There's an abnormal concentration of hemoglobin in your blood."

"Is that bad?"

"No, or at least not necessarily," the doctor said reassuringly. "In fact the more hemoglobin, the more oxygen the blood can carry to our cells, so in principle it's a good thing."

"So what's strange about that?"

"A concentration of hemoglobin like yours goes off our charts," Dr Schmidt admitted with a touch of astonishment. "On Earth, cases were reported of concentrations like these in people used to living at high altitudes, like Sherpas or inhabitants of high mountains. But what's staggered us is that there are no records of anyone showing a natural increase in hemoglobin like that in so short a time. In fact your levels of blood erythropoietin are way above normal. Which, considering they're the hormones whose job is to create hemoglobin, fits in perfectly with everything we're seeing. What we don't yet understand is why the two of you have been able to create so much of it."

Emily was thoughtful. This agreed with the theory Taro and Chad were working on: that it was the alien molecules themselves which were accelerating and favoring this organic adaptation.

The doctor was looking at her with interest. "Are you all right, Emily? What are you thinking?"

"Do you remember the famous molecules that were found on the planet?"

The doctor nodded. "Of course. In fact we've found a high concentration of them in your blood."

"Taro and Chad are looking into how those molecules affect different organisms. The results, as of today, are beginning to suggest that they're the ones that accelerate the process by which the subjects adapt to their environment."

"What? As if they were mutagenic agents?"

"Yeah, in fact I think I've sometimes heard them call them that."

"What kind of experiments have they carried out?"

"I'm not sure how far I understand what they're doing," Emily admitted, "but I know they've exposed the molecules to simple organisms, such as fungi and bacteria, and recently they've started using complex organisms, like mice and frogs."

"And what sort of results have they had?"

"I think that in a hundred per cent of the cases the organisms have survived the exposure and undergone some kind of mutation so that they can adapt to their environment. In the case of the mice, I remember they showed an increase in bone density and muscle growth proportional to their exposure to the molecules, but always in accordance with the greater gravity of the planet."

"Just a moment," the doctor interrupted her. "Are you telling me the increase in bone density is one possible effect of the molecule?"

Emily nodded. "Yes, that's right. But only because it's a natural adaptation to the planet's greater gravity."

"Some of you showed an increase in bone density."

"Right, and besides, it coincides with that time we were exposed to the molecules."

"Oh, my God!" the doctor exclaimed. "This changes everything."

"We might be looking at one of the greatest discoveries of humanity," Emily said. "Even if we don't yet know what long-term side-effects it might have."

"Now I understand about the phials and leaves the healer gave you."

"In what way?"

"Yesterday we analyzed the contents of the phials, and I didn't find anything that seemed to be useful. It looked like the dregs of a simple herbal infusion. But when we analyzed the result of burning the leaves you were given, I found something rather strange."

"What?"

"Both the gas and the liquid, taken separately, are innocuous. But once they come into contact within the organism, they produce sulfuric acid."

Emily did not react to Dr. Schmidt's revelation in the way the doctor was expecting, so she did her best to make it clearer. "Sulfuric acid is one of the raw materials which are used to induce a state of hibernation, and that's how living beings are cryogenized."

"I see," Emily said at last. "You mean the Gaal-El healer kept us in hibernation for a time until he judged that our cells had adapted to the new environment?"

"Exactly. The phials don't contain a miraculous cure, but they help to stop the host dying while the genetic change is taking place at cellular level. I read a study about this, years ago."

"Could we try something like that with Captain Beaufort?"

"Perhaps," the doctor answered thoughtfully, "but I can't risk a human life on the basis of supposition and nothing more than a general observation of the effects. And in any case, if we're right we'd need to expose the captain to the atmosphere of the planet or an indeterminate quantity of alien molecules. That doesn't sound very promising."

Emily thought about the situation, but she could understand that Dr. Schmidt was right; they would need to experiment, or at least to have more experience in the application and use of the molecules before they could even dream of using them medically. Anything else would violate her ethical and professional code.

"And suppose we do the experiments on animals?" Emily asked.

"Then we'd be violating the Manchester treaties."

"But our colony isn't subject to the same laws as governments on Earth."

Dr. Schmidt said nothing. She seemed to be trying to work out a solution.

"I know it's not the best idea," Emily went on, "but not so many years ago it was the normal procedure. Now we can't risk experimenting on healthy people. We need every single member of the expedition. And Ada will do the simulations we need, but they're costly, and we might not have that much time."

"As long as I'm assured empirically that an acceptable proportion of the test subjects have survived, enough to enable us to avoid unnecessary risks when humans are involved, I could accept using the molecules in particular circumstances."

"Thank you, doctor," Emily said with a gleam of hope in her eyes.

"But I'm not going to use the liquid in the phials you brought," Dr Schmidt added. "If we need to create a state of hibernation, we'll do it using our own methods."

"I think that's fair."

"And I'd like a geneticist from my team to take part in the investigation Dr. Murakami and Dr. Williams are carrying out," she said after thinking for a moment.

"Of course, there's no problem about that," Emily said. "Whatever's necessary."

"Anyway, I'd like to take some tissue and fluid samples. Perhaps now we have all this information, we might see some other things we might have missed."

The doctor took Emily's samples and attached the appropriate labels to them. Then Emily arranged for Chad and Taro to cooperate with Dr. Schmidt's experts. But when they were about to finish, a small disturbance interrupted them. Paula, in her cell, was restless and calling to the doctor.

"Gorka! He's waking up!"

Dr Schmidt left Emily's cell immediately and went to the one Gorka was in. At the same time she said something into the surveillance camera, but all Emily could hear was Paula shouting in the distance. She got out of bed to try and see what was happening, but when she reached the glass barrier the doctor activated the mechanism which turned the glass in Gorka's cell opaque, leaving both Paula and her with no direct view of what was happening.

"No!" Paula cried desperately. "Gorka…"

"Don't worry," Emily said in an attempt to soothe her. "I'm sure he'll be all right."

A nurse they did not know came hurriedly into the quarantine area and was lost to sight when she went into Gorka's cell. Some very tense moments followed. Paula could not stop pacing back and forth in her cell, unable to stay still. Emily could not avoid imagining the worst. The Gaal-El healer had told them that Gorka should wake up that same morning. But every human body was different, and his case might be more complicated. A hundred things could happen, including complications which might prevent him from recovering the way they had themselves. She felt a shiver when she remembered poor Rakesh. However, the glass turned transparent again and at last they could see Gorka, rather thinner than usual, sitting up in bed and waving at them.

"How are you feeling?" Paula asked him with tears in her eyes.

"Fine," he said. "Tired, with a headache, and I can't hear properly with my left ear, but in the circumstances I'd say I'm fine."

Paula had given free rein to her emotions and was sobbing with relief as she looked at him from her own cell. When the doctor and the nurse had finished examining Gorka, they let her come in to see him. They both joined in an endless embrace, which left Emily feeling touched. She was very glad they were both all right, but she could not help thinking that Robert was only two cells away from her own and she was unable to do the same.

While Paula and Gorka brought each other up to date, she decided to call Taro and Chad to tell them about her talk with Dr. Schmidt.

"Hi, guys!"

"Hello, Emily!" Taro said. "How are you up there?"

"Fine. We've had a good night's rest, and besides, Gorka has just woken up. And he's feeling fine."

"What a relief!" said Chad. "Give them a hug from us."

"I will. But I'm calling about something else. This morning I had an interesting talk with Dr. Schmidt."

She told them everything about the phials and the tests results.

Taro nodded. "Everything you're telling us fits in perfectly with what we're seeing ourselves."

"Yesterday, after we'd talked to you, we took some mice outside," Chad said. "We made use of the little habitat Director Patel built beside here to set up an improvised lab without simulated atmosphere."

"And what did you get?"

"All the subjects suffered from hypoxia to a greater or lesser extent," Chad said. "Half of them died."

"Oh dear, I'm really sorry about that," Emily said. "But I think the key was in the phials the Gaal-El healer gave us. According to Dr. Schmidt's analysis, they contain a straightforward infusion of medicinal plants. But if we mix them with the fumes from burning the dried leaves, it turns out that they produce sulfuric acid."

"Do they induce a state of hibernation?" Chad asked in surprise.

"That's right."

"And in that way…" Chad said, thinking aloud, "the host stays in a lethargic state till the molecules can do their job. Yeah, it could just work!"

"Can you put it into practice?"

"Yeah, I think we could do something."

"Oh, yes!" Emily added. "I almost forgot. A geneticist from the project is going to get in touch with you, to give you a hand."

"That's great," Chad said. "A little help would be welcome."

"And I'd also like Ada to carry out all possible simulations based on these assumptions," she added.

"I'm on the job," Ada said.

"Right, that's perfect. Will you let me know about anything new?"

"Sure," Chad said.

"Of course," Ada added.

After arranging everything so that Dr. Schmidt could validate the testing of the molecules on living beings, she relaxed a little. She was deeply unhappy at the sight of Robert intubated and in a coma. She wanted to get up, go into his cell and hug him, although she knew that for the moment she was not going to be able to. But at least that morning she was able to hope he would come out of that situation.

"Hold on, Robert, help's on its way," she said to herself.

She thought about how she could spend the time in there without going crazy, so she decided to have a talk with some of the inhabitants of the base. She needed to keep her mind busy so that she would stop thinking about the critical situation Robert was in. She called Kostas, who told her that young Karlsson was surprising him greatly. He seemed to have a special interest in everything to do with crops and was putting a lot into everything he was doing. This did not help her solve the problems she had at that particular moment, but it comforted her to know that one of the new settlers had found his place there.

Kostas also told her that Shildii had come to the base during those last few days and had been helping them with the work in the greenhouse. He had never seen any of the plants there, but he was finding more than one equivalent to the vegetables his people cultivated. In addition he seemed to have made friends with Martin, which meant that Kostas now had two helpers instead of one and they were growing new types of vegetables.

She also spoke to Erik and Min. They were working on important improvements in the exosuits. They thought it might be possible to use the energy of the batteries in a more effective way. Their aim was to increase the endurance of the exosuits by one additional day, which would be a definite improvement.

Ada brought her up to date about what had been happening on the base. Lieutenant Ortiz had doubled the military presence in the area, setting up two more defensive posts to prevent any possible retaliation by the Khaavahki after Emily's escape. In fact, thanks to Sergeant Ferrara's reports on the Khaavahki village, Commander Bauer himself was now thinking of surrounding the bases with a wooden palisade. There had been systems for perimeter defense in the arsenal which had been lost before they reached the planet, but without them and with no possibility of building new ones, they would have to turn to nature once again. Alberto was working with the soldiers, and he seemed to have some good ideas about working the wood and building a defensive palisade.

Everything seemed to be going more or less well. Or rather almost everything. James Coogan had spent his time eating and sleeping. Since Emily had deactivated his use of the gym machines, the former celebrity had decided to stop doing anything that required the slightest effort. As a result he was spending the day in his underwear, alternately taking meals and short naps and watching old movies. Emily was thinking about that particular pain in the neck when she received a call from Deputy Director Green.

"Good morning! How are you feeling today?"

"Fine, Deputy Director. I suppose you'll have heard that Gorka's woken up and seems to be fine."

"Yes, I've heard that. But you'd better tell Ada to activate your cell's privacy filter."

"What is it, David?" she asked as Ada darkened the glass of her cell.

"The probe we sent to meet the SOS signal has reached its source."

"And what was producing it?" she asked eagerly.

"It's an emergency pod from the Galileo."

Emily closed her eyes as her worst fears came true. If it was a pod, it meant there had been an emergency on the Galileo.

"I'll send you the images from the probe."

She was able to see, still some distance away and despite the probe's optical magnification, what was undoubtedly one of the Galileo's pods. Its shape and size revealed that it was intact. At the same time its exterior paintwork was deeply eroded after its journey through space and exposure to cosmic radiation and very low temperatures. But even so, it was clear that this was Pod 3C from the Galileo.

"How far is the probe away from it?" she asked.

"There are still a few hours left before it reaches it."

"What do we know?"

"So far, not very much," he admitted. "Just what we can see in the images, and the fact that we're still receiving the incomplete signal from the pod."

"It looks intact."

David nodded. "Yes, at least from this distance and from the visible side."

"The 3C is the one just opposite the control center, right?"

"Yes."

"That could mean the senior management of the Galileo is in it."

"That's what I'm afraid of, Emily. But we'll wait until the probe reaches the pod and gives us more information about what could have happened on the station."

The next hours were very tense. The probe was travelling at maximum speed, but even so, it was too slow for her. She wanted to know whether her father was inside that pod. She remembered the nightmare in which she had dreamed about an escape pod. Could she be beginning to have premonitory dreams? She dismissed that thought; it was absurd, it defied all the laws of science. It was impossible. The only thing certain was that someone on the Galileo had needed to use an emergency pod, and that might be able to cast some light on the fate of the station. The probe had begun its docking maneuver, and she knew that everyone in the command center was tense and nervous.

"In a few minutes we'll know what's happened to the rest of the expedition," the deputy director said solemnly.

The probe reached the pod and slowed down until it was almost alongside it and only a few meters away. The surface of the hull was intact: rather worn, but intact. Then it extended a series of mechanical arms which enabled it to grasp the pod and move around it. It passed above it and made a full turn.

"It seems to be intact," Captain Mei said.

"Ada, get it to look inside."

"I'm afraid that's not possible, Deputy Director. The probe's some distance away and the signal takes nearly twenty minutes to reach it. But don't worry, the probe has a very detailed set of instructions, and it's sure to do that."

Just as Ada had predicted, the probe searched for the entrance-hatch. Once it was in front of it, it brought one of its cameras close to the small circular window. The interior was not clearly visible. There was no light, and in addition the glass was eroded and dirty. The probe turned on its infrared camera, but still could see nothing whatever.

"Either it's empty," Commander Bauer began, "or else…"

"Or else anyone inside is dead," Emily said, finishing the sentence for him.

"I'm afraid we're going to have to decide whether to open the hatch or tow the pod back here," the commander said.

"Wait," Captain Mei interrupted him, "we might find out something more. Ada, can you connect with the terminal of the pod?"

"I'll see what I can do."

The probe changed its position and moved to the rear of the pod, where a screw-fix lid gave access to the terminal. The probe extended a small arm with a range of tools and manipulated the six screw-points. However hard it tried, it was unable to remove even a single one of them.

"So what do we do now?" the commander asked.

"Try to tear the lid off," Emily suggested.

Ada sent the order to the probe, and after a while it set to work. It produced a small cutting laser and went from point to point, cutting the lid at those points where the screws were fixed. It moved the lid aside and was able to gain access to the terminal.

"The pod has no power," Ada told them. "The radio only managed to work because it gets sunlight. Something seems to be wrong here: the data are incomplete. The pods don't have the same conditions inside them as the rest of the station. They aren't fitted with filters for cosmic radiation, because they're not designed for prolonged use. In an emergency the passengers would run out of oxygen long before they were affected by radiation. But prolonged exposure may have affected the terminal."

"How long would it be until that happened?" Emily asked.

"It depends on the conditions it's met on its way. Radiation isn't the same everywhere in the universe. Also, the pods themselves may not have been free from defects. When all's said and done, they're almost a thousand years old. It might even have happened to be in a bad state when they attempted to use it."

"Thank you, Ada," the deputy director said after a brief pause. "What do you think we should do now?"

"Whoever it was who used it, their chances of survival are practically nil. The pods only contain oxygen for three days, if they're full. It's taken us a little over two Earth weeks to reach it, and if we bear in mind that we've seen no trace of the Galileo, it must have been drifting for longer than that. Quite a lot longer, I'd say, judging by the state we've found it in."

"Let's open it," Emily said.

"That would be risky," the captain pointed out. "Even if there's no-one left alive, if the capsule's still pressurized the oxygen left inside will cause everything inside to be thrown out. We might lose the probe, and if there's anyone or anything inside that isn't strapped into place, we'd lose them as well."

They were all thoughtful for a few moments, but it was the deputy director who made the final decision.

"I think we ought to tow it back," he said at last. "We can't risk losing either the pod or the probe. If we can manage to bring it back here we might be able to fix the terminal and recover whatever's inside. Do we agree on that?"

The captain nodded. "Yes."

"Yes," the commander agreed.

It seemed that Emily was not going to say anything, but in the end she agreed with the deputy director. It was safer to tow it back to the station, even though it would be two more weeks before they knew who was inside the pod.

"Yes," she whispered.

33
Life or death

Several days had passed since they had gone into quarantine. Both Paula and Emily, thanks to diet and exercise, had regained a fair amount of muscle and had recovered from that little episode with the Gaal-El. Dr. Schmidt had promised to discharge them that very morning if nothing new came up. Gorka too had improved considerably, but as he had been exposed to the planet's atmosphere for longer he was going to have to spend a couple of days more in there.

All their analyses showed similar readings: there was a persistent increase in hemoglobin production, and their bone capacity seemed to have increased considerably. It could be said that the molecules had begun to prepare them for life on Kepler-442b. All the same, there were many questions still to be answered. Their bodies had been able to survive in those conditions for a few days, but what long-term consequences would that have? Would they be able to switch constantly from one environment to the other with no trouble? Dr. Schmidt was also concerned about the amount of ultraviolet radiation which reached the surface of the planet. Excessive radiation could range from severe burns on the skin to an effect on their vision, causing cataracts or even total blindness. This morning she wanted to carry out a series of tests on their eyes.

They passed through a machine which examined their eyeballs, checked their physiognomy and general state, in addition to measuring eyestrain and other relevant parameters.

"We're going to dilate your pupils now," Nurse Conte told them. "We'll administer some drops for that. You'll notice increased brightness when they take effect, but don't worry, that's normal. After that we'll administer another set of drops so that the effect passes as soon as possible."

"All right," Emily said.

Paula nodded happily. "As long as we can get out of these cells, whatever."

After a couple of minutes the solution took effect, and Emily began to notice the light becoming increasingly uncomfortable.

"Sit down here," the nurse said, indicating one of the ophthalmological machines.

Emily followed the instruction, and the machine emitted a powerful and extremely uncomfortable beam of light, first into one eye and then the other. But she was able to bear it until the machine gave a slight whistle and moved back from her face. The nurse repeated the test with Paula, and once they had both had it he applied another liquid which gradually helped their pupils to recover their normal size. Dr. Schmidt came over to them looking thoughtful, holding the readings the machine had printed out.

"What does it say?" Emily asked.

"It's very interesting."

"In what way?"

"There are some changes in your eyes. They're not too obvious, but I think that in some way the molecules are affecting your vision."

"How?" Paula asked.

"The pigmentation of your irises has suffered a very slight darkening. Imperceptible to a human at a glance, but not to a machine."

"Oh dear, I like the color of my eyes," Paula joked.

"But what shocked me most is that your crystalline lenses are three point five per cent thicker."

"Is that bad?"

"Not if we're talking about preventing ultraviolet radiation from affecting you. But a thicker crystalline lens means that light will find it harder to reach your retina, where what we know as vision is produced, In the long run you might lose some sharpness or precision. But all this is very strange. We've never been confronted with a mutagenic agent before. Perhaps that small mutation will come accompanied by others which will allow your retina to correct that loss of sharpness."

"Quite honestly, it's rather scary," Emily said. "It gives the impression that we're leaving behind being human."

The doctor sat down with them. "For the moment I'd avoid any more exposure to those molecules. I'm still not sure how to interpret all this."

"Chad and Taro are experimenting with it at the moment, right?" Paula asked.

Emily nodded. "But the doctor's right. We don't know the long-term effects. With a fairly controlled exposure our bodies are changing, we're stronger and our cells are beginning to be more efficient, but that could come associated with unwanted morphological changes."

"Are you implying that we're turning into monsters?" Paula said, horrified.

"I don't think so. But I don't know whether I want to find out either."

"I think the best thing," the doctor suggested, "would be to let Ada carry out the appropriate simulations, based on the data we're gathering about both of you and the experiments Dr. Murakami and Dr. Williams are doing."

"But what about Captain Beaufort?" Emily asked, sounding worried.

"It's very risky to expose him to the molecules without having more information about them. But we're going to try to induce a state of hibernation in him, something similar to what the Keplerians did with you. He still has plenty of molecules in his blood, and if what we've seen in Gorka and both of you is true and can be repeated, then we should notice some improvement."

Emily was still very worried about Robert's condition. He had been in a coma for over ten days and there had been hardly any improvement. She could understand the doctor's reluctance, even though she herself would have exposed him to the molecules without a moment's hesitation.

"We're doing everything we can," Dr Schmidt told her when she realized how worried she was. "I understand the situation, but we can't risk using something when we don't know what consequences it might have, not just in the long run but in the immediate future."

Emily and Paula left the medical area of the Centrifuge for good and took a long walk along the corridors.

"How d'you feel?" Paula asked her.

"Fine, I guess. I'm not dizzy, and I'm not having trouble breathing."

"I mean about Robert."

Emily paused briefly before answering.

"Messed up, worried, frustrated…"

"I can imagine," Paula murmured. "I was feeling the same way just now, and it's not easy. But you just wait and see how everything sorts itself out. I bet what the doctor just said will work."

"I hope you're right," she said with a sigh. "But he's been ten days like that with barely any improvement… and what happens if he stays like that forever? Or has irreparable brain damage?"

"Don't think about it," Paula said, stroking her friend's back.

"Robert's very strong, he'll get better, I'm absolutely sure of that."

"Thanks, Paula. It's a good thing you're here."

They chatted for a while longer, had something to eat in the mess hall and then parted with a hug. Emily was going back to the base immediately. Unfortunately the project could not be held back and there was a lot to do. Paula did not want to leave as long as Gorka was under observation, so she asked permission to stay on the station for a couple of days longer.

Emily prepared her return. There was something she wanted to do as soon as possible: something an old friend deserved. She spent the whole journey to the surface aware of the shrouded body which was traveling in the hold. She had already chosen the spot where the ill-fated anthropologist and theologian would rest for ever. The deputy director had suggested incinerating the body, following the recommended norms of the project, but she insisted that he should wait. She herself would lay him to rest as soon as she could, in the old-fashioned way.

A fine rain was falling in the clearing when they landed. Emily raised the body with the help of her exosuit and took it to the largest of the trees around, where Jonathan already lay. Here a large hole had been dug, the size of a person, awaiting its new tenant. Kostas, who had been designated to dig the grave at Emily's request, appeared shortly afterward with young Martin beside him.

Soon they were joined by the remaining members of the expedition. Ferrara, Lieutenant Ortiz, Chad, Taro, Evelyn and Pilot Balakova came over to say their last farewells to the one who had been their partner. The remaining settlers also joined the group: Alberto, Erik, Marko, Dr. Hudgens, Dr. Moreau, Emma and even James Coogan went up to the tree to pay their respects. Emily laid Rakesh's body in the earthen bed. Weeping, she put her hand on her comrade's shrouded head.

"Farewell, my friend. I hope wherever you are, you find peace."

Although she remembered his last words, when he had asked her not to blame herself for what had happened, she could not help feeling guilty about it all. She, and only she, was the person responsible for the base.

I'm very sorry to have got you into all this, she said to him, but without uttering a single word aloud.

Kostas and Martin, armed with shovels, began to replace the soil on top of the body and so take their leave forever of Rakesh Kumar: anthropologist, theologian and friend, but most of all a great comrade. Once the mound of earth was in place once again, Emily addressed the others:

"Rakesh was a simple man and a friendly one," she began. "The first conversation we had lasted for hours, but it felt so familiar that I had the impression that only a few minutes had passed. Ever since that first moment, we connected in a way I still find hard to explain. He was someone of great wisdom, someone who always knew how to say what we needed to hear and gave us very good advice.

"But now he's not with us any longer. And the way everything happened… I can't help feeling guilty…" A tear ran down her cheek. "But I know he wouldn't want me to blame myself, he wouldn't want any of us to be sad. I know he'd like us to keep going and to manage to survive on this planet. For him the survival of humanity was a lot more important than that of any individual, such was his generosity and his greatness. Rest in peace, my dear friend. We'll try to honor your memory and see that the human race prevails. Thank you for all your advice, and for the time we were able to enjoy your company,"

The whole group stayed silent for a few moments in memory of their fallen comrade. Kostas began to applaud, and although with the exosuits the effect was not the same as it would have been with bare hands, everyone else followed the biologist's initiative. Those were very emotional moments.

Once they had all left, Emily stayed a while longer at the foot of the grave of her two comrades. By then the clouds had begun to move away and the rain had given way to the first brightness of daylight. Little Lemy came over, unaware of what that had just taken place. The little creature climbed up her suit onto her arm, and she welcomed him with a small caress.

"Hi, little one," she said. "Have you missed me?"

Little Lemy managed to raise her first smile in many days. After everything that had happened, she had not felt much like smiling.

"I bet you're hungry," she said as she went to the base entrance. "I'll bring you out some food."

When she went to the mess hall she looked for some kind of vegetable to offer her little friend. However, as she was looking for one of the airtight packages they had in store, she noticed the small red metal box with its pictures of various Hindu deities. That was where Rakesh kept the tea he liked so much.

You won't be able to enjoy your delicious tea now, she thought.

So, after feeding her grateful pet she went back into the base, changed into comfortable clothes and went back to the mess hall intending to have a cup of tea. She prepared the water, took two spoonfuls of tea from the box and heated a little milk. Cup in hand, she sat down on one of the couches in the leisure area, where more than once she had found Rakesh taking a nap with his terminal still switched on. She took a small sip and began to feel comforted again.

However, life was not prepared to allow her even a moment's

peace. She had just finished her tea when she heard someone speaking to her.

"How does this work?" came the voice of the high priest Waafdiv. "Do I just have to speak?"

"Yes, that's right," Ada said.

"Emily can you hear me?" he asked without much hope of being heard.

"Hello, Waafdiv," she called.

He was surprised by this. "Oh! This device works!"

She smiled. "Of course it does, Waafdiv."

"I've been talking to Ada for several days," he went on. "It's fascinating what you humans have been able to create. A person who thinks inside a metal box: it's amazing! I'm sure the Khapabir would love to see this."

She smiled. "Yes, it's not the first time someone's told me that."

"How do you feel?"

"We're fine, we've already got our strength back, and my comrade Gorka has come out of his state of hibernation at last. Everything thanks to Iwshaj's care. Please convey my most sincere gratitude to him for everything he did for us those last few days. If it hadn't been for him I don't know what would have happened to us."

"It's the least we could do. After all, we owe it to our cult, and hence to you."

"Well, Waafdiv, about this business of being the chosen... I've had a lot of time to think about it and... I don't think I'm what you believe I am at all. A very dear comrade has died because of this madness... and it really can't be me, it's impossible."

"Emily, that isn't the question. What matters is that I myself don't have the slightest doubt of it," Waafdiv rebuked her with absolute conviction. "You are the chosen one."

She was silent for a moment. It was not going to be easy to get him to see his mistake.

"But the Khaavahki will be looking for me, and I don't want to be responsible for a war between villages."

"Don't worry, I think I've come up with how we can claim the sole command. I found the ancient writings that explain how it can be done. Long before the Great Revolt there were a number of leaders who wanted to regain sole command for themselves. In the face of the refusal of their peers, they were given the chance to

attain it if the candidate could manage to prove his knowledge or skill in every aspect of Keplerian society. In this way each leader required the candidate to pass a test. And if he was able to achieve what was required of him, the leader of the village was required to hand him his staff of command."

Emily sighed. Waafdiv was never going to admit that he was beaten.

"What kind of tests are we talking about?"

"Well, that would depend on each leader, but they could be anything from tests of intellect or skill to tests of survival, or even combat."

"But what about the Khaavahki?" she asked. "They'll go on seeing me as a foreigner, and in their eyes I'll still be a fugitive under sentence of death who escaped from their fortress."

"Don't you worry about that, I'll take charge of everything," he assured her. "According to our laws they can't refuse anyone who requests the opportunity to gain sole command."

"And what about that trial, where they accused me of that massacre?"

"Leave it to me. We'll manage to make Vaahur desist from that absurd crusade of his against the humans. Our peoples need one another."

Emily sighed again. At that moment, with everything that was going on around her, she did not feel strong enough to deal with it all. But nor did she feel like going against Waafdiv, so she said nothing more. Whatever the future might bring, it would have to include eliminating the Khol, so that they would need both humans and Keplerians united under a single command.

"All right, Waafdiv," she said resignedly.

After finishing her conversation with the high priest, she left the mess hall and ran into Taro at one of the points where the corridors crossed.

"How do you feel?" the geologist asked her.

"Okay, I guess, considering everything that's been going on lately."

"Well, if you need anything, we're here."

"Thanks, Taro. Have you been able to make any progress with the experiments?"

"In fact we have. If you have some time, we can explain in the outdoor module."

He called Chad, and all three got into their exosuits and went to the module where the scientists had set up a series of small terrariums. In them a dozen tiny white mice seemed to be sniffing and scuttling around, knowing nothing of the reasons why they had been taken there.

"The initial experiment only involved exposing the mice to outside conditions for an entire night," Chad began. "Unfortunately, half the test subjects died. We managed to save the others the following day, though they showed side-effects from the hypoxia they'd all suffered. In fact a couple of them were in a kind of coma we couldn't get them out of."

Emily was interested in those two mice, because clearly a connection could be established between their condition and Robert's.

"In a coma?" she said. "What happened to them?"

"We'll explain that in a moment. After we'd spoken to you we put the survivors into a state of hibernation, then exposed six more mice to the atmosphere to try and simulate what happened to you when you ran out of oxygen. We put the six new mice into a state of hibernation the moment hypoxia made them lose consciousness. They all survived. As for the ones who survived the other experiment, they all survived too, except one of them which was in a coma."

"And the other one who was in a coma?"

"It's this little fellow," Chad said. He pointed to one of the mice running around its terrarium, unaware of the human eyes fixed on it.

"He survived," Emily whispered.

Chad nodded. "Yes, and I have to say that all the ones who survived are in top health and form. We've carried out blood tests on them, and they all show the same morphological and cellular modifications."

"Increase in muscle mass and bone density and a substantial increase in the amount of hemoglobin," Emily predicted.

"Bingo!"

"The only drawback is that one of the mice in a coma didn't pass the test," Taro reminded them.

"It's a fifty-fifty chance of success," Emily said, thinking about its application to humans.

"If you're thinking about Robert, yes. I'm afraid what we're risking is that he won't be able to take it."

"Have you talked about this with Dr. Schmidt's team?" she asked.

"Yes," Chad said, "they're up to date with everything. We've passed on everything that's been done and the results of the experiment."

"Right, keep us updated if there's any change. I'll have a word with Dr. Schmidt to see how we can extrapolate those results to cover Robert's state. Good work, guys."

"Thanks," Chad said. "Do you want us to do any specific test?"

She was thoughtful for a moment.

"Yes," she said at last. "I'd like to know whether once they've been through the changes, they can move from one atmosphere to another without either losing their faculties or risking their lives."

Emily left them to go on with their work, even though she could not help wondering how she could use that information to persuade Dr. Schmidt, knowing that only fifty per cent of the mice had survived. Robert's life might depend on the toss of a coin. It was not a very reassuring thought.

"Emily," Ada interrupted her as she was about to take off her suit, "I think something's happened to Shildii."

"What is it?"

"These past few days he's been coming to help Kostas, but this morning he hasn't appeared. The thing is that I can see a couple of adult Keplerians carrying someone in their arms. To judge by the clothes he's wearing, I'm eighty-four per cent sure it's Shildii."

"What!" she shouted.

Ada showed her the images her peripheral cameras were picking up, and she left the base as fast as she could. She ran to the Keplerians, following the route Shildii had been in the habit of taking. As Ada had guessed, the two adults were Shildii's parents. In their arms they were carrying the body of their son, who showed multiple bruises and wounds.

"Please!" Shildii's mother said desperately. "They've beaten him almost to death! Save our son! I beg you to!"

Emily examined Shildii's body, which lay in his father's arms. His face was disfigured by the blows he had been given. He seemed to have a broken bone or two, because a glance was enough to show that his left arm and right leg were at unnatural angles. But what worried her most was the blow to his head, which made her fear some kind of fracture. He was unconscious, but still breathing.

"Oh, my God!" she exclaimed. "Who did this to him?"

"We don't know who they were," his father said, "but a crowd of Keplerians went up to him and beat him up."

"My son!" the mother sobbed. "You can all save him! Please!"

"We can't afford to waste any time," Emily said urgently. "Follow me."

She took Shildii's body from his father's arms and hurried to the base as fast as she could. She tried not to shake him too much on the way to avoid worsening his condition, and tried to take special care with his head and neck.

"Dr. Hudgens!" she called on the radio. "We have an emergency!"

"What is it?" came the voice of the base surgeon.

"It's Shildii, Keplerian male, about fifteen human years. He's been beaten to within an inch of his life. Multiple contusions, broken bones and a possible skull fracture."

"Keplerian?" the doctor said. "Our facilities and technology aren't set up to treat Keplerians."

"We could use the operating theater, with a bubble stretcher to adjust the level of oxygen to something like what's outside."

"Yes, but we'd have to do everything manually. The surgery robot doesn't know anything about Keplerian physiology. In fact even we don't know anything about it, we have no idea what a Keplerian's body is like.

Nor do we have any blood of his type for a transfusion in case we needed one."

"Doctor, I know I'm asking the impossible," Emily insisted, "but this is someone very important to me. He's dying. He needs urgent medical assistance. I doubt very much whether any of his own people can do anything to save his life. You're his only hope."

"All right," she said. "We'll see what we can do. Bring him to the entrance. We'll start setting everything up."

"Thank you, doctor. We'll be there in two minutes."

Emily and the boy's parents, who could barely keep up with her, reached the door of the facilities at last. Dr. Hudgens and Dr. Moreau soon appeared at the door, wearing their exosuits and pushing a bubble stretcher. Evelyn and Lieutenant Ortiz came to join the group.

"Help us arrange him on the stretcher properly," the surgeon said to Emily.

With the help of Evelyn and Dr. Moreau she put Shildii inside the stretcher and sealed the bubble around him. Dr. Hudgens adjusted the level of oxygen in the cylinder which formed part of the stretcher itself.

"The oxygen concentration in the planet is twelve per cent, right?" she asked, and Emily nodded. "Right, I think that's it. In we go."

Emily decided to stay with Shildii's disconsolate parents. His mother was very much affected, despite his father's unsuccessful attempts to calm her down.

"Come with me," she said. "You can't go in there, and it'll probably be hours before they tell us anything. We'd better wait somewhere where we can sit down."

She led them to the small isolated module where Chad and Taro had been carrying out their experiments with the mice. She made sure to turn the lights off so that the brightness would not trouble them and invited them to sit in the chairs around the table.

"Would you like me to bring you some water?" she asked. "Or something to eat?"

"Water would be nice, thank you," Shildii's father said. He looked tired after carrying his son in his arms all the way from their home, which was several kilometers from there.

Emily brought two glasses and put them down on the table in front of them. The father downed his at once, but the mother was still disconsolate and could not stop mumbling about how anyone could do such a thing to an innocent creature like her son. Emily excused herself for a moment and went to the main building in search of something to eat. She took some nuts and a couple of slices of cake and brought them back to the little module.

She put them all on the table. "I know it's not the best moment, but you might want something to eat. Is there anything I can do for you?"

"No, all I want is my child back," the mother said sadly. "All this is your fault. If you hadn't lured my son here, no-one would have taken any notice of him."

"But I—"

"I warned him this might happen. No foreigner's to be trusted."

"I…" Emily stammered, taken aback. "I'm really sorry, I never meant any of this to happen."

What Shildii's mother had said had hurt her deeply, but what was even more painful was that this heartbroken Keplerian was verbalizing what she herself was already thinking in some way. She had turned into a threat to anyone who came anywhere near her. She had dragged Rakesh to his death, Robert was in a coma because he had tried to rescue her, and now Shildii could die at any moment. And that too was her fault.

It was one of the worst moments in her life. She was unable to comfort Shildii's parents, she felt guilty about everything that was happening, and at the same time she had to wait for news from the operating theater.

"Emily?" came Evelyn's voice on the radio.

"Evelyn! How's Shildii?"

The nurse made no attempt to sugar-coat the situation. "He's in a very bad state. We need blood from his parents. I'm on my way."

"All right. I'll tell them what to expect."

She explained to the boy's parents what they needed, and both of them agreed without hesitation or reluctance. This meant that Evelyn was able to extract half a liter of blood from each of them. The father was a little dizzy afterward, so Emily urged him to eat something of what was on the table to restore his strength. Several hours went by with no news from the operating theater. The light was growing fainter and fainter, a sign that the day was nearly over. By now Shildii's mother was a little calmer, but she still said nothing to Emily. His father on the other hand was a little more approachable, and even thanked her for taking care of his son.

The operation lasted for nearly nine hours. When Emily had already started to think about putting up Shildii's parents in the module guestroom, Dr. Hudgens called her. She went out of the habitat so that the parents would not hear the conversation.

"We've finished," the doctor said, sounding tired. "It was very complicated, I won't try to pretend otherwise, and Shildii's still in a serious condition, but I think we've managed to stabilize him. The next hours are key, but at least he's still with us."

"Thanks, Melissa," she said from the bottom of her heart. "You've no idea how glad I am about that."

"You can tell his parents their son is all right, but when you're finished I'd like you to come in. I need to have a word with you."

"What about?"

"See to his parents," she said. "I suppose this can wait."

Emily went back to Shildii's parents, who got up from their seats and looked at her hopefully.

"Your son is alive. His condition is serious, but our doctors have managed to stabilize his condition and at the moment he's resting in the other building. The next few hours will be the key to his survival."

"Thank you, Emily," Shildii's father whispered. He came forward to embrace her. "Thank you, from the bottom of our hearts."

"It's the least we could do," she said sadly. "Your wife is right. I'm the only one who's responsible for all this."

The mother was still overwhelmed. "Can we see him?" she asked

"Not yet, I'm afraid. I'm sorry, but for the moment our doctors would like to keep him under observation for a while, just in case there's any complication. And I'm afraid you wouldn't survive conditions inside our buildings."

Shildii's father took his leave, as their younger son was at home by himself and he needed to go and fetch him. Emily offered them the guestroom with four beds so that they could spend the night there if they wanted, but he had decided that he would come back the following day with their other son. Shildii's mother did not want to be separated from him, so she accepted the offer, and Emily prepared the room for her and showed her how everything worked.

Once the mother had had something to eat and settled down, Emily excused herself and went to the other building to talk to the doctor.

"What was it you wanted to tell me?" she asked.

"Come with me, there's something I'd like you to see. But first things first: how are the parents bearing up?"

"Very worried, naturally, especially his mother. She didn't want to go home and she's going to spend the night here, in the outer module."

"Poor thing, it's natural that she should be worried."

The doctor took her to the observation room, where Shildii was lying intubated and with a mass of bioactive bandages to encourage scarring. When she saw the state he was in, Emily covered her face with her hands.

"Oh, my God!" she cried. "Poor Shildii, what on earth happened to him?"

"Apart from the multiple fractures in his arms and legs, he has several broken ribs and all kinds of bruises. There was also an internal hemorrhage which luckily we were able to stop. But there's no doubt that the most worrying injuries were those to his nasal passages and the severe

315

skull damage. We had to open an airway so that he could breathe more normally, and I was very lucky with the cranial fracture. A few millimeters more and we wouldn't have been able to do anything."

"How horrible!"

"But in fact that's not really what I called you about," she added.

"No?"

The doctor operated her terminal and showed her a full scan of a human body.

"This is a normal human body, like yours or mine," she explained. "When you brought the patient in I presumed that as an alien, his physiognomy would be very different."

The doctor clicked a few keys on her terminal and showed her Shildii's full scan.

"However, I found that despite the differences, there are many similarities between us and them."

Emily saw that the scan showed two lungs within a very similar thoracic cavity, though there were fewer ribs and these were slightly thicker. The Keplerian heart was in the exact center, and despite the differences, there were several organs that were clearly identifiable.

"I'm no expert on alien life, and I'd imagine the project will have some specialist who's far better prepared than I am. But what are the chances that an alien race, separated from us by over a thousand light years, would turn out to have so many similarities?"

"I… I'm as amazed as you are," Emily muttered as she bent forward to look more closely at what the surgeon was showing her.

"We've asked Ada to analyze the genome of the Keplerians, but we already know they have twenty-four pairs of chromosomes, one pair more than us. I'm no geneticist either, but quite honestly I expected that other forms of life, even if they were carbon-based, would be a lot more distinct from us."

"I've finished sequencing the Keplerian genome now," Ada said at that moment.

"What did you find?" Dr. Hudgens asked.

"There's a ninety-eight per cent similarity to the human genome."

"That's… that's impossible," Emily said.

"There must be some rational explanation," the doctor said.

"If there is one, I don't know it," said Ada.

The adventure continues in the next book:

Acknowledgements

I would like to thank everyone who made this book possible. It's very hard to condense into a few lines what all the support and good advice I've been given since embarking on this journey have meant to me. And even at the risk of not doing it justice, I'll give it a try:

To my great friend and mentor, Pedro Urvi. You showed me the way and helped me walk it. All of this has been possible thanks to you. A thousand thanks.

To the entire Peterson Publishing team. Especially to Mon, Luis, and Kenneth for pushing me to follow the yellow brick road. None of this would have made sense without you. Many, many thanks.

To Ana C., Miguel G., Andrea E., and Nuria M. for being the best alpha readers anyone could hope for. Your advice, corrections, and ideas have been vital to bringing this project to completion. Thank you so much!

To David C., with whom I embarked on this adventure. None of this would have happened without you. I hope our paths continue to run parallel and that we can enjoy the journey together. See you at the end of the road!

To Susana R. L., if Pedro is the father of this book, you're the mother. Your advice and corrections have allowed me to get this far. I treasure your teachings. I hope to be a worthy student of the best teacher possible. Thank you so much!

To Pilar García, for designing the covers that allow this drop of water to stand out in the ocean. Thanks for everything!

To Tanya, Christy and Peter, for being the guardians of language, the sentinels of perfection. None of this would be the same without your skills. A million thanks!

To Aitor C., for your explanations and ideas on orbital mechanics and astrodynamics. Thanks to you, everything is much more realistic. Truly, thank you!

To my parents, whose efforts made me who I am. I hope you're

proud of what I've achieved. Thank you for giving me everything.

To my sisters, for always being there when needed, encouraging my crazy ideas, and supporting me every step of the way. A thousand thanks!

To the rest of my family—nieces, nephews, uncles, cousins, brothers-in-law, and everyone else—thank you so much!

To all my friends, for always being there. A little piece of this novel is yours too. Thank you!

To you, the reader, for choosing my books. I hope you've enjoyed the journey and that you'll join me for the adventures ahead. Once again, I'd like to ask you to leave a positive review so others can enjoy this wonderful world we've created. Thank you from the bottom of my heart.

And finally, to Yuvi, the light that guides my steps, my inspiration. The only person capable of putting up with my nonsense. All this is for you.

Thank you very much, and with warmest regards.

Frank J. Cavill.

Note from the author:

I really hope you enjoyed my book. If you did, I would appreciate it if you could write a quick review. It helps me tremendously as it is one of the main factors readers consider when buying a book. As an Indie author I really need of your support.

Just go to Amazon and enter a review.

Thank you so very much.

Frank J. Cavill

Author

Frank J. Cavill

I would love to hear from you.
You can find me at:

All my books: relinks.me/FrankJCavill
Web: frankjcavill.com
X: @FrankJCavill
Facebook: facebook.com/frankjcavill
Threads: @frankjcavill
Instagram: @frankjcavill
Tiktok: @frankjcavill
Bluesky: @frankjcavill

Mail: frankjcavill@gmail.com

Thank you for reading my books!

See you in:

Galileo's Legacy (Project Orpheus, Book 4)

Printed in Dunstable, United Kingdom

65376860R00184